Running Elk

E.A. Porter

For Marcella "Whitekiller" Ketcher
Čhaŋkú lúta máni, mi khola wašté

Chapter One

Running Elk watched from where he had hidden himself, behind a large rock, as the woman picked over the beautiful desert flowers abundant in the early spring. Her clothing clung to her curves with every breath of the wind. The warrior had seen more than his fair share of white women, yet from the moment he laid eyes on her, he could tell that she was different. She was beautiful, young, and graced with a very appealing body. But there were many women like that. Maybe more importantly, plenty of his own kind. He had a wife at the camp, though she was growing fat and miserable with being left alone so much.

Running Elk's life revolved around hunting. He was happiest when alone on the prairie; just he and his gods. They blessed Running Elk more often than not with the sight of his expertly-honed arrow piercing the soft flesh of a strong, free-roaming animal. However, the sight of the white woman picking flowers was proving to be too much of a distraction for him to concentrate on his mission.

He was aware of the men in close proximity to the woman and knew remaining hidden was the prudent thing to do. Still, the woman was a pleasing sight, so he chose not to disturb the tranquil scene but instead prayed for the opportunity to see her again.

She had hair the color of sun-ripened wheat. It was long, though not as long as his. Her eyes were a striking green and her skin was not as white as most of the *tahbay-boh* he'd seen. Hers was a darker hue, a healthy sun-kissed glow. Above all else, the woman seemed to be fearless. The knowledge made him smile. And for reasons he couldn't begin to understand, he wanted nothing more than to see her again.

Running Elk watched as she swept her forearm across her brow, her skin glistening in the midday sun, and had to command his body not to stand. It was amazing that the woman could be so unguarded in a land so full of bloodshed and heartache. She was the most interesting person he had ever come across.

Noises from the men approaching caused him to decide it was time to leave her to her flowers.

The woman consumed his thoughts as he rode back to his camp. Never before had he allowed a woman, let alone a white woman, to affect him. Knowing nothing of the woman, except for the fact that she excited him in a way he hadn't felt in years, cemented the knowledge that tomorrow would be another good day for hunting. Only he wouldn't be bringing home any meat. Running Elk would be hunting for more information.

Once he arrived at the camp, he immediately went in search of the Shaman. He knew he could trust the spiritual leader more than anyone; the holy man was his brother.

He held both his older brothers in the highest regard. They were powerful men among his people.

After entering the tipi's open flap, Running Elk took a seat by the crackling fire in the center of the home.

White Wolf looked up at his little brother before lighting the pipe. "Running Elk. I can tell from your thoughtful look that you have seen the white woman."

Running Elk couldn't conceal his surprise. His brother had always had a special relationship with the gods. They allowed him to see things before they took place and gave him the guidance to help his people. But White Wolf's visions had never before included him.

"What do you know of the woman?" Running Elk asked eagerly.

"She pleases you. I know that much. I also know Morning Star could never arouse your emotions like the white woman has."

"Brother, I took Morning Star to my lodge for the wrong reasons. But I am duty bound to take care of her. No matter what, she will be taken care of," Running Elk vowed. His wife might not have held his heart, but she never wanted for anything. Except Running Elk's company.

White Wolf watched his little brother closely through the smoke from his pipe. His first inclination was to warn Running Elk of the dangers of bringing a new white woman to their camp

"Do you understand the harm it will cause if you act on your impulsive thoughts?" the shaman asked as he handed Running Elk the pipe.

"And just what do you think I am thinking?"

"You are thinking about bringing her here. How would Morning Star feel if you did?"

"A lot of men have more than one woman. Why am I so different?"

"Not white women. The only white left in our camp is Sparrow. And honestly, there is no remnant of white left in her. She has given Kicking Bird three fine sons and has spoken out against being given back to her old family. Taking a white woman now would cause us to break a treaty with the Great Father in Washington. The soldiers would come for us and destroy everything."

"I understand, but I am still free to come and go as I please. I think tomorrow I will hunt again, and it will please me greatly," he said, standing and walking to the doorway.

"Tomorrow the raiding party returns. You should be here to welcome our brother back," White Wolf strongly suggested.

Running Elk knew his brother was attempting to delay the inevitable, but he wasn't going to be put off. "I will be in our village tonight, but that means I will be leaving again shortly. I will hunt either way."

Running Elk departed the company of the shaman and thought about his devoted wife with braids to her knees and round, soft face. Her height was matched only by her width and her smile was the brightest in the camp. Morning Star's eyes revealed her every thought; she had nothing to hide.

Like always, she had his meal waiting for him. Yet, instead of thanking her, he ate in total silence. When he finished, he picked up his bow and looked to his long-suffering wife. Running Elk quietly appreciated her silence.

"I am going out again. Tomorrow, Kicking Bird returns. I will be here to welcome him home."

"Will you be gone all night?" she asked him, noticeably attempting to keep her disappointment in check.

He could see the tears forming in her eyes. Her distress made him angry, as did knowing he could not do better by the woman. She was not his first love, nor would she ever be able to fill his heart. Their union had been one of convenience to their people. Years earlier, when he was a much younger man, his best friend had been killed in a raiding party against the Kiowa. Doing what was expected of him, Running Elk had taken the woman to his tipi. He always did what was best for the Comanche and, without him, Morning Star would have been without a mate.

"Go to sleep. I will be back when the sun rises."

After calling his mount, he directed his pony towards the white man's camp.

***

Running Elk walked his horse behind him as he neared the people sitting huddled around a small fire. When he saw her, he stopped walking. She seemed uninterested in what was going on around her. The striking woman was looking out on the prairie, watching the setting sun. He hadn't noticed the stunning beauty of the end of the day until then.

It was a spectacular sight which gave the entire sky a golden hue. He took a few seconds to thank the gods and then fixed his attention back on the woman.

She was wearing a sun-colored dress and black boots. Running Elk's immediate thought was that the captivating woman would be much more comfortable in his people's clothing. The attention she demanded caused him to lose sight of the rest of the group. There were two men and another woman. He looked at the other woman. She was attractive, but he wasn't drawn to her in any way. He was spellbound by the woman with yellow hair and faraway eyes. Instead of worrying about the others in her party, he decided they would not be a problem as long as he could draw her away and speak with her alone.

It was when his attention turned back to her that their eyes met. He held his breath, hoping she wouldn't scream at the sight of him. Instead of screaming, she looked him straight in the eyes with what he assumed was terror.

Chapter Two

The days had been long and uneventful for Alexandria. After the third day of traveling she'd lost any desire to keep track of the passing time. She thought the journey would never come to an end. The wagon supplies were becoming threadbare, and the herds of animals were getting thinner as the miles passed. Food was scarce, although being close to water and fish was a blessing. Everything she owned was covered in dust, and she longed for her tub back in Virginia. She still wasn't convinced that leaving her home and most of her comforts behind had been the right thing to do. Her husband, Richard, loved her with all his heart. She was sure of that. The problems in their marriage were all on account of her. She loved him like a brother, not a lover. She had been against going West from the beginning but knew if her husband left her in Virginia, she would be all alone. Her final decision was that she would rather die than be abandoned. She had determined the reason her husband hadn't informed her of their destination was due to his fear of her backing out. He always called her irrational; she preferred the term *free spirit*.

After readying the camp and feeding her companions, she climbed up onto the front of the wagon to rest. Being alone gave her time to think about the feeling she couldn't shake. She had been sure she could feel someone's eyes on her while she was picking flowers earlier, and then again when she was watching the most beautiful sunset she'd ever seen. Instead of being worried or frightened by the suspicion, she was intrigued and found herself searching the area for signs she'd been right. She found him almost immediately. His close proximity caught her off guard.

The man was the most exquisite man she'd ever seen. He had coal-black hair which was almost blue in the dusk. His hair reached the bottom of his back with loose strands hanging over his muscular shoulders. His eyes were brown and incredibly deep. She could tell just by looking at him that he'd seen many things. The hardness of his features assured her that the Indian had seen his share of pain and death, suffering and loss. His face was strong but handsome. His nose came to a bit of a point; his cheekbones were high and well formed. His lips were full and well defined. He was wearing only a breechcloth and moccasins that tied at the knee. His smooth skin was almost the color of caramel. He was an impressive man.

After slowly looking the man over, her eyes moved to his necklace. The blue-beaded choker he wore was exquisite. She found herself smiling at him instead of screaming and alerting the others in her party. After cautiously glancing back towards the people by the fire, she jumped down from her perch and walked in their direction.

She couldn't explain the overpowering feeling of excitement she was experiencing as she neared her friends.

***

Running Elk watched her with doubt in his mind. Instead of leaving the people in peace, he stayed where he was and observed the unfolding scene. His muscles involuntarily tightened when he watched the woman speak to the others before making a gesture with her arms and walking away. He wondered what she was doing, but didn't see any sign that the woman had alerted the others to his presence. He didn't plan on letting her out of his sight. The white men were fools to allow her to walk away. There were wild creatures out in the forsakenly frightful night. The sparse landscape offered little protection from man or beast. There were anemic trees sprinkled here and there, and large rocks jutted up from the hard ground. The most abundant life held itself close to the ground. Tall thin blades of prairie grass and muted flowers helped cover the ground and maintained the little moisture brought by the morning dew.

Running Elk wondered if the rest of the traveling party cared about the woman's safety at all. After watching her walk behind a large rock, he followed. The intriguing woman had stopped and waited for him. Her actions caused him to run into her, forcefully. She let out an audible gush of air.

"Sorry," she said quietly.

Running Elk could both speak and understand the white man's language. He had learned it when Sparrow had come to live with his brother. For the first time, he was thankful for the knowledge.

He wanted to say so many things to her, but his first question was the most logical.

"Why are you not afraid of me?" His accent was rough, he knew, but she seemed to understand him perfectly.

"I'm not sure. I know I should be. But you don't seem inclined to hurt us, or you would have already."

"I am called Running Elk. What do they call you?"

"My name is Alexandria Standish."

"Alexandra," he said, mispronouncing the word. Names had always given him trouble, and he decided to find a more fitting name for her. He would call her Two Fires.

"Close enough. Your necklace is very nice. What is the stone?"

As she spoke, she moved closer to him and reached to touch the jewelry

When her hand made contact with his skin, he felt desire well inside him. It was a feeling he had forgotten he could experience. He knew at that moment that he would have the woman, and she would come to him willingly.

"The stone is turquoise. It is protecting to my people," he said, touching her hand where it held his necklace. "I have worn this for many summers, but now I give it to you."

"I would love to have it, but it's your protection," she said, letting the choker go. A blush covered her cheeks when her hand grazed his chest.

"I believe that I will continue to be protected by my gods. I have many other stones at the camp and will have another one when I return to you. You keep this. You and your party need protection more than I."

After quickly removing the pendant, he laid it into her outstretched hands.

"You shouldn't wear it now. The others will most definitely be curious as to where you found it. Are you aware of just how dangerous this country is? Where exactly are you and your party going?"

He seemed to be regaining some of his senses and needed all the information she would give him. The only thing he was sure of at that very moment was that the woman would be his.

"I told them I needed some privacy. And as for the Indians, you are the only one any of us have seen."

"No doubt because I was the only one wanting to be seen. You must be very careful. Now where are you going?" he asked again.

"We are going west, that's all I know. I am with them, but I don't know if they are sure exactly where they … where we are headed." She explained as she located the nearest felled tree and made a seat out of it.

He could hear the frustration in her voice when she spoke.

He knelt down so that he could look her in the eye. The desire to believe the woman was overpowering, but her answer was making it difficult. No one could be so foolhardy as to venture west with no idea of where they were going; not even settlers.

"Do you belong to one of those men?"

"Yes, I am married to the man with the dark hair. His name is Richard," she replied, lowering her head.

Running Elk thought he could detect annoyance in her tone. It was the same tone he took on every day when he spoke to Morning Star. Maybe they had something in common. Before continuing the conversation, Running Elk moved silently and looked in on the rest of the traveling party. They were all talking as they sat around the fire. He took the briefest of minutes to look at the dark-haired man. He was tall and stocky with eyes as black as night. The man seemed a bit jumpy, and not particularly smart.

"Why did you marry if you do not love him?"

"I do love him."

"Then why are you here with me?"

"He's my best friend. I love him like that, not as I should love my husband."

"You are unhappy? You do not appear to be unhappy. You seemed to not have a care in the world when you were alone in the flowers."

"The open prairie calms me. I feel so close to nature when I'm away from the city. You're the only uncertainty I've encountered. Have you been following us?"

"I am not following them. I am following you. I cannot explain why. The gods have brought us together for a reason," Running Elk stated with resolve.

"I, too, feel drawn to you but I must get back to camp. I don't want them to come looking for me, and I cannot explain my absence if I'm gone much longer. When will I see you again?"

Her question filled Running Elk with hope. The woman wanted to see him again. "I agree, you cannot tell them about me, and do not let your husband see the necklace. Go now. I will find you again soon." He spoke softly as he moved behind the rock before disappearing into the darkness.

***

Alexandria felt a chill when she realized he was gone. She looked at the choker before holding it to her breast. Richard had never made her palms sweat and her knees weak simply by being near her. Surprising as it was, she had to admit to herself that she was actually looking forward to seeing the handsome, kind Indian again. And strange as it was, she also found herself wanting to tell Richard about meeting him. On her way back to the others, however, she decided that telling Richard anything would only cause a fight that would end as they always did, with him calling her irrational. She didn't want to taint her meeting with the handsome Indian, so she stayed quiet.

Her mind was full of thoughts of Running Elk as she sat by the glowing fire after returning to her friends. While her traveling companions talked of the land they would soon farm, Alexandria looked into the night sky. She'd never appreciated the beauty the night held when she was living back in Virginia.

Chapter Three

Running Elk took his time returning to Morning Star. A smile crossed his face when he remembered the way Alexandria looked at him. Most women looked at him twice, but not many would speak their thoughts so openly. He enjoyed the effect he had on the white woman. He was also savoring the effect she had on him. Women aroused him quite frequently; he was a normal man. But the need he felt for her was as powerful as anything he'd ever experienced. The white woman was so firmly in his mind that he decided to speak to Sparrow when he reached the camp. His sister-in-law surely remembered some of her old ways, and he found himself hungry for knowledge.

The women and children in the camp were wandering about in an anxious manner as he rode in. There was more activity than usual as the people moved in various directions in a rapid fashion. The air had a feel of uncertainty to it, and he seemed to be the only one without knowledge of the cause. Before doing anything else, he took a moment to say a silent prayer for his oldest brother.

"Running Elk," he heard someone call as he dismounted from his horse.

He knew the voice well. He felt his muscles stiffen as he watched Morning Star's approach. When he saw a smile cross her face, relief flooded through his tense body. If she was smiling and calm, then he was sure his brother was well.

"What is going on here?" he asked, walking toward his tipi.

"Kicking Bird and the other warriors are back. White Wolf has sent for you. Did you have any luck with the hunt?" Morning Star asked as she followed closely behind her husband.

"Luck?" he asked, looking at her.

The irritation of simply speaking with her was rapidly becoming too much for him. He did everything in his power to quell the sudden onset of anger towards his wife. The irritation he felt was unfounded and would do neither of them any good.

"Luck in hunting?"

"Does it look like I killed anything, woman?" he asked. "Did you see any dead animals when I rode up?"

"No," Morning Star answered, casting her eyes downward.

"I will be at the council. Do not wait up." It seemed even the guilt he felt when addressing the woman wasn't enough to take the acid from his tongue. While he was walking towards his brother's tipi, he decided he was going to attempt to be more charitable with her. She was a good woman, just not the right woman for him.

When he was admitted to his brother's tipi, he saw both White Wolf and Kicking Bird sitting near the fire. The outside of the shaman's home belied the spirit of the inside of the dwelling. The inside of the hide was painted with mysterious scenes of spirits and symbols unknown to most, but sacred to the tribe. Inside, natural lighting, almost eerie in its prevalence, penetrated throughout. Drawings told anyone entering the tipi that its owner was a man of sight and immense healing powers. White Wolf's home smelled of sweet, burning herbs which he liberally tossed on the fire.

Running Elk's brothers were both great men and he loved and respected them, so he showed his reverence by dipping his head before making himself at home and sitting by the flames. It was good to see Kicking Bird return unharmed from the raiding party against the Apaches.

"How did you fare?" Running Elk asked, making himself comfortable.

"We were able to capture over a hundred ponies," Kicking Bird answered with pride in his voice.

"No one lost their life?" Running Elk continued, asking the questions he knew he was supposed to.

"Jumping Beaver broke his arm, but White Wolf says it will heal nicely."

"I am pleased to hear that. While you were traveling, did you happen to spot any buffalo?" Running Elk continued.

"No, we didn't. But I still consider the outcome of the raid a good one."

Running Elk didn't completely agree with his brother's last statement. "No buffalo in fifty miles and you act as if that isn't something to be concerned with? More than worried, we should be angry."

"What good would anger do? My dissatisfaction is not going to bring the animal back," Kicking Bird declared, looking from White Wolf to Running Elk.

"No, I suppose it won't, but you seem too calm. The herds were so prevalent a few summers ago that if someone had told me they would begin to disappear, I would have laughed and called them crazy, but it is happening. I miss the hunt," Running Elk said, realizing he was anxious to hunt once again. Buffalo were a challenge, and hunting them carried the strong possibility of death. Knowing that made him feel alive.

It was then that Running Elk realized he hadn't given much thought to actual hunting since he saw Alexandria. Two

Fires. As soon as her image entered his mind, a smile crossed his face.

"Running Elk. Smoke the pipe with us and tell us of the game nearby," Kicking Bird suggested.

He did as he was told and took the pipe offered by his oldest brother.

"It is good to see you again, my brother," Running Elk greeted before he lit the pipe.

"It is good to see you too. Now that we have discussed the buffalo, tell me about the game near the camp. Is it plentiful?"

"There is no abundance of game, but I have never had a problem," he informed his brother with a hint of superiority.

"We are aware of your abilities, but we must know if there is enough game to feed our people through the summer," White Wolf pointed out.

"Honestly, I don't believe there is. We need to hunt for buffalo," Running Elk admitted, surprising himself with the confession.

Going on a hunt that would take him away from the white woman was one of the last things he wanted to do. But if he was going to leave with the hunting party, he vowed to see Alexandria one more time before leaving.

Running Elk noticed White Wolf didn't bother to hide his shock at his little brother's sudden interest in hunting.

"At least you are still thinking of our people first," White Wolf said.

Kicking Bird watched both men before speaking. "Something happened while I was absent. Tell me what it is," he demanded after taking a long pull from the pipe.

"I have met a woman," Running Elk answered.

"Met? Running Elk, please tell me you haven't spoken to the white woman," White Wolf spoke in a chastising manner.

"White woman? What white woman?" Kicking Bird asked.

"Why wouldn't I speak to her? I plan on doing much more than that."

"This nonsense will stop now!" Kicking Bird said angrily. He was not used to being left out of a vital conversation. Both his brothers stopped talking and gave him their complete attention. "White Wolf, what is it about the woman that alarms you? Did you say she was white?"

He was shocked that his little brother would want anything to do with a white woman.

"White Wolf, please do not speak until I have had my say. It is my right to explain the situation."

The shaman wasn't pleased, but he nodded his head in agreement.

"Kicking Bird, I saw a woman today, a white woman. She is traveling with two men and another female. She has an intoxicating spirit and I am drawn to her in a way that, to be honest, is foreign to me. I returned to the camp to share my news with White Wolf, and he informed me he had seen the woman in his visions. I just returned from her. I did speak to her, and she wasn't frightened by me."

As Running Elk told the story, a smile crossed Kicking Bird's face. "Brother, I have never seen you so intent on anything other than hunting. If White Wolf has had a vision, it must be taken into account. What worries you about this woman?" Kicking Bird asked White Wolf.

"If we allow Running Elk to bring the woman to our camp, then war will break out with the white soldiers. This is what I have seen. Brothers, our time as free people is coming to an end. Soon, we will not have our land. We will be forced to live the way the white man sees fit. Having that woman here will only hasten that very outcome. Do not get me wrong, there is no evil in the woman. I have seen that she has a truly loving spirit. The others in her party will cause the distress. And for that, I am very sorry. It is the way it is. I am sorry, Running Elk, but we cannot change the will of the gods or slow the advancement of the whites."

Running Elk had to convince himself that White Wolf did not want to hurt him. He knew White Wolf had the whole tribe's interest to think about, but so did he. It was always the good of the people, first and foremost.

Kicking Bird stayed silent, but the look on his face was one of saddened agreement. Things were going to change, and there was little any of the nations could do about it. Although that very fact had led to may spirited debates in the past, it didn't seem the time to begin another one.

"White Wolf, Kicking Bird," Running Elk said, standing and addressing both brothers. "I have always done what was best for our people and will continue to do so. I will not bring her here. But I will be with her. I feel I must. I have never felt this kind of need before. The urgency I feel is as confusing to me as it is to you. Tell me when you decide to leave for the hunt. I am going back to her and will return by midday."

"Running Elk, I know how you feel. Sparrow is my reason for breathing," Kicking Bird said, standing beside him. "I believe I will ride with you tonight. I find I must see the woman that incites such passion in my younger brother."

Running Elk stood, exited the tipi, and walked until he was standing outside of Kicking Bird's home, impatiently waiting while his brother talked to his wife.

Sparrow walked out with her husband and embraced Running Elk. The woman was tall and tanned. Her beautiful light green eyes were the only remaining clue to her race. "I am truly sorry, my brother," she said in perfect English.

"There is a way for this to work, Sparrow. I just need some time to think this through."

"You are speaking the white man's language well. I must be a good teacher." He knew his sister-in-law was attempting to make him smile, and he appreciated her effort. "If this was meant to be, it will be. Please do not keep my husband too long. I have missed him."

Running Elk followed his brother to his horses. They mounted two of the finest and rode away. Kicking Bird looked back at his wife until she was but a shadow.

***

The ride was uneventful. There were small green bushes that had taken hold haphazardly throughout the visible landscape and patches of out-of-control prairie grass growing anywhere it could find enough moisture. Every once in a while, the rhythmic sound of the hooves was interrupted by the occasional rabbit or fox running through the grass in search of the day's dinner. The weather was perfectly comfortable and welcomed them to the vast expanse of emptiness lying ahead.

The brothers had ridden almost halfway to the white man wagons before Running Elk thought about Morning Star. He had again left her without saying a word. It bothered him to think she could so easily slip his mind. The woman tried to be a good wife to him. Always there, reliable, and caring. But he had taken her to his tipi for all the wrong reasons. He had been young at the time and in love with another. But the woman who had held his young heart had been in love with everyone in the camp except for him. The responsibility of taking Morning Star to his tipi had come at the right time. There had been passion at first, but, for him, it had soon faded. She was always willing, but most women were with him. The damning prophecy his brother spouted would not deter him. He would have Alexandria. The passion he felt for her was strong and pure. He had to be as one with her. And he was sure it would happen.

"You are deep in thought but still smiling," Kicking Bird observed. "If the woman has affected you this strongly in the days since you met her, I believe I will need to seek some guidance. When we return, and after I have reacquainted myself with my wife, I will speak to Quanah on your behalf. You know as well as I do that Quanah will know what to do. He straddles both worlds."

Quanah Parker was the son of a white woman, Cynthia Parker. Cynthia Parker had been recaptured by soldiers when the warriors were away from the camp. The woman begged to be permitted to stay with her new family but the soldiers chalked her resistance up to brainwashing and didn't listen to her. She was dead less than a year after they forced her to return to her white family. Quanah was sure his mother had died of a broken heart.

Running Elk slowed the horse and dismounted as they neared the camp where the four whites were greeting a new day. A large fire burned behind the unimposing barrier the settlers had made of their wagons. The smell of coffee and bacon was thick in the air.

Running Elk looked in the direction of the water and saw Two Fires preparing to bathe. The morning was warm and sunny. It held promises of a hot day. Running Elk watched as she carefully placed his necklace around her neck and gently caressed the beads with her fingers. Given that she was putting on the necklace, rather than taking it off—probably because he'd warned her not to wear it around the other members of her party—he felt certain that, as she slipped the necklace on, her mind was with him. Her actions embolden him to move nearer, knowing Kicking Bird would follow close behind.

Her expression changed when she saw he was with someone. Her eyes displayed her confusion. Seeing Running Elk touch his neck where his necklace used to lay seemed to settle her dismay. He was smiling, and so was the other man. Running Elk watched as the woman decided the new man was not a threat.

"The woman is unusual, and very interesting." Kicking Bird finally said after watching his brother communicate with the golden-haired woman from afar.

"She looks even more appealing when she is unclothed. I am going to her."

"No," Kicking Bird objected, touching Running Elk's shoulder in an effort to stop his uncharacteristically impatient brother from going. "It is not safe. It's not the right time."

"You watch the others for me. Then it will be safe."

"I do not want trouble with them just for you going to look for her."

"It has to be now. We will be leaving for the hunt soon. We might be gone for some time and if I do not go now, if I don't take this chance, I may not get another one."

"She is not worth dying for," Kicking Bird said sternly.

"She might be."

Running Elk dove into the water without making a splash before Kicking Bird could say anything else to him.

***

A gasp of surprise slipped from Alexandria's lips when she realized he was beside her in the water. She could feel her throat tighten and her knees start to tremble. Her body's reaction to his presence was confusing to her but not at all unpleasant.

"Good morning," she whispered, looking him straight in the eyes.

Her breathing had become labored and her voice sounded strange to her ears.

Running Elk smiled at her and touched her cheek. She quickly moved her hand to cover his. His hands were so sensual. His fingers were calloused and he looked as if he hunted frequently, and the way his touch made her feel was almost too much to bear.

His other hand grasped the back of her hair as he cautiously pulled her closer to him. She moved willingly into his embrace.

"This has to be perfect," he declared, moving her hair away from her face and gently kissing her neck, right above where the necklace lay. His eyelids were heavy when he kissed her.

The kiss was gentle and simple until her arms came around him. She seemed to cling to him for her life. He had to pull away from her before he took her right there in the water.

"Where are your clothes?" he whispered, kissing her earlobe.

***

Alexandria felt like, at least, if nothing else ever took place between them, she had had this kiss and felt his touch. Yet she desperately wanted it to continue. She attempted to calm her breathing and pointed to a large rock. She watched Running Elk move silently through the water and pick up the blanket she'd brought with her. After moving closer to the water's edge, he placed the blanket on the ground and watched as she slowly walked out of the water. Alexandria had come from modest people, but as strange as it was, she wasn't bothered by her nakedness. The man definitely made her lose her reasoning. Nothing was said between the two as she sat beside him and melted into his muscular arms.

"Now," he said, as he laid them both down and kissed her again.

She could think of nothing but him. She had been touched before, but never had she felt her body burn. She carefully ran her hand down his chest. He was much more muscular than Richard. His stomach was like a washboard.

"I must have you," he said hoarsely in her ear.

"Then please, take me." Her voice was even shakier than earlier.

"My only regret is I won't be able to fully worship your body. You have been gone far too long already. His voice sounded gravelly and his breathing was labored.

He rolled over on top of her and kissed her neck, then moved down to her stomach. Alexandria thought she was going to cry out. She had never wanted any man like she wanted him. His hands were on her thighs and gently pulled them open. When he entered her, she could no longer be still. A hushed whimper escaped her lips.

"Everything about you excites me," he breathed.

Alexandria was still breathing heavily. While she was absently playing with a strand of Running Elk's hair, she realized what all her girlfriends said was true. Making love could be quite enjoyable

Running Elk slowly looked up at her and smiled. "I would lie here with you all day, if I could. We must get you back."

"I know. Will I see you again?"

It was the first time Alexandria had thought about a future with him. All she knew was that she was not ashamed of what had taken place. But she did wonder what Running Elk felt about her. Respectable ladies did not go running off with Indians. She worried that he might think her a loose woman.

"We will be together, I promise you that. But I must know where you are going," he said, helping her to her feet and unenthusiastically helping her dress.

"I told you, I don't know. If I started showing curiosity now, they would all know something was different," she explained. "Why can't I just go with you?"

As soon as the words left her lips, she regretted the question.

***

Running Elk stood and took a step backward, watching her as she finished covering herself. He couldn't take her, at least not yet. He had to lead the hunt and had no idea how long that would take. But he knew if he left her, there was a strong possibility that he would lose her.

Running Elk reached for the woman and held her at arm's length. It was then that he realized the name he had given her was perfect. Her eyes were unusual. They were bluish-green with a fleck of yellow invading her right pupil. While he was looking into her eyes, he realized he could see her soul and that was on fire too.

"I have decided to call you Two Fires," he informed her before moving closer and kissing her deeply.

"Two Fires?" she asked breathlessly when Running Elk moved from kissing her lips to kissing her collarbone. "That is beautiful, but why?" she asked in a whisper.

"You have fire in your eye and a fire in your soul."

When he felt her knees weaken, he kissed her again.

"Listen to me," he said in a husky tone. It was growing increasingly difficult to convince himself not to disrobe her again, but he knew he needed to impress upon her how important his next statement was. "My band is going on a hunt in a few hours. I will ask a friend to keep an eye on you as you continue your journey. Do not look for him. He will remain hidden. But he will keep you safe if need be and he will be able to tell me where you are. I will find you; you have to believe that. But I cannot take you now. It would mean breaking a pact with your government. There is a strong chance it could cause a war, and I do not want to bring pain to my people. That does not mean I will not find a way. I promise we will be together again. Now you must go."

"Running Elk," she said as she held him tight to her. "I have never felt this way before, but I don't want to cause a war ..." she began choking up as she spoke.

Running Elk placed his hand under her chin and gently moved it so that she was looking in his eyes.

"I will find a way," he promised, turning her so that she was facing the way back to her small caravan. "Now you must go."

She hadn't taken more than a few steps when Running Elk heard the gunshot. The warrior moved quickly, knocked Alexandria to the ground, and covered her with his body.

Chapter Four

Kicking Bird wasn't happy about having to keep an eye on the three interlopers, but he knelt down behind the broken tree trunk and took in the scene.

Two white men and a woman slowly began to roll up their packs. They didn't appear to be in any hurry to continue their trek.

"Go ahead and put the fire out. If Alexandria wanted more coffee, she shouldn't have run off to bathe. I swear ta God, the woman is always cleaning herself," the dark-haired man said as he stood by one of the horses before beginning to harness the animal.

"I told ya she wasn't gonna cotton to the trip before we left, didn't I?" a lighter-haired man asked, clearly amused with himself.

"Stop picking at Alexandria. She has been a real trooper so far. Although it would be nice if she didn't daydream quite so much." The only woman present spoke as she reached for a silver-colored water can.

Kicking Bird was quickly drawing the conclusion that the woman his little brother was so taken with wasn't popular with her traveling companions. But he didn't have long to dwell on his thoughts as the woman emptied the can over the fire.

Kicking Bird knew her next move would be to go to the lake to refill the jug, and he couldn't let that happen. He tensed his muscles and watched as the dark-haired man moved closer to the woman before taking the can from her hands.

"I'll do it. I gotta fetch my wife anyway," the man said with a grin.

Kicking Bird carefully moved toward a tree he could conceal himself behind.

The man stopped at the wagon and grabbed a shotgun before looking at the other two people. "Go ahead and finish up. I won't be long."

Kicking Bird knew he couldn't stay hidden any longer. Before shooting his gun in the air, he took a second to pray.

***

Running Elk rolled off Alexandria and, after silently explaining the importance of staying where she was, stood up and saw his brother had been the cause of the alarm.

When Kicking Bird caught sight of his little brother, his expression changed from disgust to pure anger.

"This could very easily cause a war," he said through gritted teeth when Running Elk neared him.

"What happened?" Running Elk asked, not bothering to hide his confusion.

"After you foolishly left my side, I decided to watch the others. And you should be glad I did. The one with the dark hair was on his way to look for his woman. I knew you were with her, so I did the only thing I could do. I fired my gun. I expected the group to put up more of a fight. The dark one dropped his gun and instantly put his hands in the air. The others began praying and crying. I don't understand why white people fear us. They are the ones who started this war.

"After I made myself known, I had to tie them up. The dark one started yelling, saying something about how if I didn't kill them, he was going to send for the cavalry. Which is funny because he dropped his weapon fast enough. So, the loud one is gagged for obvious reasons.

"I have not taken a life, so our treaty will stand. Although I may still kill someone before the sun rises," Kicking Bird calmly explained, ending his statement with a warning.

Running Elk felt bad for the distress he had caused his brother but was still quite happy with the events of the morning, so his brother's threatening did not hold the weight it usually did.

"It will be all right, brother. I will go get Two Fires and tell her to tell the others she was bathing in the pond. I will also explain the marking of a Creek war party to her. That will allow the settlers to place the blame elsewhere."

Kicking Bird didn't appear to be much happier after Running Elk explained his plans. He huffed and began walking towards the trees. "You do that. I will meet you back at the camp. I have missed Sparrow and will put off our reunion no longer."

As soon as Kicking Bird was out of sight, Running Elk returned to where he had left Two Fires. She was sitting in a patch of particularly lush grass.

Because he didn't want to alarm the woman, he tried to hide his concern as he sat beside her.

"The gunshot was my brother, but everyone you travel with is unharmed. If my brother hadn't been close by, we might have been discovered, and that would not have ended well. When you return, you must assure them you are unharmed. If your party sends someone out alone, it will be dangerous. Staying together is the best plan. Can you make them understand that?"

She nodded but remained silent. Running Elk could tell she was fighting back tears. He knew if she spoke, she would cry again.

After kissing her, he pulled away. "I will find you again. You have my word," he promised before standing and offering her his hand to help her.

"I believe you," she said as her fingers untied his necklace. "I will be waiting, and I will tell them everything you told me."

"Go," he said half-heartedly.

She turned and began slowly walking away from him. He watched as she tore her sleeve and rubbed grass on her dress. He stayed until he saw her running towards her friends, shrieking. As he mounted his horse, he said a silent prayer that the woman who held his heart was good at deception. She was their only hope to keep the whole situation from blowing up.

***

Running Elk was in no hurry to return to the camp, so he let the horse walk at a lazy speed.

Once he entered the encampment, he dismounted and walked towards White Wolf's tipi. His mind on his task, he walked with purpose between the rows of tipis and around the bustling natives finishing with the day's work. It was late afternoon, so most of the night fires had burned out and the cooking fires had been lit. Younger children were playing while the young men were being trained in the ways of the warrior.

White Wolf did not immediately grant his little brother entry. Running Elk knew this delay was due to the shaman's anger, but he was willing to wait his big brother out.

Running Elk walked the length of the camp before returning to White Wolf's and was relieved to see his brother's tipi flap was now open.

Once inside, Running Elk closed the flap and took a seat next to his brother on the large buffalo hide which covered most of the tipi's floor. The air was thick with ire.

"When do we leave for the hunt?" he asked, getting straight to the point of his visit.

"So, tell me, brother, was she everything you expected?" White Wolf asked as he glared at his brother.

"She was. I would still be in her company if there was a way."

White Wolf made a grumbling sound at his brother's admission. "Kicking Bird told me of the trouble. You know the actions taken tonight could still cause problems," he said, standing and walking outside.

Running Elk followed. "I believe she can deal with the others and control the outcome."

"Brother, do you really think the white men will listen to her? They care only that their women can cook and clean. Do you not remember how they think?"

"I have told you, she is different. Two Fires is an amazing woman, capable of handling herself in any situation. She will deal with this. All that is required is that she keep them calm until they have traveled one more sleep."

"You had better be right. I do not have a choice now but to trust your judgment."

"I know I am right about her, but I have a favor to ask of you."

White Wolf looked at his brother with skepticism but allowed Running Elk to finish his thought.

"I ask you to send someone to watch over her until her party gets to where they plan to settle. If not for the importance of the hunt, I would do it myself."

Running Elk knew just how much he was requesting from his brother but it didn't stop him from asking.

After letting out a long sigh, White Wolf spoke. "I will ask for a volunteer. But that is all I will do. As you know, most will be joining you on the hunt. If someone is willing, I will allow it. But only if Kicking Bird has no objections."

While the two were speaking, White Wolf directed them towards Running Elk's tipi.

"That is acceptable," Running Elk said, keeping distance between the two. "When do we leave?"

"With the sunrise. Now I suggest you go spend some time with your lonely wife."

Running Elk balked at the command. "No, brother, I will not. I am going out to hunt. Morning Star will need food when we are gone. After I return, if there is time, I will spend it with her."

"I do not understand how you can be so cold to Morning Star. All she asks is for a small amount of attention from you. Do not hunt now. You need to rest before the party leaves. You must not attempt to see her yet again." White Wolf tried to temper his anger, aware that his brother was stubborn and lovesick. "I will go and speak to Kicking Bird now about a volunteer. If you must go, do not be gone for long. At least promise me that."

"Brother, my marriage is not your concern. I will bring the game to your tipi. Will that be enough for you? I know I cannot see her again. It would endanger our people, and I am not willing to do that. Even for her."

"You know I do not like to see you unhappy, brother. But you are right. Your first obligation is to our people."

Running Elk nodded and walked inside his home. Morning Star was nowhere to be seen. During the day, she had a lot of chores to keep her occupied, but she was usually curled up on the furs at night. Instead of worrying for her, he was pleased he didn't have to explain his leaving again even though he knew she deserved an explanation.

He walked quickly to retrieve his horse. The sun was beginning to welcome the darkness, so he knew he had to be quick. What he didn't expect to find was several women bathing in the river. It was not difficult to spot his wife among them. She was smiling and giggling. He had always thought Morning Star's smile was beautiful. Truth be told, she was a very attractive woman, but Running Elk couldn't give her any more of himself than he did. Yet even feeling the way he did, he did not want any other man to touch her, and that confused him.

When he pulled himself from his thoughts, he realized he had been staring at her and her smile was directed only at him. She left the others and began wading through the waist-deep water toward him, greeting his horse when she neared.

"You never come in search of me," she said, smiling.

"As you know, I am leading the hunting party in a few hours. I cannot leave you with no food. My hunting has been lacking, and I will make sure you have enough. The hunt we are going on could take many sleeps. If there is time when I return, I will spend it with you."

"I will prepare a wonderful meal," she said, reaching to touch his arm.

"I'm sure you will. Now let me leave," he said as gently as possible before he mounted his horse and rode away.

***

She loved him so much that hearing there was any chance they would have some time together later was enough to make her happy. She was already planning the meal they would share. And she could hardly contain her excitement.

As he rode out of sight, Morning Star watched until Running Elk disappeared from view. She was so attentive to her husband that she failed to notice White Wolf standing behind her. He touched her shoulder gently and smiled at her.

"I am truly sorry he is so hardhearted to you," he said.

"I know he loves me. He just doesn't like to show his feelings." Morning Star turned to look at her brother-in-law.

White Wolf was taller than Running Elk and had a very different temperament. White Wolf was a holy man who interacted with the people on a daily basis. Running Elk was a hunter and seemed to be happiest when he was alone on the prairie. They shared physical features. They both had high cheekbones and pointed noses. But White Wolf's lips were thinner. He had a softer look. In Morning Star's opinion, the gods had chosen the right brother to give second sight.

"If you will allow me, I would like to walk you back to your home," he offered as he waited for Morning Star to fetch the water containers she'd collected while cooling herself from the oppressive heat. "I cannot understand why you do not take my brother's breath away," he spoke under his breath.

***

Running Elk soon learned he could not stay away from Two Fires. The woman was causing him to act completely out of character, but fighting the urge to see her wasn't something he could do. Taking into account that his presence wasn't helping to ease the tension he was sure the travelers were experiencing didn't sway his actions. He was driven to learn if the other whites believed her story. Accepting that they would have little time together didn't deter him in the slightest. His horse was moving in the direction of her camp. Even with his mind so filled with the woman, he knew he was going to have to catch some game. Knowing rabbit was easy and plentiful, he decided that would have to do. Morning Star did not need food. He may not have given her much of his time but she was never hungry. Her needing food was just an excuse he had given White Wolf.

Two Fire's party had only moved a small distance and were setting up their camp for the night. The men carried their rifles in their arms and were nervously watchful. Running Elk smiled at their actions, knowing he could still have picked them off before they knew he was there. The thought crossed his mind more than once. White people, in general, had never held a place in his heart. There were exceptions: Quanah, Sparrow, and Two Fires. But as a whole, he really didn't want them around. White Wolf had told him the whites would come no matter what any of the nations did. It really did seem a bleak outlook.

He lay on his stomach in the grass and watched her sitting at the front of the wagon, looking out onto the vast prairie. The breathtaking woman had a faraway look in her eyes again.

Chapter Five

Alexandria took a deep breath and ran into the small camp. She was greeted with the sight of her traveling companions, all sitting with their hands bound behind their backs, tied to the wheels of the wagon.

Peter and Mary shared a look of relief when they saw her, but Richard looked angry.

"What happened?" Alexandria asked as she hurried to untie everyone.

"An Indian was spying on us and when I tried to fight him, he shot his gun and then tied us up," Richard answered, sounding braver than everyone gathered knew he was as soon as Alexandria took the sock from his mouth.

"I didn't see anyone," Alexandria stated as she looked around the camp.

She even managed to fan herself in an effort to convey worry, but wasn't sure it was working.

"That sounds frightening," Alexandria said as she began packing the kitchen into the wagons.

"Oh, he was plenty frightening. I think we should send Peter back towards the closest fort. Someone needs to know we were attacked," Richard said as he finished reining the animals before taking his seat beside Alexandria.

Before Alexandria could reply, Peter spoke.

"I'm not going anywhere on my own. I think we just need to move along. And thank God above that we lived through the whole experience. If we come across any soldiers, then we can tell our story. Maybe I'm a coward, but I want to move along."

"I wonder why he attacked us," Mary said as she shakily returned to packing up.

Alexandria knew Peter was making sense whether he was talking out of fear or not. She was also aware that Mary was hoping nobody would dwell on her husband's statement. The man hadn't sounded like a coward to Alexandria, but it was clear Mary worried about just that.

Nothing else was said until the four were ready to move. Alexandria attributed her companions' silence to shock.

Richard made a clicking sound and snapped the reins to signal the animals to move along.

"Maybe we should move a bit. We could have been interfering with his hunt, or something as simple as staying too close to their water supply. And since no one was hurt, I think we should all be thankful. What do you think, Richard?" she asked, loud enough for the party in the following wagon to hear.

Alexandria wasn't used to being deceitful but was amazed at just how well she was doing it. She knew if the others decided she was correct in her suggestion, she would have a few hours to convince Richard that staying together was the best plan.

After a few minutes of silence, Richard spoke. "I'm grateful you weren't harmed. But what happened to your dress?"

Alexandria patted his leg and smiled. "Oh this?" she asked, looking at where she had torn her sleeve. "I fell when I was walking back. You know how lucky we were that nothing bad happened, don't you? I don't know why, but I have a feeling that everything will be fine. That being said, I would like to stop as soon as we locate another watering hole."

Richard rolled his eyes. "You are taking all of this entirely too well. But then, you weren't tied up either. We can stop as soon as we find water. Not so you can run off and bathe again but because I need a drink."

"I understand. And you're right, I wasn't tied up. I'm sure you acted like the leader you are. I will just ask one more question before we leave all this awfulness behind us," Alexandria said as she reached behind her to get a pillow. The wood was not a comfortable seat.

"Sure, ask away," Richard agreed, shaking his head. "You're not gonna be comfortable until after your furniture is in our new home, so it will be at least a year from now," Richard teased.

Alexandria smiled at him. It was difficult to act as if nothing had changed. Everything had. She was head over heels in love with Running Elk and not only that, she was planning on running off with him. Knowing Richard would be fine without her was little help. Even understanding how the actions she was planning on taking would affect everyone she knew, she was still prepared to take the leap.

"Did the Indian have any markings?" she asked after repeatedly trying to convince herself she was not the worst person in the world.

"No. I don't think so. Besides, what if he did?" Richard asked, not hiding his confusion.

"I was just asking. When we do come across a soldier, it might be helpful if you can describe the man."

"He was an Indian. Isn't that a good enough description?"

Instead of showing Richard her disgust, she moved to the back of the wagon. "I think I will try to nap."

"My little pioneer," Richard said under his breath.

***

Alexandria woke when the movement of the wagon stopped. She had no idea how far they had traveled but was covered with sweat, so she knew it was late afternoon.

"Did you sleep well?" Mary asked, offering to help Alexandria down.

"I guess I did. Where's the water?" she asked as she jumped to the ground.

Mary smiled and pointed over her shoulder. "But that can wait. Let's get some food started."

Alexandria went about doing the chores and while the group ate dinner, she listened while each recounted the attack. Every time they spoke, the story got bigger and more action-packed.

She did her best to act surprised and terrified when her friends recounted the events of the morning, but her heart was alive with excitement. She ached to see the handsome Indian again. After picking at her beans and coffee, she excused herself to sit on the wagon and look out at the marvelous prairie. Words really could not describe the beauty. Richard and Peter partook in a few drinks while Mary sat by the fire and picked at a biscuit. Alexandria welcomed the breeze and wished she could share her thoughts with Running Elk. She was swept up in the beauty of the rising moon when she felt his presence. Her heartbeat quickened as she attempted to locate him.

***

Running Elk saw the woman's expression change and smiled. He knew she felt him near. That was the way it should be. She jumped down from the wagon and walked to the people as she had the day before. This time, the dark-haired man stood with her. Running Elk watched as Alexandria attempted to calm him down. Finally, the white man sat down, but not before forcing Two Fires to take the gun. She took the rifle and walked behind the wagons.

Running Elk slipped silently around the white people and made his way to her. She turned when she heard a tree branch splinter. He was beside her before she could speak and took her in his arms. "Are you all right? Did you manage to keep the group together?"

"I am perfect, and yes, everyone is here. It was a terrible shock, but they're just glad they weren't hurt. How did you get here? You said I wouldn't see you again for a while. What has happened?"

"I am hunting so that Morning Star has plenty of ..." He stopped talking when he realized he had spoken his wife's name.

"Who is Morning Star?" she asked him.

He could see the hurt in her eyes. "Two Fires, you have my heart. But I have a woman. I have never cared for her, but she stays in my tipi and I make sure she wants for nothing. You must know that only you consume my thoughts. I want you. No matter what. You knowing about her can't change anything. You are with a man, and I am with a woman, but soon it will be only you and me."

"So you don't love her?"

"Yes, I suppose I do love her. But not like a man loves a wife. I wish the nights were longer, but I must go. I needed to know you were all right. My brother, White Wolf, will send someone to watch over you and keep you safe on your journey. I will find you as soon as it is possible. You will be present in my thoughts constantly. I promise you, we will see each other again." He pulled her into him and kissed her deeply.

He longed to lie with her but reminded himself her absence needed to be short. Surely the others would be on alert.

Running Elk slowly returned to his horse, looking back only once before mounting up.

"Don't forget about me," Two Fires said quietly.

"I would sooner forget to breathe."

***

Alexandria watched him leave and found herself confronting feelings she didn't know she was capable of. The man was different than anyone she had ever met. He made her heart race and her soul sing. But she knew their coupling was fraught with dangers. Not just for her, but she was sure he was facing obstacles too.

Knowing he would remain on her mind until she saw him again, she held his necklace in her hands and said a prayer for him.

"Please keep him safe," she whispered as she looked up at the quickly disappearing stars. She would have been quite happy staying where she was, leaning against the wagon, if Richard hadn't appeared.

"Alexandria Hazel Standish. What is wrong with you, woman? Are ya going soft in the head? You do realize you are standing in the middle of nowhere, surrounded by savages?" he asked angrily. "And just why is the rifle lying on the ground?"

Although it was clear that Richard wasn't happy, she couldn't help but smile when she looked down at the heavy weapon lying in the dirt at her feet. She reckoned it had fallen out of her grip when Running Elk had held her in his arms. She was certain of one thing. The handsome Indian made her lose her sense of reason.

Chapter Six

Running Elk was anxious to get back, so much so that he only killed four rabbits. His thoughts were consumed with learning whether White Wolf had found someone to watch over Two Fires' party.

He quickly made his way through the quiet camp. Most were in their homes, sleeping, or visiting. A few of the elders sat outside their tipis and smoked their pipes. They nodded their greetings as Running Elk made his way towards White Wolf. The warrior dropped the game by the door of his brother's tipi.

The flap on the tipi was closed, which meant White Wolf did not want to be disturbed, but Running Elk walked in anyway. The fire was only glowing ashes, and the dwelling smelled like sweet herbs. His brother was in a deep meditative state and oblivious to his presence. It was infuriating to say the least.

Knowing he would get no answers, he turned and left, picking up his game as he walked.

As soon as his home was in view, he saw Morning Star standing in the entrance, eagerly awaiting his return.

"It is good to see you. Come in. Our meal is ready," she said, smiling brightly.

He tried not to let his wife see his irritation.

Running Elk sat cross-legged in front of the fire and waited until Morning Star served him. The woman smiled proudly as she handed him a bowl of deer meat cooked with sage and potato. The food smelled heavenly, but it always did.

"I hope the hunt doesn't last for too long," she said as she sat beside him.

"It will last longer than I want it to. I never thought we would have to go to such lengths to find our food source," he said in between bites.

"You are a great hunter, husband. I am sure you will locate a herd in no time."

He planned to revisit White Wolf when he was finished eating and was doing his best to have a normal conversation with Morning Star but found his mind roaming.

In his haste to be with Two Fires, he had not given the situation with Morning Star much thought. He had given his brother his word that she would be taken care of, but hadn't thought much past that. He wanted to ensure that Morning Star's reputation stayed untarnished and once things were settled, he would speak to everyone and explain that the parting was his fault entirely.

"The food was superb, like always. Thank you," he said, handing her the plate. "I will be back after speaking to White Wolf."

Running Elk stood and walked out of his tipi.

Morning Star didn't say anything, but Running Elk heard the deep sigh.

When he made his way through the camp and saw the open flap on White Wolf's tipi, he was sure things were going to start going his way.

"You have never been impatient before, little brother. Has this white woman changed you so much?" White Wolf asked. "Before you speak, let me finish. I have found a volunteer to watch the white men's wagons. Now let's go outside and walk. The dawn promises to bring a beautiful today."

Running Elk bit his tongue and followed his brother outside. "Your mood has improved."

"I talked to Kicking Bird and we both came to the same conclusion. This hunt will be good for you."

"You would know these things. You are the shaman," Running Elk said through gritted teeth.

He did not like thinking his family was sure the woman would simply leave his thoughts because of absence. She was burned into his heart and brain. He wasn't crazy about the tone of White Wolf's voice either. "Do you not see the future? Why even speak to Kicking Bird? You have all the answers."

Running Elk stopped himself before he said something he couldn't take back.

White Wolf stopped walking and turned to his brother. "Running Elk, I see only bad things when I see you with the woman. Morning Star loves you. So much so that she would give her life for you. Why can't you love her? She would not cause any trouble for you. Or for our people, for that matter."

"Because I cannot. Morning Star is not the woman for me. And I will leave as soon we return from the hunt. But know that if I do leave, I will not return. That way, Two Fires will not be blamed for anything. I will go to her!" He stopped talking when he realized just how loud his voice had gotten.

***

White Wolf wasn't sure if his brother was venting or if he might actually leave his family, his people, for a white woman. He was so consumed with wonder that he left Running Elk where he was standing, walked into his tipi, and closed the flap. He needed to pray and seek guidance from the gods.

It was apparent that he and Running Elk were not seeing things the same way, so he was surprised when his little brother followed him inside and sat next to him before reaching for the pipe.

"Running Elk, we will speak no more until we say our farewells," White Wolf said in a dismissive tone as he lit the pipe and drew in the vision-giving smoke.

Chapter Seven

Running Elk backed out of White Wolf's home and walked in the direction of Kicking Bird's home. Before he reached the tipi, he saw his oldest nephew grooming one of his horses.

The boy was becoming a fine man. The hunt would be his first, and he was already showing signs of being a gifted warrior.

When Gray Eagle saw his uncle, he walked towards him in a hurry with a smile on his face.

"Have you heard the news, uncle?"

"What news is that?" Running Elk asked, slowing his pace but not stopping.

"Father and White Wolf have allowed me to watch the party of whites traveling through our land."

The boy was excited to have been chosen. Running Elk could tell his nephew thought it was quite an honor to be trusted with the task. He had mixed emotions when he heard his nephew's declaration. On the one hand, he knew his nephew would take the job with the seriousness that only a family member would, but on the other, Running Elk was worried the young man was not actually up for the task.

He kept his thoughts to himself and smiled at Gray Eagle. "This is an extremely important task. Are you sure you are up to it?" he asked, putting his arm around his nephew.

"I can do it, and I am up for the job. How difficult can it be to watch a group of whites?" he asked, sounding like he knew the answer would be "not difficult at all."

"Usually it would be a fairly easy job, but these people are different. There is a woman with them with yellow hair. She is called Two Fires ..."

"Why do you call a white woman a name for our people?" his nephew interrupted.

"Because I know the woman, and her soul is mine. She must not be harmed. And you must stay with them until they reach their destination."

Gray Eagle didn't look convinced that his uncle hadn't been in the sun too long, but he didn't voice his suspicions. "I will do the job I have been given."

"Good. Then, on the hunt, I will have nothing to worry about. She is in good hands."

"Good luck on the hunt, Uncle," Gray Eagle said, walking back to his waiting horse.

"I will see you soon," Running Elk said, suddenly realizing there was no reason to speak to Kicking Bird.

His oldest brother cleared his throat at the same time as Running Elk turned to wander back to his tipi with the intention of gathering the supplies and arrows he was sure Morning Star had packed and waiting. Even knowing his job was finished and that it would be a quick in and out of his home, he was relieved when he heard his brother's attempt to get his attention.

When he turned, Kicking Bird was standing close enough to have observed his conversation with Gray Eagle. His brother was smiling. "I am on the way to say farewell to White Wolf. Would you like to join me?"

"No. We don't seem to agree on anything anymore. Besides, I was just there, so I don't see the point of returning," Running Elk informed him.

"The only thing you don't agree on is the white woman," Kicking Bird corrected, steering Running Elk in the direction of White Wolf's anyway.

"Two Fires is not the downfall of our people. The whites who will take our land and kill all of our food for sport before leaving it to rot under the noonday sun are our enemies. Not Two Fires," Running retorted, his voice again growing in volume.

Kicking Bird stopped walking, turned to his brother, and held him by his shoulders. "My brother, do not be angry with White Wolf or me. We are trying to hold onto our way of life and listen to the signs the gods give us. We are more than willing to die for our land, our beliefs, and our people. But we will not invite trouble. If White Wolf has seen that as an outcome of bringing the woman here, then there is nothing you, or I, for that matter, can do. I know it is not what you want to hear. The heart wants what it wants," Kicking Bird began his speech in anger, but as he finished talking, Running Elk could tell his brother would go to the ends of the earth for Sparrow.

"I understand that times were different when you found Sparrow, but would that have mattered? If you saw her today, would you just walk away from her?"

Kicking Bird smiled sadly. "I remember every detail of our meeting. She was lost and frightened. Her family had all died from a sickness on their way to a new land. I still can't explain how I saw her hiding in the tall grass, but I did. As frightened as she was, she looked me in the eyes when I jumped from my horse and offered her my hand. And with that look, I knew we would share our lives together. All that aside, I can't say I would leave our people for her, then. Though now, I wouldn't want to greet the rising sun without knowing she was with me."

"You loved her from the first time you saw her. Why are my feelings so different? The woman holds my heart. You know how strange these feelings are for me. I have given the people everything they asked, and if you and White Wolf are convinced nothing good will come of our being together, then I have to leave," Running Elk explained, doing his best to not raise his voice.

"Let us table this difficult discussion until we return from the hunt," Kicking Bird suggested. "White Wolf's visions have never been wrong, but we will not think on it just yet."

"His vision is wrong now. I will leave, brother. If that is the only way." Running Elk hoped his brother understood it was a last resort, but one he was willing to take.

Kicking Bird loosened his hold on Running Elk's arm and looked to the sky. "You feel that strongly for a woman you have only seen twice?"

"I do. I am just not sure what will happen to Morning Star."

"You know full well that if you leave, she will be disgraced. You go gather your supplies; I am going to speak to White Wolf. Maybe he can pray on this and find a way around it all. Too many people will be hurt if you leave. When we return, you should seek out Quanah. He might be able to see this situation from a fresh angle. I will meet you shortly."

Running Elk nodded as his brother walked away. He didn't see how Quanah could possibly be of much help. The chief was a well-respected warrior and half white, but Quanah had given his word no more whites would be taken. But Two Fires would willingly join the band, so he held onto some hope.

Before pulling the flap open on his tipi, he said a quick prayer, asking the gods to keep Two Fires safe, and then walked in, to both greet and say goodbye to Morning Star.

Morning Star shadowed her husband's movements but stayed silent as he gathered the packed supplies.

When he turned to face her, she looked at his chest where his necklace should have been. A look of worry crossed her face. "Where is your necklace, husband?"

He attempted to smile a calming grin. "I lost it earlier today, but do not fear. I am sure it is not a bad omen."

"I will keep you in my prayers," she said, casting her eyes downward.

Running Elk knew tears were forming in her eyes. And that knowledge angered him. It seemed there was nothing he could do that didn't cause her anguish.

"I will return, woman," he said as gently as he could manage.

He kissed her on the cheek quickly.

When Morning Star opened her eyes, he was gone.

***

On his way toward the gathering hunting party, Running Elk scanned the area for Gray Eagle. He wanted to restress the importance of the young man's task but in a way that did not undermine his nephew's confidence.

A smile crossed Running Elk's face when he saw Gray Eagle approaching. The young man was already mounted up and ready to depart.

"Uncle, I am leaving now. Father has spoken to me, and I know how important the woman is to you. I will protect her with my life."

Running Elk nodded. He had no doubt Gray Eagle was telling the truth, but prayed it wouldn't come to that.

"Then she is in good hands. I will see you soon."

Chapter Eight

Gray Eagle had no trouble locating the whites. The wagons making their way across the prairie made enough noise to alert anyone close by that they were there. From the clanging of bells to the loudness of their voices, everything about them told Gray Eagle that the whites were not as concerned with being attacked as they should have been. He kept his distance as the wagons trudged their way through the buffalo grass.

Gray Eagle was sure he had located the right group because his father had described them down to the smallest detail. After settling his horse into a slow pace, he began to wonder why he hadn't seen the woman his uncle and father had tasked him with protecting. The young warrior disliked the dark-haired man from the second he laid eyes on him. Kicking Bird had stressed the dark, loud one was the most dangerous of the bunch, but Gray Eagle found he hadn't needed his father to tell him that. He felt the anger and fear emanating from the man, even at a distance. Gray Eagle found his emotions confusing. The fear, he understood. Kicking Bird had told him of the man's actions when his father had been forced to fire the gun. But his anger was a curious thing. Unless the man was angry that he had acted so cowardly.

He considered watering his horse, knowing a pond was close by, but quickly decided staying with the group, until he saw the woman his uncle called Two Fires, was his best course of action. As soon as he was sure she was well, he would ride ahead and find a good place to camp for the night.

Her appearance took longer than he hoped. It was noontime before the two wagons stopped for a meal. As soon as they stopped, Gray Eagle dismounted and crouched down while the settlers moved about, ignorant to his presence.

When the yellow-haired woman walked from the back of one of the wagons, she seemed to sense he was near. Immediately, he felt a kinship with the white woman. He quickly decided his uncle was a lucky man; the woman was a striking beauty. He even allowed himself a moment to be envious of Running Elk. Gray Eagle had never encountered a white person who was so relaxed on the open prairie. Most he'd seen were on guard and nervous; much like the dark-haired man. Even though he had been told to stay hidden, he knew he would break his word. Just not until he had found a place to make a camp and the white man's wagon had stopped moving for the night.

He watched with fascination as the women in the group started a small fire and began carrying black metal pots and pans to the flame. From the looks of it, the cooking vessels were heavy and cumbersome. The next thing he saw was a clumpy, reddish liquid fall from a tin to the waiting pan. He had never seen any food source placed in a silver container before. His lunch would consist of dried berries and pemmican. The difference in their diets was something he would ask his mother about when he returned. The white man's food was strange, but it did smell interesting.

It was almost dusk when the settlers set up camp. Gray Eagle knew his campsite was close enough to hear if there was trouble. That was a real possibility since the fire they built was easily visible for miles. It was not smart to let a flame grow to such size. He decided to try to explain that fact to the woman when he introduced himself. If she hadn't run at the sight of his fierce-looking uncle, the young warrior was sure she wouldn't be scared of him.

While he spied on the settlers, he took the time to look at some of their belongings. Wooden pieces were tied to the back of the wagons. The men had pulled a heavy rectangular piece from the wagon when they set up camp. Although he thought some of the furnishing was interesting, he didn't understand why it was needed. His people had little in material goods. Blankets for warmth, clothing for special occasions, cooking vessels that weren't so heavy they weighed your arms down. Everything they owned was a gift from Mother Earth, except for the guns. The guns were needed even more with each passing day.

It wasn't long before he saw the dark-haired man give the yellow-haired woman a rifle before kissing her on the cheek and walking to the back of a wagon. He quickly realized the group was seeking sleep for the night. Soon, the woman called Two Fires would be alone and then he would put his plan into action.

The woman waited for a few minutes and then stood. After looking around, she began walking away from the camp. She took three steps before turning back to retrieve the forgotten rifle before continuing walking into the night.

Once she was some distance from the fire, the woman leaned back and looked to the heavens. It was embarrassingly simple for Gray Eagle to sneak up on her. He stealthily placed one hand on her shoulder and the other gently over her mouth before turning her to face him.

The woman jumped from fright but didn't appear to be on the verge of screaming. So, he moved the hand, stopping her from speaking. But not until he quickly shushed her, just in case he was reading the situation wrong.

The woman remained silent as she turned to get a better look at him. She was a remarkable-looking woman. Her face was quite appealing, but her eyes were breathtaking. The young warrior once again found himself envying his uncle.

"Running Elk sent me to watch over you. I will be your shadow until you get to where you plan to settle."

"Is he well?" she asked, holding tightly to a familiar necklace in her dainty hands.

Seeing his uncle's good luck stone in the white woman's hands surprised him. "Did my uncle gift that to you?"

She smiled and held the necklace tighter. "He did. The very first time we met. It gives me comfort. I'm sorry. I am being terribly rude. My name is Alexandria. What do they call you?

Gray Eagle had to stop himself from smiling. The woman was indeed a strange one. "My name is Gray Eagle. I am son of Kicking Bird, and Running Elk is my uncle. The bauble you hold so tightly is the only thing my uncle has that belonged to his father."

The statement seemed to touch the woman deeply. "He did tell me it protected him but insisted that I needed protection more than him."

"I am certain he will be fine without it," Gray Eagle assured her, trying to sound more convinced than he was.

The woman smiled and sat on the grass.

Gray Eagle kept an eye on the wagons. "You must know that my presence is to be kept between you and me. They cannot know. If you like, I will continue to visit you when it is safe. But for now, I must go."

"I won't tell them. Gray Eagle." She spoke as he turned to leave.

He turned to look at her.

"Do all Indians speak our language?"

He smiled. "No, only a few in our village. Mainly my blood relations," he explained as he picked up his bow and arrows.

"How did you learn?" she asked quickly. Gray Eagle was getting the feeling the woman would talk to him all night if he allowed it.

"My mother, Sparrow, is white. No, she no longer holds to the white man's way." He corrected himself. "She was white; now, she is Comanche."

The pride was thick in the young warrior's voice when he spoke of his mother. In his mind, she was a strong, brilliant woman, and he would not have chosen another mother if he had the chance.

Chapter Nine

Kicking Bird was usually single-minded. The hunt would normally be the only thing occupying his thoughts. Yet his brother's white woman was weighing heavy on his mind. He honestly hoped the problem would simply go away. He would have been overly pleased if the white people completely disappeared, but he knew neither one of those things was going to happen.

When his little brother met the assembled group, Kicking Bird looked to the heavens and asked the gods to give him patience. But even after praying, he knew he was going to hear about the woman the whole trip.

As soon as the ten top hunters were gathered and ready to leave, White Wolf walked to the center of the group. He looked at the men and said a prayer for a successful hunt.

Once he was finished, he looked towards Running Elk. "Brother, I wish you much success on the hunt."

Running Elk nodded and looked the shaman in the eyes. Kicking Bird could see the anger simmering in his youngest brother.

"I have spent a great deal of time in prayer over the last day. And believe me, I will continue to commune with the gods while you are absent. I do not want us to be enemies."

"I appreciate your words," Running Elk replied. "But words are not actions. As angry as you make me, we could never be enemies. We are brothers. If you can keep an open mind about Two Fires, I am sure you will find a way to allow our union to happen. We will see each other soon." He mounted his pinto and turned in the direction of the open prairie.

***

Running Elk tried to concentrate on the hunt, but Two Fires was eternally in his thoughts. For the first time in his life, he felt disconnected from his people. He rode behind the group and tried to think of a way that he and Two Fires could be together. Even though he had never wanted anything more, there seemed to be no easy way to accomplish his dream. The other worry that plagued his thoughts was her traveling through Kiowa country. He could only pray Gray Eagle was watching closely.

At night, when the others would sit around a small fire and tell stories, he would lie on his blanket and remember how good it felt when she was in his arms.

Kicking Bird left him to his thoughts for the first six days of the hunt, but when he saw his brother riding his way, Running Elk knew his peace had come to an end. His brother's expression meant they were going to talk, whether Running Elk wanted to or not.

"I feel today we will find a sign of the buffalo," Kicking Bird said as he rode by Running Elk's side.

His brother's opening statement wasn't what Running Elk expected, but it was at least a topic that couldn't possibly end in angry words. "That would be good."

"It would help if your mind was on the hunt," his brother added. "A buffalo could have walked in front of you, and I don't think you would have noticed."

Running Elk fought the urge to prod his horse to run. Instead, he rolled his eyes and looked at his brother. It would seem he had been wrong about assuming they wouldn't argue. Since Kicking Bird had brought up the subject, Running Elk decided to share what had been bothering him the most. "I am worried that the Kiowa might stumble over Two Fires' wagon. The thought has been weighing heavily on my heart since we left. I don't know why I hadn't considered how real the threat was before. If they do find the settlers, they will not just tie them up like you did. They will simply kill the men and take the women."

"That is a possibility, but Gray Eagle will watch over her. Have a little faith in your nephew. My son is growing into a fine warrior."

"It is not Gray Eagle's ability I doubt. I need to know she is safe."

Kicking Bird made a grunting sound, denoting his unhappiness with his brother's statement. "We may get lucky and find the buffalo today. If we do, the rest of the camp will follow once Otter has informed them where we are," he reminded him. "So, pray that this will be over in a short time."

"A short time feels like an eternity."

Kicking Bird rode away, leaving Running Elk to return to his unsettling thoughts.

Running Elk was preparing to lay his sleeping hide out when Kicking Bird returned. "Brother, come walk with me for a bit."

"What is there to speak about?" Running Elk asked as he turned to his brother.

"We are family. There is always something to talk about. Let's talk about hunting when we were young," Kicking Bird suggested. "Do you remember the excitement? Everything was different then. I miss those times," he said, allowing sadness to enter his voice.

Running Elk heard a noise and quickly put his arm out to stop Kicking Bird from taking another step. He stretched out on the ground and crawled to the edge of the hill. In the valley below was a small herd of buffalo. They were lazily eating grass and enjoying the coolness of the evening. Kicking Bird, who had crawled beside his brother, began silently backing away before Running Elk.

Running Elk was experiencing mixed emotions. He was overjoyed they had found the animal but saddened by the size of the herd. The hunter knew the reason; the white man was killing off their main food source for fun.

After quickly counting the number, he realized he had never seen a group so small. When he was young, his father would tell him that the buffalo would be great in number until the end of times. For the first time since he lost his father, he was glad the man wasn't alive to witness the annihilation, not only of the animal, but maybe even his people.

Kicking Bird sent Otter back to alert the tribe, and Running Elk was left to watch the herd.

"Brother, the camp should be here in two or three days," Kicking Bird informed him.

"I am going to ride ahead. I need to clear my mind. But do not worry; I will keep an eye on the buffalo," Running Elk said, moving away from his brother.

He was in no mood to talk. The dreams that had awoken him in the night were impossible to shake. He had seen Two Fires being taken and watched helplessly as his nephew was killed trying to stop the abduction. He had never been given a vision before and prayed the night terror wasn't his first.

While Running Elk was watching the herd, he fought with what his next course of action should be. There were plenty of men present, and with the smallness of the herd, he wasn't needed. It was the first time he'd ever considered not being a part of a buffalo hunt. But his choice was a surprisingly easy one.

He reined his horse in the direction of the hunters' camp and decided to share his dream with his brother before telling him he was leaving. Kicking Bird wasn't difficult to find. He was sitting around the campfire with two other hunters, sharpening his arrows.

After dismounting from his horse, he walked behind Kicking Bird and placed his hand on his shoulder. "Walk with me, brother."

Kicking Bird stood and followed his brother. As soon as Running Elk was sure they were out of earshot, he told his big brother about his dream. Kicking Bird stayed silent during the retelling.

"You saw my son's death?" Kicking Bird asked, interrupting the story.

Running Elk could see the news, whether it was true or not, had taken a piece of his brother's soul. "I did not. It was just a feeling," he lied to his brother. "I am not gifted with sight. But you have to understand the need to assure myself everything is all right."

"Did you see who did it?" Kicking Bird asked in a tone that led Running Elk to believe his brother wasn't sure he wanted to hear the answer.

Running Elk was glad Kicking Bird had calmed down. He had never lied to his brother before, but it had seemed to help. He waited until his brother lit his pipe before answering.

"They were Kiowa. I couldn't see the markings on their faces quite clearly, as badly as I wanted to see the one that took Two Fires. If I had been able to see him, it would be a face I would never forget. But I am sure the dream was merely a manifestation of my concern."

"I suppose my next question should be ... do you honestly believe the dream was not a vision?"

Running Elk took a deep breath. "I have given it much thought, brother. It may be a sign that I am needed there for some reason. Most probably it is an overactive imagination. Whatever it was, I feel that I am not vital to this hunt. You know as well as I do that the men here can handle this without me. I am sorry if you don't understand, but I must leave. I will not be able to rest until I know the truth. If all is well, I will find the camp before I make a decision on what to do next."

"When will you return?"

Running Elk knew Kicking Bird didn't want him to go. Maybe it was fear that he had lost his eldest son; maybe it was worry that Running Elk would make good on his threats. But whatever his brother was feeling, he was still leaving.

He began walking towards his waiting horse before looking back at his brother. Kicking Bird was standing beside his horse, watching Running Elk as he rode away. The alarm that was etched into Kicking Bird's face was all caused by him. Running Elk prayed that if the dream had been a vision, he would be able to get to the wagon train in time to stop it from happening.

Chapter Ten

Alexandria opened her eyes slowly and was readying herself to stretch before climbing from the wagon when she heard the strangest whooshing sounds followed by screams and moaning coming from one of the men. Before thinking her actions through, she cautiously slid back the loose material blocking the exit and peered out.

Everyone in Virginia had told her stories about how being captured by Indians was a death sentence. When Richard had informed her they were going West, he had promised to kill her if they were attacked, just to save her from the horrors she would have to endure if the Indians took her. Yet even before meeting Running Elk, she'd had a hard time believing the stories. It was alarming to think any humans could be so heartless and barbaric.

As soon as her eyes adjusted to the brightness of the morning, Alexandria saw two Indian warriors. Nothing could have readied her for the sight.

Her friends were all on the ground. Richard had been shot by two arrows and was lying face down. She didn't know if he was dead or alive.

Peter was lying on his back while two Indians poked his chest with sticks. Although there was no blood on the ground around him, Alexandria was pretty sure he had been shot with an arrow or two himself.

Mary was curled up in the fetal position by the fire. The woman was rocking back and forth, silently mouthing words. She didn't appear to have been hurt yet; just traumatized.

While Alexandria was frantically scanning the camp, she saw a third warrior. The two men who were yelling had half of their faces painted red, but the man leaning against her wagon had a face which was painted white. His lips were black, and he wore what looked like turkey feathers on his head.

She was both terrified and saddened by what was happening to her friends. Her hand was firmly over to mouth to try to stop herself from screaming. Alexandria had a very important decision to make. Her options were simple enough. She could try to help. But then she might be seen.

She could also attempt to sneak away and find Gray Eagle. Maybe he could help get her husband and friends out of the mess they were in.

Since the three Indians were all busy, she thought she had a pretty good chance of being able to walk quietly and quickly to the grass line and then hide herself before looking for Gray Eagle. Alexandria was sure the young warrior had to have heard the commotion. As soon as she made up her mind, she turned around and stepped out of the wagon.

No sooner had her foot hit the dirt, than she felt an excruciating pain in the back of her head. The next thing she knew, she was being held up by one of the warriors.

Alexandria fought fiercely to gain her freedom but the man had a steel grip. After realizing her movements were doing no good, she stopped fighting and hung her head. While she was doing her best to convince herself everything would be fine, she noticed there were more than three warriors. The whooshing sound happened again and she watched as three other Indians showed themselves. As each one rose and hollered, they were hit by an arrow.

The warrior holding her yelled something, and two other Indians fanned out in the grass to find the sniper. While they were searching, she was forced to watch the two warriors with the red paint on their faces while they scalped her husband. Before throwing up and fainting, she said a prayer for Gray Eagle and thanked God he had been close. The arrows had to be coming from Gray Eagle's arrow, and she hated to admit it, but she was overjoyed that the arrows made their mark. She knew Gray Eagle was attempting to help her, but failed to locate him in the commotion. The two had become close during their time together. Over the days, he had freely shared many stories of his people and his uncle. All she could do was pray he survived the attack.

When she was awoken from her daze by being shoved onto a horse, she watched as Mary was scooped up by one of the warriors.

Alexandria's head was swimming, but she thought they were moving eastward. The men talked amongst themselves, but she couldn't understand a word they said. After her captors yelled at her several times, they seemed to realize speaking louder wasn't helping.

When the men stopped for water, she was yanked from the horse and Running Elk's necklace fell out of her dress pocket. As soon as she realized what was happening, she fell on top of it. The jewelry was the only thing she had left. It was her most precious possession and she was willing to die rather than lose it.

The Indian who she'd been riding with kicked her out of the way, knelt down, and grabbed it. She begged him to let her keep it but was sure he didn't understand her any more than she understood him. The man laughed and threw it into the river. She rolled over and cried. Losing Running Elk's gift was more than she could bear. She was truly lost, and stayed in a fetal position until the tears wouldn't fall anymore.

As soon as she stopped whimpering, she was placed back on the horse while her captor walked beside the animal. She wanted to run, but knew she wouldn't get far. As they rode further from her old life, she repeatedly tried to convince herself that Gray Eagle was alive and would be there soon.

Chapter Eleven

Running Elk rode day and night, stopping only to tend to his horse. After traveling for several days, he noticed thick gray smoke in the distance. Fear gripped his heart as he prodded the horse to a full run. The smell of the smoke invading his nostrils was not that of a campfire but, instead, reminded him of the smells of battle. Nearing the camp, he quickly realized that the settlers had been attacked and knew it must have been the Kiowa. He could see what remained of the wagons, still smoking, looking more like meatless buffalo than something built by the white man.

The next thing he noticed was the abundance of arrows protruding from the ground. The markings on the arrows proved to be of the Kiowa tribe. Among them were several that were not Kiowa; they were his nephew's arrows. Gray Eagle had been involved, and his aim had been true enough to take the lives of more than one of the attackers. The only sound of life in the camp was the hum of the flies and the calling of buzzards gathering in the sky above. Looking over the scene, he found the bodies of the two white men. Their twisted bodies were bloody and beaten; their scalps and eyes removed. His heart ached for Two Fires. She must have been witness to the death of her husband.

Running Elk dismounted and began surveying the camp on foot, looking for any clue to the fate of Two Fires. The cooking fire still crackled, keeping warm the uneaten food from that morning's meal. Stepping over the slain bodies of Kiowa warriors, his pride for Gray Eagle brought a faint smile to his face. His nephew had used his abilities well. He searched in vain. Neither his nephew nor Two Fires were there. The signs of struggle near the wagons convinced him that the women had been, taken and were possibly still alive. He knew the attack had happened only hours earlier and that knowledge made him more angry than sad. He could have saved her if he had been quicker. If he had left when he woke from the nightmare, he might have been able to save Two Fires. That knowledge caused him to consider what needed to be done before leaving to find Gray Eagle. He decided that a burial for the men was not necessary as the animals would ensure the bodies were not left in peace for long. Finding his nephew and Two Fires was more important.

After saying a quick prayer and vowing he would find the woman he loved, he went in search of Gray Eagle.

***

Running Elk searched for three days he located his nephew. The young warrior was weak, but he was alive. Running Elk walked up on Gray Eagle sleeping by the water's edge. A Kiowa arrow had found its mark in his leg, and Gray Eagle had lost a lot of blood, but he was alive. It looked as if he had broken the arrow in two and pulled it through the wound.

Running Elk walked with trepidation toward the motionless Indian before kneeling and lightly touching the young man's shoulder. Gray Eagle was burning with fever. The young warrior was pale and sweating.

"Gray Eagle, it is Running Elk. Can you hear me?"

Gray Eagle opened his eyes and smiled faintly at his uncle. "I have not lost her. Just this morning, I saw the party. There are only three Kiowa warriors and Two Fires. They killed everyone else," he said, sounding as if he were struggling to breathe before closing his eyes again. "The other woman was taken but continued to be disrespectful to her captor. Yesterday, he had enough of her mouth and threw her from his horse. They took turns beating her until she expired. Even at that distance, I could hear Two Fires begging them to stop. I also found this in the river."

Running Elk opened his nephew's clenched hand to find the necklace that he had given Two Fires.

Mixed emotions ran through Running Elk when he held the stone. Did the necklace's reappearance indicate that Two Fires was alive or prove she was gone? "Gray Eagle, listen to me. You must tell me, have they hurt her?"

"They are Kiowa; they treat all white women as slaves. No, they have not beaten her. You have to go to her. I just need to rest for a few minutes and then I will follow. We will t—" He did not finish his sentence before he lost consciousness.

After wrapping his nephew's wound and ensuring Gray Eagle was comfortable, Running Elk left to gather materials for building a shelter. The resulting structure was a sturdy lean-to of limbs and leaves. He was grateful for the warmth of the night and the light provided by the full moon.

Building the shelter took longer than he expected, because his thoughts were not on his job; they were with Two Fires. Returning to his nephew, he understood that he had an extremely difficult decision to make.

Gray Eagle had fallen from a sitting position to lying on his side in the dirt. The wrap Running Elk had placed on his leg was red with blood. He thanked the gods when he saw the shallow rise and fall of his nephew's chest. Running Elk knelt down and took Gray Eagle in his arms. As he carried him to the shelter, he remembered when Gray Eagle was just a child and he would carry the boy back to Kicking Bird's tipi after he had followed Running Elk around the camp all day. The memory made his heart hurt. Gray Eagle was like a son to him. He had been active in the boy's training. The pain Gray Eagle was experiencing had been caused because of his admiration for Running Elk.

Running Elk knew Two Fires was close, but his responsibility was to his brother's son. He vowed that as soon as his nephew had recovered, he would go in search of the Kiowa party and put an end to it. He had to help the boy regain enough strength to return to their people. Knowing the decision was the correct one didn't mean it wouldn't haunt him forever. It would take many moons before he would be able to start searching for Two Fires again.

The warrior sat beside his sleeping nephew and lit his pipe before praying that Two Fires remained safe until they could be together again. While he smoked, he placed the necklace he had gifted her back around his neck.

Chapter Twelve

The ground was hard underneath Alexandria's sore back as she stared up at the night sky and attempted to count the stars instead of reliving, yet again, the events of the last few days. A gentle breeze brought with it the warmth and smell of the small fire. Alexandria knew she had been with her captors only four days, yet it seemed like forever to her. The murders she had been forced to watch haunted her every thought. The horrors of her capture only increased her prayers that Gray Eagle was alive and that Running Elk would be there soon. Her hope of rescue was slowing being overcome by doubt.

The Indians had treated her badly. Bruises spotted her body, and her limbs ached, but at least they had quit yelling at her. Her dress was torn, and the multitude of holes made it look more like a rag. One boot had gone missing days ago, and her hair was caked with mud. For the first time in a very long time, she had begun to not care what happened to her.

At night, the angry Indian whom she had been forced to ride behind would tie a rope around her hands and affix the other end around his body. She had not slept for more than minutes at a time. As she lay awake, waiting for the man lying beside her to move, she tried to believe Running Elk would be rescuing her soon. It was becoming more difficult with each passing moment.

Every muscle in her exhausted body tightened when she felt her captor stir. The only thing she was sure of was that she was not looking forward to another day.

***

The Indian untied the rope from his body and stood up. He looked down at the woman lying on his robe. He had many questions for the woman. None were being answered, and he was not known as a patient man. He needed to find a way to communicate with her. After making a noise that was a mixture of anger and irritation, the Indian leaned down, grasped her by the shoulders, and pulled her to her feet. Staring intently, he studied her face carefully and inquisitively. The woman was strikingly beautiful, but her eyes were exquisite. It was difficult not to get lost in them. He appreciated her spirit but was pleased to see that she was beginning to resign herself to her fate.

***

Alexandria stood toe to toe with the man as he looked in her eyes. He was taller than Running Elk and not as muscular. It was apparent, no matter what she thought of the man, that he was a warrior. A man who could, and did kill, with no visible sign of regret. Although she had been terrified at first, her fear subsided as her indifference grew. The warrior seemed to sense her change in attitude and smiled. His face changed dramatically when he smiled. His angry face softened, as did his eyes. The best she could do was stare at him blankly. It was the same look she had tried desperately to display from the moment she was captured.

Another man walked towards them and pulled her captor away toward the far side of the camp, speaking a language foreign to her. She stood where she had been left and watched as the third man joined the conversation. It occurred to her that, if she was going to attempt an escape, there would not be a better time. Knowing she could easily die before reaching safety was not as much of a deterrent as it would have been a week before. Without Running Elk or Gray Eagle's help, she was lost. Still, she knew she couldn't live with her captors. She had seen their brutality firsthand and was sure it was only a matter of time before they bestowed the same treatment upon her. Before her thoughts were completely sorted, she began taking small steps backward towards a grove of trees.

The conversation the men were having was getting louder, and they didn't seem to notice her movement until the man who seized her turned away from the others with a disgusted look on his face.

***

Standing Bear was not in the mood to continue to quarrel about the white woman. He had already decided she was going to live with him in his tipi. His conviction was strong, even if he couldn't explain why he felt the way he did. As soon as he had an explanation, he would tell the others. He was well aware of the repercussions of wounding the Comanche who had tried to stop the abduction, and of the possibility that the woman would be sought out. A warrior from another tribe, attempting to protect white travelers, was a strange occurrence. It wasn't one he had seen before, but Standing Bear was still hopeful there would be no more bloodshed. If the Comanche had had any interest in the wagon train for himself, he would have surely made his move earlier.

Because of his preoccupation with the argument, he was shocked when he realized the white woman was not standing where he had left her. The woman was attempting to escape and, for the second time that morning, she made him smile.

"She has run away," he informed the others with amusement in his tone. "I will find her. You two ride ahead. If you come across her, leave her be. This is my problem to take care of. Tell my father I am a day behind you, but do not tell him about her. I am sure he will feel the same as you both do about the situation, so allow me to speak to him first. Then you can say your piece. "

The other men were already on their horses, waiting for Standing Bear to finish his request. He knew that they were his friends before anything and that they would grudgingly follow his request. He also knew they were concerned about the actions the Comanches would take. The nations had worked many years to coexist and stop the fighting between their tribes.

Standing Bear watched as they rode away. The woman was brave, but not very good at avoiding recapture by a trained Kiowa. He retrieved his pinto and walked towards the trees. Instead of packing the camp, he left it as it was. He was sure she hadn't gotten far.

Chapter Thirteen

Much to Running Elk's disappointment, Gray Eagle was no better the next morning. The young warrior had called out many times during his fitful sleep. Running Elk stayed by his side and slept little through the night. The furthest the warrior went was to the river to gather water in hopes of cooling his nephew's fever. He was angry about the situation but knew if nothing else turned out like he wanted, he had to keep the young man alive.

As dawn was breaking, ushering in a new day, Running Elk walked back from the river with a wet piece of cloth. He was surprised when he saw his nephew attempting to sit up. For a moment, he allowed himself to be hopeful that the boy was on the mend, but quickly realized the strength Gray Eagle was employing to make the simple movement. Running Elk shook his head in disappointment and quickly walked over to help.

"Why are you here?" Gray Eagle asked hoarsely. "Where is Two Fires?"

"Lie down. You are still very weak. I will search for her once you have regained your strength," Running Elk explained as he gently pushed his nephew back down. The truth was, Two Fires had never left his thoughts. But he didn't want to worry his nephew more than he already was.

Gray Eagle put up a fight in an attempt to show Running Elk that he was feeling better. It was a good sign, and Running Elk said a quick prayer of thanks.

"Uncle, did I manage to kill any of the Kiowa?" Gray Eagle asked as he attempted to make himself comfortable as possible.

Fighting amongst nations was nothing new. It had been happening since the dawn of time, but the question forced Running Elk to understand that that way of life wasn't what he wished for his nephew. The realization was hard to swallow. It was their way of life. Before the white man came, some nations had fought over everything from horses to game. With the incursion of Europeans, the fighting had only gotten more frequent and barbaric. For a brief moment, Running Elk wondered if the nations could put aside their differences if the people might have a chance at fighting off the white men.

"Does your silence mean I did nothing to help?" Gray Eagle asked, interrupting Running Elk's train of thought.

Running Elk could hear Gray Eagles disappointment at the thought. "You did a brave thing and yes, you did help. As far as I can tell, there are only three Kiowa left alive."

"That's good. If I was only a little quicker or a better aim, I might have been able to save Two Fires."

"Gray Eagle, listen to me. What happened isn't your fault. The blame lies with me. I will see you safely back to Kicking Bird and Sparrow before I search for Two Fires. Everything will be fine. Do not worry. Here, drink some water, it will help."

"Leave me. I will be fine. I cannot say that about Two Fires," Gray Eagle argued weakly as he slowly swallowed the water from the buffalo skin.

"I will not leave you. I made my decision and will not second-guess myself. Now rest," Running Elk said, trying to convince himself he had done the right thing.

"Tomorrow, I will be strong enough to ride. We can leave then. To find ..." Gray Eagle fell into a slumber before he could finish his thought.

Running Elk was glad for the silence. He knew Gray Eagle wouldn't be strong enough to ride for days and was glad not to have to argue with his nephew further.

He leaned against the temporary shelter and closed his eyes. Seeing Two Fires' smile caused him to experience both happiness and great sadness.

Chapter Fourteen

Standing Bear easily followed the trail left by the white woman. It couldn't have been much clearer if she had intentionally left it for him. Even so, he was surprised at the distance she managed to put between them. Deciding that the woman had earned the right to have a drink at the nearby river, he slowed and again smiled. She was unlike any woman he had ever encountered.

The woman ran as far as her legs would carry her. Standing Bear knew she had to be sore and tired, but she managed to keep moving. He watched as his two friends rode past her. They had seen her but didn't bother to look her way. He appreciated them having enough faith in him to do as he asked.

The woman's face displayed relief. She took a moment to rejoice in her good fortune. When she saw the clear, inviting water she seemed to consider jumping in and washing the dust and death from her body. Standing Bear knew he couldn't allow her to get too comfortable. A drink was all she would get.

The woman slowly neared the water's edge, looking in all directions as she did. As she knelt down to scoop up the inviting water, her gaze traveled further down the bank. Her movements reminded Standing Bear of a deer. The Kiowa warrior allowed his muscles to relax and smiled until he saw her stand up.

Standing Bear was aware there was a small encampment across the river and knew he couldn't allow the woman to call out. He was not ready to lose her. He had seen the Comanche warrior his captive was so willing to call out to but did not know his name. He knew he couldn't take any risks with her; he just didn't know why he felt the way he did. He also knew his actions could quite possibly cause more trouble. But none of that mattered. He wanted to keep her.

The woman's behavior suddenly changed. She went from being frightened of the water to barely being able to conceal her excitement. Standing Bear didn't understand the change but knew he couldn't allow her to act on her impulses. Before she was completely to her feet, he moved behind her and put his hand over her mouth. She thrashed about in her grasp but he held her tightly. He even managed to keep his hand firmly over her mouth when her teeth sank into the meaty part of his palm. Standing Bear pulled her body against his and waited until her flailing body calmed and he felt her go limp. Once he was sure the fight was gone from her, he carefully picked her up and carried her to his waiting horse. While he carried the unconscious woman, he tried to understand the scene he'd watched unfolding.

The woman was obviously not afraid of the Comanche. He was sure he'd seen her smile before she started to stand. If he were honest with himself, it was more than a smile; it was a look of relief and love. Standing Bear knew there was more to the story. Two Comanches being close to the woman was more than a coincidence. Still, he felt a strong desire for the woman and wasn't willing to let her go. He was sure all his unanswered questions would be answered when he could communicate with her, and that couldn't happen until he was back amongst his people.

When he returned to the makeshift camp, he laid the woman near the fire before covering her with one of his robes and beginning to pack up. She was still unconscious when he finished, so he sat beside her.

As he moved a piece of dirt-caked hair from her face, he took the opportunity to really look at her. It was then that he vowed to win the woman's trust and, if he was extremely lucky, maybe even her heart. He found himself longing for her to look at him like she looked at the Comanche. But Standing Bear knew that in order for that to happen, he would have to start treating her with kindness. The white women in his camp were treated poorly. His brother kept one as a slave and she ran away at every opportunity. A few warriors took their captives to their tipis and started families with them. He wanted that kind of relationship with the woman lying beside him.

After deciding to begin treating her gently, his desire was that he wouldn't have to chase her again. He wanted the woman to be with him willingly, to be there when he returned from war parties. The white woman lying beside him exhibited a spirit he had never encountered before. Everything about her was special. The longer he looked at her sleeping form, the harder it was not to touch her. Knowing he could cause her to call out wasn't enough to stop him from gently touching her cheek before tracing the outline of her lips.

The woman didn't open her eyes. But he knew she had regained consciousness when she rolled away from his touch.

***

Alexandria knew it wasn't Running Elk's touch, as much as she tried to convince herself otherwise. Her heart was shattered. She had been so close to him, and now it seemed she had lost him forever. There was no point in trying to be strong any longer. Instead, she curled into a fetal position and cried into her hands.

As she sobbed, she felt a hand on her back. It was a gentle touch, but it didn't calm her in the slightest.

The man spoke words she couldn't understand, but for the first time, they were gentle and soft instead of harsh and loud. He might not have been yelling and throwing her on his horse, but that wasn't having any effect on her feelings towards him. And yet, her curiosity still got the better of her.

She rolled to face him and found she couldn't contain her anger and hurt any longer. "Why are you trying to be nice now? You should have killed me by the river. At least then the last thing I would have seen was the man I loved! But no, you couldn't even give me that!"

Her abductor smiled at her outburst and that angered her even more.

Her mood didn't seem to be translating as well as she would have liked because the man gently grabbed her arm and pulled her to her feet before guiding her towards his horse.

Alexandria stood in stunned silence as the warrior rolled the blanket and placed it at the back of the animal.

The man's sudden change in behavior was confusing but it didn't lessen the hatred she felt towards him. She watched as he took the reins of his horse and motioned for her to walk in front of him. After running, she would have much rather have ridden the animal but knew doing as the man said was easier. Since nothing mattered any longer, she sighed, looked down at her wrists, and held them out, waiting for him to tie her arms.

He shook his head and waited for her to begin to move. She wasn't going to celebrate his sudden trust in her; instead, she steeled herself for whatever was going to happen next.

***

The next three days were spent in silence. They walked, rode, and ate with no words passing between them, and Alexandria was fine with that. He slept away from her, but not far enough that he wouldn't wake if she decided to run again. Little did he know, she had nowhere to run. They had traveled too far for her to believe she could find Running Elk again. By the fourth day, her resolve was wearing thin, and she had to admit to herself that she longed to be able to communicate with her captor. It wasn't because she liked him any better. She hated the man, and didn't see that ever changing, but she could tell his feelings were softening towards her. Her hatred was still strong, but she also felt lost and more alone than ever before in her life. Alexandria was sure she would go insane if she didn't talk to someone, soon.

When they rode together, she was so close to him that she could feel every muscle in his back and legs tighten anytime she readjusted herself to get more comfortable. Alexandria knew her captor had to be aware of her every movement. Every few minutes, he would turn to her with a mixture of confusion and compassion on his face. She promised herself she wouldn't allow her feelings to change toward him no matter what he did. He had taken everything from her. He had killed her husband and stopped her one chance at reuniting with the man she loved. Her future wasn't important. There would be no happiness in her life, no matter how long it lasted.

Alexandria was pulled from her maudlin thoughts when her captor pointed to a rather large collection of tipis. It was a remarkable sight. There were women and children moving in every direction, while men and rode in and out of the village.

She watched as tipis were pulled down and travois were attached to horses. It appeared the people were moving their camp.

Alexandria sighed deeply and took a minute to pray Running Elk would find a way to come for her.

***

Standing Bear stopped his horse and dismounted in an effort to try to decide just what he was going to say to his family. How he was going to attempt to explain his captive was something he had put off thinking about, but he was out of time. The only thing he was sure about was that he was going to do everything in his power to keep her with him.

Chapter Fifteen

Running Elk knew the trip to his people's new location would take twice as long because of his nephew. While Gray Eagle grew stronger, Running Elk took the time to build a travois to carry him. There was no way the young man could ride, but pulling his nephew behind his horse would mean the best they could do was a mere mile or two a day. Choosing to look on the bright side, he told himself a mile was better than nothing. Gray Eagle was still apologizing for the outcome of his task and pushing to leave. Running Elk appreciated his nephew's desire for him to be back with Two Fires but found being constantly reminded of their separation was not helpful to his mood.

Yet, the stronger Gray Eagle got, the more he stressed the fact that Running Elk should be looking for the woman he loved.

"What are you going to do once you see me home?" Gray Eagle asked from his position behind Running Elk's horse.

"I will inform Kicking Bird and White Wolf that I am going in search of Two Fires. I want my woman. And I will have her," he answered through gritted teeth. He had answered the same question many times.

"What if they forbid it?" Gray Eagle asked. "We have a truce with them, and they have proven to be helpful against the advancing white man."

Running Elk was beginning to think he had enjoyed his nephew's company better when he barely spoke. The boy was asking questions Running Elk didn't want to answer. But the queries made him think, and that was something he needed to do. The actions he chose to take from this moment on couldn't be knee-jerk. How he decided to go about locating Two Fires needed to be determined before he rode his horse away from his people; perhaps for the last time.

"Do not fear, Gray Eagle. Nothing else will stop me from finding her," he said, hoping his words were more than mere comfort for the both of them.

As they neared the village, they saw women gathering water at a nearby river. Running Elk spotted Morning Star almost immediately. When she saw him, she dropped the water vessels and ran in his direction. He could see she was crying and desperately tried to quell his rising anger.

Running Elk slowly dismounted from his horse and began walking slowly but deliberately. He knew Kicking Bird would arrive momentarily; the women had alerted the whole village to their presence.

Morning Star fell into step beside him and gently touched his arm. She was a good wife, and he knew she wouldn't cause him any grief about what had happened. He definitely couldn't say that about his brothers.

Kicking Bird ran toward him when he realized his son was on the travois behind Running Elk's horse. He quickly untied his son, making sure not to cause the boy any further pain before peppering the young man with questions.

Sparrow was also at her oldest son's side. She smiled through her tears and gently touched Gray Eagle. "It is good to have you home," she whispered.

Kicking Bird helped his son stand and embraced him.

"It is good to be home," he said, smiling bravely at his mother before turning to his father. "Do you think you could help me the rest of the way, Father?"

Running Elk watched as the family slowly made their way towards their tipi. Not a word was said to him, but he wasn't going to let that fact deter him. After handing Morning Star his horse's reins, he began walking towards White Wolf's home.

Once he'd taken several steps, he turned back towards his long-suffering wife. "I will be back soon. I have to make peace with my brothers."

He was surprised to see the man he was looking for walking towards him.

"It is good to see you again, brother," White Wolf said, embracing him.

"Gray Eagle was wounded. When I found him, he had lost a lot of blood. I feared he wouldn't live, but the gods were kind. He is still extremely weak, but I believe he will fully heal," Running Elk explained as they walked.

He hadn't realized they were walking towards his tipi, and not his brother's, until he finished explaining the events that had taken place.

"Why did you bring me here?" Running Elk asked, feeling the familiar mix of anger and confusion he seemed to have whenever he was in either of his brothers' company.

"You have not rested. Go now and get some sleep. We will speak tomorrow."

"No! I want to talk now! I will not be put off any longer! I have done my job. Gray Eagle is home and safe. If you do not wish to speak, I will find another horse and ride to the Kiowas' camp." Running Elk finished his statement a little quieter than he began.

"You will not go into the Kiowa camp. It could cause a war. We cannot continue to fight each other when the whites keep moving west. They are building more forts every day. It is not something I will allow you to do. No!" White Wolf shot back through clenched teeth.

"No?" Running Elk repeated his brother's answer in disbelief. "No?"

"When will you quit being so selfish? What you are thinking about doing will affect the whole camp. If you walk into the Kiowa camp and demand the white woman, it could easily cause the death of our people."

Running Elk snorted in disgust and walked away from his unbending brother. Instead of entering his home, he began walking in the direction of Kicking Bird's.

Before he took too many steps, he heard White Wolf call to Morning Star.

Running Elk stopped, turned, and saw the pained expression on his wife's face.

It was apparent that she had heard the heated words the brothers had exchanged. He could see the pain in her eyes. But his anger quickly and unexpectedly turned to shock when White Wolf took the woman in his arms to comfort her.

"I am truly sorry that my brother is so cruel and ungiving to you. You deserve so much better."

After seeing his wife accept the comfort White Wolf was offering, and being forced to accept the fact that he didn't know how he truly felt about the scene, he turned and continued walking towards Kicking Birds.

The flap was open, so he walked in. The small place was abuzz with activity. He moved to where his brother was standing over Gray Eagle. When Kicking Bird looked at Running Elk, he could tell from his brother's expression that Gray Eagle had told him the whole story. Running Elk could also see that he was going to have to fight with another brother if he wanted to leave.

"Running Elk, I cannot thank you enough for saving my son. There is no way I will be able to repay you for your actions."

"There is a way you can repay me. We must talk. I will not be put off. I did what I needed to do. And believe me when I say I do not regret nursing Gray Eagle back to health; we are family."

Kicking Bird nodded and patted his son on the arm before answering Running Elk's demand.

"We can go to the river. Come." Kicking Bird led the way out of his home.

Running Elk found it too difficult to stay silent until they reached their destination. "White Wolf has informed me I cannot go rescue Two Fires."

"You can't. I understand that you don't want to accept that, but it is the truth. We need the Kiowa as allies. And she was not taken from your arms. You have no true claim to her."

"How can you not demand revenge for what they did to your son? Are you no longer a warrior? They left him for dead, and they knew he was Comanche!" Running Elk lost his temper once again.

"Calm yourself, my brother," Kicking Bird said, holding onto his brother's shoulders. "You are frustrated, I understand that. But you need to accept the future. There is nothing that can be done. There is no longer a reason for you to leave us. If she can communicate with them, and if she speaks of you, then the Kiowa will surely come to us. I am truly sorry it has to be this way. If it were any other time, I would be on your side."

Running Elk walked away feeling more frustrated than ever before. He had to have Two Fires back, yet he would not be the cause of bloodshed.

He walked into his tipi, expecting to see Morning Star waiting for him. When he saw she was gone, he considered looking for her but quickly decided he would enjoy the peace. After sitting by the dying embers, he pulled out his pipe. While he was building the fire back up and looking around his dwelling, he realized that not only was Morning Star gone, but so were her sleeping furs, clothing, and several of the cooking vessels. It was clear that she had left him. Running Elk wasn't surprised by her actions after she heard the heated discussion between him and White Wolf. What did shock him was that he felt no desire to attempt to locate her. Until that moment, he had been a jealous man; even if he didn't want her, he wouldn't have her with anyone else. However, with her timely exodus, he made up his mind that, in the morning, he would depart, whether his brothers liked it or not. But not before seeking Morning Star out and making sure she was cared for.

He knew he would be no good to his people without Two Fires by his side. If he couldn't have her, he would be on his own; no longer a Comanche. Maybe then he could enter any Kiowa camp and not bring their wrath down on his family. When he did locate the woman who consumed his every thought, he would barter for her and would not stop until she was his again. He had to maintain the belief that it would all work out, or he wouldn't be able to go on.

***

When he woke, Running Eagle went in search of Kicking Bird and told him of his decision. His brother attempted to stop him. He repeated more than once that Running Elk was not considering his people and reminded him that the Kiowa would come to their camp willingly if they were asked. In the last few months, the two bands had fought side by side.

"I understand what you are saying, but I cannot wait. I promise I will do nothing to endanger the truce. I am alone now," Running Elk stated, finding it strangely difficult to admit to his brother that Morning Star had left him. He was a prideful man even when he was in the wrong.

"Morning Star will be taken care of. I know where she is, and I believe she will find her happiness."

Running Elk felt the familiar knot grow in the pit of his stomach when he heard the news. "She has found a man so soon? It would seem she was no happier than I was."

It had never entered his mind that the woman he called his wife might have been carrying on with another man, but once it did, he was furious.

"You don't seem pleased with the news. You never loved her and were never truly with the woman. She had no idea the man she is now with was enamored with her. The woman was faithful to you. The man she is with has longed for her from afar since you took her into your home."

"Huh. Tell me where she is staying," Running Elk demanded. He knew his reaction made little to no sense, but that didn't make it any easier to calm himself.

"If you must know, she is with our brother. You should be glad, or at the very least, relieved."

Running Elk quickly covered the shock he was experiencing. All of the advice White Wolf had offered over the years made sense. Instead of dwelling on his brother's betrayal, he stayed focused on the reason he was speaking to Kicking Bird. "I should do this. I can't do that. I am growing excessively tired of being told what to do. I am my own man. My own blood deceiving me like this just shows how alone I am."

Even though Running Elk was well aware his outburst was totally uncalled for, he was too far in to stop and apologize. Accepting that he was making more of the situation than he had a right to, he turned and walked away before Kicking Bird could say anything further.

***

Kicking Bird watched his little brother leave with a heavy heart. Running Elk was hurting and in need, but there was nothing he could do to aid him. He prayed his little brother would be able to work through his demons and return soon.

Chapter Sixteen

After walking down the ridge and entering the packing encampment, Standing Bear led his horse to a colorful tipi. It was covered with a painting of a bear and a buffalo. Once they reached the entrance, he dismounted and reached for Alexandria. She leaned toward him cautiously. Her legs gave out when she put weight on them. Standing Bear scooped her into his arms and carried her inside. While she was being carted in, she could hear people speaking. Although she had no idea what the words meant, it seemed to her that people were shocked and slightly agitated about something.

Standing Bear sat her down on a thick brown fur in the back of the dwelling, moved back to the front and picked up some logs. Without looking up at her, he readied a small fire in the center of the home and walked out, pulling the flap closed behind him.

Alexandria was alone for the first time in over a week. She remained sitting and slowly surveyed her surroundings. She was sitting on top of a soft, thick brown fur. They were dotted throughout the tipi. There were colorful paintings on the walls. The main focus was a bear and a herd of animals. The dwelling was like nothing she'd seen before. It was a large circular structure held in place by numerous tall wooden beams. Everything about the tipi was different than anything she'd imagined. There were no chairs, or even tables. After taking in her surrounding, she again focused on just had lost she was. The fear she was experiencing was almost choking her. After swallowing several times, she decided to try to stand. Her legs were still shaking, but thankfully they held her weight. Her body was weak, and her mind was spinning, but at least she was standing on her own.

After making her way to the fire, she sat down and attempted to warm her cold, shaking hands. Her first coherent thought was the realization that she had been left inside her captor's home. The hatred she felt towards the man hadn't lessened, but she did have questions for him. He had been so very cruel at first and then had suddenly softened. After he'd recaptured her, his demeanor had changed and he had seemed to almost care if she was comfortable or had enough to eat. While she was initially grateful when he left her alone, she soon learned she didn't care for such isolation.

"Where am I?" she whispered, looking up through the hole at the top of the tipi. "Where are you? Dear God, what is going on?"

"Maybe I can help answer some of yer questions," a voice spoke from the entrance. "Stay there, we'll come ta you. You are in a Kiowa camp, and this man here is Standing Bear. He wants ta know what they call you."

A white man sat on one side, and Standing Bear sat on the other. Her first reaction to seeing a white man was relief. If she could talk to him, surely he would help her.

"Thank God you're here."

The white man was older. And from the looks and smell of him, it was safe to assume he hadn't had a bath in months. He had gray hair and a long straggly beard. His eyes were a clear, deep blue. He smiled a toothless grin when she reached for his hand.

"Well, I can't remember the last time I was welcomed like that. But Standing Bear here wants ta know your name, and he's not a man I would call patient."

Alexandria turned to face the man who had stolen her life. The white paint that had covered his face for the entirety of their trip was gone. He wasn't nearly as fierce-looking as Running Elk, and yet she was still scared of him. "Your name is Standing Bear? My name is T … Alexandria. Now that the introductions are over, ask him why I am here. Then inform him that I need to go. I have to find Running Elk," she explained, turning from the warrior to the old man.

The trapper looked around her and addressed Standing Bear.

Alexandria kept her gaze on the old man, refusing to turn back to Standing Bear.

After the warrior spoke, she waited for the trapper to interpret.

"He says he has heard of Running Elk. But he doesn't want ya, or he would have come for ya by now. It's proly best if ya forget about him. Standing Bear here is a warrior in fine standin'. He don't want ya as a slave neither. I reckon you should consider yerself lucky. Proly on account yer so perty. Anyway, Standing Bear wants ya, and it don't seem like you have much of a choice in the matter."

Alexandria listened to the man but her brain refused to allow the words to sink in. She shook her head. "No. Running Elk and I were meant to be together," she explained as calmly as she could manage.

The old man ran his hand through his straggly beard and looked to Standing Bear before replying.

"If ya know what's good fer ya, you'll be happy here. These boys enjoy torture. In fact, they are known fer it …"

Before the trapper could finish his warning, Standing Bear interrupted.

Alexandria stubbornly kept facing the white interpreter.

There were a few sentences that passed between the Indian and the trapper before the old man spoke again.

"He says you'll warm ta him. You will be staying here, in his tipi. In a bit, he is gonna bring another white girl in here so that she can teach ya a few words and get ya cleaned up. Ya really don't have any say in the matter. But remember what I told ya. You are lucky. I gotta get goin' now," the man said as he rose and quickly backed out of the dwelling.

"But …" She stood quickly, but Standing Bear was quicker. He was blocking the exit before she was able to take a step.

He smiled and led her back to the fire. After gently pushing her back down to a seated position, he joined her and attempted to speak her name several times. The closest he got was a broken *Alax*. She sat in silence, staring into the fire, while he practiced butchering her name.

When she heard a voice from outside the tent, Standing Bear said something and a white girl entered cautiously. Alexandria looked at the young woman. She couldn't have been more than eighteen and was short and thin. Her hair was orange and freckles ran from her cheeks to her nose.

Once the young woman was standing across from Alexandria, she spoke. "Hello."

Alexandria stood quickly and grabbed the girl by her thin arms. "You have to help me. I have to get out of here. Please tell him to take me to Running Elk. Please, please. Don't you see? You have to help me."

Standing Bear walked to Alexandria and put his arm around her waist. She tried to pull away from his embrace but

Standing Bear's grip was so tight that if she had moved any further, it would have caused herself an immense amount of pain.

He quickly spoke a few angry words to the white woman before waiting for her to tell Alexandria what he said.

"Alax, Standing Bear wants you to realize that you belong to him now. He is a great warrior. You should feel honored," the girl said, never raising her eyes from the dirt floor.

"No. You have to understand. I love another man. Does that not matter?" Alexandria asked in near panic.

"Standing Bear has taken you to his tipi. He is a good man. Now come and we will get you some clothes and a bath before we begin packing the tipi," the woman answered calmly.

Alexandria was so frustrated, she was on the verge of screaming. She understood everything she had been told, but the people she was talking to seemed to not hear her. Was she supposed to do nothing? Follow their instructions blindly? Was she meant to just fall into living with another man she didn't love? At least she had been friends with Richard. She could barely tolerate Standing Bear and vowed not to be his wife. That was something she simply would not do!

"Come now, you will feel much better once you are clean," the girl urged nervously.

When the girl reached for her hand, Alexandria attempted once again to break free from Standing Bear's grip. "What is your name?" she asked as soon as realized the warrior had loosened his hold to allow the tiny girl to pull her towards the exit.

Standing Bear walked back towards the fire and nodded before saying something else to the woman that Alexandria couldn't understand.

Alexandria felt beaten. She had run out of ideas about what to do. But having clean clothes, bathing, and washing her hair didn't sound like a terrible thing. While she was cleaning up, maybe she would find a way to convince the girl to help her out.

"My name is Abigail. Abigail Thompson. And you are called Alax."

"Well, that's close. I'm Alexandria Standish," she corrected weakly then smiled. "But that doesn't fit me like the name Running Elk gave me."

"Is Running Elk the man you love?" Abigail asked.

"Yes, and I know he will come for me. He promised we would be together. He has to come. And how will he know where to look if this camp is moving?" Alexandria asked as tears filled her eyes.

Abigail stopped walking and put her arm around Alexandria. "We are moving like we do with the change of season. And I'm sorry, but I do not think anyone will come for you. If they do, Standing Bear will most probably not give you up. But your pain will be a little less with every passing day. Believe me, I know what I am talking about. I am lucky. I have an adopted family that loves me." Abigail said before beginning to walk again.

They walked to a plain-looking tipi and Alexandria waited while Abigail walked in and returned with a bundle of clothing. The women of the camp were busy pulling down the tipis, but they all stopped what they were doing and looked at her. Their expressions varied from interest to disgust.

"You and I are lucky we are not being mistreated. Remember that."

Alexandria fell in step slightly behind Abigail. "Abigail, I will not be with that man. He killed my husband and friends. And if that wasn't horrible enough, he forced me to watch. Every time I look at him, my mind replays the scene."

"I understand what you are saying. But please, try to accept your fate. We all must. Now bathe, I will be right here.

While you are cleaning yourself, maybe I can try to teach you some words in Kiowa," Abigail directed as they walked to the water's edge.

The water did look inviting. Alexandria didn't say anything as she looked around to ensure she wasn't being spied on before quickly disrobing and running into the cool, crisp water. Once she forced herself to stop shaking, she began washing up. It felt good to be clean. She took time washing her hair, making sure all the dirt was gone. Just as she was thinking about stepping out, she realized Standing Bear had joined Abigail.

Alexandria could see they were talking and turned around to hide her nakedness from the warrior.

Before turning away, she saw a look of disappointment cross Standing Bear's face.

Alexandria didn't turn around until she heard Abigail calling her name. She slowly turned to look at her new friend and realized Standing Bear was gone. Abigail met her at the water's edge and helped her dry her goose-bump-covered body before helping her dress. The clean clothes felt good against her skin and whether she wanted to admit it or not, the soft tan-colored buckskin dress and beautifully beaded moccasins were comfortable. She let Abigail braid her hair and they walked back towards Standing Bear's tipi. Abigail was silent, and Alexandria was once again busy trying to think of a way out of her new life.

***

Standing Bear was waiting for them when they arrived at his home, but the tipi was gone. All that remained was the circle of stone that had been at the center of his dwelling and the dying embers of a fire. Alexandria was shocked at how quickly a group of people could be ready to move their homes. Abigail patted Alexandria on the back and mounted one of the two ponies Standing Bear was holding.

Alexandria attempted to mirror Abigail's movements but learned that not having a saddle made the task a little more difficult than normal.

"No," Standing Bear said, smiling with pride.

It was evident he was proud of himself for speaking a very simple English word.

"No?" Alexandria asked, not allowing herself to be slightly impressed. After all, she didn't know the Kiowa word for no.

He spoke to Abigail in his language.

"He said you will ride with him. In front of him, were his exact words."

Something in Alexandria snapped. "And there is nothing I can do? I do have a mind, you know. How can you not have one? How can you sit there and smile at me? Does it not bother you to blindly follow their orders?" she asked, trying to break free of Standing Bear's grip.

He pulled her body tightly against his before looking Alexandria in her eyes and speaking.

"He said that you can't fight him forever. That he will be good to you, but that you must not run. Alexandria, he speaks the truth. If you run and they catch you, and they will, you could very easily be killed," Abigail added her insight at the end. "I like my life here. I hope to make a marriage pact one day. I have learned to be content with what life has handed me. And he is a handsome man. The most handsome and desired warrior in the camp."

Alexandria listened to Abigail but still attempted to break the embrace. The warrior held her with very little effort on his part.

"If he is so wonderful, then you take him."

Standing Bear lifted her onto the horse and mounted behind her.

"He has chosen you. Now, while we ride, let's try to learn some words."

After riding for hours, Alexandria was convinced she would never learn to communicate with anyone other than Abigail. That didn't stop Abigail from pointing at objects and saying words. After the first hour, Alexandria was pretty sure the Kiowa word for man or warrior was *ch'i*.

"Why is it so important that I learn the language?" Alexandria asked, frustrated.

"Because you live here now, among people who speak this tongue. And more importantly, because he wants you to learn."

"Teach him English," Alexandria spat.

"He is learning. He already told you no. After you have rested your mind, we will try again. But now I am riding ahead to speak to my mother," Abigail informed her before she rode away.

Alexandria looked across the open prairie through tear-filled eyes. As much as she tried to reassure herself that there was a way to escape, she still felt desperate.

The wind blew suddenly and Standing Bear's hair covered her face. She pushed the errant stands away from her without looking back.

Her captor had been silent the entire trip, but Alexandria was sure the reason was because Abigail was attempting to teach her the language.

In between introducing words to Alexandria, Abigail had repeatedly told her how handsome her captor was. But Alexandria had never been able to look at him for long. She knew when he smiled, his face softened, but she definitely didn't consider him handsome. He was a monster.

Abigail was also convinced Running Elk wasn't coming for her. Alexandria didn't understand why the woman was so sure her rescue wasn't a possibility and hoped with everything inside herself that her new friend was wrong.

Chapter Seventeen

Running Elk left the encampment and rode in the direction of the Kiowa. After traveling until sunset, he made camp for the night, lit his pipe, and tried to digest everything that had happened to him over the last few weeks. From the first time he'd laid eyes on Two Fires, his life had spiraled out of control. He had always been close to his brothers, and now, whenever he thought of White Wolf, his emotions turned to rage. He was glad to be free of Morning Star, but that didn't stop him from being angry about the whole affair. If his brother wanted his wife, then why hadn't he told Running Elk years earlier? In Running Elk's opinion, it would have saved a lot of heartache on everyone's end.

Over the last few years, he had killed many Texans. They killed Comanche and almost completely destroyed their food source for sport. Yet he never felt hatred towards Two Fires. They had been together twice, but here he sat, after giving everything up for her. All Running Elk could do was say a prayer for her safety. He was well aware of how the Kiowa lived. He also knew if they had mistreated the woman he loved, he would kill them with his bare hands. If he was going to walk into any of their camps, he would have to get his emotions in check. After smoking his pipe, he closed his eyes and hoped for sleep.

The Comanche had just nodded off when he heard a noise. As he was slowly opening his eyes, his right hand was reaching for the knife he wore tied to his leg. When he opened his eyes, he saw a pair of moccasins. He stood quickly and faced the intruder, silently hoping it was a lone Kiowa warrior.

"Running Elk, it is good to see you again, my friend."

The intruder was his friend, and one of the Quahadi war chiefs, Quanah. The chief was tall and intimidating. But Running Elk knew him to be a fair man. Running his camp meant Quanah was always in high demand, so Running Elk was shocked the man had come in search of him.

"Quanah, what are you doing here?" he questioned, allowing his tense muscles to relax.

"I have come to see you. Your brothers have both sought my counsel. Sit, we will smoke to ensure only truth is spoken between us," Quanah answered, sitting on the robes that had served as Running Elk's bed only seconds earlier.

"What did my brothers want? Did they tell you I was going to walk into a Kiowa camp and cause war?" Running Elk asked as he paced in front of his visitor while Quanah built up the dying fire. Running Elk attempted to not allow his emotions to break through but failed miserably.

"Sit. Calm yourself. Running Elk, you forget, I understand what you are going through. My mother was very much in love with my father. When the whites came into our village and took her, he wanted nothing more than to go after her. It took many wise men to talk him out of it. Still, he never stopped loving her. I wanted her back more than anything, but the safety of our people must come first. That is the way it must be …"

"No. I will find Two Fires, and nothing you or anyone else says will stop me," Running Elk interrupted as he sat beside the chief and took the pipe he was offered.

"The truth is, we need you Running Elk. The white men want us to touch the pen to yet another paper. Our band has made the decision not to go to the meeting. Of course, we will be classified as hostiles. I ... we need you to help fight if that is the outcome. They may very well send soldiers when we do not show up."

"I will be no good to you if my heart isn't in the fight. And my heart is with Two Fires."

"If you will give me until the first snow, I will send out a messenger to all the Kiowa camps to seek your white woman. They will bring us the information you desire. My way will get you results without causing friction," Quanah explained, smiling.

"Will your scout bring her back to me?" Running Elk asked, allowing himself to hope.

"If she is willing, yes. I will make sure the scouts know the story, and they will do all that they can. Is that a satisfactory plan? Will you return to the camp?"

Running Elk stood and walked a small distance from the burning fire. "I don't know how well I will be able to fight beside White Wolf. I want us to be brothers again but am not sure we can, after all that has passed between us."

"Your brother loves you, but he also loved the woman you took as a wife. She has joined him in his tipi. You must let go of your anger. Their union is better for you anyway. And we will have news of your white woman soon."

Running Elk had felt lost for a long time and was pleased Quanah had given him a small amount of hope. Quanah was a wise and generous man but also a warrior. He demanded respect even from the Kiowa. Although Running Elk wasn't convinced of his importance to his people, he decided he would return home with his friend.

He followed Quanah through the camp until the chief decided which men he would send to the Kiowa camps. People were carrying on with their lives and paid little attention to Running Elk. He was pleased to move amongst his people without causing a stir. He was sure the camp thought him crazy. He wasn't; he was in love.

***

The warriors Quanah handpicked met in the war chief's tipi and shared a pipe.

"There are four encampments for the Kiowa, and each one of you will ride into one," Quanah began before passing the pipe to his right. "We are looking for a white woman who was taken from a wagon train. We don't want to be too demanding, but let their leaders know I am serious in my search."

The chosen four nodded and took turns drawing from the pipe.

"And if we find her?" the warrior across from Quanah asked.

"Bring her here. Buy her, if you must," Quanah answered, looking to Running Elk.

"What if they don't want to sell her?" the warrior seated to the left of the war chief asked before returning the pipe to him.

Running Elk bit his lip but managed to stay silent.

"Then return here, and we will decide what to do from there. You will depart with the rising sun," Quanah said, emptying his pipe on his moccasin. The action was a clear sign he was finished talking to the group.

Running Elk would have been happier if the scouts were leaving immediately but knew pushing the subject would do no good. He had been many things in his life, but impatience was new to him.

After waiting for everyone else to leave, he thanked Quanah for his help. Holding onto a renewed hope, he walked towards Kicking Bird's tipi.

His brother looked both surprised and pleased to see him. "I am glad you have returned. What changed your mind?" he asked, welcoming Running Elk inside. "Gray Eagle, your uncle had returned."

"It's good to see you again, Uncle," Gray Eagle greeted from the robes he was resting on. "I can walk with the help of a strong branch now. I tried yesterday."

The young man looked much better than the last time Running Elk had seen him. His color was back, and he sounded determined to fully recover.

"I am pleased to hear that. You will be healed in no time. Kicking Bird, thank you for seeking Quanah's wisdom. He came and spoke to me."

Kicking Bird smiled and escorted his little brother outside.

"I owe my son's life to you. It was the least I could do."

"Quanah thinks we will be fighting soon. What do you think?"

"I think I want our old way of life back. But I do not see any chance of that happening. The white man will not be satisfied until he has taken everything of ours. Even the land we walk on. Yes, Quanah is correct in his thoughts. We need you with us. You do understand we will be fighting side by side with the Kiowa. What if you aren't reunited with your Two Fires by then? Will that hinder your fighting ability?" Kicking Bird asked.

"No, I don't believe so. I can use their company to my advantage. When we are camped, I will speak to them and ask them questions. I do feel much more at peace than I have since I met Two Fires."

"Now, brother, I don't want to bring this subject up, but I feel I must. You do know there is a distinct possibility she was killed, right?" Kicking Bird asked cautiously, not sure what kind of reaction he would receive.

His big brother's question felt more like a punch in the gut than words.

"I would be a fool not to have considered her death. I try not to dwell on the thought, but I will know something soon. I feel in my soul that she still lives. She was their only captive, so I have to believe they kept her alive for a reason."

"Will you go after the warriors if you find out her spirit has moved on?"

"With a vengeance, brother."

Chapter Eighteen

"How can it have been two months already?" Alexandria asked Abigail as she picked up the robes before taking them outside and shaking them.

In eight weeks, Alexandria had mastered the Kiowas' language. She and Abigail had become fast friends and because Standing Bear had been absent since the camp was relocated, Alexandria was beginning to calm down. The lightheadedness and queasy stomach were even lessening every day.

Abigail had moved into Standing Bear's tipi as soon as the camp moved and the two had spoken about Running Elk at length. Although Abigail said she understood Alexandria, she continued to remind Alexandria that Standing Bear was the most handsome man in camp, not forgetting to add how pleased Alexandria should be with her situation.

As the days passed, the two fell into a schedule. Alexandria watched and shadowed Abigail while her friend completed the daily chores until she thought she could accomplish them without help.

The first day Alexandria gathered the nerve to walk to the river to fetch water, she knew the other women in the camp resented her. The knowledge made her want to finish her task just to show the women she was not a fragile flower and that she was quite capable of doing some hard work. After filling the skins, she made it back to the shoreline before her eyesight began clouding until all she could see was nothingness.

When she regained consciousness, she was lying on top of her fur bed.

"It is good to see you are awake. The women wouldn't have kept picking at you if they'd realized you were carrying a child. Why didn't you tell me?" Abigail's voice was a mixture of excitement and anxiousness.

"A child?" Alexandria asked quickly. "No, that's impossible …"

Alexandria stopped speaking and allowed herself to consider the impossible was actually possible. If she was as the Kiowa women said, then there was only one possible father.

She smiled and touched her stomach. She was shocked and scared when the words sank in. Fear quickly moved to joy. The universe might have been trying to keep her from the man she loved, but that would never happen now. "Abigail, I believe I am carrying Running Elk's child."

Abigail was not pleased with her friend's news. "What is Standing Bear going to say?" she asked, sounding concerned.

"He can't say anything. This is my child. He said many times that he would be kind to me so that I would be with him, right?"

"He did say he was doing that," Abigail agreed after giving it some thought.

"Then he will have to accept this. I am overjoyed, Abigail. I will have Running Elk with me forever. But how did the women know?"

"When you fainted, Willow, an elder, looked at you and said you were with child. I don't know how she knew, but she was sure she was right. Even when I said that it was impossible."

"I'm glad to know. This is the first time since I was captured that I haven't felt lost and alone. No offense, I am grateful for you, but I was always trying to find a way to leave here. It might have been crazy, but I couldn't imagine living without Running Elk. Now I have him with me," Alexandria gushed before standing and walking the perimeter of the tipi.

"I am glad you are happy, but please don't tell Standing Bear the minute he returns. Why not show him how you have learned his language?" Abigail suggested, watching her friend instead of resuming grinding corn.

"The man killed my husband and friends, took me from the man I love, and tied me up for days. And you want me to consider his feelings? I don't know why you cannot understand this; I do not love Standing Bear."

"I understand your feelings, but Alexandria, he loves you. Everyone can see it in his eyes when he looks at you or has even just been in your company. I'm sure his absence hasn't changed that fact. And now I feel I must tell you … he is back."

Alexandria stopped her mindless walking and looked at Abigail as she felt the color drain from her face. "Why didn't you tell me that earlier?"

"Because we were discussing important things. Now I am leaving but will return in the morning. Try to be kind to him," Abigail said as she gathered her few belongings and left the tipi.

Alexandria watched her friend leave without speaking because her mind was reeling. She was overjoyed at the news she was pregnant, but as soon as she knew Standing Bear was back, she began to worry about what his reaction to the news might be. She sat by the fire for a few hours, deep in thought. After deciding fresh air might help her thinking process, she stepped outside.

Chapter Nineteen

Standing Bear watched as the woman walked out of his tipi before stretching and sitting cross-legged by the opening. When he looked at her, he realized how much he had missed being in her company. He hoped that in his absence she had learned some of the ways of his people. It was obvious she was more at peace than she had been when he'd left. As much as he wanted to go to her now, he knew before visiting with Alax, he needed to speak to Abigail. The woman would have all the information he desired, so he went in search of her. After listening to Abigail, he was pleased with everything she told him. Yet he could sense the girl wasn't telling him everything.

"What are you keeping from me? Does she still speak of the Comanche?" Standing Bear pressed.

"She does," Abigail answered, lowering her head. "But not as much, and that is surely a good sign. As time passes, she will understand just how lucky she is."

Standing Bear smiled at Abigail when she looked up at him. The woman had been adopted by his uncle's family when she was captured. Standing Bear had always accepted her as one of the family, but it was obvious the young woman had deeper feelings for him, whether she knew it or not.

"I will take any good news. I am not sure myself why I am so drawn to Alax. But if she will have me, then I am the lucky one. Thank you for helping. I will seek her company now."

***

Alexandria watched as Standing Bear walked towards her. For the first time, she allowed herself to look at the man without allowing blinding hatred to cloud her judgment.

He was a handsome man. His hair fell loose around his shoulders. She noticed it was a habit for him to place it behind his ears. He had a confident walk and carried himself like a warrior. His face was long. He had high cheekbones and a nose that rounded at the end. His eyes were deep chocolate brown. His body was hard and muscular, though he was not as imposing as Running Elk. The Kiowa warrior wore only a breechcloth, moccasins, and a feather that hung from his hair.

As he neared, she stood up. "Standing Bear, how have you been?" she asked, attempting to be civil.

He stopped and smiled when he realized he could understand the words she was saying.

"Alax, I am pleased we can finally talk without help. Let's go inside," Standing Bear said, smiling, as he ushered her back inside his home.

"Abigail is a good teacher, and you have been away for quite some time."

"Please, sit. My absence is something you are glad of?" he asked, sitting beside her.

Alexandria didn't look away from the fire. "You killed my husband and my friends and took me from the man I love. While it is obvious that your feelings have changed towards me, I still see death when I look at you. I know you've been kind to me since I got here and that my treatment could have been a lot worse. I also realize that you are not going to take me back to Running Elk. So, to answer you, your absence has given me time to learn of your people."

"That was not an answer. If your Running Elk wanted you, he's had time to come. But he has not. You must accept that and move on. That is the reason I gave you this time. Now, you and I will get to know one another. I am not so bad," Standing Bear said gently, touching her leg and smiling.

Alexandria pulled away from his touch and his smile disappeared.

"If Running Elk had come for me, would you have told me?"

"Yes, you would have been informed. The tribal elders would have given you to him. But again, he has not come," he repeated as he stood. "You cannot hold onto memories forever. And yes, I have killed white men, but they drew first blood. This is war and sadly, people die." His voice was getting angrier with every word he spoke.

"Oh? I can and will carry my memories with me forever. You see, I am carrying Running Elk's child," Alexandria spoke with defiance thick in her voice. She stood when he spoke; it was more of a symbolic gesture than a threat.

Alexandria watched as Standing Bear's features grew dark. The change in his appearance frightened her. Since she had caused his anger, she knew there was nothing she could say to quell it.

The warrior slowly stood and walked out of his home without a backward glance. As soon as she was alone once again, she realized she had been holding her breath.

Alexandria hadn't planned on telling him the news in such a blunt, hurtful manner, but the man had a way of infuriating her. Once he left, she began to worry that he might give her to someone else. Maybe she had crossed a line that she couldn't return from. For the first time since she had been a captive, she realized her situation could have been worse. Although the fear she was experiencing was close to paralyzing, she knew she couldn't just let the man walk away. She had no idea how she was going to fix her situation, but after gathering herself, she went in search of Standing Bear.

Alexandria found him standing by the river, looking out at the horizon. It appeared the warrior was deep in his thoughts as she cautiously moved towards him. Alexandria stood beside him and waited for him to acknowledge her presence. He seemed to not notice her.

Alexandria knew she needed to say something but had no idea how to start another conversation. The only movement the man was making, other than breathing, was the steady clenching and unclenching of his jaw. Instead of speaking, she decided to just stand beside him and wait for him to either speak or move.

Almost immediately after reaching her decision, the warrior made a grumbling noise and began walking away before turning back to her.

"If you are so sickened by my touch then you should be somewhere else."

The words sent renewed fear coursing through her veins. "Where?" she asked, not wanting to hear his answer.

"Why should I care? I will see to it. Wait in my tipi."

"Standing Bear, please do not do this. I will try to be good to you. I promise," she pleaded as she moved towards him and reached for his arm.

It was the first time she initiated contact with the warrior and when she realized what she had done, she pulled her hand back.

"You want me now? Is this change in your attitude only to save the child?" Standing Bear asked angrily.

Alexandria had convinced herself that Standing Bear would not hurt her child, but she couldn't be sure other warriors wouldn't. It was a terrifying realization, but she knew sharing her thoughts wouldn't help with her situation. Instead of saying it outright, she chose her words as carefully as her panicked brain would allow.

"It doesn't matter why. Does it? I am willing to try my best. Abigail says you care for me. If that is true, please, take me as I am."

The warrior looked at her for a moment, but his expression stayed the same. "Go back to the tipi. I will return later," Standing Bear directed, leaving her with no idea what his decision would be.

Alexandria walked back to Standing Bear's tipi, full of worry and regret. If she had just kept her true thoughts to herself, their reunion would have gone smoother, but she hadn't, so she was stuck pacing back and forth until she was too tired to continue. Her body was telling her she needed to rest, even if her brain was full of questions and concerns. After convincing herself that, no matter what happened, she needed rest, she took off her clothes, covered herself with the furs, and fell into a fitful sleep.

***

Standing Bear stayed outside and watched as the stars began to shine. The news the woman had hit him with was something he'd never considered. He was well aware Alax had said she felt love for the Comanche but hadn't considered the two could have lain together. The information was difficult to digest. He knew raising the child as his own would be easy enough, but only if Alax was willing to be his. He was also aware of the importance that no one know the child wasn't his. Living a lie in order to keep the woman who ate at his heart and invaded his soul was something he was surprisingly willing to do.

The depths he was prepared to go for the white woman surprised him.

After arriving at his decision, he returned to his tipi in the hopes that the two could conclude their conversation. As soon as he returned, he saw Alax was asleep and the fire was dying. The nights were beginning to get colder, and he was pleased there were enough robes to keep her warm. The woman had dealt with numerous changes in a few short months. He knew she was not used to being out in the elements. If knowing Abigail had taught him anything, it was that white women sometimes struggled with the Indian way of life. Even after accepting the woman was not truly his, he knew he would do anything in his power to keep her comfortable. Keeping his distance was difficult, but after stirring the embers to allow some extra heat to flow, he grabbed an old blanket and lay by the fire.

Before falling asleep, he heard the woman stir. Standing Bear looked in her direction and saw that when she'd moved, she had revealed her bare shoulder. Desire gripped Standing Bear when he realized she was naked underneath the robes. He fought the overpowering need to go to her, thinking if he did, he would be left unsatisfied. That outcome being a probability still didn't stop him from kneeling beside her and pulling the robes back up to cover her exposed shoulder. As soon as his hand touched her, her eyes opened. Standing Bear stopped moving while the woman blinked several times before smiling at him.

He returned a weak smile, knowing her reaction meant she wasn't fully awake. The warrior wasn't proud of himself but quickly found he couldn't stop from taking advantage of the situation. Knowing the woman would be fully awake soon enough, he stood and disrobed before lying beside her. She had closed her eyes and returned to a state of sleep when he gently ran his hand down her face. Her breathing changed and she once again opened her eyes when he moved the hair from her face.

He knew it wasn't the best situation to put her in, but he was desperate with need, and he couldn't force himself to leave her.

"If you can do this … if we can be together, then you can stay. I am sorry, but it has to be this way," he said gently as he caressed the length of her arm underneath the covers.

Chapter Twenty

Alexandria didn't say a word. It was as if the lump that had formed in her throat wouldn't allow her to speak. The man had snuck into her bed while she was sleeping. Her mind desperately held to the thought that he was unbelievable. But her mind wasn't in charge; her body was. It had been too long since she'd been touched in tenderness.

His strong hands gently caressed her breasts before he moved down and took her nipple in his mouth. Her back arched as she pushed into him.

"I want to see you," he said hoarsely as he gently held her chin.

Alexandria could see the relief and gratitude cross his handsome face when he realized she wasn't going to fight him.

"It will not be so bad, I promise," he spoke before taking her mouth with his.

Her arms moved slowly, almost mechanically, but she was embracing him, even dragging her nails down his spine.

Standing Bear moved from her mouth to her neck, covering her with kisses. Without her brain's consent, her body took over. She pulled his hair and moaned. Her actions excited him more.

***

He gently rolled her over before looking at her breathtaking face. She was even more beautiful when her eyelids were heavy. While looking her in the eye, he traced her stomach with his finger, stopping at the opening of her thighs. He wanted to be easy with her. But more than anything, he wanted her to beg him to make love to her.

While he was cautiously parting her legs, she was digging her nails in his back. He leisurely moved his hand back to her breast.

Her hands grasped the sides of his face, "Don't stop," she whispered, looking him in the eyes.

She looked confused by her plea, but the last thing Standing Bear wanted to do was ask why.

"You don't know how long I have longed to be with you. You will be mine," he said as he trailed kisses down her stomach.

Alexandria wiggled underneath him, driving his need to new heights.

As he shifted his weight, his knee moved to open her legs. He entered her slowly and gently, not wanting to hurt her. He wanted her to enjoy the experience as much as he was.

Standing Bear had been with his share of women but never had he wanted one so desperately. He moved slowly as he developed a rhythm. Alex moved with him until she began making noises that sounded like heaven to him.

Afterward, she rested silently in his arms while he ran his fingers through her beautiful yellow hair.

She hadn't run away or broken out in tears after making love, and he knew she'd enjoyed the act, but he still had doubts.

Standing Bear did not want to say anything that might ruin the experience, but his pride wouldn't allow the question to go unanswered. "Were you thinking of him or me?"

She lifted her head from his chest and pulled away from his embrace. As soon as she was aware of her nakedness, she pulled the fur up to cover herself.

He thought he saw a tear fall down her cheek before she answered him. "As badly as I wanted to fight it, my body is yours."

He smiled, pulled her down against him, and gently laid his hand on her stomach. The woman hadn't given him her heart, but he was overjoyed hearing her admit she had given one part of herself to him. "You are showing signs of the baby. When will he be born?"

"I've been doing some counting, and I would guess that I have about five more months," Alexandria answered.

"Then he will be born with the coming of spring. It is a good time for birth. Am I always going to have to keep you in bed to ensure that you will quit pulling away?" he asked with a small amount of playfulness in his tone.

She didn't answer.

"Let's sleep. We will talk and make love again when we wake," Standing Bear promised as he held her close to him.

***

While lying in Standing Bear's arms, her thoughts returned to Running Elk. Alexandria couldn't shake the thought that she had betrayed him, even if the man she longed to be with didn't know what she'd gone through. The fact that her body would betray her so easily was confusing at best. The only solace Alexandria took from the situation was that her child would be cared for.

Sleep had just taken hold when she was woken by Standing Bear's breath on her neck. She sleepily rolled over to face him.

"If your body is mine, I've decided I would like to possess you again," he informed her as he rolled on top of her.

She fell into his embrace willingly, knowing resistance would do nothing to guarantee her safety or the protection of her unborn child.

When Alexandria woke again later that morning, she was alone on the pallet, but not completely by herself. Abigail was placing more wood on the fire.

"Where is Standing Bear?" Alexandria asked as she wiped her eyes.

"You asking about him is a change. Yesterday you wanted to know nothing of the man, and now you ask about his whereabouts. What has happened? And don't tell me nothing. Come to think of it, Standing Bear looked extremely pleased when I saw him earlier."

"He was happy?" Alexandria asked.

"Blissfully. But you didn't answer me. Yesterday, when I left, you were filled with worry; today, you are both changed. I'm guessing you didn't tell him about the baby."

"No, I did. And I'm pretty sure we have come to an agreement," Alexandria explained while she was dressing.

"The agreement seems to be good for you too. You have not looked this calm since I met you," Abigail informed her as she began fanning the flames.

"I am calm because of the child."

"No. I think it is more than that."

"You didn't answer me. Where is he?"

"I don't know where he was going, but I'm sure he is still in the village. Now, come, we have work to do. Kiowa women do not stop working because they are with child. And you are a Kiowa woman."

Alexandria was taken aback by the statement.

"Abigail, I have to ask you a question, and you must answer it honestly. Can you do that?"

Abigail stopped tending the fire and looked Alexandria in the eyes. "Yes. What is it?"

"If Running Elk ever comes into the village, please help me get to him. I will always love him, no matter what I have done. Will you help?"

"I will. You have my vow. Now tell me what took place between you and Standing Bear last night.

"We came to an agreement … twice," Alexandria said, keeping her gaze on the ground.

"So, his touch doesn't sicken you anymore?" Abigail asked.

"No. I enjoy his touch, and yet still I stand here professing my love for Running Elk." Alexandria's mood began to darken before Abigail grabbed her hand and pulled her out of the tipi.

"I gave you my word that I will help you if the time comes. For now, try to be happy. You are very pretty when you smile. And I'm sure Standing Bear thinks so too."

"He does," Standing Bear walked into the tipi before pulling Alexandria into his arms.

Much to Alexandria's surprise, her arms held tight to his lean, muscular body.

Abigail watched the scene with a dumbfounded look on her face. After a few moments of silence, the young woman cleared her throat in an obvious attempt to be heard.

"Abigail, we are going to Medicine Lodge Creek to meet with the whites. We need to show Alax how to dismantle the tipi and pack everything."

"You don't need to help. These things are women's work," Abigail said, not bothering to hide her surprise at the warrior's offer.

"I will help. Besides, this way, I will know Alax is being taught the right way," he said, teasing his cousin.

Alexandria watched and listened to Standing Bear and Abigail's exchange until she could no longer hold her tongue. "Why are we going to Medicine Lodge?"

Standing Bear's attention was focused on Alexandria as soon as she asked her question. "The white man once again wants something from us. We have all been summoned, and our band has decided to attend. Others have decided against it. In the past, I would have argued to hold out, but I believe I have lost some of my desire to kill. Besides, the mostly useless trip will give us time to enjoy each other's company. Or does the thought of that still sicken you?"

Alexandria stood before the warrior and only then began to realize just how correct Abigail's words had been. Standing Bear seemed almost playful. She forced herself to smile and in doing so, realized it wasn't as difficult as it had been earlier in their relationship.

Chapter Twenty-One

The trip to Medicine Lodge was interesting for Alexandria. Standing Bear took every opportunity to point out important places and landmarks. He also taught her what some of the flowers and berries were called and what they were used for. When she looked at him, she saw love in his eyes. She couldn't help wishing she was riding behind Running Elk, but did her best to stay engaged with Standing Bear and hoped he couldn't see the doubt in her eyes.

When the band arrived at the clearing where they would camp for the night, Standing Bear helped Alexandria erect a lean-to before suggesting they bathe in the nearby pond. The water's edge was striking. The leaves still clung to the branches and were a brilliant red and yellow color.

The bath was cold but refreshing. When the two arrived back at their accommodations for the night, they saw that Abigail had left a warm pot of stew hanging over the fire.

"She is good to you," Alexandria said as she huddled in a buffalo robe by the fire.

"She is. One day she will make a lucky warrior a wonderful wife. Do you realize you have never cooked for me? I believe my woman should learn to feed me in every way."

"I think Abigail is the better cook," Alexandria assured him, ignoring the sexual connotation of his words.

During the remainder of the trip, they were almost always together. Standing Bear asked about her life before she met Running Elk. The warrior made sure she understood he did not want to hear any more about Running Elk.

She learned about Standing Bear's life too. He admitted that he had been in love before, but that the woman had been killed when the Texans raided his village. Alexandria felt the slightest bit guilty when he confided that he'd never imagined he would want another woman but she had changed his mind.

As they neared Medicine Lodge, Alexandria could see Indian tribes setting up camp. There were more horses than she'd ever seen, and the number of tipis rivaled many of the small towns she'd visited.

Children were playing while the women were either beginning to gather water or finishing erecting their homes. There weren't many men walking around, and Alexandria assumed their absence was because they were all visiting with other chiefs.

"We will set up over there. My father's tipi is already up. I do not want you kept awake because of the meetings we will have. They can get heated. So, let's set up nearer the water," Standing Bear suggested while he scanned the area carefully.

Abigail was still trying to grasp the vast number of Indians gathered. She knew they were there to sign a treaty, but Standing Bear had made it clear he didn't believe the government would stand by its promises, so she wondered if he was in the minority. The people in attendance had stopped their lives and gathered where they were asked to. She didn't think too many towns would move if they were asked. Her admiration for the Indian people grew every day.

"How many people are here?"

"Many. There are Kiowa and a few Comanche. We have gathered here more to meet with other chiefs than to listen to more of the white man's lies."

"If you are so sure they are lies, then why are you here to listen?"

Standing Bear stopped his horse, turned around, and moved a stray hair away from Alexandria's face. "Because there are more of you white people than we thought, and there are fewer of us. Disease from the white man has touched most villages, and war has taken many lives. Perhaps it is time to try another way. And if nothing else, the Kiowa can visit with bands we don't often see. We are the last to arrive, so we will need to hurry. I need to learn what has taken place."

"If there are soldiers here, aren't you worried that I will run?" Alexandria asked as Standing Bear helped her from the horse.

The question made Standing Bear's muscles clench. "They will not see you. And if you do plan on running, you have to know the child you carry would be an outcast. You would be worse off with your own people than with mine."

"Will Running Elk be here?" she asked, wishing she hadn't the second the words left her mouth.

"He could be," Standing Bear said, visibly trying to control his growing anger. "This would be a place to find you, but he won't. He has moved on. You know in your heart I speak the truth. You are mine, little one."

Chapter Twenty-Two

Two of the scouts sent out to locate Two Fires returned empty-handed. Both had the same story: "there were no new white women in any of the bands." Running Elk simply would not accept the thought that his Two Fires had vanished. There was no questioning that she had been taken by the Kiowa. That knowledge meant her life could be in constant danger. And yet, he still prayed daily that she wasn't being mistreated. The one thing he wouldn't allow to seed in his mind was her death. That was something he just couldn't permit.

Quanah suggested Running Elk remain calm and reminded him there were still two men yet to return, but Running Elk didn't like the odds.

At Quanah's suggestion, the two warriors sat on the edge of a small hill and smoked a pipe.

"We will be going on a raiding party soon. Your people need you," Quanah informed Running Elk while he handed him the pipe.

"And in helping with the raiding, I will once again lose sight of Two Fires," Running Elk stated with aggravation clear in his tone before taking a long draw from the pipe and handing back to Quanah.

"This will not take long, and the other two scouts will be back when we return," Quanah promised, taking the pipe and tapping the ashes out.

"It could take many sleeps," Running Elk objected as he stood and dusted the dirt from his legs.

"It could, but fighting might just be the only thing that will take your mind from your woman," Quanah stated, looking up at Running Elk.

Running Elk had spent most of his time since his return to the camp in the company of Quanah and saw him as a friend, someone he could place his trust in. The war chief's statement was true. If Running Elk put some of his pent-up anger towards a fight, it would be good for him.

"Of course I will go with you. But if we don't have any information on Two Fires' location by the first snowfall, I will seek her out on my own," Running Elk decided.

"Good, now go visit your family. They miss you, and you have been avoiding them. There is never a guarantee we will return, and I know you don't want to cause your brothers undue pain," Quanah directed, standing and patting Running Elk on the shoulder before walking towards the camp.

Quanah was a wise man. Running Elk had been avoiding his family. He just wasn't sure why. Maybe their happiness caused him pain; perhaps he felt like they thought of him as weak because he cared only for a woman. Whatever the reason, he had mastered the art of being gone when either brother was around. After a short time, neither brother had continued to seek him out.

He would occasionally run into Gray Eagle and always took the time to ask about his health. The young man was returning to his old self and Running Elk couldn't have been happier with the outcome of his nephews' injury. Gray Eagle was now stronger than he had been before he got shot with the Kiowa's arrow. Speaking to his nephew was relatively easy, but he knew he needed to speak to both his brothers before leaving.

Kicking Bird was easy to find. He was on the outskirts of the camp, shooting with Gray Eagle.

"Brother, I am sorry I've acted so out of character." Running Elk began talking before reaching his brother and nephew.

Both looked surprised by Running Elk's sudden presence, but they smiled warmly at him.

"Come shoot with us," Kicking Bird suggested as he embraced his little brother.

"Are you going on the raiding party?" Gray Eagle asked as he loaded his bow and carefully took aim.

Kicking Bird looked at Running Elk in question.

"I am. Are you coming?" he asked Kicking Bird.

"Not this time. I plan to stay close until Gray Eagle has completely healed. But we will celebrate your return soon. Have you spoken to White Wolf yet?" Kicking Bird handed Running Elk a spare bow.

Running Elk took the bow, loaded it, and fired, splitting a fallen horse apple in two. Gray Eagle made a noise of awe and Kicking Bird rolled his eyes.

"No, but I am going to see him next."

"May the gods watch over you until we meet again," Kicking Bird said, physically turning Running Elk in the direction of the camp.

Running Elk heard Kicking Bird laugh as he was walking away.

While walking to White Wolf's, Running Elk realized Kicking Bird had been easier to approach. He still held onto hurt feelings because of White Wolf's actions, even if he knew there was no reason to.

Morning Star was happy where she was, and White Wolf was overjoyed. Their coupling had saved Morning Star from any hurtful gossip. The people of the village appeared to still question

Running Elk's actions, but none spoke to him about their thoughts.

On his way to the shaman's tipi, he rehearsed what he would say. When he reached the doorway, he saw Morning Star leaving. The woman had never looked happier. Seeing her caused the speech he had memorized to leave him. All he could manage was a smile and a nod of his head as she walked past him. Morning Star appeared to be blissful, but she didn't look him in the eye.

White Wolf was behind Morning Star but stopped his forward movement when he saw his little brother near his door.

"Come in," the shaman offered, backing into his home once again. "Sit and tell me how you have been."

Running Elk sat and looked at his brother. "I am sure you know everything that has happened since I returned," he said with no anger in his tone. "I wanted to make peace before I left with the raiding party. I know I have been preoccupied, but I need you to know I am happy for the both of you."

White Wolf smiled and put his hand over his heart. "Thank you for that, brother. I know you have been forced to deal with many obstacles lately but ..."

Running Elk knew if he let his brother continue to talk, they would end up arguing, and he wanted to avoid that outcome. "I will see you when we return," he interrupted before standing and walking towards the door.

"We will see each other again, brother," White Wolf stated before Running Elk left.

***

The next morning, fifteen warriors and Quanah rode away from the camp in search of blood.

Running Elk's bravery during the raids quickly earned him a name for himself. The people, who had been questioning his worthiness and loyalty only days before, saw him as more than a gifted hunter. His medicine was growing stronger, and with each battle, he was becoming a well-respected and feared warrior.

Running Elk knew he had Quanah to thank for his new reputation. But while others were in awe of his stunts, Running Elk's bravery was all on account of the fact that he fought with a reckless abandon. Without Two Fires, he didn't care if he lived or died.

Chapter Twenty-Three

Standing Bear spent the next seven days meeting with friends and family. At night, when the discussions were finished, he stayed in his father, White Buffalo's, tipi.

It was difficult to keep his distance from Alax, but he knew it was the only way to ensure she wouldn't be found by either the soldiers or a Comanche. Every morning, he left food outside the tipi where Alax and Abigail were staying but managed to not look in on them. Knowing Abigail was keeping Alax company lessened his worry but did nothing to ease his desire to spend time with her.

He occupied some of his time trading pelts for beads he thought Alax might like. No matter who he spoke to, the conversation always turned to talk of the elusive buffalo, but none came up with a way to rectify the situation. He'd heard Running Elk's name several times, and everyone who spoke of him seemed to hold the man in high regard. Every time the man's name was mentioned, Standing Bear did his best to change the subject.

Listening to the soldiers wasn't a top priority for him, so he relied on the gossip at the end of the night to learn all he could. When the people arrived at the summit, some still wanted to believe the government would keep its promises. They were quickly becoming the minority. Two crucial questions that remained unanswered were why the Kiowa and Comanche should be forced to relocate and how their relocation would stop any more death.

By the sixth day, Standing Bear knew his father would not touch the pen. The Kiowa didn't know what to make of his father's decision. Before finding Alax, he would have relished the thought of more bloodshed, but she had changed him. He would have much rather just been left alone to grow old and fat with the woman.

During the visit, Standing Bear was forced to listen to everyone who had any knowledge of his relationship with Alax repeatedly voicing their objections. White Buffalo talked to his son for hours about the same subject, but in the end, he told Standing Bear to find happiness wherever he could.

The morning the official signing was to take place, White Buffalo found his son and informed him they would be leaving.

"Then I will go speak to Alax," Standing Bear stated, quickly finishing combing his horse.

"There is more news. Several scouts from Quanah's camp have been visiting the other bands. And they are seeking information about your woman."

"Has anyone been to visit you?" Standing Bear asked, suddenly desperate for the answer.

The warrior had intentionally kept Alax from interacting with his friends and family and, after enduring the views of everyone he ran into, he knew he'd made the right decision.

"No, not yet. But I think it is only a matter of time. Surely by the time we have set up our winter camp, the scout will locate us."

White Buffalo's voice held no judgment. He was answering his son and nothing more.

"Let me think on this. Right now, I am going to my woman," Standing Bear decided before patting his horse.

"Do not take too much time reacquainting yourself. Remember, we will be classified as hostile once the soldiers see us leaving. It is best to all move together."

Standing Bear nodded his understanding and walked towards his home. It was still an hour before sunrise, and he hoped he would be able to at least hold Alax before she woke for the day.

He was surprised to see the woman awake, sitting by the fire while Abigail was sleeping.

Fear gripped him. "Are you well?" he asked, moving quickly to sit beside her.

Alex didn't move away from him when he sat close to her, and her reaction emboldened him. He was quickly convincing himself he was doing the right thing by hiding her and asking others to lie.

"I am fine. Just couldn't sleep. What are you doing here?" she asked, allowing him to wrap his arm around her.

"It is over. We will leave in the morning. And this is my home. Am I not welcome here?" he asked, smiling.

"Of course you are. But I haven't seen you since we arrived. Is everything finished? Have the soldiers left?"

Standing Bear stood and walked towards the bed. He didn't want to answer her questions; he wanted to feel her naked body against his. "Come to bed and let me warm you. I have missed you. We will talk about the meeting in the morning."

"Standing Bear, we can't. Abigail is here," Alexandria protested.

"Her presence will not stop me from holding you for a few minutes. Now come and lie down," he said, patting the robes beneath him.

The woman appeared to be thinking about denying him her company.

"Just for a short time," he urged as he watched her stand and look to her sleeping friend before cautiously moving closer to the Standing Bear.

He was pleasantly surprised when she slipped into bed and quickly disrobed.

Standing Bear held her in his arms and breathed her into him. As soon as he heard her breathing change, he allowed himself to relax and think about all the events of the last week.

He knew his father was right. The Comanche scout would find them soon. What he wasn't sure about was how he was going to handle the situation.

Standing Bear did not want to betray Alexandria, but he felt he couldn't allow her to be taken either. While he was nestling himself into her loose, flowing hair, he made the decision to take a more scenic route back. At least then he could postpone any betrayal and lies he would have to tell her. Never before would he have willingly endangered his people, but he was prepared to do anything to keep the woman in his lodge.

***

The long, scenic route postponed their return to the village until the first snow whitened the prairie. He took the opportunity to continue to teach Alax about various plants and animals. The woman soaked up his knowledge like a sponge and even seemed to be enjoying his company. They moved at a leisurely pace during the day, and at night, he made her body his own.

By the time they neared the winter camp, Standing Bear was able to convince himself the woman thought of him more than she did the Comanche.

After helping Alax set up their home, he suggested she find Abigail while he was greeting his father.

"It's been a few weeks since you've spoken to anyone but me. I'm sure the two of you have missed visiting." Standing Bear walked in the direction of his father's lodgings as he spoke.

"It will be good to see her again," Alexandria agreed, walking towards the waterway.

Once Standing Bear reached his father's, he gathered himself before entering.

White Buffalo was sitting around the fire with two of Standing Bear's closest friends, Big Tree and Sleeping Otter, and a man he knew was the Comanche scout.

"Sit, son," White Buffalo greeted, pointing to an open space beside the Comanche.

Standing Bear's mind was swimming. He had no idea what he'd walked into and was anxious for an explanation.

"What is going on?" he asked, attempting to sound disinterested.

Big Tree cleared his throat and passed White Buffalo the pipe. "This man, Black Cloud, is here about a white woman …"

Standing Bear looked from his friend to the Comanche.

"We have told him we have no white women here who aren't family, but he has asked to see them," White Buffalo interrupted.

Standing Bear was overjoyed at his father's words. He was beginning to think his friends had said more than they should have. He turned and looked at the Comanche for the first time.

"I will walk her through the village at sunset. Do not attempt to speak to her. She is my woman. I am only allowing you to look on her because I value the peace our tribes share," Standing Bear declared before standing and looking at his father and friends before departing.

White Buffalo hid his emotions well, but Big Tree and Sleeping Otter were both looking down at the ground.

**

Once Standing Bear was outside, he began walking in the direction of his home, hoping he had done the right thing. Before entering his dwelling, he heard Abigail's voice.

"Look at the size of you," Abigail squealed. "I have missed you!"

"I have been growing larger every day. But that is plain to see. How have you been?"

The two friends were so caught up in their conversation, they didn't notice Standing Bear. Instead of interrupting their reunion, he quickly stepped inside.

"We will go find wood as soon as we get this water back to your home," Abigail said as they neared the open doorway.

After helping Alax inside, he spoke to Abigail. "Abigail, I will accompany you to fetch some wood. Alexandria can set up the bed; she looks like she needs to rest," he said to his cousin before placing a kiss on Alexandria's forehead.

Alexandria's arms encircled his body. "I will be here."

Standing Bear wanted nothing more than to stay inside their home and hold her close to him, but instead he slowly pulled from the embrace and ushered Abigail outside while he thought through what he was going to say. He thought the outcome of the visit with the Comanche scout was the best he could hope for, but he was also aware that he might need Abigail's help if Alexandria was going to be kept completely in the dark.

Abigail spoke first. "Standing Bear, there is a Comanche here. He has been waiting for your return. He wants to talk to you about Alexandria …"

"I am aware. I just left him and Father," Standing Bear interrupted his nervous, whispering cousin. "You have not said anything to him, have you?"

"No, not really. I did say the woman with you is happy. I once promised Alexandria I would help her if something like this happened. And yet, I did not. I know what she means to you, and honestly, I don't want to see her go either," Abigail confessed as she lowered her head.

"Listen to me. You and I are the only ones who know the baby she carries is not mine. Before I let the scout look at her, I will tell him the baby is mine. Running Elk will not want her then. But she must never know anyone from his camp was here," Standing Bear said, gripping his cousin's shoulders. "I will not lose her. I can't lose her."

"I will never tell her. But are you sure the messenger will be satisfied with just your word?"

"That is my only chance. He has to."

Abigail looked conflicted but stayed silent when Standing Bear turned and walked away.

***

Before seeking out the Comanche scout, Standing Bear stopped by his tipi and informed Alax that he wanted to take a walk later. She agreed to his suggestion without question, not bothering to stop her cooking.

"Standing Bear, I do have one more question for you," the Comanche scout said as soon as he caught sight of Standing Bear.

"Ask your question," Standing Bear said as he stood beside Black Cloud.

The Comanche stopped combing his horse and looked Standing Bear in the eye before continuing. "People are closed-lipped, but I have a feeling the woman you hold is the one we call Two Fires."

Standing Bear was stunned by the man's statement but he said nothing while he waited for the question.

"Why do you want her when you know she belongs to Running Elk?"

"I have never heard the woman speak Running Elk's name," Standing Bear lied. "Besides, she carries my child. From what I've heard of the warrior, he doesn't sound the type who would want a woman who carries someone else's offspring."

Black Cloud watched Standing Bear closely. "If the woman is with child, then I will return to Running Elk with the news." The man stated, not looking convinced Standing Bear was being truthful.

"We call her Alax. You may see her but may not speak to her. I do not want you frightening her while she carries my child."

The Indian nodded in agreement and Standing Bear spoke again. "I will walk her through the camp at sunset. Remember, do not try to speak to her. She is my woman," he warned, leaving Black Cloud before the scout could argue.

Chapter Twenty-Four

The first snow did not bring Running Elk's departure from the village. Since the meeting at Medicine Lodge, there had been sporadic skirmishes almost weekly, and Running Elk volunteered for each mission. He found that as long as he was fighting for his life, he wasn't dwelling on Two Fires.

The group of warriors sat around a fire, remembering those they'd lost and praising the ones who showed bravery on their latest mission. Running Elk wasn't in the mood to join the other warriors. Until he'd met Two Fires, he had been considered friendly, but she had, by no actions of her own, managed to change his personality. After finishing the rabbit meat he'd cooked for dinner, he decided to seek the comfort and warmth of his hides.

"Running Elk, can we have a word?" Quanah asked as Running Elk was putting his small fire out.

"Of course," Running Elk answered, looking to the chief to decide whether they would walk or sit.

"This won't take long. We should be back at the camp in two days. You have shown great bravery over the last months, and I wanted to make sure you know how much the people value you," the war chief declared as he retied a piece of leather around the otter fur that secured his braids.

"I have done nothing anyone else wouldn't have if given the opportunity," Running Elk argued. "But if you say all that as a way to keep me from looking for Two Fires, it isn't going to work. If the scout isn't back, then I will leave."

Quanah shook his head before patting Running Elk on the back. "I will see you in the morning."

The next two days were miserable. The snow was blinding, and the wind was brutal. Instead of stopping for the night, the warriors slept on horseback. Once they returned to camp, all Running Elk wanted to do was get warm and sleep.

When he woke the next morning, he found a clean, dry outfit placed beside his sleeping pallet. He knew Morning Star had been there but didn't know why. After he dressed and ate breakfast, he went in search of White Wolf.

"Come in, brother," White Wolf said when he saw Running Elk approaching.

"Yes, come. Sit and tell us of your bravery," Kicking Bird suggested as soon as Running Elk entered the dwelling.

While he still felt uneasy around his brothers, he knew his feelings were caused by his actions, not his brothers'. Before he left, he had tried to make amends for his behavior and hoped the three could avoid all conversation that would result in harsh words.

"Thank you for the clothes," Running Elk called to Morning Star before she walked out of the tipi. She blushed, nodded, and smiled.

Before the brothers could begin any conversation beyond greetings, Quanah spoke from outside the dwelling.

"The scout has returned and has information for you."

"Has he seen her?" Running Elk asked hopefully, standing and walking outside without saying a word to his brother.

"I have not spoken to him. He has just now returned. As soon as he comes to my tipi, I will send him to you," Quanah said, patting his friend on the back and giving him a hopeful smile.

"I will be waiting."

For the first time in many months, Running Elk allowed himself to feel excitement. The warrior didn't get to enjoy the feeling for long.

Black Cloud entered Running Elk's tipi and began spinning an unbelievable tale. The warrior shook his head as the messenger finished the story.

"She is carrying the Kiowa's baby? No, it was not her. She would not do that! She could not. I do not believe you!" Running Elk was on his feet, yelling at the man.

"Running Elk, she is with a warrior named Standing Bear from White Buffalo's camp. If you don't believe me, go see for yourself. I am sorry that I had to be the one to deliver this news," the man said, walking out of the tipi.

Running Elk swallowed back the gut-wrenching pain and hurt, packed the necessities he would need, mounted his best pony, and rode to the front of Quanah's tipi.

"I will return, but I have to see for myself. Do not worry, I will watch from afar. I have to know the messenger spoke the truth." Running Elk informed Quanah when the warrior stepped out into the cold.

The war chief nodded his head. "Do not forget you are needed here."

"I cannot go on if I do not see for myself," Running Elk said through gritted teeth.

"Be watchful, my friend," Quanah said as he pulled his robes tighter against himself.

The rage coursing through Running Elk's body kept him from feeling the biting cold. He couldn't believe the woman he had given up everything for was carrying another man's child. The woman had plagued his thoughts, both waking and sleeping, and he wasn't ready to accept the fact that she had betrayed him so quickly. Had he not promised her they would be together? Did she not have faith in his words? Being forced to consider the fact that the scout had spoken the truth, he was driven to see with his own eyes the Kiowa warrior who had caused his woman's love to fade.

Running Elk rode his pinto as hard as he dared, sparing no time in finding the Kiowa camp where Two Fires was supposedly living. When he arrived, the camp was still sleeping, so he crouched behind a large tree and waited for the village to come alive.

When Running Elk saw her open the tipi flap and walk outside, all the memories of their time together came flooding back. He fought to keep his body in a crouched state; the desire to stand was almost uncontrollable. Over the last months, he had thought of nothing but her, and promised all others who would listen that he and Two Fires were meant to be together. But watching her calmly stand in front of another man's tipi was almost more than he could bear. After straining to see if she was hurt or showed signs of abuse, he realized she was most probably being treated well. She was obviously not seeking a way to escape and appeared to be almost serene.

He couldn't look away even though somewhere, deep inside, he knew he should. She turned and pulled the blanket tighter against her body. The roundness of her belly proved the scout had spoken the truth but was devastating to Running Elk nonetheless.

He knew the intelligent thing to do would be to leave, yet he stayed and watched as she returned inside the tipi. Even when she was gone, he fought with the notion of staying put. But the longer he was there, the angrier he got. So he slowly backed up.

As he was moving back, he saw Two Fires open the flap once again. She stepped outside and looked directly at him.

Running Elk didn't fight the need to stand any longer. Just as he prepared to show himself, he saw a man gently place his arms around the woman who held his heart, and pull her back inside. The warrior felt his chest tighten and a knot grow in the pit of his stomach. Not caring if he was seen any longer, he rose and ran back to his waiting horse. He half hoped one of the Kiowas had spotted him. Then he would at least be able to get some of his aggression out.

He was consumed with rage as he rode to his camp. Running Elk knew the only thing the fury was good for was to make him a better warrior. He also accepted the fact that he would never love again. The woman he called Two Fires had made sure of that.

Chapter Twenty-Five

Alexandria woke in the morning feeling restless. She had been more likely to stay in the warmth than venture outdoors lately. But she felt a strange compulsion to step outside and breath the fresh, crisp air. When she began carefully pulling out of Standing Bear's embrace, he woke.

"Where are you going?" he asked, pulling her closer.

"I need some air. But I promise I will be right back."

"Then I will keep the bed warm," he mumbled as he closed his eyes and rolled over.

Alexandria ran her hand over his exposed shoulder before standing up. Before stepping into the frigid morning, she wrapped herself tightly in a blanket and walked outside to greet the new day. The day had not begun but the birds were awake, and their song was a warm greeting.

While she was enjoying the musical cool morning, she had the strangest feeling someone was watching her. It had been a long time since anyone tried to look at her without her knowledge. After pulling the blanket closer, she took a deep breath and returned to the warmth of the tipi.

As soon as she was back inside, she felt the overwhelming desire to look back outside one more time.

There were three trees to the east that held her gaze. Just as she was about to put her hand above her eyes, to get a better look, she felt Standing Bear's arms reach around her and gently pull her back inside.

Standing Bear swooped Alexandria up in his arms and carried her to their sleeping mat. After laying her down gently, he climbed in beside her.

"You shouldn't be out in the cold for so long," he said, snuggling close to her.

"I am here," she spoke in a whisper, but smiled at Standing Bear even though inside she was feeling numb.

Alexandria couldn't shake the feelings she was experiencing. Her heart raced and her palms sweated just like they had every time she'd found Running Elk. For a split second, she allowed herself to hope her feelings weren't deceiving her. She had even gone back outside to have another look. Whether she wanted to freely admit it, she had given up hope the man would come for her. But this morning, the feeling was so strong. She also knew bringing Running Elk's name up would only upset Standing Bear. The knowledge was not enough to deter her from questioning the handsome warrior who was cradling her in his warm arms.

"Have you still had no word of Running Elk?" she asked timidly, not sure the level of anger she had caused.

Standing Bear pulled away from her and stood. She didn't move from where she was lying.

"No. I told you that I would tell you if anyone was looking for you. I will not hear the man's name again!" he yelled.

Standing Bear stormed out before she had time to roll over. Instead of praying that she and Running Elk would soon be reunited, Alexandra said a prayer that one day Running Elk would know she had given him a child.

Alexandria learned how angry Standing Bear was when he stayed away for the next two days.

His absence gave her time to finish beading the cradleboard she was making for the baby and to gossip all day with Abigail.

Standing Bear returned the afternoon of the third day to find Alax hunched over, holding her stomach, and sweating.

Alexandria didn't notice his appearance until she heard Abigail shout an order at him. "Standing Bear, go get Willow!"

***

"You had an easy birth. The boy wanted to come into this world. He is healthy and big for coming so early," Willow said as she handed Alexandria her son.

The labor might have been easy, according to Willow, but the pain had been so great that Alexandria made up her mind not to ever go through the ordeal again.

The elder smiled a toothless grin and handed Alexandria her baby. Alexandria took her son and held him close to her heart.

"Standing Bear will be so proud," Abigail gushed, joining the conversation. "Willow, why don't you go and get him? They need to give their son a name."

"Abigail! Can I have a word?" Alexandria demanded more than questioned.

Abigail knelt down by her friend. "They need to believe the child is his. It is best this way, believe me. Your son will be raised by the Kiowa people. Now calm yourself and let me see him," she whispered hurriedly, hoping Alexandria would say no more on the subject.

"I cannot have these people think that. He is Running Elk's son."

Abigail sighed loudly before speaking broken English to her friend. "Standing Bear has been good to you. He has given you everything. It will hurt nothing for the people to believe he is the father," Abigail repeated, a little more intensely than the first time. "Think of where you would be if he had just given you up once he learned you carried another man's child. No one would have accepted you. You wouldn't have had Willow's birthing experience; you would have been a slave left alone in a field to have your child."

When Standing Bear entered the tipi, he interrupted the scolding Alexandria was receiving from her friend.

"I have come to see your son. A healthy boy is something to be proud of."

Abigail handed the bundle to the warrior. Alexandria watched as the man cradled her son. Her heart felt as if it were breaking. Standing Bear was being gentle and speaking lovingly to the child. Tears rolled down her cheeks. She wasn't sure if they were tears of joy or tears of defeat. It was at that very moment that she gave up hoping for a different outcome and decided if Running Elk couldn't be a father to his child, Standing Bear would be a fine stand-in. Knowing it was best if Standing Bear didn't see her crying, she wiped her eyes with a blanket before looking at the two again.

"Does the boy have a name?" the warrior asked as he knelt down beside Alexandria with the child still resting securely in his strong arms.

"I would like to call him Gray Eagle. Is that all right with you?" Alexandria asked, watching Standing Bear's expression change little.

"We will call him Little Eagle. This way you can hold onto your past and I can look upon the child with love," he decided as he handed the child back to his mother.

Standing Bear placed one hand on his heart and the other on Little Eagle's head. "Little Eagle, my son, you have come into this world in a turbulent time. You will be a warrior, like your father, but I am not sure how many raids you will ride in. By the time you have grown to manhood, all of this could be gone. You may never know the joys of roaming the prairie free, but you will always be proud of who you are. We are a proud and giving people," he said, emotion thick in his voice.

Alexandria couldn't stop the tears when she heard Standing Bear's blessing.

Standing Bear sounded choked up himself as he knelt down and showed Alexandria her son. She pulled the robes from her baby's face and really looked at him for the first time.

He was beautiful. He had Running Elk's caramel-colored skin, a head full of jet-black hair, and her greenish-blue eyes. They even shared the strange yellow fleck in their left eye. She was sure Running Elk would have been proud of the child. And was grateful Standing Bear accepted him.

***

Standing Bear watched Alexandria place the babe to her breast before gently pulling Abigail nearer to the fire.

"Cousin, I am going to ask Alax to be my wife."

He was still unsure of what Alexandria's response would be, but Abigail was overjoyed with the news.

"When?" she asked excitedly.

"As soon as she has healed from the birth. I want Little Eagle to have a father."

"He does," Abigail said quietly. "And he will never know the man because of our lies."

"Abigail, I will not lose her now," Standing Bear vowed through gritted teeth. He pulled his cousin outside the tipi so that they could finish their conversation.

"I do not want to speak about the untruths we have told. Forget about them. What is done is done."

Abigail nodded and looked to the ground. "I can't help feeling guilty for what I've done, but I will do as you ask. Mostly for selfish reasons. I don't want to lose her friendship," she promised softly.

"We have done the right thing. Do not think on it any longer. Now go and help her with the child. I am needed at council," he said, kissing her on the top of the head before walking away.

***

Alexandria had managed to sit with her back again the leather wall. It was painful, but her discomfort was lessening with each passing minute. She was curious about where Standing Bear and Abigail had gone but kept busy talking to her son as she held him to her heart.

"He will be over-proud if you aren't careful," Abigail teased as she walked into the tipi.

"No. He will never be over-proud. He will be good and fair and giving. Where did you go?"

"You will spoil him if you aren't careful. In this world, a child learns from experience. You have a lifetime with the child. Do not fill his head with such things too early. Take your time. I walked to the river to fill another container," Abigail said, taking the baby from Alexandria's tight grip.

"I see Running Elk when I look at him," Alexandria said tearfully.

"You will be spoiled. There seems to be no stopping your mother," Abigail said, ignoring Alexandria's observation as she laid the child on furs closer to the warmth of the fire.

Chapter Twenty-Six

Standing Bear would have much rather stayed close to Alax and her baby. He hadn't expected her to be ready to birth the child when he'd sought her out earlier in the day. He had gone to find her simply because he didn't want to be parted any longer. He just wanted to be in her company before attending the council meeting.

White Buffalo had not come right out and explained what the meeting was about, but he had managed to convey to Standing Bear that it was going to be trying for his son.

Before walking into the meeting, Standing Bear took a moment to be thankful Little Eagle's birth was an easy one. When he entered the council lodgings, he was taken aback by the number of men in attendance.

His father had already begun speaking, so Standing Bear sat near the back of the tipi and listened.

"… to ensure the soldiers stay away from our camp, we will meet them as far from here as we can." White Buffalo stated before going silent and stony-faced as he looked around the area and waited for someone to speak.

Several warriors made noises of anger and others cleared their throats.

"I agree we need to keep them from our women, children, and the old, but this is only a temporary patch. Even if we turn them back towards the fort, they will return," Standing's Bear old friend, Sleeping Wolf, declared.

Most of the warriors nodded their heads in agreement.

"We either fight them or we surrender. I, for one, am not ready to give up our way of life yet," White Buffalo explained. "But we do nothing if all are not in agreement. Before we vote, you need to know we will not be alone in our fight. The Quahadi band will fight by our side."

The news appeared to lift the mood in the dwelling, but Standing Bear wasn't pleased to hear the news.

"My vote is to fight," he stated as he stood and left the tipi without looking at his father.

After leaving the council meeting, Standing Bear took a walk to clear his mind. He knew the Quahadi band was Quanah's, and Running Elk was one of his warriors. Along with that knowledge came the understanding that he would once again be forced to lie to Alax. There was no question about his participation in the upcoming battle. But there was no way he was going to tell Alax he would be fighting beside Running Elk.

His deepest desire was that the woman would give her whole heart to him, but as much as he hated knowing it, Alax still remained in the Comanche's steel grip. She might have given him her body, but her soul still remained with the father of her son. Standing Bear knew if he had any chance of keeping the news from Alax, he would have to ask for Abigail's help once again. He didn't relish demanding more from his cousin but saw no other option. He had to keep Alax, because he would be nothing without her. The woman had opened his heart to love after he'd lost all hope. His decision didn't mean he wasn't wracked with guilt.

***

During the two months before the warring party departed, Standing Bear stayed close to Alexandria and Little Eagle.

Between his constant presence and Abigail's help, the two managed to keep Alex in the dark about the reason Standing Bear was actually leaving. He decided to tell her he was going on a scouting trip just to watch the blue coats' movements.

Since Alex had given birth, her mind was centered on only the child so the lie was not difficult to keep on top of. The days flew by, and each night Standing Bear thanked the gods for keeping Alex and Little Eagle healthy and fed.

The day of departure seemed to catch Alex by surprise.

"I will return as soon as I am able," Standing Bear said as he reluctantly pulled the furs from his warm body.

"I know you will," Alexandria said, reaching for his waist.

Standing Bear's heartbeat quickened at her touch but he knew there was no more time. He could hear the snorts and neighing from the horses and knew he was already running late.

Instead of crawling back in bed, he leaned down and kissed her deeply before standing and quickly dressing.

"I will see you off. Give me a second to dress," she said, following him.

Seeing her naked was a picture he hoped to hold onto for the duration of his trip.

Alexandria stood outside their home with Little Eagle in her arms and watched Standing Bear depart. His heart filled when he saw tears form in her eyes. Once he'd learned of the warring party, he'd decided to put off asking her to be his wife until he returned. But as he rode away from the camp, he wondered if he might have made a mistake.

Standing Bear's group rode alone until midday when Quanah's band joined the ride. He recognized Running Elk immediately. His nemesis was riding between Quanah and another man. The man carried a look of determination and anger. Standing Bear knew it was only a matter of time before the two were sharing a pipe and planning the attack. He was glad he'd thought ahead and told his band he didn't want to be called by his name. After explaining his reasoning—if Running Elk did know of him by name, then his presence would surely cause trouble—the others in his camp agreed. If everything went as planned, the Kiowa warriors would call him by his son's name.

Although he thought he'd done everything in his power to remain anonymous, Standing Bear hadn't been prepared for the guilt he felt when he remembered Abigail's words. "Little Eagle has a father, but he will not know him because of our lies and deception."

After seeing to his horse, he walked towards the fire. A hundred battle-hardened warriors were sitting close by and all were listening to Quanah talk about his childhood.

Standing Bear was relieved when he spotted a space across from Running Elk. He found himself interested in the man. For the next hour, he listened to stories of hunting and reminiscing but nothing of the upcoming battle and nothing from Running Elk. The Comanche remained silent during the meeting.

Running Elk smoked the pipe when it was handed to him and appeared to be deep in thought as he memorized the faces of all those gathered.

Before the meeting broke, a scout returned with information that a small party of soldiers was only half a day's ride ahead. Standing Bear was relieved by the news, but he noticed Running Elk's steely expression didn't change. If everything worked out right, he would be home within two days' time. He hadn't left Alexandria alone for a night since the baby was born, and sitting in such close proximity to Running Elk only made him more anxious to return to her.

***

When Standing Bear crested the hill the sound of the gunfire was deafening. The battle had only just begun but smoke hung thick in the air. The horses' swift movements only added to the poor visibility.

The weapons the soldiers fired had more power than anything the Indians carried. They were also deadly accurate at a distance. The raiding party was taken aback by their power.

Standing Bear rode into the heat of the battle just in time to witness Running Elk fall from his horse. Standing Bear clenched his legs, rose up from the back of the horse, and took aim quickly, not having time to aim properly, and fired at the prone soldier whose gun was responsible for killing Running Elk's horse.

His arrow found its mark and hit the soldier in the neck. As soon as he was sure the white man wouldn't fire again, he steered his bay in the direction of the fallen Comanche. When he reached Running Elk, Standing Bear grasped for him and pulled the Comanche onto the back his horse before quickly riding out of range of the big guns.

Standing Bear didn't say a word until Running Elk dismounted from the back of his horse.

"I have heard stories of your bravery. It is good to know they were not falsehoods. It is an honor to fight beside you."

Running Elk looked uncomfortable with the praise. "You showed bravery as well. I owe my life to you," the Comanche said as he extended his hand to the Kiowa warrior.

"I did what anyone would. You owe me nothing. Do not give it a second thought," Standing Bear said, releasing the grip he had on the Comanche's arm before kicking his horse and returning to the battle.

When the battle was over, the Indians camped for the night. Instead of taking part in the celebrations, Standing Bear sought solitude. He wanted to take some time to reflect on the day's events. It was obvious that saving Running Elk had been the right decision, but he soon realized that in doing so, it had caused his guilt to grow to an unmanageable level. His only comfort was thinking that saving the warrior might have counted in some small way as repaying Alex. He had kept the man she loved breathing; that had to count as something. His confused thoughts were interrupted when he heard someone approaching.

"They tell me you are called Little Eagle," Running Elk greeted. "I have come to sit and smoke with you," he continued as he took a seat beside Standing Bear.

The two men smoked and talked for hours. Standing Bear found Running Elk to be a proud, intelligent man. The guilt that had momentarily subsided crept back the longer they talked. When the visit became torture, Standing Bear stood, patted Running Elk on the shoulder, and prepared to lie down.

"We will meet on the next raid, Little Eagle. It is good to know you," Running Elk said as Standing Bear was turning his back.

After a fitful sleep, Standing Bear mounted his bay and rode in the direction of home and Alex. He rode through the night, not wanting to delay their reunion any longer than he had to. There was an important question he planned to ask her, and his guilt wouldn't stop him from doing so.

Chapter Twenty-Seven

As soon as Quanah's party returned to their camp, Running Elk sought the solitude of his tipi. Almost immediately, he heard a familiar voice outside.

"Running Elk, it is White Wolf. Can we talk?"

Running Elk's muscles tensed. "Brother, I would rather be alone," he spoke, his blunt answer devoid of emotion.

"I would like to speak to you about Two Fires," White Wolf continued talking, totally ignoring his brother. "I know it is still a rather prickly subject for the two of us, but there are things we need to discuss. They are a great burden to my mind."

Running Elk didn't want to talk about Two Fires with anyone. He had to force the woman's memory to the back of his mind in order to deal with his everyday life. Talking with his brother would not aid him in accomplishing that goal.

"Your burdens are your own," Running Elk said.

"Running Elk, please. My heart is heavy. We are brothers; we should be able to speak of anything," White Wolf spoke into the closed flap of his doorway.

"I need time to myself. Come back later," Running Elk said after a long pause. After taking a deep breath, he stood and opened the flap. "Come back later," he said, looking White Wolf in the eyes. "You must know how difficult it is for me to talk about her after all that has happened."

"We got past you anger over Morning Star. You accepted the fact that Morning Star is happy. You said over and over you didn't love her. I do, and probably always have. I do not want you to be lonely and bitter. Please talk to me. What I have to tell you will settle your heart as well as mine." White Wolf said, trying his best to persuade his stubborn brother.

"Later. Come back later. We will talk then. I will be ready to listen later," Running Elk said, touching White Wolf on the shoulder before reentering his home.

Pushing White Wolf away didn't give Running Elk the peace he sought. His mind was full of questions about what White Wolf thought so important he dared to risk his wrath. They had not had a conversation about Two Fires since he'd returned to the village after seeing the woman pregnant.

Instead of being angry when he heard the footsteps return, he was almost relieved. White Wolf couldn't have walked more than twenty steps before he returned.

"Running Elk, I will not be put off. We need to speak immediately."

"Come in," Running Elk said as soon as his brother sought permission to enter a second time. "Sit," he said, pointing to the ground beside him.

"Thank you," White Wolf smiled as he sat beside his little brother. Running Elk couldn't remember seeing his brother more at peace. "We have much to talk about."

"Then you start talking while I load the pipe," Running Elk suggested, attempting to not sound desperate for the conversation to begin.

"The visions I received when you met Two Fires were not true visions." White Wolf stopped talking when he saw the change in his brother's expression. "Now, before you interrupt, let me speak, and all of your questions will be answered. I believe now that I was misinterpreting the visions because of my feelings towards Morning Star. The thought that I could have allowed such a thing to happen is intolerable. I now feel that I was to know of your meeting and nothing more. I am responsible for your separation. And I am truly sorry for that. But I have seen her again," he added at the end of his thought, hoping it would calm Running Elk's rising anger.

Running Elk stood quickly and began pacing back and forth. "So what I am hearing is it would have been fine to bring her here when I wanted to? Is that right?" he asked, trying desperately to control his rage.

He knelt down in front of his brother, looked him straight in the eyes, and clenched his teeth together firmly. "Well? Is that what you are telling me? All of the pain I've experienced was for nothing?"

"I cannot express to you how sorry I am," White Wolf stated, holding his brother's glare.

"Sorry?!" Running Elk yelled before rising and pacing again. "Is that all?"

"No. There is more. But first I have a question for you. Why did you not attempt to find Standing Bear when you were with the warrior from White Buffalo's camp?" he asked, picking his words carefully.

"She has another man's child now. She is no longer thinking about me," Running Elk answered, avoiding his brother's gaze. Admitting she was gone was difficult for him.

"How do you know these things?"

"I have seen it with my own eyes. Not through some vision. She was clearly with child and quite comfortable there. Now tell me what you came to say."

"Running Elk, the woman haunts my visions," White Wolf said, standing to face his brother. "Your time with Two Fires is not over."

Running Elk laughed painfully. "I think your visions are wrong. I am tired. You should leave now," Running Elk suggested as he walked towards the exit.

"I will leave, but how can you be sure the son she bore was not yours?" White Wolf asked as he left the tipi, leaving Running Elk standing alone, unable to speak.

"White Wolf!" he yelled after his brother.

White Wolf stopped and turned to face his brother.

"She had a son?" Running Elk questioned quickly.

"She did, and the vision I was given showed me he will be important to our people," White Wolf said, smiling, before turning and continuing to his home.

Running Elk went back inside, filled his pipe, smoked a bit, and allowed the blocks he had placed to drop. Two Fires was, once again, front and center in his mind. He hadn't allowed himself to even consider the child Two Fires carried was his. He was angry that he had so easily allowed himself to accept the woman had forgotten him, and livid that his brother hadn't come to him earlier.

After much thought, he decided the next time he saw Little Eagle, he would question the man. Even though he knew the next skirmish wouldn't be too long in coming, he was still impatient. The small battle that had just taken place between the twenty soldiers and themselves wouldn't stop the blue coats for long. It was becoming clearer and clearer that nothing would.

Chapter Twenty-Eight

Standing Bear had every intention of asking Alex to be his wife the minute he rode into camp, but when he realized the earliness of the hour, his plans changed. He wanted to surprise the woman he'd missed so badly but didn't want to wake her, so he slipped into the bed beside her and gently kissed her forehead. She rolled over and murmured something in her sleep.

"I am here," he whispered.

"Running Elk," Alexandria mumbled, smiling a smile Standing Bear had never seen before.

Anger and guilt coursed through his veins, but he knew he was to blame for the emotions so he carefully left their bed and went fishing until the sun rose. He understood the woman had been sleeping and was unaware of what she had said, but acceptance did little to calm the anger he experienced. Still, he wasn't going to find Alex and offer to return her to the man she loved, so he swallowed his emotions, picked up the three fish he'd caught, and returned to his tipi.

"I am back," he stated as he dropped his catch in a woven bowl by the door.

"It is good to see you," Alexandria said, moving towards him.

"Is it? I am needed elsewhere." Standing Bear found it impossible to stay in the company of the two women and maintain his sanity.

After grabbing a blanket, he began walking towards the exit.

"What is the matter with him?" He heard Alexandria ask Abigail.

Abigail's response was polished and well-rehearsed. "He has many pressing issues on his mind. I am sure his anger will pass."

Standing Bear again experienced mixed emotions when he heard Abigail lie for him. He wanted nothing more than to be happy and live life day by day, but all he seemed to be doing in his search for happiness was causing everyone else involved grief.

Since he knew there were no easy answers to his situation, he found his best horse and began combing her mane.

He had almost been able to stop his pounding head when he heard Alex.

"Standing Bear, have I done something to upset you?" she asked as she walked closer to him, gently resting her hand on the horse's neck.

"No," he answered, not looking away from his work. "Why do you ask?"

"You know why I am asking. You've been gone for days, and when you return, you are angry and cold," Alexandria stated as she moved her hand from the horse to cover his.

Her touch made liquid fire course through the warrior's veins. He turned and took her into his muscular arms, before gently cupping her face in his hand and leaning down to kiss her. When he felt her fall into him, he picked her up and carried her to his tipi.

Standing Bear watched as Abigail scooped up the baby with a smile before vacating the home quickly.

Standing Bear undressed her swiftly and laid her on their bed.

"Your body would bring any warrior to their knees. I cannot help but love you," he said, his voice thick with need.

He leaned on his elbow to look at her closely. His heartbeat quickened when she lazily ran her hand down his well-defined chest.

"Tell me you want me. Alax, call me by my name," he begged before leaving a trail of fire down her stomach until he reached the top of her thighs.

She lifted her head and pulled him to her. His hair fell over his shoulders and fell across her face and breasts. "Standing Bear, I want you," she said breathlessly.

He took no more time in granting her wish.

Alexandria lay on his chest afterward and traced the muscles on his stomach.

Standing Bear had hoped hearing Alex say his name and almost beg him to quench her thirst for him would ease his guilt. But as he lay with the woman, while she mindlessly traced his ribs, all he could be sure of was that he had only claimed her body.

Knowing the next question he planned to ask her would either lessen some of his emotions or make his life miserable, he did his best to speak without allowing his emotions to bleed through. "I am going to ask you a question and I need the truth. Can you promise me that? The truth, no matter what it is," he began.

Alexandria raised her head and looked at him with a puzzled look on her face. "I promise, if it is that important to you."

Standing Bear sighed deeply, slowly moved away from Alexandria, stood, and began dressing.

Alexandria sat up and covered herself with the robes, waiting for him to ask the question that seemed to weigh so heavy on his mind.

"Do you love me?" he asked, turning away from her.

"Of course I do," she answered quickly, before standing to move beside him. "You know that."

A warmth filled Standing Bear when he heard her answer. It was the one thing he had prayed he'd hear since they had been together. A tear threatened to fall, so he wiped his eyes quickly.

He turned when he felt her hand on his arms.

"What is the matter?"

"You are naked," he observed, bending to place a kiss on her collarbone before moving to the nape of her neck. "I believe we can finish this discussion later," he decided as he attempted to lift her into his arms.

Alexandria pulled away. "No. I want to finish this."

Standing Bear wasn't happy with her demand but moved away to continue to dress. She had said she loved him, but he still couldn't allow himself to be happy. After he tied his knife to his leg, he spoke again. "Do you love me the same way as you love Running Elk?"

The lengthy silence his question received forced him to slowly face the woman.

"I love you as I have any other man in my life … except Running Elk," she answered quietly.

Standing Bear was hurt, but again, his emotions were all his fault, so he nodded before speaking, just to ensure he would be able to keep his voice even. "I asked for the truth, so it would seem I am going to have to live with it."

As he spoke, he claimed her in his arms.

"I know I owe you my life and my son's. I will continue to be happy with you. How could I not be? You are a good man," she spoke into his chest as she held him tightly. "I miss my son. Would you come to Abigail's with me?"

Standing Bear knew being in his cousin's company wouldn't help with his guilt, but he was slowly realizing nothing would help as long as he held so tightly to Alex. "No. I have to speak to my father. But I will return soon. Tell Abigail hello for me," he said before leaving the tipi.

***

Alexandria slowly dressed, rethinking the conversation she'd just had with Standing Bear. It was not like him to speak Running Elk's name, but he had stressed how badly he wanted the truth. She hadn't wanted to hurt the man, but it seemed she had. She might have given up on Running Elk coming for her, but she would never stop loving the man, no matter how hard she tried.

Only a week after the war party returned, they were planning on leaving again. Standing Bear had brooded the whole time he was with Alexandria. He was absent during the days, and at night he would lovingly beg Alexandria to speak his name when he took her as his.

Alexandria didn't care for being alone and had asked several times that he spend more time with Little Eagle and her. His response was the warrior and elders needed him to help prepare for the coming battle.

The morning he was to leave, Alexandria lay in the sleeping warrior's warm, muscular arms and attempted to vanquish the dream that had awoken her. As hard as she tried to do just that, she soon realized she couldn't shake the images of Standing Bear being killed in the battle. Thinking that getting some fresh air might help, she attempted to slip away to go outside. As soon as she moved, he pulled her closer. Alexandria knew from the change in his breathing that he was awake. He slowly opened his eyes and saw the look of terror on her beautiful face.

"What is the matter?" he asked sleepily.

"I want you to stay home. Do not go today. Stay with me," she pleaded, trying to stop the tears from forming in her eyes.

"I would if I could, but I am needed," he explained, cradling her close to him. "We will not be gone long."

"I don't want you to go. They will be fine without you. Please stay."

"Alexandria, I will be home soon," he promised as he ran his hand through her golden tresses before kissing her deeply.

"I pray you are right, Standing Bear."

"Fear not. Now get out of bed, you lazy woman, and help me prepare to leave," he said teasingly.

"If I get up, will you stay?" she asked hopefully as she grabbed the warrior around the waist.

"Woman, I don't have time to play," he said, gently throwing her on the pallet and rolling on top of her.

"Make time. I really want you to stay," she said, pulling his face close and kissing him deeply.

"I would if I could. But you are a warrior's woman. Instead of enticing me to stay, be proud of me." His tone was slowly turning from playful to concerned.

"I am proud of you. I just have a bad feeling. It isn't about me doubting your fighting ability," Alexandria said, kissing him again before standing and dressing. Banishing the visions from her dream wasn't easy, but she knew he was right. She had to be strong and have faith he would return to her. It wasn't the first nightmare she'd had, and she was sure it wouldn't be her last.

"It is normal to fear for those who leave, but you will be back in my arms very soon," he assured her as he walked towards the sleeping Little Eagle. "I will see you soon, son. Take care of your mother and keep her safe," he said, gently patting the sleeping child's chest.

The Kiowa warrior grabbed his pack and walked outside.

Alexandria followed. "We will be awaiting your return," she said, holding him one more time.

Chapter Twenty-Nine

Standing Bear hadn't let Alexandria see just how much her begging him to stay affected him. Her words were tearing his heart out. If not for the shame it would have brought to his family, he might have considered staying. Between the nagging guilt, and the shameful need for her, he hoped the ride to Quanah's Quahadi band would give him time to think.

By early afternoon, the Kiowa ranks doubled in size. The Quahadi warriors slipped into step, almost silently.

As soon as the group melted into the ranks, he heard Running Elk's voice behind him.

"Little Eagle, I need to speak to you," the Comanche warrior voiced as he rode beside Standing Bear.

"It is good to see you are well," Standing Bear greeted halfheartedly as he slowed his horse's pace.

"And you. I would like to ask you a few questions. Do you know of a white woman with golden hair in your camp? Her name is Alexandria." Running Elk began his interrogation without giving Standing Bear time to say no.

Standing Bear couldn't help but notice how the Comanche warrior's voice softened when he said her name. He had hoped that their meeting would be much like the previous one, yet Running Elk's question was putting an end to that possibility.

Standing Bear took a deep breath before answering. "Alaxandra," he repeated the name as Running Elk had spoken it. "There are many white women in our camp. I do not know all of their names," he lied.

"From what I have gathered, she lives with a warrior named Standing Bear. He is supposed to be one of your best warriors, and yet I heard none speak of him the last time we were together. He was with your band this winter."

Standing Bear quickly looked at Running Elk. "How can you be sure?"

"I saw her. She is the woman I have lived for, and when I was told she was with child, I had to see for myself. I rode to your camp and saw her standing outside of the man's tipi. When I watched him put his arms around her, I left," Running Elk explained.

"Did you see the man?" Standing Bear asked, knowing if the Comanche had, they would not be having this civil conversation.

"No. I felt it was time to give her up. And I honestly tried to. But my brother came to see me and informed me that I should question my rash decision."

"What did your brother say to you?" Standing Bear asked as he stopped his horse.

Running Elk stopped beside him. "Do you know of the man I seek?"

"I do," Standing Bear admitted after a long pause. "What do you want to know about him?"

Standing Bear noticed he and Running Elk were now alone. Everyone else had moved on while they talked. He wasn't sure he was happy about the situation, but he had already answered Running Elk and knew there would be other questions. If the two were alone, maybe it would be easier to tell another untruth.

"Where is he?" Running Elk asked as he dismounted from his pinto. Standing Bear couldn't miss the excitement in the man's voice.

"He is not with us. He stays close to the woman," Standing Bear lied as he dismounted so that he could be on Running Elk's level.

Disappointment crossed the Comanche's features. "Is the child a boy? Why does he risk dishonor by staying with her? Is he afraid she will run? When I last saw her, she didn't seem to be in distress."

Standing Bear listened to the list of questions and kept his attention focused on the trail the two were walking.

"I believe the child is a boy. Why do you ask?" he inquired, trying to hide his surprise.

"My brother, the shaman, told me as much. At least he saw that right," Running Elk said, more to himself than the Kiowa. "Why does he stay with her?"

"From what I hear, he loves the woman powerfully," he answered quietly, still not facing his walking partner.

"I can understand that. She is easy to love. Now tell me, Little Eagle … does she love him?"

Standing Bear took a second to answer the question. "I believe so. She stays with him. From what I've seen, she does not appear unhappy. Running Elk, I do not know the answer to that question!" Standing Bear growled. He was finding it increasingly difficult to speak of Alexandria.

Running Elk heard the irritation in the Kiowa voice.

"I have touched a nerve, haven't I? You know the warrior better than you have been letting on. You must answer my questions," Running Elk said, grabbing his walking partner's arm. "You have to know how important this information is to me," Running Elk stressed.

"I know nothing more than I have told you. The woman does not seem unhappy," Standing Bear said defeatedly.

"Then tell me of the boy. Does the child look like the Kiowa?" Running Elk continued, undeterred.

"I have heard he does look like his father. And it is said the child has her strange eyes."

"The babe has a fire in his eye?" Running Elk asked, letting go of his hold on the Kiowa. "I called her Two Fires because of her eyes," he informed Standing Bear.

"The name seems just," Standing Bear spoke as he remounted his ride. He knew if he didn't put some space between them, he would not be able to keep his voice level. "There are more important subjects to speak about. It is not good to have a woman on your mind when preparing for battle. Nothing good will come of it. You need to clear your head. I do not want to make a habit of saving you," Standing Bear said quickly, in hopes Running Elk would see his sound reasoning.

"You are right. But we will speak more about her later," Running Elk informed him before kicking his horse and putting some distance between the two.

Standing Bear was relieved Running Elk was gone. He wasn't sure how much longer he could have kept talking about Alexandria without giving himself away.

He quickly decided to listen to his own advice and attempt to push the whole situation to the back of his mind until after the battle. Then he would try to find a way to deal with Running Elk before returning to Alexandria.

Chapter Thirty

Running Elk rode from the tight-lipped Kiowa warrior to Kicking Bird's side.

"Did you learn anything new?" his brother asked as soon as Running Elk's horse fell into step beside him.

"Maybe … I couldn't tell. I will speak to the man more later," Running Elk answered, not attempting to hide the confusion he was feeling.

"I know this might be difficult to hear, but maybe you should not seek the man out again until the battle is over. I understand your situation, but we all know our minds need to be sharp."

Running Elk considered his brother's words. As badly as he wanted news, he had to admit Little Eagle had saved his life, so he owed the man.

"I know you are right, brother. I will stay away from him tonight."

Kicking Bird smiled an appreciative grin. "I believe we are almost ready to rest for the night."

Running Elk looked in the direction his brother was staring. Quanah and White Buffalo had stepped down from their horses and were in the middle of laying a blanket on the ground.

"I will catch up with you all in a few minutes," Running Elk declared as he pulled his horse in the direction of the trees.

Running Elk wasn't the most spiritual man, but he wanted to be alone while he prayed for Two Fires. The steps he had taken to locate her were excruciatingly slow, but they were movement. After praying, he dispatched several squirrels and carried them back to the others.

When he returned, he found Kicking Bird stoking the cooking fires. The sight made Running Elk laugh and, with all he was going through, it felt good.

After the warriors finished their meal and laid out their furs, they again began gathering in the center of the makeshift camp.

Before everyone had settled, the runner returned and informed both Quanah and White Buffalo that the soldiers were breaking camp. Moving at nightfall was not something soldiers usually did, but chasing the men wasn't the best option either. The gathered warriors quickly decided it was best to surprise the men before they could leave.

Running Elk and Kicking Bird each held the end of a long leather strap and began felling the tents. He noticed Little Eagle stayed at the fringe of the melee.

Once the row of tents was down, the brothers separated and began riding back to the beginning of the camp. Running Elk rode past Standing Bear, yipping as he passed the Kiowa.

The resistance the soldiers were putting up was more than Running Elk anticipated. Bullets riddled the air and the only light was from the moon. Running Elk prepared to follow three soldiers as they ran towards their horses. The Comanche knew the men would not find their animals. They had been freed before any warrior rode into the temporary base.

Excitement coursed through Running Elk's body. He noticed Standing Bear riding beside him at exactly the same time he watched a bullet smash through the Kiowa's arm.

The force of the impact alone threw the Kiowa warrior from his horse. Running Elk masterfully changed his horse's direction and reached for the wounded man.

Little Eagle was in an immense amount of pain but managed to grab ahold of Running Elk. As soon as he positioned himself behind Running Elk, a second bullet embedded itself in the Kiowa's back.

Running Elk felt the impact first and, seconds later, he felt the weight of the Kiowa as he leaned into Running Elk. The Comanche quickly steered his horse away from the battle.

As soon as they reached a distance that was safe from the soldier's powerful guns, Running Elk gently pulled the Kiowa from his horse. He laid the wounded warrior on the ground and tied a piece of leather around his arm in hopes of stopping the bleeding, or at least lessening some of the man's pain, before cradling Little Eagle's head in his arms.

"Little Eagle, I am truly sorry I could not repay the favor and save you."

The Kiowa shook his head before speaking. "I ... am ...Standing Bear," he admitted through labored breathing. "Alax ... lives with ... me. She ... she ... loves you. I used your ... son's name ... as my ... own. He was named ... for Gray Eagle."

Running Elk had watched far too many of his people die, but none had given him such life-changing information. It was difficult to hide his shock.

"You have been telling me falsehoods this whole time? Are you the one who wounded my nephew?"

"No. The boy was collateral damage, and I am sorry he was hurt. Go to Alax ... tell her ... my love was ... real. She ... wasn't unhappy ... with me. But ... her love ... her love ... for you is still ... strong. I am dying. And ... I am ... asking for ... your forgiveness."

Running Elk held the Kiowa warrior in his arms and knew if the warrior hadn't been on the back of his horse, he would be the one mortally wounded. The Kiowa had once again saved Running Elk's life but had been lying to him the whole time. His emotions were confused and jumbled.

"Standing Bear, I will mourn for you. You were a brave warrior. Your name will be remembered amongst your people. As much as I want to hate you, I cannot. Now go to the great beyond with peace in your heart."

Standing Bear winced in pain and swallowed hard. "Go … to her. Tell her … I did what I did … because I … love …"

Standing Bear didn't finish his thought before he was gone. The Kiowa warrior's last thought had been of the woman he loved.

***

Running Elk stayed with the lifeless warrior until the battle was finished. Watching Standing Bear fall had caused him to lose the taste for bloodshed.

When the dust settled, Running Elk handed Standing Bear's body to White Buffalo.

"I know the truth," he informed the Kiowa. "This brave warrior is Standing Bear, your son, not Little Eagle. I will give Alexandria time to mourn, then I will come for her … and my son. Tell her nothing. We will be reunited soon enough. She must remember this brave man with friendship, not the hate she will surely feel when she learns the truth."

Running Elk spoke calmly, but his heart was racing. He knew in a short time he would once again hold the woman he loved in his arms. The decision to give Two Fires and the warrior's family time to mourn Standing Bear was not an easy one. But after enduring all the obstacles placed in the way of their union, he felt a renewed optimism. After leaving the Kiowa elder, he went in search of Kicking Bird. He found himself excited about sharing his news with his brother.

Chapter Thirty-One

Alexandria hadn't been able to think of anything but Standing Bear since his departure. Her mind was not on her work, and she knew Abigail could sense she was worried as they sat grinding corn to powder.

"Are you well?" she asked.

"I have a bad feeling. I had a terrible dream last night. Standing Bear was killed. I know it's silly, but I can't seem to force the vision from my mind," Alexandria answered, looking from her work to her sleeping son who was laying on a robe next to her.

"The Kiowa claim dreams are visions. We can only pray your dream wasn't one. Did you tell Standing Bear of your dream before he left?"

"No. But I did ask him to stay. He said he had to go, but he has been so strange lately. I know he still loves me, but something seems to be weighing heavy on his mind," Alexandria answered, wiping the powder from the stone before adding a new handful of dry corn.

Abigail listened to her friend's concerns and nodded her agreement before speaking. "He had a lot on his mind. I am sure he will be fine in time. War parties tend to color warriors' moods. But I can tell you Standing Bear does not seek death like he once did."

"If you would have said that to me when I first arrived, I would have called you crazy. I know he is the same man who killed my husband, but at the same time, he has changed. It is almost like he is two different men."

"You have changed him. He loves you, there is no question about that."

"I do know I will be pleased to see him return."

"I believe he was right when he said that you would learn to love him," Abigail said, smiling.

"I do care a great deal for him. And I am so very grateful that he loves my son. Little Eagle is the most important person in my life."

Abigail was noticeably surprised by the absence of Running Elk's name but said nothing. Alexandria figured her silence was out of fear that if she brought him up, the two would talk of nothing else.

"Will you watch Little Eagle? I think I will go sit by the water for a bit."

Abigail didn't stop working but smiled and nodded her head.

While Alexandria slowly walked to the water's edge, she again attempted to shake the feeling of doom. By the time she sat at the bank, she was covered with sweat. The day was hot and muggy. The sun unsuccessfully attempted to break through the thick gray and black clouds. Thunder booms could be heard in the distance. The absence of wind made the heat almost unbearable. She wiped her sweaty brow and walked into the water, fully clothed. The temperature was closer to bathwater than cooling, but she dipped her body underwater anyway, hoping the change would clear her mind. It didn't. Her mood seemed to mirror the weather.

As she was walking from the water, the wind began gusting, but it brought little relief. She stood dripping wet on the banks of the tranquil river and let the wind dry her hair and clothing. Before returning to her work, she prayed the sun would be shining when Standing Bear returned home.

The threatening rain held off until late in the night. From inside the tipi, it sounded like buckets were falling from the sky. The noise was so loud that Little Eagle woke and immediately demanded his mother's attention.

Alexandria was sitting by the fire, feeding her son, when Abigail burst through the closed flap.

From the look on Abigail's face, Alexandria immediately knew something was terribly wrong. Abigail's eyes were red and swollen and the young woman was shaking uncontrollably.

"What's the matter?" Alexandria asked, placing Little Eagle on the fur nearby the fire before pulling her friend into an embrace.

Abigail pulled out of her friend's grip and covered her mouth with her hand.

"Abigail, if you don't tell me what's wrong, I can't help."

Abigail shut her eyes tightly and shook her head.

Alexandria was quickly learning she could no longer speak calmly to her friend. "Tell me!" she yelled.

Little Eagle cried out when his mother raised her voice. Alexandria went to pick her son up and while comforting him, she tried to calm her raw nerves so that she wouldn't yell at Abigail again.

When she returned her attention to her friend, she realized Abigail had left.

Alexandria knew she couldn't go out into the downpour with Little Eagle in her arms, so she was forced to stay inside and pace as she lulled her son back to sleep.

She had just laid her son on the bed when Abigail returned.

Abigail was still in the same state of mind as she had been moments earlier. The only change Alexandria could see was that now Abigail was shaking uncontrollably.

"Abigail. Sit by the fire and calm yourself. Tell me what has happened," she said softly as she gently guided her friend to the center of the tipi.

Abigail allowed Alexandria to pull her into a seated position but her hand remained firmly affixed over her mouth.

"Breathe," Alexandria suggested as she pulled a robe over her friend's shaking shoulders.

"He is … gone. They are preparing his burial scaffold. Oh, Alexandria … our people … white men … killed him," Abigail blurted before collapsing into Alexandria's arms.

Alexandria thought for sure her heart stopped beating when Abigail's words sank in. She had tried to convince herself that the wind and rain had been the source of the noises she'd heard. When she heard her friend's, declaration she wondered if it hadn't been the women of the village, wailing when Standing Bear returned. "Are you telling me Standing Bear is gone?" she asked quietly, not wanting to hear the answer.

Abigail nodded and once again fell into hysterics.

"Oh my God," Alexandria breathed.

She pulled away from Abigail, stood, and walked to the bed she shared with Standing Bear. She fell to her knees and picked up the roll Standing Bear had rested his head on. Her emotions were running amuck. She was sad, hurt, angry, and scared. She had no idea how Standing Bear's death would affect her but knew whatever her future held, she first had to say goodbye to the man who had loved and protected her. After breathing in his scent for what she knew would be the last time, she walked outside into the rain.

Abigail followed, "Where are you going?"

"To be with him. Watch my son, please. Is he in White Buffalo's tipi?" Alexandria asked in a calm voice. Her exterior was calm, but her mind was going a hundred miles an hour. She hadn't felt these exact feelings since Standing Bear and his friends attacked her friends and family. Accepting that her actions were a good sign she was in shock, she was grateful for any buffer.

"I will stay. Yes, he is with his father," Abigail said, backing into the tipi.

Alexandria began walking in the thunderstorm. It didn't matter that she was getting drenched. She didn't care about being wet. The only thing she cared about was finding a way to protect her son. Nothing but him mattered anymore. She was relieved to see Standing Bear's father's tipi flap was open. Standing Bear had kept her segregated from his family and friends for the most part, but Alexandria had always thought White Buffalo was a fair and caring man. Her hope was that the people gathered didn't view her as an intruder.

After taking several deep breaths in order to calm herself, she entered the tipi.

There were others gathered in the dwelling, but she only saw Standing Bear. He was lying near the fire at the center of the dwelling. The warrior's face had been painted for battle. Seeing his face covered with white paint made it hard for her to breathe. It was the way he'd looked when they had first met, but he hadn't allowed her to him that way since. The clothes he was wearing were exquisite. The shirt and pants were made of white leather. He wore a bone-chest plate over his shirt and beautifully beaded moccasins.

Even in death, he was an extremely handsome man. Swallowing back tears, Alexandria quickly scanned the home, looking for a friendly face. When she made eye contact with Standing Bear's father, the man walked towards her.

"My son's last thoughts were of you," the elder said, attempting to comfort her.

Hearing the words made it impossible for her to keep the ever-threatening tears from flowing.

"I am sorry," she said between sobs. "Was he in much pain?"

"No. He was shot twice. But he died in peace. Now come and say your farewells. My son holds something in his hands that he wanted you to have," his father said gently as he guided her in the direction of Standing Bear's body.

Alexandria could see the pain etched into White Buffalo's face. The man was a well-respected elder, but Alexandria knew losing his son would have lasting effects.

"I am so sorry the white man took him. I will miss him greatly. He took good care of my son and me," she murmured through tears.

"My son loved you. But love can blind a person to many things. Now say your goodbyes," the old man said as he backed away.

Alexandria knelt down and laid her hand on top of Standing Bear's. As soon as she felt the cold, she pulled her hands away. While she was moving away, she felt something sharp poking out from in between his fingers. She cautiously lifted his interlaced fingers and saw Running Elk's necklace. She was sure Standing Bear had thrown the jewelry into a river when he had taken it from her. Tears flowed down her face unchecked as she carefully removed the necklace from Standing Bear's hands.

Before standing, she placed a kiss on his cold lips. "I am sorry that I couldn't tell you I loved you. I would have if I could. But know you took good care of me, and I will never forget you." She spoke to him as she wiped the tears away with the back of her hand.

Alexandria said goodbye to the warrior's father and walked back to the tipi she shared with the man they were preparing the scaffolding for.

Her heart hurt. But she didn't want Little Eagle to feed off her grief. So she slowly walked back to her home. White Buffalo's actions hadn't led her to believe she and her son wouldn't be cared for by the Kiowa people, and that was calming. But knowing she still had a home didn't stop her from feeling terribly alone.

When Alexandria returned to the tipi, she saw Abigail was still crying. "I know you're upset," she said, walking to her friend, "but you have to stop crying. It will not bring him back. If crying would bring him back, I would gladly join you. He is gone, and we must accept it."

Abigail looked at Alexandria and suddenly stopped crying. "Did you see him?" she asked, wiping her eyes with her hand.

"I did. He looked like the great warrior he was. White Buffalo promised me Standing Bear wasn't in pain when he passed. I find comfort knowing that. Look what he was holding this in his hands." Alexandria began talking, doing her best to heed her own advice and stay strong. It wasn't easy; tears were pooling in her eyes. But because of Abigail's distress, Alexandria found her grief a little easier to deal with. While she was trying to comfort Abigail, Alexandria placed the necklace around her neck.

"What is that?"

"It was the necklace Running Elk gifted me. He told me it would protect me. And I thought I lost it when Standing Bear took me. But White Buffalo just told me Standing Bear wanted me to have it. He also said I was the last thing he thought of … before … he died," Alexandria explained, holding the tears back for as long as she could.

Chapter Thirty-Two

Running Elk found Kicking Bird and Gray Eagle together. They seemed subdued as they prepared to ride back to their camp. Running Elk knew the battle hadn't gone as well as they hoped, but he had heard news that made it impossible not to smile.

"Kicking Bird, wait. I have something to talk to you about," Running Elk said, attempting to stop the men from mounting their ponies.

Kicking Bird looked towards his brother. "I heard the Kiowa warrior, Little Eagle, was killed. I am sorry for his loss. We lost ten warriors ourselves. So I have to ask, why are you smiling?"

"I am sorry for those who have passed over," Running Elk said as he dismounted from his horse. "But Little Eagle was not the Kiowa's true name. Little Eagle is what they call my son. He was named after you, Gray Eagle," Running Elk explained, keeping most of his excitement to himself.

"Where did you hear these things?" Gray Eagle asked, making himself part of the conversation while he laid his back on his horse. "Have you heard more of Two Fires?"

"The Kiowa who saved my life was, in fact, Standing Bear. He confessed everything to me while he lay dying. Two Fires stayed with him, but her heart still belongs to me. And I will go retrieve her soon. I have instructed the Kiowa to say nothing to her so I can explain what has happened for myself. Kicking Bird, I have a son," Running Elk explained.

Kicking Bird hugged his brother. "I will ride into the Kiowa camp with you when you go," he said, sounding genuinely pleased at his brother's turn of fortune.

"I would like that. Gray Eagle, would you like to join us?" Running Elk offered.

"Nothing could stop me. I will be well pleased to see Two Fires again. She named the baby after me, uncle. Maybe I hold a special piece of her heart," Gray Eagle teased.

Running Elk smiled. "You do not need to worry. Her heart is mine. I have loved that woman since the first moment I laid eyes on her. Now, time is the only thing that keeps us apart. So let's go home and say goodbye to our brother warriors and celebrate my private victory," he said as he mounted his ride.

Running Elk's mood remained elevated after he returned to his camp. He immediately began preparing for his reunion with Two Fires and his son. He felt so good about his sudden fortune that he even decided talking to White Wolf and Morning Star wouldn't try his patience. He found Morning Star first.

While he was shaking his extra furs out, he saw her walking back towards the camp with water bladders in both her hands. The woman looked as if she'd lost weight and appeared to be humming to herself. Running Elk was pleased she was happy.

He quickened his pace and took the containers from her grip.

She stopped walking and humming before casting her eyes downward.

"Morning Star, how have you been?" he asked, gently guiding her face upwards so he could look her in the eye.

He desperately needed to know he was right when he assumed living with White Wolf made her happy, and her eyes never lied.

When she looked at him, he knew Morning Star was happier than she'd been in years, and also that his presence still affected her.

He smiled and put some distance between them. "I have sought you out to tell you I am happy you found love with my brother. You do love him, don't you?"

"I do," she answered quietly. "I am pleased that you are no longer angry with me. It has been too long since we have spoken," she added, holding his gaze.

"I have not been much for talking lately. But I want you to know that soon, Kicking Bird, Gray Eagle, and myself are going to the Kiowa camp to bring Two Fires here. I … you were a good wife, Morning Star. I was not a good husband," Running Elk explained, finding it hard to express his true emotions, but he felt the woman who was once his wife deserved his best attempt.

"Marriage takes two people being in love, Running Elk. Thank you for telling me these things. If I can be of any help when your Two Fires returns, let me know."

"I thank you. Now, have you seen White Wolf? I need to speak to him as well."

Running Elk walked beside her towards his brother's home.

"He was here when I left. But he seems to be gone. I know he didn't sleep well again last night," she explained, taking the water container back from Running Elk. "But knowing you have found a way to be with Two Fires again will please him."

"I will search for him clscwhcrc. And I am pleased we finally spoke," he said, turning from his brother's home.

"What about the child?" Morning Star asked from inside the tipi.

Running Elk stuck his head back through the entrance. "I have a son. He is called Little Eagle," he informed her proudly.

"Little Eagle," Morning Star repeated. "White Wolf said she had a son. I am happy for you."

"I know when she is safely in my arms again, I will believe it," he said before realizing his words could very easily hurt Morning Star. "I will go find my brother," he said, leaving. He had searched the woman out to ease her mind, not cause her undue pain.

Running Elk located his brother walking the outskirts of the camp with Quanah and immediately realized the two shared the same expression: worry. He considered turning around for half a second. Even though he wanted nothing more than to hold onto his good mood, he slowly walked towards the two anyway.

"Quanah, White Wolf," he greeted.

"Is this the first time you are seeing White Wolf since we returned?" Quanah asked.

"No. That is what I am doing now. That is if your business is concluded."

Quanah nodded his head. "It is, at least for now. After you and White Wolf are finished speaking, I would like to see you," the war chief expressed as he began walking away from the brothers without a parting word for White Wolf.

"So, what have you to say? Did you speak to the Kiowas while you were away?" White Wolf asked.

"Come with me to my tipi," Running Elk suggested. "The story is much better if you are sitting down."

After Running Elk told his brother about the events that had happened since he left for the battle, he waited for his brother to speak.

"I am well pleased that events are going so well. I knew the boy was yours," White Wolf said after a long silence.

"We will leave soon. I find it increasingly difficult to wait the proper amount of time," Running Elk confided in his brother.

White Wolf's lighthearted expression did not match the tone of his voice. "The soldiers are coming, brother. We will have to fight again soon."

Running Elk could tell White Wolf hadn't wanted to dampen his spirit and only spoke the words to prepare him for his meeting with Quanah.

Running Elk sighed loudly. "As soon as we return, I will again go into battle. I have given my people everything they have asked of me, but this will be postponed until she is with me again."

"I wish we didn't have to continually fight, and I know you will be here when we need you. Our outcome is so bleak, brother," White Wolf said, sounding melancholier by the second before looking at Running Elk and forcing a smile. "We will see each other before you leave, right?" White Wolf asked, standing in preparation to leave.

"I will make sure of it, and don't worry, brother, we are in the hands of the gods," Running Elk said, patting White Wolf on the back as he followed his brother outside.

"Is that supposed to calm my concerns?" White Wolf asked.

"You know, I am beginning to believe what you and Kicking Bird have been foreshadowing. I had held onto hope that they would simply stop needing more land, but now it seems the white man will stop at nothing to have all the land. They already have most of it. What is to stop them from taking more?"

"I don't know," White Wolf admitted with defeat in his tone. "I hope to have an answer to your question soon, if the gods are merciful." White Wolf finished his thought and turned in the direction of his home and Morning Star. Running Elk was glad the woman was a great comfort to his older brother.

Running Elk walked to Quanah's lodge, hoping the discussion they were going to have would not dampen his mood even more than his talk with White Wolf had.

He understood that they were living through difficult times, but all he was asking was to be able to spend time with the woman he had been separated from for almost a year. He wanted to get to know his son and hold his woman in his arms. Running Elk found himself wishing once again for times to return to the way they were when he was a boy.

Before entering Quanah's tipi, he did his best to calm his mind. The war chief was sitting by his fire, filling his favorite pipe.

"Come in, sit down," Quanah invited when he saw Running Elk in the doorway.

Running Elk did as he was directed. "What is it you wanted to speak to me about?" he asked, thinking the direct way was the best.

"We have reports that the white soldiers have left the fort and are heading our way …"

"What?!" Running Elk shouted as he stood and found a place to stand at the back of the tipi, near where Quanah slept. He suddenly needed distance between the two. Quanah's words felt more like a punch in the stomach than words. "Let me guess. You and my people are in need of me. Right?"

Quanah stood and walked to him before placing his hand on Running Elk's shoulder.

"Calm yourself," he said, smiling. "If you had let me finish, you would understand there is no reason for your outburst. I am not going to try to keep you from your woman. I understand how important she is to you. I do ask that you keep an eye out for the soldiers' movements though. We may have to move quickly. I will not allow them to attack our village. Our women and children mean too much to me for that. You know as well as I do that the soldiers care not who they kill, as long as they are Indians."

Running Elk heard the same concern he had heard in White Wolf's voice. "I don't need to take Kicking Bird and Gray Eagle if they are needed here," he quickly decided.

His anger had subsided as quickly as it rose.

"You should not go alone. Just keep your eyes open for signs of the soldiers' movements. We have scouts out now."

"We will leave for the Kiowa camp in three sleeps. Will the scouts be back by then?"

"They should be, and if so, I will let you know what they report. Stop by and let me know when you are leaving."

"Quanah, what are our children going to have to look forward to? Are they ever going to know about hunting and freedom? Are they even going to know the true meaning of freedom?" Running Elk asked, growing serious with his friend.

"The question weighs heavy on my mind. I wish I had the answer, but all I can say is we will have to wait and see," Quanah said, walking away from Running Elk and back to the pipe he had been smoking when Running Elk arrived.

"We will talk later. Maybe I will go hunting for small game. It may keep my mind busy with something other than my upcoming trip. Would you like to join me?" Running Elk asked before walking into the heat of the beautiful summer day.

"I would like to, but I have many matters here to keep me busy. I remember the days when our lives were our own. You were able to be a hunter, and not a warrior, before the whites moved closer. You were a fine hunter, if I remember right."

"I still am. Now I am gifted in many areas. I have a son, you know," Running Elk said, joking with his friend, attempting to lighten Quanah's mood.

"I believe I had heard that you are a father," Quanah said, smiling. "Do not stand half in and half out. Go about your day, and good luck with your hunt."

"I will seek you out before leaving for the Kiowa encampment," Running Elk assured him before walking back towards his home.

***

Quanah watched his friend walk away and realized he was looking forward to meeting the woman who had eaten away at Running Elk's heart. He prayed that Running Elk would be at last reunited with Two Fires. But couldn't help wondering if Running Elk had given any thought to what life on the run would be like with the white woman in tow. Quanah knew the soldiers would take her if they reached the Comanche village. Just like they had with his mother. His mother had begged the soldiers to leave her with the people she loved. But they had not listened to her. The soldiers had forced her inside the wagon and taken her back to what they called civilization. He prayed events would work out better for his friend.

Chapter Thirty-Three

Abigail moved into Alexandria's tipi the night the war party returned with Standing Bear's body. Her family didn't fight her on the idea, White Buffalo even seemed to think the two white women were good for each other.

Being able to share her grief with Alexandria made her sadness more bearable. In the month that had passed since Standing Bear died, Abigail stayed close to Alexandria, not leaving for more than a few minutes at a time.

Alexandria filled her days and nights taking care of Little Eagle. Abigail helped with the baby when asked but found working helped calm her mind the most. Watching Alexandria's reaction to losing Standing Bear forced Abigail to confront her true feelings.

Abigail slowly realized she had loved Standing Bear, and not in the way one loves their family. He was the first thing on her mind every morning and the last person she thought of before falling asleep. He was the reason she had lied to Alexandria so easily. Abigail had lied to her best friend so that the man she loved would be able to hold onto a woman who was unable to return his love. As the days slowly passed, Abigail was realized the wisdom she had imparted on Alexandria the first day they met was not far from being the truth. The pain lessened with each passing day. As her agony subsided, Abigail realized the best thing she could do for her friend would be to work up the courage to tell Alexandria everything she knew about Running Elk. But

Abigail was too afraid to tell Alexandria anything that might cause her to lose her only friend.

Every night, Abigail would listen as Alexandria called out to Running Elk. The necklace somehow caused Running Elk's memory to grow stronger. Abigail still couldn't understand why Alexandria couldn't love Standing Bear, but she was convinced the Kiowa warrior had done nothing but dull Alexandria's memories of the Comanche.

***

Alexandria tried desperately to delay opening her eyes as long as possible. When she slept, she was with Running Elk. They were riding across the prairie with the wind whipping their unbound hair. She held him tightly as their bodies moved in unison with the rhythm of the horse. The images were so real, she could smell the musky aroma Running Elk's body naturally gave off. She rolled over and imagined laying her head against Running Elk's bare back while clinging to him tightly.

"Alexandria, you can't stay in bed all day! Get up. We have work to do," Abigail expressed loudly.

Alexandria shut her eyes tighter and pulled the fur over her face in an attempt to block out Abigail's voice.

"Alexandria. Get up! Maybe you should go to sleep earlier tonight," Abigail repeated, walking to her sleeping friend and shaking her body gently.

"Go away," Alexandria barked.

"No. We have work to do, and Little Eagle is awake," Abigail said, walking to the cooing boy. "Good morning, Little Eagle. Your mother does not seem to care that the day has begun. She is becoming lazy," she informed the child, making sure her voice was loud enough for Alexandria to hear.

Since Alexandria was unable to summon her dream back, she moaned and kicked the covers from herself. "All right. I was having a dream and didn't want to wake. I'm sorry," Alexandria said, finishing her thought with a note of irritation.

"You have been dreaming a lot," Abigail observed.

"I have been," Alexandria agreed. "I don't mean to be cruel to the memory of Standing Bear. He was a wonderful, giving, brave man. And I know Running Elk has gone on without me. I do wish I knew why he gave up on me so easily though. He is the father of my son, and wrong or not, I will always love the man. I will forever ache for him to hold me in his arms. I can't help it. See," Alexandria explained as she opened her hand to show Abigail her palms were damp, "My heart beats quicker when I talk about him too. And if Standing Bear couldn't make me fall in love with him, I am certain no one else will take his place. My problem is deciding where we belong."

Abigail's eyes widened. "What do you mean, where you belong?" she asked, walking to her friend and handing Alexandria her son.

Little Eagle's hand reached for the necklace his mother wore.

"You both belong here. Where else would you go?"

Alexandria watched as Little Eagle began chewing on Running Elk's necklace. "I don't know, but I know we can't stay here. Before long, I will be taken to another tipi. I hold no special place in the tribe," Alexandria reasoned.

"Little Eagle is a great warrior's son," Abigail objected.

"Little Eagle is a Comanche's son. Not Standing Bear's," Alexandria corrected gently.

"Our people believe he is Standing Bear's. You will always have a place here. You aren't thinking of going to the soldier fort, are you?" Abigail asked, not wanting to believe her friend would consider doing something so disastrous.

Alexandria placed Little Eagle in his carrier and strapped him to her back before leaving the tipi without answering Abigail's question.

"You can't be considering that. Alexandria, they will never let you teach Little Eagle the ways of his people in a city. You can't do that to him. I am white but would prefer to die than live amongst those people again," Abigail said, following Alexandria into the unyielding sunlight.

"Abigail, I am not sure what to do. I want to do what's best for my son. I want him to have the best life has to offer," Alexandria explained, trying to make her friend understand.

"Promise me you will think on this long and hard. And please don't do anything without talking to me first," Abigail pleaded.

"I do very little that you don't know about," Alexandria reminded her friend. "After the work is done, why don't we go for a swim? Does that sound like a good idea to you?" she asked, changing the increasingly frustrating subject.

"That sounds like a plan. We can begin teaching Little Eagle to swim. Everyone needs to know how," Abigail said, also glad the conversation had changed course. She would do whatever she had to do to keep Alexandria from going to the fort. Even if that meant telling Alexandria the truth about everything. She only hoped the truth could be avoided. Because the longer Abigail held onto the lies, the surer she was she would lose her friend.

Chapter Thirty-Four

Running Elk woke early the morning of their impending departure. Forcing his brain to slow was nearly impossible. Knowing once the three warriors departed for the Kiowa camp, it would take three sleeps to get there, wasn't aiding in his anxiety. He knew he wouldn't be able to push his horse as hard as he wanted because he didn't want to take any chances that the reunion with Two Fires would be postponed yet again.

While he waited for the camp to awaken and begin the day, he busied himself with packing the supplies he would need for the journey. After he could find nothing else to do, he packed his horse and hoped it wasn't too early to seek out Quanah. When he turned to begin his search, he saw the war chief approaching him.

"You are awake early," Running Elk smiled as he greeted his friend.

"I am an endlessly busy man," Quanah said with a hint of humor in his tone. "The scouts haven't returned," he continued. His tone grew more serious. "I know the soldiers are closing in, yet my scouts can't tell me where they are. You must be watchful for any signs. On your return, watch for our movements. We will be forced to move, I am sure of that. I just don't know when."

Running Elk saw the concern etched in Quanah's face. His friend was a brave and wise man. The kind of man who still wanted to fight to maintain their way of life. Yet as of late, the war chief seemed to be bending towards peace. He was thinking more of the children. The worries Quanah shouldered were more than enough to bring a normal man to his knees.

"We will be on guard. Remember, I won't be alone. Do not worry for us. I won't allow anything to get in my way this time."

Quanah nodded. "When you return, come to my tipi immediately and tell me everything you have observed," Quanah gently ordered as he watched Running Elk mount his pony.

"You are my friend, and I would do almost anything for you, but I believe I will send my brother to give you the report when we return. I plan on being occupied," Running Elk said, smiling.

Quanah stood with his arms crossed and shook his head. "Be careful, my friend," he stated as Running Elk steered his pinto away from the smiling chief.

When Running Elk arrived in front of Kicking Bird's tipi, everyone was already gathered outside.

"Running Elk, I am pleased you will be bringing Two Fires home," Sparrow said as she petted the side of the horse.

"I can hardly believe this is finally happening," Running Elk admitted as he smiled down at his sister-in-law.

"Kicking Bird and Gray Eagle have talked of nothing else since yesterday," Sparrow whispered.

"I have thought of nothing else for almost four full seasons. I am pleased they are accompanying me. Pleased they wanted to."

"They are your family, and they love you. They would do anything to help you. Do try not to keep them away too long. You know, I believe I miss them already," Sparrow said lovingly, patting her brother-in-law on his leg.

"I will be in a hurry to get home, sister," Running Elk informed his brother's beautiful wife.

When they returned, there would be two white women in the camp. Both loved by Comanche warriors and both with children. He felt comforted knowing Two Fires would be welcomed by his family.

"Wife. Come and tell me how much you will miss me," Kicking Bird said. Running Elk heard his brother's attempt to be stern with Sparrow. He couldn't hide his amusement when he realized his big brother had failed miserably.

Sparrow smiled. "First I will tell my son to be careful and that I love him. You, I will get to in a moment," she said playfully.

The love and tenderness his brother's family so easily displayed tugged at Running Elk's heart. "Come, Gray Eagle, we will ride ahead. Your father can catch up," Running Elk suggested once Sparrow had said her goodbyes. "I am getting no closer to Two Fires sitting here."

"I will see you soon, Mother," Gray Eagle said, reining his horse and following his uncle.

***

The first day's ride held few surprises. There was no sign of soldiers' movements. The trio saw a miserably small herd of buffalo. Not a word was said between the three men for hours after witnessing the scene. They were all deeply affected by the sight.

Gray Eagle finally broke the silence. "I am beginning to believe my children will not be able to hunt the buffalo. They will surely all be dead by then. I cannot understand why the whites kill them and leave them to rot in the sun."

"I don't understand many of the white man's ways, son," Kicking Bird confided.

"Mother doesn't understand either. I am half white, yet I know I could never fit into that world," the young warrior declared with vengeance in his voice.

"Gray Eagle, remember the circle. We are all part of a bigger event. We will survive as a people, that is the one thing I am sure of. We are too proud not to," Running Elk told his nephew.

Running Elk was familiar with the emotions that were awakening in the young man and tried to comfort him as much as he could.

The second day of the journey wasn't as peaceful as the first. The three were awoken by thunderclaps. The sky was gray and menacing. The thunder seemed to shake the earth. Running Elk knew they would not be able to cover much distance but insisted they keep moving.

Gray Eagle rode ahead to scout the terrain.

When the young warrior rejoined his father and uncle, Running Elk immediately noticed Gray Eagle's expression; it was one that led him to believe that something had happened.

"What is it?" Kicking Bird asked his son as soon as he reached them.

"Soldiers are camped not far from here. They have many guns. They must be afraid of getting wet though, because there was little movement," Gray Eagle informed the two as he attempted to keep his emotions in check.

Running Elk let out a deep breath and looked to the heavens. "Why?!"

Kicking Bird turned to his brother when he heard the outburst.

"We must do something. The soldiers are only a day's ride away from our camp," Gray Eagle stated, speaking more to his father than his uncle.

"I know, son, I know."

Kicking Bird moved his horse closer to Running Elk until the two brothers were side by side. "I will ride back to the camp.

You and Gray Eagle go on without me," he offered, attempting to break the trance Running Elk had entered. "This does not have to come between you and Two Fires."

"Am I supposed to ride away from the soldiers without a second thought? I must keep an eye on them. Even with you leaving to alert the camp, I have to do something. I should try to free their horses. As much as I want to, I can't ride away from them. The gods must truly want me to be miserable," he barked at his brother angrily.

"Just this time, go. Don't think of anyone except yourself. She is only another day's ride from you," Kicking Bird tried to convince his brother. "There is nothing the two of you can do against a whole camp."

"How many men were in the encampment?" Running Elk asked Gray Eagle, ignoring his brother's words.

"I did not stop to count, but I would guess at least seventy-five. Why?"

"There are more, close by. They never come in small numbers. It is my guess that those men have broken away from the others," Running Elk surmised as he began to accept that yet another obstacle had erupted to delay his reunion with the woman who held his heart and his son.

"What you are thinking will delay your arrival at the Kiowa camp by days." Kicking Bird objected.

"I will go in search of the other soldiers. Ride quickly, Kicking Bird. I am growing weary of all these interruptions," Running Elk demanded as he slapped his brother's horse's backside with an open hand.

As Kicking Bird departed, Running Elk's attention focused on his nephew. "You, stay out of sight. The soldiers will also have scouts. Do not let them see you. I will return by nightfall," he said, riding off in a southern direction. "Be careful, Gray Eagle," he warned, looking over his shoulder.

***

Running Elk rode until dusk without seeing any sign of additional soldiers. He was sure there were more but couldn't find where they were located. Instead of continuing on, he headed back to his nephew. Running Elk knew Gray Eagle was becoming an impulsive man, and he didn't want the boy to get any ideas.

"I hear you, uncle," Gray Eagle whispered with amusement when Running Elk attempted to sneak up on him.

"Then you have become a fine warrior. Not too many hear me when I don't want them to," he boasted as he took a seat behind the rock Gray Eagle was sitting against.

"Did you find the others?"

"No. Have you heard any movement from the camp?" Running Elk asked, motioning in the direction of the soldiers' temporary camp.

"No. It has been a peaceful day, except for the thunder. I wish the rain would fall, just so the thunder would quiet."

"Don't tell me that thunder frightens you," Running Elk questioned, doing his best not to laugh.

"It doesn't scare me, but it does put me on edge," Gray Eagle corrected.

"I find comfort in the thunder," Running Elk shared. "If not for the sound, I believe I might have lost my senses today."

"I hope we can see Two Fires soon," Gray Eagle said, changing the course of the conversation drastically.

At the mention of her name, Running Elk laid his head against the rock, closed his eyes tightly, and pictured her in his mind. He saw her looking up at him with passion-filled eyes. "You cannot possibly want that more than I," he finally responded to the statement as it hung in the air.

"I will take the first watch. Why don't you try to sleep?" Gray Eagle offered.

"No. You sleep. I couldn't now. My mind will not allow it," Running Elk said as he slowly stood and walked in the direction of the soldiers. "I am only making sure they are still there," he said when his nephew looked at him in question.

***

During the night, the stars slowly crept from behind the clouds and the bright full moon occasionally lit the night sky. The clearing sky didn't stop the thunder Gray Eagle heard when the wind gusted.

"Did you hear that?" he asked Running Elk while the two sat and ate pemmican.

"Hear what?" Running Elk asked as he stopped chewing and gave his nephew his full attention. Running Elk hadn't heard anything, but he knew from the previous night that Gray Eagle's hearing was keen.

"It sounds like thunder when the wind is right. I've heard it for a while. You don't hear it?" he asked, beginning to believe it might be his imagination.

Running Elk could see Gray Eagle was second-guessing his senses. The sun was shining, so it did seem strange that the thunder would linger.

"Do you hear it now?" Running Elk asked, concentrating.

"No. Wait … there, did you hear it?"

Before Gray Eagle could finish his question, Running Elk was on his feet and running towards his horse.

"What is it?" Gray Eagle asked with concern thick in his voice as he mounted his ride.

"It is not thunder you hear. That is gunfire coming from White Buffalo's camp," he informed his nephew, trying unsuccessfully to keep his rising panic under control.

"I am right behind you," Gray Eagle yelled as they rode their horses at full speed.

Running Elk slowly began to realize that even with the horses moving as fast as their legs could carry them, they would not be able to make the camp in time to help the Kiowa. His only hope was that White Buffalo's camp hadn't been caught by surprise. He slowed his horse and pressed his hands against his temples, attempting to stop the unbearable pounding in his head.

He slowed so abruptly that Gray Eagle sped by his uncle. When he turned his horse around, he saw his uncle once again looking towards the heavens. He also couldn't help but notice Running Elk's expression was blank.

"We must continue," Gray Eagle urged excitedly.

"We cannot leave Kicking Bird with no word on our whereabouts," he reminded his overenthusiastic nephew.

"But if I go back, there will be no one to help you," he objected.

"Gray Eagle, it hurts my heart to admit this but there is nothing ten warriors can do, let alone the two of us. The distance is too vast, and the battle is more than likely already ending. I will ride ahead and see if there is anything I can do. When you meet up with your father, tell him what has taken place and return to our camp. I will return soon."

Running Elk knew by Gray Eagle's expression that the young man wanted to argue. It was obvious that he was concerned about Running Elk. Running Elk was concerned himself. He had never heard his own voice sound so broken.

"Will you be all right?" he asked meekly, clearly not wanting to anger Running Elk but intending to show his concern.

"At least this will be an end," Running Elk answered.

"You think they are dead, don't you?" he asked in horror.

"I know she is out of my reach, yet again," Running Elk admitted.

"Ride as fast as you can to her and your son. Do not give up now!" Gray Eagle implored, trying to keep his excited pony under control.

"I will not stop until I reach the Kiowa camp. And I will meet up with you two later," Running Elk said, spurring his horse forward with his moccasin-covered feet.

***

Gray Eagle sat atop his ride and watched his uncle quickly depart. He listened for the gunfire he'd mistaken for thunder, but the wind had changed direction.
"May the gods be with you, uncle," he said in a normal tone, hoping the wind would carry his words to Running Elk's ears.

Chapter Thirty-Five

Running Elk was holding Alexandria closely and confessing his love when a loud noise interrupted the peacefulness and yanked her from her dream. The noise was incredibly loud. As much as she wanted the noise to be nothing more than angry thunder, she knew it was not. She could hear the cries of the other women. The sounds of a battle beyond the skin of the tipi quickly brought her to her senses and pulled her from her dream-like state. Pulling the buffalo robe around her naked body, she carefully pulled back the flap, fearing the worst.

What she witnessed was total panic. Women were running in all directions with screaming babies in their arms. Hastily-armed warriors were quickly mounting their horses. Her newfound kin were falling all around her as she tried to make sense of the scene. What was happening and why? It was clear that she must abandon the camp and put as much distance as she could between the melee and Little Eagle. When she didn't see Abigail, she grabbed her clothes, picked up the wide-eyed Little Eagle, and ran outside with him.

Not sure what to do, she headed straight for the tree line as fast as she could move, still not grasping what was happening. She could hear the women screaming about the white soldiers but couldn't figure out why the cavalry was firing on the Kiowa. As soon as she felt safely hidden among the foliage, Abigail suddenly appeared next to her. Alexandria, in her frightened state, was startled. She took a firm grip on the girl's sleeve.

"What are you doing here? Why didn't you stay in the tipi?" Alexandria asked as she pulled her friend deeper into the trees and away from the soldiers' eyes.

"I dreamt of Standing Bear. In the dream, he told me to find a place for us to hide. I did what he demanded, not really believing we were in any danger. But now I realize he was sending me a vision. He is still looking over you, Alexandria."

"What is happening?" Alexandria asked, full of fear, as she situated her son in her arms.

"The soldiers are here," Abigail answered flatly.

"I can see that. But why?"

"Because we don't live on reservation land. After this, the ones they capture will be forced to live there. We can only hope most of the warriors escape. I don't think the soldiers will search us out. We should be safe. I will not go back to the white man's civilization, Alexandria. I cannot."

"I don't understand any of this," Alexandria said, trying to stop the tears from falling. "Why are they trying to kill us? We were sleeping."

"We are considered hostiles. They do not care whether we were sleeping or not. Now stay still and do not look out there. You don't want to witness the killing," Abigail said in a barely audible voice.

Alexandria wrapped Little Eagle to her chest with leather straps, knowing she would need to be as unrestricted in her movements as possible.

After a short time, the gunfire grew louder, and the screams quieted. The cries of war were replaced by the cold barking of orders from the white commander telling his men to stand down and capture those who remained. The smell of burning wood and fur was thick in the air, and English words replaced the native tongue. Alexandria strained to hear what was being said. It seemed strange that her own language could sound so foreign to her. She had to concentrate to make sense of rapid-fire commands and banter between the men.

One particularly loud voice said something about white women being in the camp. He ordered that they be found and put in the wagons away from the savages.

Alexandria was having a difficult time understanding how the soldier could call the Kiowa savages. The soldiers were the savages. The battle was over before it could begin. The only savages present were the ones who had entered the sleeping camp armed to the teeth. Knowing that a number of the warriors had been able to escape the carnage gladdened her heart. She considered anyone who had gotten away lucky. The hatred she was feeling toward her own people was unprecedented.

***

During the next couple of hours, the sound of the soldiers preparing to move their captives could be heard. The rattling of chains made it evident that the soldiers were untrusting of their prisoners.

The soldiers offered the white women horses. Alexandria could hear them refuse, saying that they would rather walk. The rejection was answered harshly, and they were unceremoniously thrown onto the horses.

Alexandria and Abigail were starting to breathe a little easier when the soldiers began to depart. Alexandria let out a sigh of relief. As if Little Eagle sensed her relief, he cried out. She held his head to her body in an attempt to suppress his cry and kissed him gently on the head.

"I know they heard that," Abigail whispered. "We have to run. They know we are here. They will come for us," she said, attempting to pull Alexandria deeper in the woods. Her words were quiet, but her voice was terrified.

Alexandria didn't move. Instead, she reached for Abigail and took her friend's face in her hands. "No, we will not go with you. They know about Little Eagle and me, but not you. You've said it yourself; you do not want to go back," Alexandria said with urgency in her voice.

"But they will not allow Little …" Abigail began to object.

"Come on out, or I'll start shootin'," a masculine voice yelled, interrupting Abigail in midsentence.

"Go. I will raise my son right. Run, my friend," Alexandria whispered as she neared the break in the trees. "Don't shoot me, I'm white," she called out, her acquired native accent becoming evident for the first time.

"You don't sound white," the voice said, sarcasm thick in its tone.

"I have been with the Kiowa a long time," she explained as she broke into the open. "I am white."

Her words were spoken in defiance.

The dumbfounded soldier backed away from her and let her pass without saying a word. She looked around her home and saw the destruction caused by the invasion. Lodgepoles that, only hours earlier, had held homes erect were burnt to the ground. The bodies of her tribesmen cluttered what used to be a peaceful encampment. Flies gathered around the dead, and crows were circling above. Alexandria choked back the bile in her throat and held tightly to her son. As she walked past the carnage and charred belongings, she felt a hand cautiously touch her shoulder.

"Ma'am, my name is Captain Percival Armstrong," the tall, athletic, blue-eyed soldier greeted, removing his hat. Long blond hair fell past his shoulders. "And, your name is?" he asked from a slightly bowed position.

Alexandria couldn't decide if the man was being serious in his gallantry or if he was playing some kind of cruel joke on her.

She stood in front of him, rocking her body back and forth in a subconscious manner to soothe Little Eagle. The captain stayed semi bent and patiently waited for her answer.

"I am called Alexandria Standish," she answered, watching him suspiciously.

"Ma'am, I am pleased to meet you. Is that your child?" he asked, peering at the sleeping baby securely wrapped to Alexandria's chest.

She backed a step away before answering. "Yes. He is my son. His name is Little Eagle," she proclaimed proudly, pulling the blanket away from the child's face.

"He is a good lookin' boy," Captain Armstrong stated. "Can ya ride and hold him at the same time?"

"I believe the chore is one I can handle with ease. I have lived among the Kiowa long enough to learn simple tasks," she said, walking toward the horses.

"Then go ahead and pick one out," the captain said, pointing towards the herd. "And you are more than welcome to ride with me if you'd like," he offered, sounding as if he thought he were being generous.

Alexandria scanned the herd until she spotted one of Standing Bear's horses. She walked towards it, gently petted his neck, and blew a puff of air into his nostrils. The horse responded with a nod and knelt slightly, allowing her to climb onto his back easily.

Once she was settled, she addressed the officer's proposal. "I would prefer to ride at the back. I have many memories to clear from my mind," she admitted quietly as she rode away from the captain.

From her vantage point at the rear of the pack, she counted over a hundred Kiowas being taken to the reservation against their will. Alexandria looked down at her son who was awake and grabbing at his father's necklace. "I will give you the best life I can," she vowed as her eyes filled with tears.

***

The journey gave her time to consider her split-second decision to surrender. She worried that she might have caused undue hardship on her half-native child. It was difficult to stay positive with soldiers yelling at the proud but weary people to keep up and stay in line. She was so deep in thought that she failed to realize Captain Armstrong was riding beside her.

"Ma'am, I'm just checkin' to make sure you're doing all right," he said, tipping his hat once again when she acknowledged his presence.

He surprised her with a heart-stopping smile. His voice was deep and velvety and unquestionably Southern. Along with his shiny hair, sleepy eyes, and beautiful smile, he had a nicely groomed mustache and goatee. She shuddered when she realized he was the perfect white man.

"Captain, I am not all right," Alexandria spoke after a long silence. "I love and respect these people and what you are doing is wrong."

The captain looked at her in surprise. "All I'm doin' is following orders. Nothin' more, nothin' less. It's my job."

"How can you do a job that includes killing women and children?" she asked angrily, not caring if he was upset.

"I don't, but my men can sometimes get out of control. I will do my level best to discipline the men who did the unnecessary killin'," he informed her.

She knew there would be no punishment for anyone except the Kiowa.

"Tell me this, Captain. Do you believe taking their land is the right thing to do?"

"You're asking a personal question, ma'am. I am unable to answer that now. I'll be happy to discuss that with you when we stop for the night. That is as close to being off duty as it gets," he said, smiling again.

"Will you force me onto the reservation too?"

"No, ma'am. Why would you think that? You ain't an Indian," he asked in shock.

"Then where will I go?" she asked, looking across the prairie; her home for the past year, and the only place her son knew. A pain emanated from her heart to the pit of her stomach.

"Don't ya have family?"

"Not here. I have a sister in Virginia, but we were never close. I believe I would rather stay with the Kiowa. At least my son will be accepted."

"Well, ma'am, that's not entirely true. He is a half-breed. They are the ones who have trouble fittin' in anywhere."

Alexandria looked at the captain with hatred in her eyes. "My son was conceived in love, and I will raise him to be proud of who his father is."

"I wish ya the best of luck. But I gotta tell ya, it ain't gonna be easy," the captain said before nodding his head and departing.

Alexandria watched him ride away and prayed he'd been wrong in his opinion. She had heard from everyone she came into contact with that she would not be allowed to have an easy life. After forcing the negativity from her mind, she said a prayer for Abigail, asking that she be safe and find happiness. While allowing her mind to linger on her friend, she remembered Abigail's final words. Had she ruined any chance of a normal life her son had? The longer she was left to her thoughts, the more Alexandria questioned if her decision had been the right one.

Her thoughts also turned back to Running Elk. He might not have come for her when he had the chance, but she had never given up hope. As hard as she tried, her heart wouldn't allow it. Yet her rash decision had ended any chance they would ever be together again.

When she pulled herself from the depressing thoughts she saw four soldiers riding near her. All shared the same look of disgust. Their reaction to her cemented the realization that no matter what her actions led to, she had to make the best of it.

When the formation stopped moving during the heat of the day, the handsome captain once again sought out Alexandria's company.

Alexandria slowly turned in his direction. "Yes?" she asked, not bothering to stop feeding her child.

"I was making sure you're still all right," he stammered, not hiding his discomfort while actively avoiding looking at her.

She was shocked by his modesty. "I have to feed my son when he is hungry. The act is not obscene or sexual; it is merely a fact of life."

"Yes, ma'am, I understand that well enough. I'm just not used to seeing it. I'll be over here," he stammered, pointing in the direction of the horses. "Call me when you're finished. If ya don't mind."

"I will," Alexandria said, not able to keep a weak smile from crossing her face.

Percival shook his head before replacing his hat and walking towards the horses the soldiers had captured.

Alexandria watched as he approached Standing Bear's finest stallion. For reasons she couldn't understand, she suddenly wanted nothing more than for the soldier to move away from her horse. Little Eagle had fallen asleep, so she called out to him.

"Yes, ma'am," he called in reply before walking towards her again.

"You said you wanted to speak to me. My son is asleep."

The soldier sat beside her, keeping a respectable distance. "Well then, I guess my first question is, why did you pick that horse?"

"The horse belonged to someone very special to me," she stated simply.

"Who?" he continued.

"His name was Standing Bear. Why do you ask?"

"The horse is well taken care of. Was Standing Bear the boy's father?" he asked, pointing to the sleeping child.

"Not that it is any of your business. But no, he isn't my child's father," she answered, attempting to keep the conversation civil but finding it increasingly difficult.

"You said earlier the boy was conceived with love. Are you in love with one of these Indians?" he asked.

"Captain, what difference does that make?" she asked, looking him in the eye.

"You are a fascinating woman. I find myself wanting to know about your life," he confessed as he stood and walked in front of her. "I don't mean to upset you, but most women would be thanking me for rescuing them from the savages, but not you. Hell, you even asked to stay with them. I find it hard to believe, that's all. And please call me Percival."

"Once again, they are not savages," she said angrily as she stood to face him. "And believe me, if I thought I could have been back with Running Elk, I wouldn't have allowed you to catch me," she informed him.

"Running Elk? Is that the baby's father?"

"Yes. I only saw him a few tim—"

"He fights alongside Quanah Parker. He's a Comanche, and a damn good fighter from what I've heard," Captain Armstrong interrupted her.

She could hear the respect in his voice when he spoke of Running Elk and that made her swell with pride.

"You know of him? Tell me what you know," she begged as she reached out to the soldiers' crossed arms.

"I don't know much more than I've already said. He fights with the war chief Quanah Parker," he informed her.

"And he is brave?" she asked, imploring him to continue.

"Running Elk is what I like to call dangerous. The Indians say he has strong magic. So, if he is the baby's father, what were you doing in the Kiowa camp?" he asked.

"Because Standing Bear took me from our wagon train to the Kiowa village. He told me Running Elk would come for me if he wanted me, but he didn't," she explained quietly, avoiding his eyes.

"He left you there? Are you sure he knew where you were?"

"Standing Bear said he would know. He never came for me. Abigail promised to tell me if she heard anything about his arrival."

"Abigail? Who's Abigail?"

"My friend. She is white also, but she is still with what's left of the Kiowa."

"How? No white women rode away,"

"She was with Little Eagle and me. She ran away," she divulged, thinking that the information she had just shared with the captain would do nothing more than aggravate him.

"Why? She had the chance to come back to civilization, and she chose to stay in the wild," he said, sounding as if he didn't believe what he was hearing.

"Because civilization to her is with the Kiowa. She told me she would rather die than return to the white world," she answered defiantly.

"I was right. Those Indians have a way of brainwashin' white women."

"Are you crazy?!" Alexandria screamed at him. "You understand nothing. They are just like you. They are people. We are the ones taking their land and their way of life. But that isn't where it ends. White people want the Indians to forget where they came from. We are the ones in the wrong!"

Captain Armstrong backed away from Alexandria as her speech gained speed. "I suppose I can see some of your points," he admitted after a lengthy silence. But ma'am, I gotta do my job. We need the land," he added quickly.

"No, I don't believe that. If you would open your mind, you would realize I am right. The job you have is to wipe out an entire race of people," she said in a muted tone before she sat down and began preparing to strap her son to her chest with the leather straps Standing Bear had taken such care to make.

"No, ma'am. We don't do nothing to them that they don't do to us. So they are murderers too," he said, crouching down to her level.

"Captain, I am tired of this. All I ask is that you realize the Indians are people first. I would appreciate it if you started treating them like it," she explained, allowing doubt to creep into her statement.

"I will do my best, but you gotta quit calling me a murderer. Do we have a deal?" he asked, flashing a smile.

"Yes, Captain, you have a deal," Alexandria agreed as she picked up her son.

"Please call me Percival," he asked again. "May I call you Alexandria?"

"Yes, Captain. You may call me Alexandria. How much further do we have to go?"

"By nightfall, two other companies will meet up with us and then we will have two more days, at least. Will you ride beside me this time?"

"Again, thank you for asking, but I am not very good company. Maybe tomorrow," she offered, hoping her answer would be enough for the captain.

"We'll be moving out in the next few minutes. I'll come back and check on you once we've started moving," he stated before he mounted his horse and rode away.

Alexandria looked around and realized only one soldier was left to guard her. She wondered what had brought about the change but decided against questioning the soldier riding towards her.

"Stop playing around and get on your horse," he ordered rudely.

"I was just about to do that," she assured the soldier with hatred in her voice. The man clearly didn't like her, and he was not going attempt to hide the way he felt. Knowing there was nothing she could do about the soldier's attitude, she decided the next time she spoke to the captain, she would ask him to change her guard.

After riding a few minutes, Alexandria realized just how defeated she was. Even with one guard near, she didn't feel the desire to escape.

Chapter Thirty-Six

Abigail waited until the sounds of the soldiers were gone and only then cautiously stepped into the clearing to view her old home. Tears flowed unchecked down her cheeks as she realized the devastation. Finding it difficult to remain standing, she found a felled tree and sat down. She slowly rocked back and forth and cried into her open hands until she heard the faint sound of horse hooves. As soon as she convinced herself she wasn't hearing things, she stood and ran back to the trees. All sense of time was warped. It felt as if she'd just sat down, but her screaming muscles told her a different story. Her body ached, but she wasn't going to let that stop her from hiding. She planned on staying hidden until she could identify the rider.

Abigail waited and prayed the visitor was a warrior coming back to view the damage left by the soldier's predawn attack.

She spied a fierce-looking warrior atop an exhausted pony. The man wasn't a Kiowa. He was a Comanche. Abigail held her hands to her mouth in hopes the man wouldn't hear her breathing. She watched as the Comanche ran through the charred remains, cautiously observing the dead as he moved. The look on his face was a mixture of great pain and great relief.

Once he had checked all the lifeless bodies, he looked to the sky, raised his arms, and wailed a name.

Abigail watched the man, thinking she was safe to reveal herself, but didn't move until she heard the name the warrior called out. As soon as she heard the name, she showed herself with hesitation.

"Are you Running Elk?" she asked quietly, unsure of how to even begin the discussion they needed to have.

Running Elk turned and ran towards Abigail. "How do you know who I am?" he asked with urgency.

"I know Alexandria. She was my best friend," she answered, crying into her open hands.

Running Elk pulled the woman's hands from her face, smiled gently, and asked as calmly as he could, "Where is she?"

"She went with the soldiers," she answered, wiping the tears.

"And my son?" Running Elk asked, still holding the woman by the shoulders.

"He is with her. When the soldiers came, we hid. Little Eagle cried, and she told me to run. She gave herself up so that I could be free," she explained through the hiccups that followed her crying.

"When did they leave?" he asked, making it clear he was trying his best to be patient with the shaken woman.

"I think it was around midday yesterday. They took all the horses except for the ones the Warriors were riding. A few men got away, but they haven't returned yet," Abigail explained, beginning to ramble.

"What are you called?"

"Abigail. Running Elk?" she asked, pulling away from the imposing warrior.

"Yes?"

"She never knew you sent someone to the camp to find her. She made me promise I would tell her if you ever tried, but when Standing Bear fell in love with her, and he asked me to stay silent, I did. I am so very sorry. She still dreams of you nightly. She never stopped loving you. I am so sorry they are gone," Abigail confessed through sobs.

"Then, sweet Abigail, we will find them," a masculine voice stated from behind the trees where she had been hiding only moments earlier.

Abigail jumped from fright but calmed slightly when she saw Running Elk smile.

"Gray Eagle? Show yourself. I told you to …"

"I am here also," Kicking Bird interrupted his brother as he and Gray Eagle rode into the camp, side by side.

Abigail knew all about Gray Eagle because Alexandria had told her the story over and over. Knowing the warrior was alive after Standing Bear's party shot him gave Abigail something to be thankful for. The day had been a nightmare. Her friends and family were gone, she had no home, and she couldn't think of any way out of her situation. Her brain was going a mile a minute, and the very last thing she should have been thinking about was just how handsome Gray Eagle was. He was almost as handsome as Standing Bear. Her sight was beginning to haze, so she decided to return to the seat she claimed earlier. Her thought was that if she could just sit down and take a few deep breaths, everything would be a little easier. After only taking three steps away from the Comanches, everything went dark.

She woke to find Gray Eagle sitting beside her on a robe. Her heartbeat was racing, but for a minute she wasn't bombarded by memories of the morning. She was glad no one noticed her wake. They seemed engrossed in a conversation.

"The woman said they left around midday yesterday. We can easily catch them once we have allowed the horses to rest. They cannot be moving quickly," Kicking Bird stated.

"You saw the other soldiers. They will join together. We cannot take on a whole company. But there has to be something we can do." Running Elk sounded torn with grief.

Abigail sat up, putting a stop to the talk the men were having.

Gray Eagle smiled at her. "I am Gray Eagle."

"Alexandria named her son for you," Abigail said shyly.

"I know," he stated with pride. "What does the boy look like?"

"He is the image of his father. Alexandria said that often, but now I can see she was right. All except his eyes. He has his mother's eyes. He is a beautiful child. Alexandria thought surrendering was the best option. She was sure you had given up on her, Running Elk. I should have told her the truth. If she had known there was still hope the two of you would be reunited, she would have never gone. The morning of the attack, she was dreaming of you," Abigail said, falling into tears once again.

***

Running Elk appreciated the news the woman was telling him, but her constant tears were beginning to anger him. Gray Eagle seemed to be affected differently. His nephew was hanging on every word the girl uttered, even going as far as trying to quell the woman's tears by assuring her Alexandria's surrender wasn't Abigail's fault.

Running Elk was angry, and not so sure Alexandria's surrender wasn't completely Abigail's fault. But instead of voicing his opinion, he stood and motioned for Kicking Bird to follow.

"We have come too far now. We will rest the horses for the night and then leave in the morning. Gray Eagle can take Abigail on his horse with him. She knows the direction the soldiers took," Kicking Bird stated.

"Either of us could easily see what direction they went," Running Elk said sharply.

"We cannot leave the poor girl here," Kicking Bird reminded his brother. "The Warriors have not returned. They might not ever. We must keep her with us. Besides, I believe my son is taken with her."

"Kicking Bird, she is white," Running Elk warned.

"She is Kiowa. She speaks the language. She even looks like one of them."

Running Elk shook his head but didn't fight his brother any longer. "We will leave at sunup. Now we must give these poor people a burial."

Kicking Bird nodded and followed his brother back to Gray Eagle and Abigail.

Running Elk's heart was heavy. But he knew Two Fires and his son were alive and had a pretty good idea about where they were headed. He was sure the soldiers would take their captives to the fort. He also knew it would be difficult, if not impossible to rescue her when she was guarded by soldiers. But he vowed to think of a way.

It took until sundown to bury the dead. They found a nice spot by the water and prayed the people would find peace in the afterlife before returning to where they'd left Gray Eagle and Abigail. The brothers were both stunned when they witnessed Gray Eagle sitting beside the woman, running his hand down Abigail's hair, looking as if, any minute, he would swoop in for a kiss.

"Well, Kicking Bird, it appears your son is a man," Running Elk stated, louder than necessary.

Abigail looked confused by Running Elk's proclamation and Gray Eagle looked guilty. The pair separated quickly. Kicking Bird elbowed his little brother in the stomach.

"You have a mean sense of humor," Kicking Bird said, trying to keep the amusement from his voice. "But it is good to know you still have one."

"I have decided I am not returning to our people until I have my woman and my son with me," Running Elk declared, changing the subject as he vigorously rubbed his stomach.

"Then we have a journey ahead of us, don't we?" Kicking Bird asked as he placed his arm around his brother. "I will stay with you. I already informed Sparrow of the fact. She was not happy with my plan, but she understands this is something I want to do with you."

Running Elk smiled and embraced his brother. "I am pleased for your company. Now, what are we going to do with your son? The girl needs time to mourn." he asked quietly, pulling away from their embrace.

"They can ride with us tomorrow. I will talk to him now. It might be best for Abigail if we send them to the camp. She is in need of comfort and love from other women, not my son," Kicking Bird decided, making sure the last bit of his statement was directed directly at his son.

Gray Eagle stood and walked towards his father. Running Elk moved towards Abigail, and he shook his head at his nephew as their paths crossed. When Gray Eagle lowered his head and avoided his uncle's grin, Running Elk couldn't stop his suppressed laughter from breaking through.

When Running Elk realized Gray Eagle had stopped moving, he turned back to him. "Gray Eagle, your father called you," he said lightly.

"I …" Gray Eagle began to object to his uncle's harassment but was interrupted by his father repeating his name in a sterner manner. The young warrior turned and slowly resumed walking in Kicking Bird's direction. Gray Eagle's head was held high, but there was concern on his handsome face.

"We need to talk," Kicking Bird said as he guided his son in the direction of the river.

Running Elk started a small fire and sat across from Abigail. She watched him closely but said nothing.

"Abigail. You seem much calmer now. Do you think you can answer some of my questions without crying?" he asked while he was pulling out his pipe and tobacco pouch.

"I'll try," she answered, looking as if she was trying to stop her bottom lip from quivering.

"Good. Then listen. I knew Standing Bear," Running Elk began. He discontinued his speech when he saw the shock on Abigail's face. "You see, we fought side by side. The man died in my arms. I asked your elders not to allow Two Fires to know I was coming. As he lay dying, Standing Bear admitted to me that Two Fires never loved him. Was he speaking the truth, or was he just telling me what I wanted to hear?" Running Elk asked, not being absolutely certain he wanted to know the answer.

"Standing Bear was a great man," Abigail stated. "But the truth is … Alexandria never loved him. She was glad for his kindness, but her heart was always yours. When he found out about the scout you sent to the camp, he kept her close to him until the baby was showing. He was sure you wouldn't want her if she was happy with another man. We both lied to keep her here. We knew she would leave if she thought you had any interest in her. I am so very sorry, but I was doing it for me as well. She was the only friend I had," Abigail explained, realizing that blaming Standing Bear for everything wasn't fair. She had deceived her friend and knew she had to speak of it.

Running Elk sat and smoked his pipe while he listened to the woman tell her story. He felt rage towards himself, but not for her. He could have stopped the situation if he had just ridden to the camp after Standing Bear was killed, but he had chosen to do the right thing and wait until Two Fires had time to mourn.

"Abigail, tell me of my son," he urged, keeping his eyes on the woman.

"He is a handsome child. And very well-behaved. Alexandria never lets the child out of her sight. Before she surrendered, she promised me she would raise Little Eagle the right way, even if she lived amongst the whites," Abigail said, allowing her pride for the baby to bleed through her speech.

"Little Eagle will know me," he said quietly.

"Alexandria tells her son of you. In a way, he already knows you," she responded quickly. "Did you give Standing Bear the necklace she wears after he died?"

Running Elk nodded. "He must have thrown it in the river. Gray Eagle found it shortly before I located him. When I learned who Standing Bear was, I gave it to him. I thought her having it back would give her strength to carry on until I came for her," he admitted, lighting a twig in the bluish orange flames that danced before his eyes.

"It did just that. She hasn't taken it off since she took it from Standing Bear while they were erecting his burial scaffold," she said, speaking more quietly with every word.

"Does Gray Eagle please you?" he asked, changing the subject out of fear the woman might begin crying again.

Abigail looked at the handsome Comanche warrior and smiled a shy grin. "Yes, I suppose he does. I need time to heal, but he has shown me nothing but kindness, and I am thankful for that," she answered, seeming to choose her words with care.

"He does seem to want to get to know you better, and Kicking Bird will remind the young man just what you have been through today. In the morning, we will begin to follow the soldiers. You will ride with Gray Eagle. But now you should sleep. Kicking Bird and Gray Eagle will be gone for some time. I know the conversation they are having, and it can be rather lengthy."

Running Elk smiled when he remembered the conversation his big brother and he had had many summers earlier.

"Where should I sleep?" she asked meekly.

"On that robe. I'm sure Gray Eagle won't mind sharing his things with you."

As soon as Abigail made herself comfortable, Running Elk walked to his horse and pulled another blanket down. He laid it out beside his horse. "I will be right here," he informed her before lying down.

"I'll be fine," she answered, sounding less than convinced.

"I know the memories are strong, but try to think on something else," Running Elk suggested, knowing what the woman was going through.

She didn't answer, and he could tell by her breathing that she was already asleep.

Running Elk put his arms behind his head, crossed his legs at his feet, closed his eyes, and said his nightly prayer for Alexandria and Little Eagle. He relaxed but didn't sleep until he heard Kicking Bird and Gray Eagle return. He opened one eye when he heard Kicking Bird pulling his son in Running Elk's direction.

"You will sleep with the men. Has nothing I just told you sunk into your thick head?"

Gray Eagle grumbled but followed his father's instructions.

"Brother, you have a man on your hands now. I am sure I told you that earlier. Your efforts will only delay the inevitable. Abigail is just as taken with Gray Eagle as he is with her. All that is needed is time as long as your son is patient with the girl,"

Running Elk informed Kicking Bird as he watched his brother lay out his blanket.

"Then we are in for an interesting few days. I am pleased my son has found a woman, but the circumstances could be better. How is Sparrow going to react to this news? Abigail is fragile and broken now, but she will heal. Will my son still feel drawn to her? Sparrow is not going to be happy that I allowed this to occur. But I guess I will have to accept whatever happens."

Knowing that continuing to speak about Gray Eagle's life choices wasn't getting them anywhere, Running Elk changed the subject to one he was really interested in. "Do you think we will catch up to the soldiers?"

After Kicking Bird was comfortable, he answered his brother. "I do. They cannot be making good time with the prisoners in tow. We should be able to spy them by nightfall. Now, the dawn will come early, so get some sleep. Gray Eagle took the first watch," he said yawning.

"Do you think that is wise? Given the situation with Abigail?" Running Elk didn't bother to hide his amusement with the situation his big brother was enduring.

"My son knows we have keen hearing. Anything unusual will wake us. Even with the new feelings he is experiencing, he knows how to behave. Besides, he does not want to anger me further tonight. Now sleep."

Running Elk laughed softly. "Has it been that long since you first found Sparrow?" he asked before rolling over.

"No. But my father and uncle were not in earshot, and the situation was different as well. Now please go to sleep," Kicking Bird said defeatedly.

"I will say no more tonight," Running Elk vowed, still smiling.

Chapter Thirty-Seven

Alexandria was surprised the soldiers hadn't covered any more distance than they had when they decided to stop for the night.

The horses the soldiers were atop stopped moving and the soldiers who were walking corralled the Indians they were guarding. After the convoy ground to a halt, the men began setting up for the night with little enthusiasm but plenty of speed. As Alexandria was climbing off her mount, she wondered how long it would be before Captain Armstrong made an appearance.

The soldiers guarding her threw a dirty blanket to the ground and while doing so, informed her that the filthy rag was to be her and her "Injun baby's" bed.

The man made her blood boil, but she said nothing. The captain seemed to be a man of his word and when he stopped by, she would discuss the soldier with him.

After rolling the blanket out on the ground, she decided she and her son would lie on the grass before they would touch the mucky, tatty bed. She was busy being aggravated by what the soldiers believed was proper sleeping material and jumped when she heard the captain's voice.

"I am sorry I didn't stop to see you earlier. I've been rather busy," he said before she turned around.

She turned and a look of relief crossed her face.

228 Elizabeth Anne Porter

He expression caused the captain to take a step backward. "Now, if I didn't know any better, I'd say you were glad to see me. But I'll bet you will be even more happy to see these though," he said, smiling as he handed her a clean bedroll.

"I am pleased to see you," she admitted as she took the bedding from him. "Please find someone else to guard us. I cannot bear that man another second," she explained, doing her best not to sound as if she were begging.

"I can do that. But I need to know why. Did he try to hurt you?" he inquired, concern marring his features.

"He has strong opinions and is eager to share them. I will not be leered at or have my son called an Injun. Anyone else you find will do fine, I'm sure." Alexandria stated her case.

"All right. Tomorrow, you will have someone else. But for now, will you have dinner with me?" he asked with a smile on his face as he bowed before her in a grand gesture.

"Captain, that would be nice," she decided as she unrolled the clean linen. "Thank you for the bedding. But tell me what the other Kiowas sleeping conditions are like," she asked, feeling no reason to be treated differently.

"They are pretty much sleepin' under the stars tonight. Now, you said you'd eat with me, so I will be right back with some food," he said, backing up and returning his hat to his head.

"I will be here," she said absently as she picked up Little Eagle from where he was napping on the grass and placed him on the linen. She kissed him on the head and spoke words of love before lying beside him. Knowing the Kiowa would prefer sleeping under the stars eased her mind a little.

It wasn't long before she heard the captain return.

"I'm back," he said cheerfully, interrupting her ongoing conversation with her sleeping son.

Alexandria sat up and turned to the man.

"I am hungry," she admitted when he handed her a plate before sitting beside her.

They ate in silence, and Alexandria was glad for the peace. She knew her opinions of the Indians weren't going to change and neither were his. So, it appeared they had very little in common. And Alexandria had never been one for forced conversations. There were feelings of guilt because she was sure the Kiowa weren't eating much, if anything. The food was tasteless but she needed sustenance to keep her son healthy.

"Alexandria," the captain said.

It was strange to hear him call her by her name and not the customary *ma'am*.

She looked at him, waiting for him to continue.

"Will ya ride with me tomorrow?" he asked hopefully.

"Please don't think I don't appreciate the offer, but I'd like to stay back, if you can find another soldier to guard me," she answered cautiously, hoping her constant rejection wouldn't anger him. He seemed like a good ally.

The captain nodded, but didn't bother to hide his disappointment. "I've already found another soldier. His name is Corporal Scott, and he will be sleeping over there," he said, pointing at the sleeping man's figure. "I should get back to the boys. But before I take my leave, I feel like I must say this. Please do not attempt to run," he warned, politely tipping his hat to her, keeping a smile across his handsome face.

"Why haven't we met up with the other soldiers yet?" she asked as he was departing. Him asking her not to run had nothing to do with why she wasn't trying to escape. She simply had nowhere to go.

The captain turned around. "They have been delayed. Which in turn has delayed my platoon. Army life is really a lot of hurrying up just to wait," he informed her in a joking manner. "Sleep well, Alexandria."

She found sleep elusive and was increasingly restless. Her mind was full of thoughts of Running Elk and Standing Bear. After tossing and turning for longer than she cared to consider, she sat up and looked at the stars that shone in the clear summer sky.

***

Not long after she dozed off, the sounds of the camp stirring to life and the bugler heralding a new day woke her.

She moved slower than normal, but at least she was moving. It wasn't until she had her pack rolled up and Little Eagle attached to her chest that she heard her new guard approach.

"I am Corporal Scott. Captain Armstrong said for me to make sure you had everything you need, ma'am."

"I'm fine, and my name is Alexandria. I prefer you use my name and not ma'am," she said, doing her best to smile at the man.

Her initial impression of the new guard was the young man would be much better than the last. At least he seemed to be polite.

As soon as the camp began its march, Alexandria saw Captain Armstrong riding in her direction with the ever-present smile on his face. She forced herself to return his grin.

"Mornin', ma'am. I hope you slept well," he said in greeting, tipping his hat and running his hand through his hair.

"I slept fine," she lied politely. "Do you think we will meet up with the other soldiers today?"

"That is the plan, but I won't know for sure for some time. I was hoping I could ride with you for a spell," he explained.

Alexandria knew the captain was paying far too much attention to her and could tell he was growing interested in her.

The last thing she wanted was to have to explain to another man that she couldn't possibly love anyone other than Running Elk and hoped speaking the truth would be enough. Having a friendship with the man could be helpful to her situation, but that was as far as she planned on allowing their relationship to go.

"Captain …" she began.

"Percival," he interrupted.

"Percival," she said, beginning her thought again. "I will never be good for you. If you are thinking I am good for anything besides company on the ride, you should stop. My child is the most important thing in my life and will be for some time."

"I understand that, and hell, I commend ya for it. All I'm tryin to do is be your friend. Whether you know it or not, you need a friend," he said, looking her straight in the eye.

"Then we shall be friends," Alexandria decided, feeling much better about the situation.

Chapter Thirty-Eight

Running Elk easily tracked the signs the soldiers left behind and knew they were closing in on the soldiers and their Kiowa prisoners. Besides the large swath of broken glass, the soldiers had also dropped everything from ammunition to canteens to food containers along their way. The blue coats hadn't bothered to pick anything up when they left where they had camped for the night.

"We are close, brother," Kicking Bird said as his horse walked over some discarded foodstuff.

"It will be good to set eyes on her again, but the frustration of not being able to grab her will be crippling," Running Elk informed Kicking Bird as he was turning to locate Gray Eagle.

The younger warrior's mind was full of nothing other than Abigail, and he had not been keeping up with the pace Kicking Bird and Running Elk set.

The last time Running Elk had seen Gray Eagle, he had dismounted from his horse and was giving Abigail freshly picked flowers. While Running Elk understood the young man's feelings, he found himself quickly losing patience with his amorous nephew.

"Gray Eagle," Running Elk whispered through gritted teeth.

The young warrior acknowledged his uncle's summons by looking in Running Elk's direction and smiling. Abigail looked around Gray Eagle and smiled weakly.

Running Elk shook his head, frowned, and turned to Kicking Bird.

"He is your son," he stated in disgust.

Kicking Bird laughed. "I remember a time not so long ago when you carried the same look as he does," he answered.

"Yes, and look at where that look got me," Running Elk reminded his brother bitterly.

"Brother, do not let allow your soul fill with hatred now. We know what we must do. You will bring Two Fires and Little Eagle home. Be happy for your nephew," Kicking Bird said, turning serious.

"They are doing us no good. In fact, they may be slowing us. We should send them back," Running Elk decided, speaking loud enough for the pair to hear his thoughts.

"No, uncle. I want to help find Two Fires," Gray Eagle explained as he urged his horse closer to Running Elk.

"We don't need your help. You are too preoccupied, and Abigail needs to be cared for," Running Elk shot back, anger still thick in his tone.

"Running Elk," Kicking Bird warned quietly.

"I will pay more attention. I'm sorry," Gray Eagle said, looking towards the ground.

"Then you are aware we are close. I must set eyes on her, and then we will ride ahead to the fort," Running Elk stated, looking in a westward direction.

"The fort?" Abigail asked in horror as she once again looked around Gray Eagle's frame.

"We can easily hide among the others. The soldiers never have been any good identifying our bands. They will never know we are Comanche," Running Elk explained.

"But I can't go back! I'm white! And I told Alexandria I would rather die than return to my people," Abigail argued as she fought tears.

"Don't start crying again!" Running Elk yelled. "You and Gray Eagle will return to the camp once we start heading for the fort. Does anyone have a problem with that?!" he asked the small group. When he saw his three traveling companions look at him in shock because of his sudden outburst, he continued in a softer tone. "Abigail, I am sorry I shouted at you. Tears have always made me angry."

The woman wiped her eyes and nodded. "I will feel safer if I know Gray Eagle is with me." She wrapped her arms around the young warrior's waist.

Running Elk rolled his eyes and attempted to hide his disgust before turning to his laughing brother. "Do not say a word," he warned before spurring his horse to a full gallop. "And do not be left behind."

***

Running Elk held his horse at a full run until he reached a ridge of rocks. He was delighted to learn he could view the soldiers from his vantage point. After jumping from his ride, he laid his bare chest against a large rock. It was a fortunate surprise to see the march had stopped and soldiers and prisoners alike were resting. He strained his eyes to see the people more clearly. His heartbeat raced when he caught sight of her. In his heart, he knew the woman he was looking at was his. She was sitting on the grass, holding their son close to her chest. Running Elk was so taken with the scene, he barely heard his brother and nephew crawling to his side.

"She is there," Running Elk said, pointing in her direction.

"I see her. But it looks like they are preparing to move once more. See that soldier speaking to her?" Kicking Bird observed as he made himself comfortable by his little brother's side.

"I know, and I do not like the soldier being so close to her. I wish there was some way she could know I was near," he said disappointedly, his eyes never leaving her form.

"The wind is at our backs, and the gusts are strong. Call to her. She will hear you. Two Fires is attuned to your voice," Gray Eagle suggested with excitement invading his voice.

Running Elk looked at his nephew and smiled. "I was wrong. You are a help to me. I wouldn't have thought of that. Kicking Bird, we are out of reach of their guns, don't you agree?"

"Yes. I have seen no signs they have big guns. Why?" Kicking Bird asked, observing the soldiers closely.

"Then I will stand and call to her. If she hears me, she will be sure I am near. Then we will ride ahead to the fort."

It took great discipline to stay crouched until he saw Two Fires mount her horse and move ahead of the soldier.

"Two Fires, we will be together again soon," he spoke confidently into the wind.

Chapter Thirty-Nine

"Just checking to make sure we didn't leave you behind," Captain Armstrong said, slowing his horse from a full run to a slow gait.

"No, as you can see, I am here. Corporal Scott is not far behind me," she informed the soldier who seemed determined to befriend her.

"Then we will talk later," he said, tipping his hat and making his way to the front of the formation once again.

Alexandria raised her arm to wave at the captain, but when she heard Running Elk's deep voice, she dropped it as if it weighed a ton.

"Two Fires. We will be together again."

When the vow reached her ears, she frantically looked in every direction. It sounded as if he were right behind her. After being disappointed he wasn't there, she looked towards the rock formation in the distance. As soon as she raised her arm to shade the sun, she saw him. He was standing atop of a large rock with his arms crossed at his chest. Without thinking, she kicked her horse and raced in Running Elk's direction. Her mind was reeling, and her heart pounding. She could just make out another man holding Running Elk back. At the exact same time that she allowed herself to feel hope once again, she felt her horse being slowed.

"No! Not again!!" she screamed hysterically. "Let me be happy! Let me go to him! You said you were my friend."

"Calm down, Alexandria," the captain said, steadying her horse as he dismounted from his. He quickly turned to look and see if the hostiles were still watching. "I am not letting you go. Calm yourself."

He reached to pull her from her horse, and she kicked and wiggled in an attempt to get away.

He forcefully pulled her to the ground, being careful not to hurt Little Eagle. "Think about your child. You are upsetting him," he said loudly, hoping she would hear him over her sobs.

Alexandria heard her son crying, pulled him from the captain's hold, stood up, and looked to where Running Elk had been standing. When she realized, he was gone, she collapsed into the captain's waiting arms.

***

When she opened her eyes, her heart was heavy. Once she could breathe a little easier, she looked for her son. What she saw was unexpected. The captain was walking back and forth with Little Eagle in his arms, clearly doing the best he could to comfort the child. As soon as the captain saw her eyes were open, he handed Little Eagle back to Alexandria with a thankful look on his face before turning serious. "You lied to me, Alexandria."

"And you lied to me. You are not my friend," she stated sadly as she cuddled her son.

The captain ignored her comments. "You told me the warrior didn't want ya. From what I just saw, I'd say that was a lie. Wasn't it?" he asked, taking a scat beside her without waiting for an invitation.

"That was the first time I've seen him since Standing Bear took me. But you did the same thing as he did. You stopped me from going to him. Stopped me from being with the man I belong with. Why?!" she asked, trying to control her ever-present anger.

"Because you are under my protection. The United States' Army's protection," he stated plainly.

She laughed at his simple answer. "Protection from whom?"

"I believe I'll ride with you today. Just to be safe," he said again, ignoring her.

Alexandria knew arguing would do no good, so she said nothing.

"Let's go. You are holdin' up the whole group," he stated, trying to be amicable while he offered his hand to her.

She glared at him and slapped away his hand before standing on her own and mounting her horse in silence.

Chapter Forty

"I told you she would hear you. She hasn't changed. Did you see her trying to get to you?" Gray Eagle asked excitedly as soon as they returned to Abigail and the horses.

"I saw. She wants to be with me as much as I want to be with her. That pleases me more than you can know. When we get to the camp, we can formulate a plan to free her. The soldier who stopped her horse will be our biggest obstacle," Running Elk said, smiling at his family. He knew Kicking Bird held him back, but he wasn't angry with his brother.

Seeing the woman brought him back to life. He had hope again. It was a feeling he had forgotten. Two Fires was not only aware of his presence; she had run to him. That knowledge would keep him strong until she and Little Eagle reached the soldiers' fort. Before moving closer to the fort, Kicking Bird and Running Elk said goodbye to Gray Eagle and Abigail. Gray Eagle was reluctant to leave, but when Kicking Bird explained how much it would help Abigail heal, he agreed.

Before parting ways, they gave the young warrior a message for Sparrow and Quanah. Running Elk's message was one of hope and promise; *we will return as a family.* Kicking Birds message to Sparrow was short and simple. *I will explain when we see each other again. And I love you.*

Running Elk and Kicking Bird watched as the two began their journey back to the Comanche.

The two brothers rode side by side in silence. Running Elk was working through several plans of action, and from the look on Kicking Bird's face, he was still worried about how his wife was going to react to a new member of the family and a possible love match. Even with his mind full of plans, Running Elk smiled at his brother's worries.

"Would you like to talk about it?" Running Elk asked, hoping Kicking Bird would continue to be silent and stoic.

"What? No, she knows I love her," Kicking Bird answered, looking to the sky as he spoke.

"Look there, brother," Running Elk said as he pointed in the direction of a small encampment.

People from Comanche and Kiowa bands who had agreed to be relocated were living in close proximity of each other. Running Elk and Kicking Bird knew they had friends among the people gathered. One was their father's best friend and a powerful voice in his own right. He still kept the free bands informed on everything at the fort and oftentimes sent scouts to Quanah's camp to tell him of troop movements. Instead of asking where they could locate the man, they rode through the small encampment in silence.

Running Elk had no way of knowing what Kicking Bird was thinking, but the sight saddened him. There was no joy in any of the faces he saw. Lame Deer's tipi was located at the far end of the camp. Instead of being covered in hide, it was enveloped in a white, thick material foreign to both brothers.

Running Elk dismounted from his horse and waited for his brother to follow suit.

"How is any of this good for our people?" Kicking Bird asked in a barely audible voice as he stood next to his brother in front of the closed flap.

The toothless old man welcomed the brothers with outstretched arms. When Running Elk explained the situation, the old man promised he would find out what he could once the soldiers returned. After sharing a pipe, the old chief offered his tipi to them. Kicking Bird gladly accepted the old man's hospitality, but Running Elk politely declined, saying he would rather sleep under the stars.

Chapter Forty-One

Alexandria said few words on the ride. She was too busy trying to figure out a way to get to Running Elk. Knowing he was near was both terribly exciting and equally frightening. She soon realized she didn't want to share her renewed optimism with anyone other than her son. Keeping it close to her heart was the best way to ensure nothing changed her feelings or endangered Running Elk further.

When the platoon stopped for the night, the captain informed her they would be at the fort by midday the next day. Alexandria only nodded her understanding and watched him ride away. After laying the roll out, she regaled her son with stories of his father, promising the boy Running Elk was close and that everything would work out in time. She had to admit to her laughing child that she had no idea how the family would be united, but she couldn't allow herself to accept that it wouldn't.

After eating alone, she laid down and allowed the events of the day to replay in her mind. Her mind had been so filled with the sight of Running Elk that she'd failed to realize she had also seen Gray Eagle standing beside Running Elk. Her day had been filled with mixed emotions, but she was relieved to know the young man was still alive. She fell asleep with a smile on her face as Running Elk's words echoed in her mind.

Little Eagle's cry tore her from a dream about the captain. It had been so vivid that she looked around quickly to ensure she was alone.

Once she was certain it was nothing more than a dream, she picked up Little Eagle and prepared to feed him. While she was attempting to lull her son back to sleep, she thought she heard footsteps behind her. Excitement ran through her body at the thought that the noise might be Running Elk. She was disappointed to learn the noise had all been in her mind. Sleep was elusive because she was trying to convince herself she hadn't heard the same noises the night before.

The sounds of the movements of the soldiers guaranteed the few hours of sleep she'd managed to get would quickly take their toll on her. She found some comfort knowing the fort was only half a day away though arriving at the stronghold didn't mean her troubles were over. Knowing Running Elk was near emboldened her, but she knew she had to be careful. Her hope was that she would be given options. If so, she would choose to stay with the Kiowa. Running Elk was bound to look for her there.

"What's the matter?" she heard Captain Armstrong ask as she tried and failed to mount her horse.

She turned in the soldier's direction but didn't bother to force a smile. "Nothing. I'm fine," she answered sharply.

"I'm worried about you. Are you sure you are all right?" he repeated.

"I'm terribly sorry, Captain. But did you not live through the same events as I did yesterday? If so, you should understand that I am as fine as I can be." She finally succeeded in mounting her ride after her third attempt.

"Alexandria, I told you, I was doing my job. I don't suspect he's going to give up on you. And that's why I am riding with you. No one will be taken from my custody. Once we get to the fort, you are no longer my problem. Not that you are a problem," he added quickly, clearly not wanting her to think the worst of him.

"I understand," she said sharply, not bothering to look at him.

"Alexandria, please don't be angry with me. You're much better off with your own kind. You're white, remember? How do the red skins brainwash so many people?" he asked, using a tone that led Alexandria to think he was serious.

"Captain. I am not brainwashed. I think I have always felt this way. The 'redskins,' as you call them, are proud and honorable people. Perhaps you should try living among them. Then you might understand," she said, prodding her horse further away from the captain.

"If they paid me, I might," he decided with amusement in his voice.

Alexandria turned to him and saw his familiar smile.

"What is going to happen once we reach the fort?" she asked, changing the subject after realizing she was going to do little to change the man's views.

"We will go find the general and then wire your sister," he answered as he wiped the sweat from his brow.

"I don't want to go live with my sister. If I ask him to allow me to stay with the Kiowa, what will he say?" she asked, growing more anxious.

"He'll probably say that you are crazy and no white woman lives on the reservation if she ain't married to a tribe member. And you aren't. You have no place amongst those people. Your son is a Comanche, and his father is still a hostile. Look at the whole picture, Alexandria. You can't have it all," he explained, attempting to reason with her.

"Then will he let me stay in the fort?" she asked, hoping she would have time to formulate a plan.

"The base is no place for a single woman. It's full of lonely men, dirt, death, and Indians," he informed her.

"Captain. Again, I have no problem with the Indians. I will ask the general if I can wait here while my sister wires me money. Do you suppose he will have a problem with that?" she asked angrily.

Lack of sleep was making her irritable, and that, combined with the stupidity of the captain's words, was making it close to impossible to control her anger.

"Calm down, Alexandria. Here, take a drink," he said, offering her his canteen. "I have no idea what the general's gonna say, but we'll know real soon. Our destination is just over that rise," he said, pointing as he spoke.

Alexandria took a drink but said nothing else.

The fort appeared as they topped the small hill. It looked like a large wooden monstrosity invading a land where it didn't belong.

Once the massive wooden gates opened and she and the captain were inside the small town, she saw the Kiowa stagger forward in rows while the weaker crowded in wagons.

The scene was difficult to look at. The Kiowa were her family, and she felt both guilt-ridden and heartbroken. "This is all so wrong," she said almost under her breath.

"They don't want your pity. Remember, they're a proud people. Beaten, but proud," the captain said.

Alexandria was surprised the captain had heard, but his answer immediately angered her. It was beginning to seem like everything the man said annoyed her.

"The general's office is just over there. Don't suppose ya want to go freshen up or anything before you see him, do ya?" he asked, dismounting and tethering his horse to the weathered wooden railing.

She glared down at him from her horse. "Am I that offensive to look at?"

"Well, ma'am, we have been traveling for days now. I'm sure we can wrestle ya up some water so you can bathe. Would ya like that?" he asked politely.

The idea of a bath sounded wonderful, but she didn't want to be treated any different than the Kiowa. "Are you offering the Kiowa baths too?" she asked, holding Little Eagle closer to her as she jumped from the horse.

"No. But once again, you are white. And I know an officer's wife that is about your size. We could get some clothes for Little Eagle too. He would enjoy a bath, I'm sure of that. Follow me," he said, guiding her away from the general's office and towards a row of buildings across from the corral.

Before she had time to voice her objections, she was being introduced to the captain's sister-in-law, had handed her son to the stranger when she opened her arms and smiled, and was sitting on a fancy chair that had been carefully transported from the East Coast. The shock was great. She had been living on the prairie for over a year and hadn't thought she missed the luxuries of the white world. But to her shock, the chair was quite comfortable, and the woman offering her tea was kind and gentle.

"Alexandria, I am going to tell the general you are here and fill him in on the trip. I'm sure he's wondering where I am by now. I'll be back soon. Let Jatana take care of you until I return," he said before bowing quickly and walking out the door.

"I laid Little Eagle on my bed. He will be fine," Jatana informed Alexandria as she sat across the table from her.

Jatana was a small woman. She stood five foot two on the tip of her toes and was thinly built. She had light brown hair and wore it in a bun at the back if her head. Her skin was light and her eyes were green, her smile warm and her manner friendly.

"Your bath will be ready in a minute. Now, while we wait, tell me about the Indians," Jatana said, leaning her elbows on the table and leaning closer to Alexandria.

"What would you like to know?" Alexandria asked as she backed her chair away from the table to give herself a little more distance from the woman.

"What are they really like?" she asked before standing, walking to the stove, and pouring more water into the teapot.

"They are just like you and me."

"What about your baby's father? Where is he now? Are you pleased to be away from him?" Jatana continued her gentle interrogation as she returned to the table.

"No. I love him very much. But I don't think we should be talking about this now," Alexandria stated before cautiously taking a sip of tea.

"Oh! I'm sorry. I thought you had been mistreated," Jatana apologized, clearly embarrassed by her mistake.

"No. I am in love," Alexandria said before changing the subject. "Do you think my bath is ready yet?"

"I'm sure of it. I laid some clothes out on the bed too. Can I ask one more question?"

"Yes," Alexandria said as she stood up from the comfortable chair and realized how much her muscles ached.

"What are you going to do now?"

"I am going to speak to the general after I have a bath and bathe my son," Alexandria answered as she walked into the room where the tub for bathing was kept. A woman who had been carrying buckets passed her in the hallway and immediately looked away from her. Alexandria didn't know how to take the woman's reaction, but she smiled in hopes the woman had been mortified by her appearance.

While it felt good to be bathing in warm water, she didn't enjoy it. Her mind was full of thoughts of the Kiowa. Knowing they were afforded no luxuries, broke her heart. Before leaving the water, she cried and prayed the soldiers would at least leave the Kiowa in peace. The people had no trouble living off the land if they were just left to it.

Chapter Forty-Two

Running Elk spent the morning walking around the camp that was set to eventually move to the newly-formed Indian Territory. Since the people were short on supplies, families shared tipis. The dwellings were shorter and rounder than he was used to. There were several communal cooking fires and beside them, white sacks filled with government flour as well as smaller ones with coffee and sugar. The people did not seem to be excited by the dark black liquid. He looked into the faces of the people as he passed them and decided they would be no better off living where the white man dictated. Nobody looked happy. No one smiled. His people's future did seem like a bleak one. How long Quanah would be able to hold out also weighed heavy on his mind. His emotions were running high. On the one hand, he was thrilled knowing he would be with Two Fires soon, on the other, he knew what he was witnessing was the beginning of the end of his people's way of life.

When he saw a group of children playing, he stopped and smiled sadly.

"Brother, she has arrived at the fort," Kicking Bird informed Running Elk.

"Good. Then I will enter the fort," Running Elk said, patting his brother on the back.

"Lame Deer says we cannot just ride into the stronghold and that Two Fires has been taken to the living quarters at the fort. She will be watched closely. I believe we have lost the element of surprise." Kicking Bird relayed the old chief's words.

"Brother, I have heard nothing but 'no' every time I mention Two Fires. It is getting old, and while I will take both Lame Deer's and your advice, nothing will stop me. All we need to do is learn where she sleeps," Running Elk said, thinking out loud.

"Where she sleeps?" Kicking Bird asked, confused.

"Yes. I am going to hold her in my arms tonight, my brother," Running Elk informed Kicking Bird with a smile.

There were many things he couldn't control, no matter how hard he tried. Running Elk knew his decision didn't come without danger. Nothing about the woman had been easy, but she was worth everything. Throwing caution to the wind was something he did during every battle, and reuniting with Two Fires was a battle no matter how he looked at it.

"You will be seen," Kicking Bird cautioned his little brother with a mixture of shock and warning.

"I am a hunter, remember?"

"You will be the hunted if you go into that fort," Kicking Bird repeated his objections.

"Then come with me and help," he suggested.

"This sounds familiar."

"Let's go and talk to Lame Deer. We have to be sure where she will be," Running Elk said, putting his arm around his brother and walking in the direction of the old man's tipi.

"Just promise me one thing," Kicking Bird asked.

"Anything," Running Elk answered, not slowing his pace.

"Promise me that this time, while I am looking out for you, it will not come to the same outcome as before," he said, attempting to be lighthearted.

"I will gladly promise you anything but that. You know how unpredictable the white men are," Running Elk replied, smiling.

"I hope you know what you are doing," Kicking Bird stated quietly.

"I am going to be with the woman I love. And you don't need to come. I will go on my own," Running Elk said, his voice devoid of anger.

"I wouldn't miss this, brother. I just want to make sure you are using your brain."

Chapter Forty-Three

Alexandria was physically and mentally exhausted by the time she finished cleaning herself and Little Eagle but knew there was no time for sleep. Being dressed in clothes that belonged to Jatana's sister felt strange and constricting to her. The boots were too small and pinched her toes. After taking less than five steps, she decided to take them off and put her moccasins back on.

Once she was more comfortable, she put a cloth hand-stitched diaper on her son. Alexandria watched as he wiggled against the ties. The boy had only known the feel of soft leather and milkweed, so Alexandria understood his reaction. Since she had shocked his system already, she decided against dressing him further. Once Alexandria thought the two were presentable, she ventured into the drawing room.

Jatana dropped her knitting, failed to hide her surprise, and quickly offered Alexandria another cup of tea. Alexandria politely declined the offer and ignored the woman's shock. She couldn't be bothered to ask what it was about herself or her son that offended the woman.

"We have an extra bedroom if you'd like to stay for the night. Percival sleeps there sometimes, but he won't mind giving the room to you. Would you like to stay?" Jatana asked with sincerity in her tone. If she had been shocked by Alexandria, it was clear she was attempting to make her up for her lack of manners.

"That would be nice. But only if you are sure it's all right with your husband," Alexandria said, shifting Little Eagle in her arms.

"Ben is on a mission with his men. I don't know when he will return. The life of a soldier's wife is a lonely one. I would be glad for the company," Jatana confessed.

"Then I will see you when I've finished speaking to the general. Thank you," Alexandria said as she walked towards the exit.

"Percival said he would be back to fetch you," Jatana said, walking towards the doorway in a blatant attempt to slow Alexandria down.

"I have my own mind, and I am ready to speak to the general. This shouldn't take long. And again, thank you for your hospitality and generosity."

"But that isn't how things are done on a fort. You don't …"

"Jatana, I do," Alexandria interrupted and walked out the door. "I will see you later."

***

Alexandria took a deep breath and walked towards the general's office. The heat of the day had passed, and the wind had begun to blow so she enjoyed the walk. She couldn't help but notice the people looking at her. Their stares were steely and she wondered again if the soldiers found her or her son more repugnant. Whatever their problem was, the whole situation shaded her mood.

The fortification was a perfect replica for any of the small towns Alexandria had seen. Everything was made of wood, and there was everything from a large mess hall to a drinking establishment. Several small homes were sitting close to the back fence, but it looked as if most of the soldiers stayed on the main street in buildings that looked like hotels. The place was bustling, but it lacked color. The buildings were the same color as the fence, a dull, weathered, tannish-gray.

When she reached the building belonging to the general, she walked inside to find the captain's hand attached to the doorknob on the other side.

He opened the door with a shocked look on his face.

"Alexandria," he said quickly. "What are you doing here? You look real nice except for the shoes."

"Thank you. And these shoes are comfortable. I have come to see the general," she informed him as she walked passed him, leaving him still holding the doorknob.

"The general is a very busy man. You can't just expect him to jump because you're here," the captain said as he shut the outer door and quickly caught up to her.

The inside of the office was as bleak as the fort. The walls were adorned only with a large cuckoo clock and a painting of George Washington.

"Have you told him about me?" she asked, moving Little Eagle to her hip.

"Yes," he said, reaching for Little Eagle's outstretched hand.

Little Eagle didn't pull away from the soldier's touch but after all the man had said about her son, Alexandria wasn't thrilled with their contact. Knowing she needed to behave, she said nothing about the feelings she was experiencing.

"And what did he say?" she asked, hoping to loosen his lips on the subject of her life.

"He said he would meet with you after he settled the Indians in. He's already gone. Would you like to take a walk around while we wait for his return?" the captain asked, still holding Little Eagle's chubby hand.

"How long is he going to be?" she asked impatiently.

"Not long. Did I tell you how nice you look in that dress?" he asked, changing the subject.

"You did. I suppose we could walk for a bit, but I will not be put off, Captain. I will have this settled by tonight," she warned him.

"Yes, ma'am," he said as he held the door open for her.

***

The walk was uneventful and tiring. By the time they had toured the small town, Alexandria was convinced the place was depressing for more reasons than the bleakness. Nobody spoke when they crossed paths on the walkway. But she had to wonder if that was on account of her presence. Alexandria knew the captain was speaking, but she was far too busy rehearsing her plea to the general to actually hear anything.

"Oh, he's back," she heard the captain say.

The officer accompanied Alexandria to the general's door and was then dismissed.

When she saw the man sitting behind the desk, she was pleased with his appearance. He was an older man; she would have guessed around fifty. He had gray hair and a full beard and mustache. He reminded her a little of her own father. It was clear the general had once been a huge man, but age and war had bent him slightly. He looked at her with a corncob pipe clenched tightly between his teeth. Alexandria was sure the captain had mentioned the general's name, but she had no idea just who she stood before.

"Sir, my name is Alexandria Standish ..."

"Sit," the general interrupted as he pointed to one of the three chairs that sat in front of his oversized, ornately carved desk.

"Thank you," she said, sitting down before placing Little Eagle on her lap. "As I was saying, my name is Alexandria

Standish, and Captain Armstrong found me when he invaded a Kiowa camp. I am white …"

"Yes, I can see that. And I have been told all about you. I heard you were interested in staying with the Kiowa. Well, I talked to them, and they don't want ya. You are better off going back east," he stated, interrupting her once again.

His words cut her deeply. The idea that the Kiowa wouldn't want her had never entered her mind. Was the man lying? Did the Kiowa think she would bring them more heartache? Before hearing the general's cruel declaration, she'd been sure the army would be the problem. Alexandria slowly sat back in the chair and realized her first impression of the general had been wrong. After taking a moment to digest what she'd just heard, she attempted to speak once again.

"I would like to stay here until my family sends me some money. I'm sure my sister will do as I ask as soon as I am able to wire her," she said, thinking it was sheer luck he allowed her to finish her thought.

"This is no place for a single woman. I suppose you can stay until then, but not a day longer," he said, smiling at her. "Captain Armstrong tells me the boy's father was a brave Kiowa warrior. It's a shame you'll be strapped to the kid forever. It ain't gonna …"

"Excuse me, sir," she said, standing and speaking louder than necessary. "My son is a blessing, and I love his father …"

"Alexandria." Captain Armstrong busted through the doorway as soon as Alexandria's voice grew in intensity.

"Captain, I believe it would be best if you got her out of here. Let her wire her sister," the general said as he walked to the front of his desk.

Alexandria's expression mirrored her anger. "General, it has been anything but a pleasure."

Captain Armstrong wrapped his arm around her waist and pulled her out of the general's office.

"Have you lost your mind?" he asked when he finished dragging her out of the building.

"Get your hands off me!" she said, struggling the best she could and still maintaining a grip on her son.

"You are crazy," the captain said, releasing her from his grasp while she continued to wiggle.

"I will not have my son talked about like that. That man is an idiot, regardless of what the army calls him," she informed the captain as she backed away from his grasp in an attempt to stop him from reaching for her again.

"Well, ma'am, the army calls him a brave and much-decorated general. I call him Dad," he answered with a smile.

Alexandria tried to hide her disappointment. "You know, that really doesn't surprise me."

"Now that you know he is my father, can I expect an apology for the 'idiot' remark you made?" he asked, turning serious.

"I am sorry your father is the way he is," she said, looking him straight in the eyes.

Captain Armstrong replaced his hat and shook his head.

"Let's go wire your sister," he suggested, walking closer to her.

"Is all your family here?" she asked, allowing him to walk beside her, but out of his reach.

"My family is the army. Did Jatana ask you to stay with her?" he asked, stopping in front of a small wooden shack.

"Yes, and I thanked her for doing so. I just hope your father doesn't have a problem with my son sleeping there," she said, allowing the anger to grow.

The captain held the rickety door open for her. "My father and I don't share the same opinions on everything," he whispered near her ear as she walked between his tall, lean body and the entrance.

Alexandria left his declaration hanging in the air as she walked to the smallish man who sat behind a poorly constructed wooden desk.

***

Once the wire was sent, she returned to Jatana's and fed Little Eagle before laying him down for the night.

The sun had set, and there was a coolness to the air she hadn't felt in months. Her mind was full of unanswered questions, but she managed to make polite conversation with Jatana as she sat and ate the best meal ever. Alexandria had never been a good cook, no matter if it was white food or Indian fare, and thanked Jatana over and over between compliments.

Jatana directed the conversation from 'this is lovely gravy' towards Captain Armstrong. It was clear to Alexandria that the woman was attempting to learn of Alexandria's feeling towards her brother-in-law.

"Jatana, I am in love with Running Elk. Your brother is a kind man … sometimes," Alexandria stated honestly as she finished her last bite.

"Percival is here, and your brave isn't," Jatana continued to push as she cleared the dishes away.

"I have taken that path before and it only ends up in heartache. If you don't mind, I think I will take in some air. I will hear if Little Eagle wakes," Alexandria said, standing up.

"At least take a wrap, the wind is chilly," Jatana suggested as she picked up a white crocheted square that was laying across the couch.

As soon as she stepped outside and the crisp wind blew, she instantly felt wide awake. She had been tired and irritable all day so she had hoped fresh air would do the trick and was overjoyed to be outside. The sky was cloud-cast and there was an eerie glow over the crescent moon. The stars she'd grown accustomed to seeing were barely visible through the gray clouds. Even being outside, it was not peaceful like the prairie. As she was readying to return inside, she heard her name being called.

She knew the voice belonged to the captain and stayed where she was with her hand remaining on the worn brass doorknob.

"I was just stopping by to see if Jatana had any more of that prize winnin' pie," he informed Alexandria as he closed the gap between the two.

"I'm sure she has. I'm going to bed. I will see you in the morning," she said quickly, entering the home to keep as much distance as possible between them. Now that she knew his feelings towards her, she knew he hadn't heard her when she told him over and over that she loved Running Elk and no one else. The captain was a handsome man, but so was Standing Bear, and her heart had been untouched by him. Before shutting her eyes, she prayed that Running Elk would appear again soon.

Chapter Forty-Four

Running Elk and Kicking Bird observed the scene in silence, not even turning to see each other's expressions. When most of the movement had slowed, they moved closer to the building they'd watched Alexandria enter with the soldier. Running Elk quickly looked into a window at the back. The room was dark and empty. Kicking Bird knew there were people in the front of the house and cautiously looked into the only remaining window.

There was a dim light emanating from the room. Kicking Bird watched until his eyes adjusted to the area. The room was crowded with furniture. He scanned the area quickly and noticed a sleeping form on top of the bed. As soon as he saw the child, he knew he was looking at Little Eagle; the sleeping toddler was the image of his father. Kicking Bird was sure he was looking into the room his brother desired, so he ducked under the glass-covered opening and moved to Running Elk's side.

When Running Elk looked at Kicking Bird, his brother pointed to the window and then to an area where the warrior could easily hide.

Running Elk slowly moved toward the window and peered in. When he saw his son sleeping on the white bedding, he pushed his face closer to the glass. The warrior quickly scanned the room to locate Two Fires. He found her lying on the floor on top of a blanket. A smile crossed his face and his breath quickened. Before he could act, he heard the voices in the front of the house and pulled away from the opening.

"Jatana, she is gonna stay here if her sister sends her some money. Stop matchmaking, all right?" he heard the man say.

"Do you think she will ever be with Running Elk?"

When he heard his name, he strained to hear everything more clearly.

"He's a hostile, but I kinda hope he does show up. It might make an interesting game."

Running Elk waited until the door shut and the noises in the house were silenced. He knew walking in the front door would be difficult to do without being caught. The blue coats were walking about too much. His need for her was so strong, he might have done just that if he hadn't found one of the windows at the front of the house open.

After slowly pushing away the linen that hung in the opening, he slid in, silently making his way down the short hallway to Two Fires' door.

As soon as he was inside, he picked his son up. A tear fell down his cheek. He had never felt such pride as he did when he held his son close to his heart. After placing the sleeping child back on the soft bedding, he knelt down and gently laid his hand on Alexandria's back.

Running Elk stretched out beside her and ran his hand through her tousled hair. His finger found his necklace tied around her slender throat. She rolled over, still embracing sleep.

He placed his lips close to her ear and repeated her name in his language. He knew she spoke Comanche well enough to understand him. Abigail had told him Alexandria demanded she teach her all the Comanche she knew.

"Two Fires, I am here," he repeated as he nibbled her earlobe. As he spoke, his hand ran the length of her long, lean body.

Running Elk sensed Two Fires' change in breathing and his heart skipped a beat. She was awake, and he repeated her name.

***

Alexandria didn't want the dream to end so she held her eyes tightly shut.

"Two Fires, look at me. It has been too long to play games. My body aches for you," he breathed into her ear.

"Running Elk?" she whispered.

Running Elk could see her rapid heartbeat in her neck. "Please be here," she begged as she rolled over.

Hearing her speak in his language made him love her more. It was clear to him the woman was more Indian than white. And he felt pride in her.

"I am going nowhere for now," he said, pulling her closer to him with his muscular arms.

She couldn't stop the tears from flowing as he kissed her cheeks and eyes gently before moving to claim her lips.

"This time, we will take our time, my love," he said as he loosened the ties to her white nightgown, kissing her collarbone as soon as it was exposed.

She ran her hands up and down his body and kissed his bare chest as he pulled the nightgown from her shoulders to expose her bare breasts.

Running Elk stopped breathing momentarily. "I had forgotten just how beautiful you are."

She was lying beneath him, naked from the waist up. He kissed her breasts and then moved down her stomach until she was squirming beneath him. When he raised up to continue to remove the long gown, he noticed the look of disbelief on her face.

"Two Fires, say something to me," he whispered as he began kissing the inside of her thigh. It never dawned on him that the shock of his appearance might have been too much for her.

"I love you," she said, barely audible as she ran her hands through his long, silky hair.

"Uh ka-muh-kuh-tuh nuh," he said, parting her legs with his knee after hearing the words he'd longed for.

She held him tightly as he slowly entered her. When he began moving, he became lost in a world that was all their own.

Running Elk knew the dangers of speaking above a whisper and gently placed one of his hands over her mouth when Alexandria started making the noises he loved hearing.

Afterward, he lay in his arms until her regular breathing returned.

"You have given me a wondrous son," he whispered as he caressed her body.

"I still can't believe you're really here. When can we leave?" she asked when he began to move away from her.

"I am here, but we cannot leave now. If they found you missing, they would look for you, and I'm afraid there would be bloodshed. What have they told you?" he asked, picking up the nightgown he had discarded, before thinking better of it. He enjoyed her being naked, so he lay back down and held her close to him.

She nestled into his warmth before answering him. "They told me I can't live with the Indians," she said, a little louder than Running Elk was comfortable with.

"Shh," he warned quietly. "Then you must get them to let you leave the fort. I can't take you from here. It is too dangerous, and I will not lose you again."

"When should I leave?" she asked before pulling him into a deep kiss.

***

Alexandria had sorely missed the way he made her feel. Her heartbeat hadn't slowed since she heard his voice in her ear. Everything about the man made her weak. His voice was deep and strong, his spirit courageous and bold, his body as hard as stone, and his hands could play her body like a fine-tuned instrument.

"In two moons. We will be ready and waiting for you. We will be together, and I will take you where we can be safe," he explained as his fingers toyed with her nipple.

She was finding it increasingly difficult to pay attention to his plan but wasn't about to ask the man to stop doing what he was doing.

"We? Is Gray Eagle with you?" she asked before moving quickly and sitting on top of his hard stomach.

***

"Who?" he asked, allowing Alexandria to understand she had the same effect on him as he did on her. "Oh no, my brother is with me. His name is Kicking Bird …"

"Gray Eagle's father?" she asked, interrupting him.

"Yes," he answered, laughing softly. "I forgot you knew Gray Eagle for a moment. You do drive me to distraction."

Alexandria slid back down to a lying position and began tracing his stomach muscles with her fingernail. "When I realized it was him standing beside you, I was so happy. I worried that he was dead."

"He is fine. In fact, he is with your friend," he said, holding her hand in his.

"What friend?"

"Abigail. They seem to be taken with one another."

Alexandria sat up and looked down at Running Elk in shocked disbelief. "How do you know Abigail?"

Running Elk was preparing to answer the question when he heard the banging on the door.

"Jatana! Open the door!"

Alexandria stood up and frantically began dressing. Running Elk was doing the same.

"You have to get out of here," Alexandria whispered frightenedly.

"I will be fine," he promised before he kissed her again. "Now lie down and I will hide under your bed."

She nodded and pulled the blanket over her. Trying to slow her breathing was more difficult than she'd imagined. Especially when she heard the footsteps and the captain's voice approaching.

Alexandria jumped when she heard the knock, even with prior knowledge it was about to happen.

"Alexandria," Captain Armstrong said through the closed door. "I need to speak to you. It is very important."

"Do you have any idea what time it is?" she asked, doing her best to sound as if he had awoken her.

"Yes, ma'am, I do. But like I said, it is important," he insisted impatiently.

Alexandria stood, covered her nightgown with the blanket, and moved towards the door. Little Eagle began crying so she reached to pick him up. As she leaned at the foot of the bed, she felt Running Elk touch her bare foot.

"Give me a second. You woke my son," she stated as she slowly opened the door.

Captain Armstrong quickly scanned the dimly lit room before centering his attention on Alexandria.

"I have had word that your brave is near," he said, watching her features closely.

"He is?!" she asked, not hiding the excitement she knew was expected from his statement.

"So it would seem. This is the first time you are hearing this news, right?" he asked suspiciously.

"It is," she skillfully lied. "Can we go look for him?"

"No, I'm afraid not. He is a hostile, and if he is seen he will be taken prisoner," he explained through clenched teeth.

"Does he know that?" she asked, worried.

"I'm sure he does. I told you he wouldn't give up on you," he said, speaking louder to ensure he was heard over Little Eagle's wails.

"Well, as you can see, he isn't here. And he shouldn't be here if he can go to prison. We will speak more in the morning," she spoke just as loud as the captain had.

"I don't see him, that's true enough, but you look a mess," he said, slowly backing out the door.

"I was having a nightmare," she explained before closing the door and letting out a breath she hadn't realized she was holding.

Alexandria sat on the bed and tried to comfort her angry son. She waited for Running Elk to sit beside her and speak before she said a word.

"I will be fine," he whispered, putting his arm around her and placing his hand atop his son's head. "It will be more difficult for you to leave now that they know I am here, but you must try. In two moons, we will be waiting."

Alexandria nodded. "How are you going to leave?" she asked, her voice thick with concern.

"The same way as I came in," he said, pointing to the window.

"Are you sure that's safe?" she asked, moving closer to him.

"I'm sure. I must leave now though. The sun will be up soon, and I need the darkness to hide me. We will be together again soon," he said before kissing her passionately.

While Alexandria was trying to catch her breath, Running Elk laid a kiss on his son's forehead.

She didn't watch him leave. She couldn't. All she wanted was to run with him. Every other time she'd let him leave her, something had stopped them from reuniting. As hard as she tried to banish the thought that she would never see him again from her mind, she couldn't.

Chapter Forty-Five

Alexandria held her son close and told him his father loved him very much. The boy fell asleep as the new day was dawning. She knew her body couldn't function much longer with so little sleep and decided to ask Jatana if she minded if she slept a little later. When she ventured into the kitchen, she saw Captain Armstrong sitting at the table, drinking coffee. He greeted her with a smile.

"Good morning."

Alexandria ignored his greeting. "Jatana, I didn't sleep well again last night. If you don't mind, I would like to stay in bed a little longer."

"I'm afraid that isn't possible," the captain answered for his sister-in-law. "Sleeping on the bed might help your sleep, by the way. You and I have a meeting with the general this morning."

"Why?" Alexandria asked, looking at the captain for the first time since she entered the room.

"He wants to discuss your future plans. But before we meet with him, we have got to talk. So please, sit down and have a cup of coffee," he suggested, standing and pulling out the vacant chair for her.

Alexandria was curious about the captain's strange tone.

"What could we possibly have to talk about?" she asked before taking a sip of the hot, bitter liquid.

"Well, the general believes your son is Kiowa and his father was Standing Bear. So you need to stick to that story if he brings it up," he said quickly.

"Why does he think that?" she asked, looking confused.

"Because if he knew you were connected to Running Elk, then he would have to put the man in jail. Christ, the man is almost doing my soldiers' job for them. He should know the dangers of being here," he said, speaking frankly to Alexandria.

Alexandria listened to him and searched his face for signs he was concerned and sincere. After looking at him closely, she was convinced he was neither of those things.

"Why are you trying to be helpful?" she asked suspiciously.

"I don't want you hurt anymore. Now, just stick to the story I told him if you want to be allowed to roam freely through the fort. I spoke to him last night and told him I would keep an eye on you while I am here. I am trying to help you, but you must stick to the story," he said, stressing the importance of keeping to the lie.

"Does he know Running Elk is near?" she asked, still watching his eyes closely.

"No. The scout who informed me doesn't think much more of my father than you do. He only told me because he is paid well to scout for me," the captain answered, looking down at his drink.

"Why did you want to know? First you tell me you are trying to keep me from being hurt, then you send someone in search of Running Elk. What is the truth?" she asked, beginning to feel the familiar anger rising.

"Because I need to know these things. Running Elk knows what he is doing. But he needs to be careful. I see this as a game between him and I. The winner will end up with the pleasure of your company," he informed her. His voice was devoid of humor. The man was totally serious.

Alexandria tried to quell the sick feeling rising in the pit of her stomach.

"What are you talking about?" she asked, pushing away from the table before standing and placing her hands on her hips.

"I'm not telling anyone he is here. If he can get to you without me stopping him, then he will win," he answered plainly.

"Does it not matter that he is the only man I will ever love?" she asked, still confused at the captain's plan.

"It does, but if he is in jail, you will need someone around, and I will be here," he explained.

"I don't like the idea of your little game and will not be a part of it," Alexandria stated as she turned to return to her bedroom.

"Well. You either play, or we will tell the general the truth," he said abruptly, stopping her forward movement.

"I will be leaving today," she said to Jatana.

"If you leave, the old man will know something is wrong and he will send you back east," Captain Armstrong threatened.

"You are not my friend," Alexandria spoke, full of anger and hurt.

"I know you were aware Running Elk was here before I was, and I did nothing about it. He will not be so lucky the next time. If he attempts to enter this home again, he will be jailed," he informed her smugly.

Alexandria tried to hide the shockwaves his words sent through her body. She had been sure Running Elk was not seen.

He had been too careful to leave any signs of his presence. After coming to the conclusion the captain was only trying to get a reaction out of her, she decided she wasn't going to give him the satisfaction.

"You were the first to inform me. I wish that wasn't true, but you have to know that if he had come for me, my son and I would have been gone."

"No, ma'am. Your brave is much smarter than that."

Alexandria turned and walked towards her room. Once she was alone, she shut the bedroom door and sat on the bed before allowing the tears to flow.

She had prayed that nothing would interfere with her reunion with Running Elk and valiantly fought the doubt that had crept in as soon as he was gone. She knew Running Elk had understood the words the captain was spewing the night before and hoped he knew just what the captain was capable of. Because she certainly hadn't been. The captain had seemed to accept her offer of friendship, yet he had just made it clear he would be there to care for her after he carted Running Elk to a cold, dark prison cell. Alexandria knew the warrior could not live in a cell. Panic was taking over when the captain's voice boomed down the hallway.

"Alexandria. The general will be waiting for us, and he is a man that does not like being kept waiting," he said impatiently.

She didn't reply to his instruction but dressed her son quickly before dressing herself. After gathering her son in her arms, she walked towards the kitchen slowly.

"I can watch your son if you'd like," Jatana offered when she walked over to greet the boy.

"No thank you. Maybe later though. I think I would enjoy a walk around, and it would be nice to know my son will be looked after. Will your kind offer still be there?" Alexandria asked, forcing a smile.

"Yes, I look forward to it," Jatana answered.

Alexandria didn't like the position she had placed Jatana in. She hoped the fake smile was enough to convince Jatana that her brother-in-law hadn't totally unnerved her.

When she followed the captain outside, she was greeted with the warm sunlight. She took a deep breath and tried to steel herself for another meeting with another Armstrong man. It was disheartening to realize she wasn't a better judge of character. And it was proving extremely difficult to think of anything other than the night she had spent with Running Elk. Her heartbeat quickened and her breath labored every time she allowed the memory to root in her overcrowded thoughts.

As they walked, she noticed the captain watching her closely. It surprised her how much hate she felt towards the man. Alexandria could only hope her sister would quickly wire the money she asked for and decided to tell the general she would gladly leave the territory as soon as she was able. It was the only thing she could think to do that could cause the general to stop watching her movements so closely. The only hiccup in her plan was that she had to find a way to get word to Running Elk, and she had to keep the soldiers from finding him.

As she was entering the general's office, she heard Captain Armstrong whisper in her ear, "Remember your story."

She pulled her arm from his grasp and waited for the general to call them into his office.

"Come in," the older man said when he opened the door.

The general seemed friendlier than he had the previous day, but his manner put her even more on guard.

"Have a seat, ma'am. Captain, pour the lady some tea. I am sorry this meeting is taking place so early, but I do have a full day ahead of me," the general said politely.

She had held her tongue as long as possible. "Sir, you were rather rude to me yesterday, and today you are a changed man. Why is that exactly?"

He seemed taken aback by Alexandria's boldness as he lit a fresh cigar. "I do apologize for my manners. You have no idea how difficult it is to keep these savages under control. Not to mention the bands that still think they can win this battle. I tell ya', some days I feel like a dog chasing his tail."

Alexandria heard nothing the man said after he described the Indians as savages. She kept her simmering anger under control and waited for him to stop talking.

"I have made a decision that I think will be of interest to you both," she began, looking from the general to the captain who had taken a seat next to her after pouring the untouched cup of tea.

She could tell by the look on the captain's face that he would rather she stopped talking. Alexandria smiled and turned her attention back towards the general.

"Well, don't keep us in suspense," the older man said.

Just as Alexandria was readying to speak her plan, the door burst open and a young, wild-eyed soldier ran inside.

"I'm sorry for the interruption, general, sir," he said in between breaths as he saluted the commanding officer.

"This had better be as important as you're makin' it look," he yelled at the young soldier.

His booming voice woke Little Eagle.

Alexandria stood to excuse herself in an effort to calm her wailing son. But she was too curious about what the soldier had to say to move far from the open doorway.

"We got one. It ain't Quanah, but he's close. He's a Comanche who has been raiding and killing us for years," the young man proclaimed proudly, still attempting to catch his breath.

Alexandria immediately felt her knees weaken. She leaned against the wall and slowly slid to the floor, to ensure she wouldn't fall, and forced herself to continue to eavesdrop. Holding onto the hope that the Comanche wasn't Running Elk, she desperately tried to calm both herself and her son.

"Well, tell me who it is!" the general demanded, walking out of his office and past Alexandria without giving her a glance. The private followed on his heels.

Captain Armstrong followed the two and reached to close the outer door of the building. He didn't make it quick enough for Alexandria not to hear the beginning of the name.

"Running ..."

She didn't need to hear anymore.

***

As soon as the captain ensured the door was closed, he joined Alexandria on the floor.

Alexandria tried to move away, but her body was just as broken as her heart.

"I swear I didn't tell anyone he was here. It ruins my game," he informed her.

"Where ... will ... they... take him?" she asked softly. She couldn't have spoken louder if she wanted to. The lump in her throat made it impossible to speak over a whisper.

"He'll be at the guardhouse. After they get done interrogating him," he answered as he fiddled with the tassels on his hat.

"Oh God! They aren't going to hurt him, are they?" she asked, knowing full well what the answer would be.

"I don't know," the captain stammered. "Yeah, most probably."

"Where is the guardhouse?" she asked as she forced herself to stand.

"You don't want to go around there," he said, still looking at the floor.

"Oh, I am going," she said defiantly. "And if you don't tell me where he is, I will find someone who will."

"Then go find him," he said, still not looking at her.

"Go to hell," she seethed before turning and reaching for the doorknob.

She ran back to Jatana's house and asked if the woman would watch Little Eagle.

"Of course, but what's wrong?" Jatana asked when she realized Alexandria was in distress.

"Nothing. I just need to be alone. To take a walk," Alexandria lied as she handed the woman her child. "Tell me, Jatana, do you know a lot about his place?"

"I've been here over a year, so I know where most things are."

"Good. Where do they take the prisoners?"

"Usually to the guardhouse. Why?"

"Where is the guardhouse?" Alexandria asked impatiently, not bothering to answer Jatana.

"By the stables. Why?" the woman asked again.

"Where are the Kiowas I arrived with?"

"Oh no. You answer my question before I answer any more of yours."

"Jatana," Alexandria said, standing her ground. "I can't tell you. I must have answers, and I'm asking you to trust me."

"Percival said you were to stay away from the Indians," Jatana reminded Alexandria meekly.

"Percival is an idiot! Will you help me or not?"

Jatana took a deep breath, rocked Little Eagle in her arms, and answered Alexandria's questions.

"The Kiowa are a few miles east of the wall in a kind of temporary settlement. There are a few friendlies, as they call them, just to the west, but they aren't from the group you came in with. It's guarded at all times, and they usually move the captives out after a few weeks. Once they leave here, they will be moved into Indian Territory. They say the Indians are given homes with walls, roofs, and everything."

Jatana answered Alexandria with more information than needed, but the news was welcome nonetheless.

"You said the guardhouse was beside the stable. How will I know which building it is?" Alexandria asked, hoping Jatana's answer would be shorter.

"Oh, you can't miss it. It's the only building on the property that has locks on the outside of the door. It's a rather dingy place ..." Jatana answered, once again elaborating more than necessary.

"Thank you," Alexandria said before kissing her son on the top of his head and smiling at Jatana. "Please take good care of him."

***

Alexandria was relieved to have the information she sought but also knew it could easily only be a matter of time before Jatana also told the captain everything she had told her.

After walking to the massive wooden gates, she turned to the guardhouse. Alexandria knew she needed to find Kicking Bird if she had any hope of freeing Running Elk. It took all her strength to pull the stubborn gates open wide enough for her to squeeze through. She walked quickly in the direction Jatana had said the Kiowa were located.

It was strange to see several tipis in varying degrees of completion and people milling around much like they had when they were free.

The government had at least allowed what was left of the band to camp near water. But the covering of the tipis didn't look like they were hide, and the poles that littered the ground weren't without imperfections. Several Indians stared as she made her way through the makeshift camp, but she didn't stop until she spotted someone she knew. When she saw Abigail's adopted mother, she ran towards the woman. Nothing could have prepared Alexandria for the cold reception she received.

"Where is White Buffalo?" Alexandria asked.

"He stays there," the woman said, avoiding looking Alexandria in the eyes as she pointed over her shoulder.

"I have heard Abigail is happy. She is living with the Comanches," Alexandria offered, still taken aback by the woman's cold attitude towards her but convinced the woman would be glad of any information of Abigail.

"That is good to know. I am busy. The man you are looking for stays there," she repeated as she pointed again towards a tipi before going about her work and dismissing Alexandria.

Alexandria walked away, still perplexed by the woman's anger but glad she had pointed out the war chief's tipi. She knew White Buffalo was the only man who could find Kicking Bird, and it appeared Running Elk's life depended on her success. Relief flooded through her body when she saw the old man sitting cross-legged outside of his home.

"White Buffalo," she spoke his name anxiously.

"Alexandria!" he said, standing to embrace her.

Standing Bear's father looked as if he had aged twenty years in the short time since she'd last seen him.

She was momentarily calmed when she received a different greeting than she had from Yellow Bird.

"I am so very glad you are well," she said honestly as she held the embrace.

"And I am pleased that you are well. Where is Little Eagle?" he asked, pulling Alexandria to arm's length so he could look her up and down.

She saw the concern on his wrinkled but stern face. "He is thriving. Don't worry, he is being cared for. I had to come find you. Running Elk is in jail and he told me his brother Kicking Bird is near. We have to find a way to rescue Running Elk," she explained, not allowing herself to breathe until she had said her piece.

"Calm yourself. Sit," he said gently as he guided her inside the dwelling.

"I can't be calm. I have to save him! I understand that you don't know everything that happens here, but this is vitally important. You have to help me. Please help me," she begged.

"I happen to know more than you think," he offered as he took a seat beside her. "You are looking for Kicking Bird?"

"Yes. Do you know of him?" she asked, praying his answer would be yes.

"Never mind that. I will send someone to the Comanche camp to search for him. I'm afraid that is all I can do. I do not have the power I once did," he said, taking her hand in his.

"You could let me take a horse and go myself," she suggested hopefully.

"The soldiers have taken all but two of my ponies, but I will send someone. Come back and visit with me in the morning," he said after giving his decision some thought.

"Thank you for your help. I will find a way to return tomorrow," Alexandria said, smiling at him. She was grateful for his help but didn't think he was moving fast enough.

"It would not be wise to try to walk to the Comanche camp," the old chief warned as he stood beside her.

Alexandria was surprised the old man had read her thoughts. "I was thinking about doing just that," she admitted, smiling sadly at him.

"In the morning, I will have news. Now go home to your son. You must miss him," White Buffalo suggested, changing the course of the conversation.

Alexandria's mood lifted slightly when the old man mentioned Little Eagle. "This is the first time I have left his side since the soldiers came into the camp," she admitted.

"Then go to him. And try to bring him with you tomorrow. I have missed seeing him," White Buffalo said with sadness shading his voice.

"I will do my best to bring him with me," Alexandria said, holding his warm embrace.

"Be careful walking back," he offered as she turned to begin her trek back to the fort. Before the man was out of her sight, she saw White Buffalo call a warrior to his side.

***

Alexandria had barely reached the outskirts of the camp when she saw the captain riding towards her. She knew she couldn't avoid the soldier on foot but was determined not to stop and engage the man in conversation either.

"From the look on your face, I'd say you didn't have any luck in whatever it was you were doing," he commented as he directed his horse to walk alongside her.

"Is there some reason you're here? Or do you simply enjoy following me around?" she asked, slowing her pace.

"I wanted you to know that Running Elk is going to be transferred to another fort for his trial," he informed her, still keeping his horse close to her.

"When?" she asked, stopping and looking up at him.

"Next Monday. They are talkin' about hanging him. He won't talk, and I was told he speaks our language. He does, right?" he asked, attempting not to sound overcurious.

"I won't tell you anything about him," she stated defiantly, bravely forcing herself to stay standing. The possibly of Running Elk hanging was paralyzing news.

"Yeah, I figured you'd say that. Now, this is not the kind of place you should be walking around unescorted," he said politely.

"It's odd that you would say that, Captain. You see, I feel quite comfortable here," she informed him as she began walking back in the direction of the fort.

"They are guarding him real close, but he has to eat," he said.

When Alexandria heard what the soldier said, she stopped walking again but didn't allow her momentary excitement show. She knew the information the captain was offering didn't come without strings. Alexandria wondered if the captain thought if he allowed her to speak to Running Elk maybe the Comanche would speak English. Wherever his sudden generosity was coming from she was sure it was another part of the captain's sick plan.

"I must know what you were planning on telling the general before all this happened," he said quickly, not giving her enough time to form an answer to his last declaration.

"It does not matter anymore," Alexandria said quickly.

"I don't suppose you want a ride back?" he offered.

Her first reaction was to say no and tell him to go away, but she was tired. Lack of sleep and worry had taken their toll on her. Alexandria didn't answer, but she didn't start walking again either.

"Is that a yes?" he asked as he dismounted his horse and removed his hat. He shook his head and his long blond hair fell around his shoulders. As much as she disliked and distrusted the man, she couldn't say he wasn't handsome.

"How about I ride and you walk?" Alexandria suggested seriously.

"Well, ma'am, that wouldn't be fair. It is my horse," he objected, once again attempting to lighten the heavy mood.

"Then I will continue to walk," she said stubbornly.

"That is your decision. I will just ride behind you until you collapse," he decided as he remounted his steed.

"I will not collapse."

She was exhausted, but her stubbornness wouldn't allow her to give in.

The captain rode beside her the rest of the way, sometimes walking his horse in a big circle around her.

He was infuriating, but she stayed silent. Once they passed the gate, she let out a deep breath. She was proud of herself for proving she didn't need the captain's help. Alexandria was sure she had proved her point.

He chuckled and directed his horse towards the stables before turning back to her. "I will see ya at Jatana's later."

As soon as he turned away, Alexandria turned and strained to see the guardhouse, but all she could see was the stables. She knew looking for Running Elk would be pointless, so she forced herself to accept she needed sleep. Her heart was with him, but her body refused to go any further.

Chapter Forty-Six

Running Elk woke quickly and unsuccessfully attempted to stand.

As soon as he moved, he felt the rope tighten around his neck and realized the soldiers had done a proficient job. His arms were tied to his feet and the little slack that the binding had hung around his neck.

The cloudiness of his mind gradually cleared, and he began remembering where he was. Once the memory of the night slowly returned, he stopped struggling, knowing it wasn't going to do any good. He could feel the wet stickiness of the blood that still trickled down the side of his face. With the return of his memory also came the return of the pain.

After slowly surveying his surroundings, he tried to figure out a way to escape. The room he was being kept in was small and had dirt walls and floors. The only window was directly across from him and too small to give him much light. No matter how difficult it would be to escape, he would not remain in the small, dark, stinky room for long. He also knew he needed to regain some of his strength before he had the slightest chance at attaining freedom.

Two Fires was on his mind the moment he regained conciseness. Despite his predicament, he was grateful they had been able to share some of the night together. It had been an answer to his prayers to be with her and meet his son. After coming so far, and with his family so close, he knew he couldn't give up no matter how bleak the odds appeared. It was obvious he had spent too much time with Two Fires. Running Elk knew he was sitting in the room because the woman made him lose his senses and yet he wasn't angry at her. He was grateful for the time they'd had.

While he was gradually understanding an escape would be difficult, Running Elk said a short prayer for his brother's safety. His prayer was only that Kicking Bird was able to escape. Instead of allowing himself to compound his troubles with more doubt, he decided Lame Deer was certain to have heard of his capture. If so, then Kicking Bird and the old Kiowa chief were bound to be planning a way to free Running Elk. Even in his position, his biggest concern was Two Fires. The soldiers surely knew how she felt about him. If so, they had the upper hand. It was a given that the man who had interrupted their reunion would bring her to him. But Running Elk did not want her to see him wounded and bound. Running Elk worried how Two Fires would react to him acting as if she meant nothing to him. It would be difficult to treat the woman he loved as if she were just like all white women, but he knew it was the only way.

Running Elk rested his head against the wall and looked up at the small bare window. When the dim light that permeated the small cell darkened, his body tensed and his hand automatically reached for the knife that was no longer strapped to his leg, and in moving so quickly he learned his restraints wouldn't have allowed him to reach the weapon anyway.

"Running Elk," the man said through the opening of the window. "I am Captain Percival Armstrong."

Running Elk stayed silent.

"I have heard you speak English. And I know you communicated with Alexandria before she was even aware of your language," he explained smugly.

Running Elk's expression didn't change, but inside his blood was boiling.

"You look like hell," the soldier continued the one-sided conversation. "Alexandria will be by later with some food. Would you like that?"

Running Elk remained silent and unblinking.

"She really is an amazing woman. While you're in prison, if they don't hang ya, I will be taking care of her and your son," he informed the silent Indian.

It was evident the captain had been looking forward to torturing Running Elk, but it sounded like the soldier's actions had not been as fulfilling as the man had hoped.

"*Nei mah-ocu-ah*," Running Elk seethed, telling the captain that Two Fires was his.

"Next time I visit, I'll bring a scout. I want to know what you are saying to me," the captain informed him before he disappeared from the window.

***

Percival walked straight to his sister-in-law's house with the sole purpose of speaking to Alexandria. He wasn't sure what was coming over him. Since he was a young man, every woman he'd ever smiled at had fallen at his feet. Alexandria was the exception, and he considered her reaction a call to arms. Shame wasn't an emotion he had experienced before. He was well aware the woman he was pursuing was beginning to hate him, and it was becoming increasingly clear there was nothing he could do to sway her. When Alexandria had described her time with Standing Bear, Percival had thought the Kiowa was unsure of himself. Yet he was doing the exact same thing. It appeared she was only ever going to love one man and, much as he hated to admit it, he was jealous of the Comanche.

Once he reached his sisters-in-law's porch, he knocked on the door and waited to be admitted.

Jatana slowly opened the door and looked at him with disappointment on her face.

"What!?" he asked irritably.

"You should be ashamed of yourself," she spoke as she let him in before following him to the living room.

"Where is she?" he asked, rubbing his forehead.

"Sleeping. Why?"

"Because I want to speak to her. That's why," he informed her testily.

"Percival, she needs to sleep. Little Eagle has just gone down for a nap, and I have no intention of waking either one of them," she informed him as she sat on the divan and picked up her knitting needles.

"I didn't ask you to wake her. What do you think I am?" he asked, plopping down beside Jatana.

"I'm not sure," she admitted. "I've never seen you like this. You were always so charming, the knight in shining armor. What has come over you?"

"She has come over me, Jatana," he admitted defeatedly. "I will stop by again later. The general said the prisoner has to eat, so will you fix something? I will deliver it to him when I return," he asked, rising from a sitting position and walking back towards the exit.

"I will do as you ask," Jatana said quietly, not looking up from her knitting.

Chapter Forty-Seven

Alexandria woke slowly, taking the time to stretch and yawn before sitting up.

The wonderful aroma of chicken being fried filled the home and forced her to realize just how hungry she was. Before getting out of bed, she reached for Little Eagle.

When she didn't see him, she wasn't overcome with worry. She knew he was in good hands with Jatana. Alexandria was grateful the woman had thought to remove her son from the room. It was the first time she had slept uninterrupted since she arrived at the fort. She hadn't realized how long she had slept until she noticed the sun had already begun to set.

After smoothing her hair and crumpled dress, she walked towards the delicious aroma filling the small home.

"Did you sleep well?" Jatana asked when Alexandria walked into the kitchen.

"I did. Is Little Eagle all right?" she asked when she saw her son lying on a pillow on the floor, playing contently with a wooden spoon.

"He was no trouble. He is a very quiet baby. Are you hungry?" Jatana asked, smiling.

"Starving," Alexandria answered. "Is there anything I can do?"

"No, everything is well in hand. Percival is coming by for dinner," she said, watching Alexandria for her reaction to the news.

"Why? To torture me some more? I'm sorry. I know he's your family, but I was so very wrong about him," Alexandria said weakly as she sat at the table and rubbed her temples in hopes the throbbing in her head would calm.

"He's never acted this way before. If it helps, I'm on your side. I wish I could say he will behave better. He did say something about taking food to Running Elk. You and I could go," Jatana offered as she thought through her new idea.

"As badly as I want to see Running Elk, I'm afraid it is some kind of trap. But even as I admit that, I still want to go. I just don't want to do anything that could cause matters to get worse for Running Elk. I'm confused, but my heart wants to go to him. You will come too, right?"

"Of course. We'll leave Little Eagle with Percival," Jatana said, even after seeing Alexandria's disagreeable expression. "As out of character as he's acting, he would never allow the child to come to harm. I can promise you that much. We just have to get him to agree to let us both go."

"And just how are we going to do that?" Alexandria asked, not believing the captain wouldn't insist on accompanying her.

"Simple. We will make him believe it is his idea," Jatana informed her with a smile as she began laying out the table settings.

"All right. But how do you plan on doing that?" Alexandria asked curiously; she was still not convinced there was anything they could do.

"By making him believe the closer he becomes to your son, the closer he will be to you. You are his weakness, plain and simple. You may have to deceive Percival to get your way."

"I will never give in to him," Alexandria replied stubbornly.

"I am aware of that, and truthfully, he should be too. But he doesn't seem to have a good grasp on reality at the moment. Maybe if you lead him on a little, you will get what you want," Jatana explained, clearly believing her idea was a good one.

Alexandria listened to Jatana's thoughts and knew a horse would be helpful when she returned to the reservation in the morning and being able to see Running Elk with no one eavesdropping was something she hadn't even considered a possibility until Jatana began talking about her plan.

After a few minutes of thought, Alexandria spoke again. "I will try it your way. But I will not have him touch me," she said through clenched teeth when she heard the knock on the door.

"I understand. You will soon see this is a rather easy thing to do. Just follow my lead," Jatana whispered before she left the room to open the door for Percival. "Percival, it is good to see you," she said sweetly.

The captain's confusion grew when he followed Jatana into the kitchen and saw Alexandria attempt a genuine smile.

"Ladies," he said, greeting both of them before removing his hat.

"Have a seat," Jatana suggested as she pushed the man closer to the table. "Alexandria, why don't you give Little Eagle to Percival while we finish preparing dinner?"

Instead of turning to Jatana and telling her she was crazy, Alexandria bent down and picked up her son before turning to the captain. "Would you mind, P ... Percival?" she asked, after swallowing the bile in her throat.

"No. Not at all, Alexandria. You know, I believe that is only the first or second time you have actually called me by my name. I like it," he said, smiling as Alexandria cautiously handed her son to the soldier.

She moved beside Jatana, who was finishing mashing potatoes at the stove. "This had better work."

Jatana turned and smiled at Alexandria before filling the first plate with food. Alexandria took it and laid it in front of Percival before turning to take her son.

"No. He can stay on my lap during dinner. Does he like fried chicken? I'll bet he's never tasted it. Well, we will fix that," he said, talking to Little Eagle more than anyone else.

Alexandria was about to object when Jatana spoke up. "Little Eagle is Alexandria's whole life, Percival. You know that. She needs to be sure you won't say anything or do anything to hurt the child," Jatana explained sternly.

"I would never do or say anything to hurt the boy," he said, sounding offended by the idea. "Little Eagle and I need to get to know each other better. Don't you agree, Alexandria?" the captain asked as he moved the child to a position where he was looking at the plate of food.

"Why … yes. Would you like to spend time with him?" Alexandria stammered, attempting with everything inside herself to sound the slightest bit sincere.

"I would. How about you two go take Running Elk his food? I mean, you can't save him, and maybe you should be able to say goodbye before he's moved. With Little Eagle's father in jail, or worse yet, dead, I believe I will be the one who will teach him things, right?" he asked, holding a forkful of peas halfway to his mouth, watching Alexandria closely.

"Percival! That isn't something either one of our guests needs to hear! Maybe it is a bad idea, leaving Little Eagle with you!" Jatana chastised her brother-in-law.

Alexandria was appreciative of her new friend's attempt to shift the captain's attention back to Jatana, simply because

Alexandria wasn't sure how much more she could take before she ruined everything.

"No, you're right. I will do better. After we're finished eating, I will give you written permission to be admitted to visit with the prisoner. Hell, the man is becoming less of a threat with every passing minute," the captain commented as he placed a piece of chicken meat into Little Eagle's chubby fingers.

Even with Jatana's help, Alexandria had heard about all she could and stood up, pushing her chair from the table as she did. Her intention was to grab her son away from the awful captain, but Jatana spoke before she could act.

"If you are getting up, Alexandria. I will take some more lemonade," she said sweetly, allowing Alexandria to see her glare.

Alexandria turned and poured the drink. While she was doing so, she realized Jatana was right to stop her from acting rashly. As difficult as keeping her emotions in check was, the captain seemed to be falling for their ruse. So after taking a few deep breaths, she bit her bottom lip and turned back to the pair.

"I think he's startin' to like me," Percival said to Alexandria as she placed the freshly-filled glass back in front of Jatana.

"He doesn't seem to mind you," Alexandria admitted, thinking to herself the only reason her son wasn't screaming was because the child was unable to decide yet who was a good person and who was a bad one.

"Eat up, Alexandria," Jatana nudged.

Alexandria ate very little but kept her eyes on her son. The captain was whispering to Little Eagle, and she found his actions infuriating. After repeatedly telling herself Little Eagle wouldn't remember anything of the man, she breathed a little easier.

Jatana pushing her chair from the table pulled Alexandria from her daze.

"We should start packing the basket for Running Elk," the woman said as she picked up her plate before placing it on the countertop.

Alexandria followed but kept her eyes on her son.

"Try not to worry so much. Soon you will be with Running Elk. Holding your tongue is paying off. I promise," Jatana whispered as she filled a basket with food. "Percival, you need to write that note," she reminded her brother-in-law.

"Right away," he said, standing and placing Little Eagle on his hip.

"Would you like me to take him while you do that?" Alexandria offered as she moved closer to the man.

"No, we're good. See? I've already finished. Now you two take your time. We'll be just fine," Percival stated as he handed Alexandria the slip of paper before returning to the table. "Oh, and take a wrap. The nights are getting nippy."

Jatana moved quickly and efficiently, but Alexandria was still concerned about leaving Little Eagle. Jatana seemed to sense her friend's apprehension and pulled her through the open door.

Once they were outside of the house, they both let out a sigh of relief.

"You are an amazing woman, Jatana," Alexandria declared, still quite shocked that the woman's plan had worked so perfectly.

"Not really. Men are all pretty much the same. Percival, thank goodness, is an easy man to manipulate. Now, let's so work some magic on the guards so that you and Running Elk can be alone," Jatana said, taking Alexandria's arm and walking at a brisk pace towards the guardhouse.

When they reached their destination, the women were met by two armed soldiers. Jatana smiled sweetly and handed one of them the note Percival had written.

Alexandria was struck motionless at the idea that she was mere minutes away from seeing the man she loved. Her temporary paralysis was broken when she heard Jatana continue to speak.

"While she is in with the savage, why don't we sit over there and have some dinner ourselves?" Jatana suggested, smiling.

Both of the men looked dumbfounded.

"Ma'am? Do you think that would be all right?" one of the soldiers asked Alexandria, looking as if he really would enjoy eating dinner with the pretty Jatana.

"Oh, I'm sure I will be fine with the prisoner," Alexandria stated, glaring at Jatana.

"Well, there you have it. Come on, boys," Jatana flirted as she laid a blanket under a nearby tree before beginning to pull food from the basket. "Go ahead and unlock the door and then come over here and eat. I hear I make the best pie around."

One of the soldiers fumbled with the keys hanging from his belt and unlocked the door as quickly as possible.

Before opening the cell door, he looked at Alexandria. "If you need anything, just yell. We will be right here," the young man assured her.

***

The air rushed into the dark cell, chilling Running Elk to the bone. He heard the keys unlocking the latch but wasn't able to hear any voices. His muscles tensed at the knowledge that someone was entering his cell. Every muscle screamed out when he tightened his body. The agony from the beating was the worst he'd ever endured. It was the worst beating he had ever taken. When he was captured, he was tied up before being introduced to the captain.

If he hadn't been bound while the captain was administering his beating, he would have held his own, but that was of little solace. All he could do to ready himself for his visitor was lift his throbbing head and watch as the door slowly opened all the way.

Chapter Forty-Eight

Alexandria's heart jumped to her throat when her eyes adjusted to the darkness. She saw Running Elk sitting slumped against a wall, his arms and legs tied to his neck with a thick rope. His handsome face was swollen and bloody and his hair was matted to the side of his face. Seeing his condition caused her to drop the basket before she ran to him.

"Oh God! Why have they done this to you?" she cried, nearing hysterics as she pulled at the rope in an attempt to loosen it.

When she realized she was speaking English, she immediately changed to Comanche.

Running Elk didn't respond to her words. Panic and anger coursed through her veins. Without thinking, she gently held his face in her hands and kissed his lips. Running Elk remained unmoved.

Alexandria scooted away and looked at him in shock. "It's me."

Running Elk lifted his head and looked at her through swollen eyes but still remained silent.

Alexandria told herself as soon as Running Elk acknowledged her, she would be able to breathe, so she spoke again. "We are alone, I swear we are. Please don't do this to me. I need you to tell me what to do! We have to get you out of here. I went to White Buffalo today and asked him to locate Kicking

Bird so that I can ask for his help. I just don't know what else to do. Please just talk to me," she whispered as she moved closer to him and spoke into his ear.

Her intentions were to stay strong, but it was proving impossible to hold back the tears.

Running Elk sighed before laying his head closer to hers. "Please stop crying. You had better be sure we are alone, Two Fires," he mumbled.

Relief ran through her when she heard his deep voice. "We are, and we have a little time," she assured him before kissing his swollen cheek.

Running Elk pulled his bound hands up to caress her face and wipe the tears from her cheeks.

Alexandria wept so much, she gave herself the hiccups. "Why? Why … did… they … beat … you?" she asked as she tore a piece of her skirt and poured some of the water from the canteen on the scrap before gently attempting to clean some of the dried blood from his face.

"Because I am a free Comanche," he answered proudly.

Alexandria could see he was in considerable pain even though he was attempting to hide the extent of his discomfort from her.

"They're bastards!" she seethed before moving the wet cloth towards the gash in Running Elk's forehead.

"Kee!" he struggled through clenched teeth. "That is too much pain for me right now. First, we eat and talk."

"Tell me what to do," she begged as she handed him a piece of bread.

She wanted nothing more than to be in his arms, listening to him tell her everything would be all right. But from the look on his face, she knew she wasn't going to get her wish. After attempting to paste a fake smile on her face, she fought to stop the tears from flowing.

The blood, the bruises, the way he was bound. Everything about the situation was wrong. Running Elk was more than a Comanche warrior. He was a man, and no man should be treated as he had been.

"My one love, they will be moving me shortly. That will be my only chance at escape. Listen to me carefully," he said quietly, leaning as close to her as his bonds would allow. "If I can't get away then I want you to return to the camp with Kicking Bird. I want our son to see his home and know his people."

Alexandria couldn't mask the pain his words were causing. "You promised me you wouldn't lose me again," she stammered, twisting the torn cloth in her hands.

"Look at me," he said sternly.

She did as he directed, wiping the fresh tears from her eyes.

"I will not be hanged like a thief. I will either die or be free before we reach the new fort. I will not be chained and imprisoned again," he explained, searching her eyes for understanding.

"Running Elk, I will find Kicking Bird in the morning after I learn where they are taking you. Just please don't speak of dying again," she begged softly.

"You and I were meant to share a life together, and we will," he said, attempting to calm her fears.

Alexandria leaned forward and gently kissed his swollen, bloodstained lips.

He pulled away quickly when he heard footsteps closing in, causing himself a great amount of discomfort. "I hope it is this lifetime," he said, wincing in pain.

Alexandria laid the food down within his reach and turned to see the soldier who had unlocked the door approaching.

"Is everything all right?" he asked, sticking his head through the opening of the door, giving Running Elk a look of warning before smiling warmly at Alexandria.

"I'm fine. Have you finished eating already?" she asked, standing and walking towards the young soldier.

"No. I just wanted to come check on ya. If ya don't mind, I'd really like to try a piece of pie. But only if you're sure that this savage ain't scaring you," he answered politely.

"The man is harmless," she assured the soldier, biting the inside of her cheek.

"No, ma'am. That's where you are wrong. That man is everything but harmless," he warned, tipping his hat. "I will be right here if ya need me," he assured Alexandria as he backed out of the doorway.

When Alexandria turned her attention back to Running Elk, she saw he was attempting to eat. He had bent his body in order to not choke himself and managed to pick up a piece of bread. She moved quickly and knelt beside him. After helping the warrior hold the food, she again tried to clean some of the dried blood from his wounds.

"Woman. Move away from me," he warned threateningly. "I may hurt you."

The intensity of his tone only made her move nearer.

"Why didn't you come for me before? I thought you had forgotten about me," she asked, breaking the deafening silence.

"We do not have time for that story now. But know I would sooner forget to breathe than forget you," he answered, avoiding her searching eyes. "I promise you, you have never left my thoughts for a moment."

His answer might not have been what she expected, but his words took her breath away. Not being able to control her desire for closeness, she laid her head on his shoulder and sighed deeply.

"I may be in pain, but your touch is awakening me. And my flesh is too weak," he said, carefully laying his head against hers.

Alexandria didn't want to put space between them, but worried for him, so she reluctantly moved slightly. "Kicking Bird will trust me, right?"

"He will. Tell him what you know and what I have told you. If all goes well, my brother will be waiting for the wagon to leave the fort. He is a good man and he will do what he can," he said, returning to the food his body so badly needed.

"Will he go to White Buffalo's camp?" she continued.

"Yes. I'm sure he's heard I was captured. He will be there and things will work out if they are meant to. Our lives are in the gods' hands now."

Alexandria hoped he was right and knew their time together was coming to an end. "I want to stay here with you," she admitted sadly.

"You cannot stay in this place with me. Where is my son?" he asked, hoping to stop the tears he was sure were again readying to fall from his love's eyes.

"I had to leave him with Captain Armstrong," she answered quietly.

Running Elk stopped chewing his food and looked at her in disbelief. "Why have you left my son in that man's care?"

"So that I could talk to you," she explained carefully. "He will not harm our son, and we are alone. I will not let it happen again. The man repulses me."

"He does not feel the same way about you. That blue coat wants you," he said angrily.

"Well, he will not have me. You see, my heart is forever with you," she replied honestly.

"I know you speak the truth, Two Fires, and I am grateful for your love, but I do not trust the man. But we do have a score to settle," he spat.

"I was only doing what was best for us. Please don't be angry," she said, touching his cheek gently.

"I am not angry with you; I am angry at the world. I don't want you to go but you have a busy day tomorrow and my son doesn't need to be with that man any longer than necessary."

"*Uh ka-muh-kuh-tuh nuh,*" she whispered as she began placing the empty plates into the basket.

"And I love you," he reassured her as he leaned back against the dirty wall.

"I will try to bring you more food when I have returned from speaking to Kicking Bird," she promised as she reluctantly stood up.

He nodded his head and closed his eyes.

After drying the tears in her eyes with her sleeve, Alexandria opened the door and walked out. Jatana and the soldiers were walking towards her.

"Gentlemen, sharing dinner with you was a rare treat. Maybe we can do it again sometime," Jatana suggested sweetly.

"Yes, ma'am. Anytime," the younger of the soldiers replied, smiling.

"I take it everything went all right?" Jatana asked, directing her question toward Alexandria.

"It was fine, but we really should be heading home," Alexandria proposed.

"Thank you, ma'am," the soldiers spoke in unison as the women began walking away.

"Well?" Jatana questioned as soon as the two were out of the soldiers' earshot.

"He told me if he doesn't escape, he will die. Jatana, I can't let that happen," Alexandria said, stopping and almost collapsing into her new friend's arms.

"Then we will do what has to be done," Jatana said, hugging Alexandria warmly. "What is our next step?"

"I am going back to the Kiowa encampment in the morning," Alexandria told her, praying with everything she had that she wasn't making a mistake by trusting the woman.

"Then we will make sure you have a horse this time. Let's go convince Percival he has come up with another brilliant idea all by himself," Jatana suggested in an attempt to lighten Alexandria's mood.

"He will follow me if he knows what I'm doing," Alexandria informed her with sadness thick in her voice.

"Then we won't tell him what you're doing. I will say we're going on a ride together. If he believes I'm accompanying you, he will not deny our request or follow you," Jatana stated as they entered the warm, dimly lit home.

The captain smiled when they entered. He was standing by the fireplace looking at photographs of his family that adorned the mantle. "Little Eagle is asleep in your room," he said before taking a seat beside Jatana on the divan.

After quickly moving down the short hallway and looking in on her son, Alexandria returned to the pair before sitting in the chair across from the divan to ensure Percival wouldn't be close to her. "Thank you," she said, laying the empty basket at her feet.

"Percival," Jatana began, diverting the captain's attention from Alexandria. "We would like to take a ride in the morning. Do you think you could get Alexandria a horse?"

"She has the horse she rode here on. Where exactly will you be going, Alexandria?" he asked.

"Nowhere, really," Jatana answered before Alexandria could speak.

"Alexandria?" the captain repeated, ignoring his sister-in-law's answer.

"I wanted to look around the land. If I plan to stay here, then I want to choose a good place," she answered, lying quite convincingly.

"Then I will accompany you," Percival declared as he stood.

"You are far too busy to follow us around. If we find a suitable plot of land, we will take you there after we return. Honestly, Percival, I never thought of you as the smothering type." Jatana said, jumping into the conversation again.

The captain smiled at his irritating sister and patted her on the back. "Alexandria, would you join me on the porch?" he asked hopefully.

"I'm tired," Alexandria replied before seeing the look on Jatana's face. "But, if it is only for a minute, I suppose it would be fine," she answered, giving in.

"Then, Jatana, I will see you tomorrow," Percival declared, smiling as he opened the door for Alexandria.

Once Alexandria was outside standing on the small porch with the captain, she felt the cold and wrapped her arms around herself.

"It would seem your talk with Running Elk has ended any thoughts of a relationship with him, and that is a wise thing. Would it be so bad to spend time with me?"

Alexandria's anger again took over, but she was able to tamp it down and looked at the soldier. "No," she lied sweetly, hoping she was doing the right thing.

"I could give you anything you want," he informed her as he closed the small gap between the two.

"I'm sorry, but I am cold. I will see you in the morning," she said, avoiding his touch as she backed into the house before closing the door.

"That wasn't very nice," Jatana teased.

Alexandria leaned against the closed door. "The man is beginning to concern me," she admitted when she moved away from the entrance.

"I understand this is difficult for you, but you need to trust me."

Alexandria listened to the woman and prayed she was being honest. Jatana already knew everything Alexandria was planning and understood she could very possibly be opening herself up for disaster, but Alexandria wanted to be able to trust someone.

Jatana seemed to read Alexandria's thoughts. "I believe in love, and you and Running Elk seem to be very deeply in love. That is the only reason I am butting into your life."

"You are not butting into my life. You have been a great help to me, and I want to believe we are friends," Alexandria stated as she sat at the table and took a sip of the tea Jatana had poured.

"I am. You'll see. But you should get some rest. We have a busy day tomorrow," Jatana said as she took the half-full cup from Alexandria's grip.

"Thank you for everything," Alexandria said as she stood and began walking towards her room.

After opening the window, she placed the folded-up blanket on the floor. The breeze was chilly, but it was easier to sleep when she was cool. Before lying on the floor, she placed another blanket over Little Eagle's sleeping form.

Alexandria had almost completely blocked out all worries about Running Elk and drifted to sleep when she heard footsteps approaching. She lay still with her eyes slightly open, looking towards the open window. Her heart skipped a beat when she saw the outline of the captain's hat. Her emotions were a mixture of relief and anger. Relief because she was sure she wasn't imagining things, and anger because he was watching her without (he assumed) her knowledge. Instead of standing up and showing him she knew he was there, she shut her eyes tightly and attempted to steady her breathing in hopes he would walk away. When she heard the footsteps growing quieter and was sure he was gone, she stood and quickly shut and locked the window.

Instead of trying once again to sleep, she dressed, dressed Little Eagle, and quietly walked out of the house.

While she was walking through the compound, she stayed in the shadows as much as possible. Only once was she stopped and asked where she was going.

Her answer to the soldier's query was that she was taking the child to a shaman. Surprisingly enough, the soldier either didn't care what she was really doing or believed her. He even showed her the way to the corral. After spotting Standing Bear's horse, she mounted him and rode towards the gates. The same old soldier who showed her the coral opened the thick wooden gates for her.

Alexandria was grateful for her luck and rode her horse at a full run until she reached the front of White Buffalo's tipi. After jumping from the horse, she kissed Little Eagle and attempted to calm her breathing. When she heard the man's voice, she jumped and quickly turned.

"What are you doing here, child?" White Buffalo asked. "The sun has not yet risen."

"Did you find Kicking Bird?" she asked, ignoring the old chief's question and still attempting to calm her heart rate.

"He did," a handsome warrior answered as he exited White Buffalo's tipi.

The man was shorter and stouter than Running Elk but the resemblance was impossible to ignore. Relief flooded Alexandria's body. "Kicking Bird, I am Two Fires," she greeted, walking closer to him.

"I am aware of who you are. And this must be my nephew," the warrior surmised as he looked to the boy who was still securely tied to Alexandria's chest. "Will you show me the child?"

"Of course," she said, loosening the leather straps and handing the warrior her son without hesitation.

"Nei mah-tao-yo, " Kicking Bird said before kissing Little Eagle on the top of his head. "Though you are not so little anymore. I have missed much," Kicking Bird said, speaking in both Comanche and English.

Alexandria watched as her son smiled at his uncle and pulled at the beautiful feather the warrior wore in his hair. Her son seemed happy to be in Kicking Bird's arms.

"He is a fine boy," the warrior decided after some time.

"He is," Alexandria agreed. "I think he looks like Running Elk."

"Very much like his father." Kicking Bird agreed. "Come inside and tell me why you are here so early."

Alexandria nodded and followed the warrior into the warmth of the tipi before turning to ensure White Buffalo was still behind her.

The war chief sat by the fire and threw more kindling atop it before looking to Alexandria. "Why are you here so early?" he repeated.

"I was planning on coming anyway, but the soldier who came for me yesterday was watching me through my window," Alexandria began explaining.

"He was doing what?" Kicking Bird asked, clearly not understanding what Alexandria was trying to explain.

"When I was trying to sleep I heard footsteps outside my window. When I opened my eyes I saw the captain watching me through my open bedroom window. He's beginning to frighten me," she explained, hoping she was making any sense.

"He watches you? Why?" Kicking Bird asked, still holding his happy nephew in his arms.

Alexandria noticed Kicking Bird had given Little Eagle the colorful leather strap he wore around his biceps, exactly like Running Elk's. Her son was happily chewing on it while watching Kicking Bird's every movement.

"Because he wants me to be his. He told me when they take Running Elk away, he will take care of me," Alexandria explained, physically shuttering at the thought.

"Does my brother know of this man?"

"Yes. He doesn't know the captain has been watching me, but he absolutely knows who the man is. Running Elk didn't trust the man before all this happened. I saw Running Elk earlier when I was allowed to take him some food," she explained, still staring at her son.

"How is he?" Kicking Bird asked quickly, concern thick in his voice.

"Not good. They beat him and he is in a lot of pain," she answered, unsuccessfully attempting to stop the tears from falling once again.

"What did he tell you?" Kicking Bird asked gently, making it apparent he didn't want to add to the woman's pain.

"He said he would either escape or die, and if he is killed, he wants me to return to the camp with you. He wants Little Eagle to know his people."

As Alexandria spoke, Kicking Bird stared into the fire. His expression made it evident he would do everything in his power to stop his brother from dying.

"I need to know when they are planning to move him," the warrior said, almost under his breath.

"I believe in a week's time," Alexandria offered, studying Kicking Bird's face.

He was much like Running Elk except that his features were softer. Being in the presence of Running Elks family caused Alexandria to experience a mixture of joy and sadness because Running Elk wasn't there.

"How are they going to do it?" Kicking Bird asked, bouncing Little Eagle on his crossed legs.

"Running Elk said something about a wagon. Tell me what you need to know and I will find out everything I can," she offered while wiping the tears from her cheeks.

"So, you plan on returning to the soldier fort even after you caught the man watching you?" White Buffalo asked, joining the conversation.

"I have to," she answered defeatedly. "If I don't, he will come here in search of me. I only came here because this is where I feel safe, even if you don't really want us here."

Both men looked puzzled at her declaration.

"Don't want you here? Why would you say that?" White Buffalo asked quickly.

"The general told me I couldn't come stay with you. He said you don't want us and we have no place amongst your people," she explained, swallowing the lump that formed in her throat.

"Yet another *tahbay-boh* lie. You are not being allowed to live with us because of them, not us. While some of my people may worry that your presence here could cause more trouble with the soldiers, you and Little Eagle will always be welcome with us," the old man reassured her.

"Thank you," Alexandria stated gratefully.

The chief's words brought happiness to her soul. Alexandria had wanted to believe the general was lying, but hearing White Buffalo's declaration cemented it. And after hearing the Kiowa chief's explanation, Alexandria understood Abigail's adopted mother's lack of warmth a little better.

"Tonight, hopefully," she answered, hoping she would still be able to talk Percival into allowing her to see Running Elk once more.

"If you can, you must tell him you have talked with me and let him know I am aware of the situation. I need to know how many guards will be escorting the wagon. Can you do that?" Kicking Bird asked, looking her in the eye.

"I will do my best. When do you want me to give you the information I am able to gather?"

"In two days', time we will meet again. And the morning they are going to move him, I want you to come here. Do you understand?" he asked seriously.

"Yes, I can do that," she said, finally breaking the trance the two were in.

"Now get some sleep. You will be safe here. You are surrounded by people who love you. And if you don't mind, I will keep Little Eagle with me," Kicking Bird said, rising as he pointed to the sleeping pallet at the back of the dwelling.

The fur-covered pallet looked far more appealing than the bed she was supposed to be sleeping on. In the back of her mind, she knew the smartest thing to do would be return to the fort, but she hadn't felt so safe and loved since the soldiers attacked her village.

"Thank you," Alexandria said weakly.

"You are my family," Kicking Bird stated.

Alexandria stood and took the few steps necessary to reach the sleeping pallet. After lying down, she watched as the two warriors sat around the fire, talking to Little Eagle. Her son was still chewing on Kicking Bird's leather strap and content with his company.

When she closed her eyes, she listened while Kicking Bird explained to Little Eagle the importance of the circle to their people. For the first time since Standing Bear's death, she felt safe, and sleep came quickly. Her dreams were of she and Running Elk frolicking in a lake on a warm sunny day. But her dream was interrupted by the sound of horses' hooves. She opened her eyes and saw White Buffalo still sitting by the fire, playing with her son. Kicking Bird was nowhere in sight. Before she could ask of his whereabouts, the flap to the tipi was thrown open.

"Thank God you are all right!" Captain Armstrong said with relief in his voice.

Alexandria looked at the man suspiciously. She had expected anger but hadn't considered the man would show concern. "You weren't invited in," she stated, trying to remain civil.

"I was worried about you! Why are you here?" the captain asked, looking down at the silent White Buffalo but acknowledging him no further than that.

"Little Eagle was feverish and I was worried so I brought him here to a shaman. I fell asleep for a few hours, and for that I apologize. Did I break some sort of law?" she asked, acting innocent and naive.

"I want to believe you. I do. But I told you about hangin' around here. These people don't want ya. Now come on and let's get you home," the captain said, holding his hand out to her.

She bit her lip and allowed him to help her up while hoping White Buffalo understood what she was doing.

"Percival, can you wait outside? I will be right there," Alexandria asked, smiling a fake but convincing smile.

"Don't be long," the captain said as he walked out of the dwelling.

Alexandria walked to the old man, sitting silent and motionless near the fire, leaned down, and kissed him on the cheek. "I am doing this for Running Elk. I will return," she whispered in his ear as she took her son from the war chief's arms.

When she walked outside, she was surprised by the brightness of the noonday sun. She knew she had slept for too long but felt better than she had in a long time and was anxious to speak to Running Elk again. But she knew she was going to need Jatana's help to learn the information she required. Alexandria might not have liked the way Jatana got things done, but she couldn't argue with results. And asking the captain outright was not an option. After tethering Little Eagle to her chest, she mounted her ride and followed the captain, hoping Jatana would know what to do.

"Would you like me to accompany you and Jatana today?" he asked as they approached the wooden gates to the fort.

"No, thank you," she answered, trying to hide the panic she was experiencing. It was difficult to be in his company since she knew he was watching her. He had to have been outside the window when she was with Running Elk, but she couldn't let him know she was aware of that fact. While she was getting down from her horse, the pieces all began to fall together.

After dismounting from his horse, the captain spoke again. "I will see you when you return then. And Alexandria …" he said, waiting for her to look at him. "Don't go to the Indians again. All right?" he asked, making sure she understood what he was saying.

"I am not accustomed to being told where I can't go," she informed him as nicely as she could manage.

"I am only trying to take care of you," he reminded her as she quickly walked towards Jatana's home.

Once she was safely in the house, she saw a worried Jatana looking at her. "Are you all right? Where did you go?" she asked quickly, not giving Alexandria the chance to answer her first question before asking the second.

"I went to see White Buffalo. Last night I saw Percival watching me through my window," she admitted as she laid Little Eagle on a blanket.

Jatana didn't hide her horror or shock. "I am so very sorry," she said, pulling Alexandria into an embrace. "I promise you he has never been like this before. I don't know what has gotten into him."

"I appreciate that, but it is not your fault," Alexandria said, pulling from the hug and sitting on the divan next to Little Eagle.

"Were you able to locate Kicking Bird?"

"I was. What I need to find out now is when they are moving Running Elk and just how many soldiers will be guarding him," she admitted with a concerned look on her face.

Jatana smiled at her friend and patted her on the back. "That should be simple enough. When do you need to know?"

"As soon as possible. I'm supposed to return to Kicking Bird in two days. But I don't think learning the information will be as simple as you believe," Alexandria answered, not at all as convinced as Jatana.

"Oh ye of little faith. I will have all the information by later this afternoon. I am going to have tea with the general, and he absolutely loves me. When I return, I will have all the material you are seeking," Jatana informed Alexandria confidently.

"Thank you so much for all your help," Alexandria said softly.

"Is Kicking Bird as handsome as Running Elk?" Jatana asked as she opened one of the living room windows.

The question caught Alexandria off guard. "He is a lot like his brother, but Kicking Bird is softer. Running Elk is more intense," Alexandria answered, full of curiosity.

"They are a handsome race. Shall we get ready for our ride? If we do not go, then Percival will want to know why we didn't." Jatana explained, slipping from one topic to another easily.

"You're right, and the weather is lovely today," Alexandria agreed. "When we return, I will take more food to Running Elk," she said, reaching for her son.

"Do you think that I might be able to meet one of your friends?"

"My friends? You mean an Indian?" Alexandria asked, still not sure where her friend was headed in the conversation.

"I would like to meet one," she admitted, looking to the floor.

"Jatana, that's nothing to be ashamed of. You can come with me tonight when I see Running Elk, if you'd like."

"Thank you. That would be nice. No matter what everyone says, I know a proud people when I see them," Jatana informed Alexandria.

Alexandria couldn't help but wonder about her friend's motives. Jatana had been extremely helpful, but Alexandria was still nagged by suspicion. Something deep inside her told her to be careful. Yet she couldn't allow Jatana to see her concern.

The ride was saddening for Alexandria. She hadn't taken time to take in the terrain before but quickly understood it wasn't anything like the Indians lived and thrived on. Her surroundings were flat and barren with no trees.

While they rode, Jatana spoke about her husband, Ben. The man had been gone for months, and Jatana hadn't heard from him in weeks. It was apparent Jatana was concerned, but the worry did not consume her. The woman told Alexandria everything about their relationship and about him. Alexandria listened to Jatana speak as she took the time to be in nature and enjoy the outdoors. The ride was pleasant enough until she saw the captain riding towards them.

"Well, it appears you were once again right about him," Alexandria acknowledged as she tried to prepare herself for the encounter.

"Ladies," the captain greeted, stopping his horse and removing his hat.

"Percival. I thought you were going to be busy all day. Honestly, I should have married you," Jatana teased coyly.

Alexandria was glad the two were engaging in flirtations because she couldn't help but roll her eyes.

"No, my beautiful sister-in-law, you and my brother are a match made in heaven," he said with regret in his voice. "Alexandria, have you seen any land that meets your expectations?" he asked, turning his attention from Jatana.

"This land is barren. No one would live here by choice," she stated plainly.

Jatana shot her a warning look.

"You'd be surprised," he said knowingly. "But I am sorry you feel that way. Maybe you can stay here with me as an officer's wife."

Her stomach flipped and nausea rose in her throat. Instead of speaking, she steered her horse in the direction of the fort.

"Percival! You do have a way with women," Jatana chastised sadly. "Let's go and find her."

"No. You have tea with Father to attend, and I am in need or a drink or two. I will see you later," he said angrily.

Alexandria rode back to the fort and handed her horse over to a soldier standing outside of the stables. Before returning to Jatana's home, she stopped by the guardhouse and informed the soldiers she would return shortly with food for the prisoner. Once they nodded their agreement, Alexandria walked towards Jatana's. After going inside, she laid her son down and sat in the middle of the floor, trying to get her nerves to settle.

Captain Armstrong frightened her more every time she saw him. Scared or not, she knew if she ran, it would ruin any chance of freeing Running Elk. Choking back tears, she convinced herself that she would be fine as long as kept her distance from the persistent officer.

After fixing Running Elk lunch, she strapped Little Eagle to her chest and walked across the fort. Once she reached the guardhouse, the soldiers smiled politely and offered to take the food into the prisoner.

When she informed the soldiers she would rather do it, they looked at her and Little Eagle with question.

"Ma'am, beggin' yer pardon. Do you think it's wise to take a baby inside with a criminal?" one of the soldiers asked, clearly uncomfortable with the whole situation.

"My son will be fine. The man inside is tied up like an animal. I do appreciate your concern, but I have Captain Armstrong's permission," she reminded the men sweetly, though seething on the inside.

One of the soldiers unlocked the door and moved away. He didn't bother to hide the fact that he was still not happy about the situation. "Do you want one of us to go in there with you?"

"No. I will be fine. If I need you then I will call out," Alexandria said as she walked into the cell.

As soon as her eyes adjusted to the darkness, she saw Running Elk sitting where she had left him the night before, attempting to smile when he saw she brought Little Eagle with her. Instead of crying, she patted her son on the back and told herself to be brave.

After clearing her throat, she spoke. "Are you hungry?"

"Hungry for you," he answered in his own language.

Running Elk sounded better, but his face was beginning to bruise and the swelling had set in. She was sure Running Elk didn't want her to dwell on his injuries so she did her best to hide her concern.

"I'm glad you're feeling a little better," she said as she sat across from him before unlacing Little Eagle.

"Thank you for bringing our son," he said with a thickness on his voice.

"You needed to see him, and I will not leave him with the captain again," she explained as she laid out the food for Running Elk.

Hate clouded Running Elk's features when he heard Alexandria's explanation. "He has not hurt our son, has he?"

"No. But I don't trust him," Alexandria answered, looking at Little Eagle as he reached for Running Elk.

"What has happened?" Running Elk asked as he reached as far as his ropes would allow.

"Nothing ... really. I need to talk to you, and I don't think we have a lot of time," she said, changing the subject to the real reason for her visit.

Running Elk didn't look convinced she was telling the truth about the captain but nodded and waited for her to continue.

"I spoke to Kicking Bird this morning. Jatana is finding out the date and time they plan on moving you. In two days, I am going to take that information back to your brother," she explained, thinking that getting her whole thought out quickly was the best way. She didn't want Running Elk interrupting.

"Do you trust this Jatana woman?"

"I don't know. I have been betrayed by everyone I ever trusted, except you, so I don't know why she would be truthful either," she confessed.

"You must trust your heart. Return to Kicking Bird with the information and then return to me and tell me what the plan is."

"I just wish you could hold me and tell me everything is going to be all right," Alexandria admitted quietly.

"I want that more than anything, Two Fires. But for now, you must return to your home," he said, watching as his son pulled a leather strap from behind his back. "Where did Little Eagle get that?"

"From Kicking Bird. He's wonderful with our son. And Little Eagle loves him," she answered happily when she saw Running Elk's proud smile.

"That is how it should be. Gray Eagle thought that way about me at one time. But he is a grown man now," he explained as he tried to move a loose strand of hair from his face.

Alexandria leaned forward and moved the hair behind his ear.

Running Elk pulled away and Alexandria quickly recoiled. She couldn't hide the pain she was experiencing.

"I'm only trying to keep you safe," he explained quietly.

"I know, but this is so difficult. I will return tonight and tell you what Jatana has learned," she said, picking up everything, placing it in the basket, and repositioning Little Eagle on her hip. "I love you," she mouthed silently, before turning and leaving his cell.

***

Running Elk was appreciative for the time he was allowed to spend with his family. But being together was no easier on him than it was for Two Fires. Running Elk had never experienced love before he met Two Fires and had not expected the pain to be as strong as the love. The warrior closed his eyes and laid his head against the wall. He missed his pipe. He felt the need to pray and ask the gods one more time for the opportunity to live with his family.

Chapter Forty-Nine

Alexandria's afternoon and early evening were a blur of activity. When she returned to Jatana's home, she bathed and fed Little Eagle before laying him down for a nap and then began pacing nervously until Jatana returned. The thought that Running Elk's life depended on the woman worried Alexandria a great deal.

When Jatana returned, looking as if she was about to burst, Alexandria knew her new friend's meeting had been a success.

Alexandria was so excited to learn the details of Running Elk's planned move that she left her son in Jatana's care and rode as fast as she could to White Buffalo's camp. Waiting had never been her strong suit and she wanted Kicking Bird to have the information right away.

She found Kicking Bird sitting atop of his horse, watching the clouds roll by.

The look of disappointment on his face was concerning until she realized his strange expression was most likely because she hadn't brought her son with her.

"Why are you back so soon? Has something happened?" he asked with concern in his voice.

"No, nothing has happened, but I wanted to move quickly so that the captain wouldn't follow."

"Have you learned when they plan to move my reckless brother?" he asked as he walked his horse beside Alexandria's.

"I have. They're moving him by wagon. He is to be escorted by ten soldiers, and unfortunately, Captain Armstrong will be the officer in charge."

Kicking Bird listened and noticed her feature change when she mentioned the officer's name. "Have you had any further trouble with the man?"

"No, not really. I'll be fine. I have to be fine, so I can keep seeing Running Elk," she explained, trying desperately to sound more confident than she was.

"Thank you for the information. I will see you and my nephew in five days' time. Come in the night and when you arrive, we will find a place to keep you hidden and safe while I help Running Elk escape," Kicking Bird stated firmly. Leaning from his horse, he grasped Alexandria by the shoulders.

"I will see you then," she said, not letting the man pull away; instead, she pulled him closer and hugged him.

Kicking Bird held her tightly. "I know you are frightened. But I am proud of your strength. It will not be long now," he reassured her as he gently pulled away.

"I will see you soon," she said, urging her horse to a full run with her moccasin-covered feet.

Kicking Bird shook his head when he realized she was wearing a white woman's dress but still wore his people's shoes.

When she returned, she was delighted she hadn't run into the captain. She was overjoyed when she entered Jatana's house and he wasn't there either.

Jatana was bursting to ask questions and began interrogating Alexandria as soon as she sat down and took a sip of lemonade.

"Is everything planned? Are you going to tell Running Elk tonight? When are you leaving?"

"Kicking Bird is taking care of everything. I don't know anything yet. He said he would contact me with the information I needed to know," Alexandria lied.

She wanted to trust her friend, but when the stakes were Running Elk's life, she decided discretion was the best way to go.

"Well, at least you will be able to tell Running Elk you spoke to his brother," Jatana said, clearly disappointed.

"Yes," Alexandria agreed. "It hasn't been long, but I miss him already."

"We can go to the jail after we eat. I imagine Percival will be here for supper."

"I guess hoping for a whole day without his company would be too much to ask," she mused as she walked behind Jatana into the kitchen with the intention of helping the woman cook dinner.

Much to Alexandria's surprise, they were able to finish their meal without seeing Percival. It seemed the longer the captain was gone, the more her mood improved.

She was all smiles when she and Jatana walked to the guardhouse.

Jatana immediately had the soldiers guarding the building eating out of her hands and Alexandria was able to walk into the cell without so much as one word of warning from the guards.

Running Elk smiled when he saw her.

It still amazed her that her heartbeat quickened with something as simple as a smile from the warrior.

"How are you?" Alexandria asked in English.

Running Elk continued to watch her as she waited for his reply.

"Oh right. I forgot you don't speak English. I'm so sorry. How will we ever communicate?" she asked playfully. "You see, the thing is, I believe I would very much enjoy communicating with you."

"To-quet," he said through clenched teeth, the muscles in his jaws tight.

The warrior looked fierce, but she could see the twinkle in his eyes when he told her *all right.*

She sat across from him in the same place she had earlier. From the looks of the dirt, she had been his only visitor. After sitting down and rearranging Little Eagle on her lap, she began laying out the food for the wounded man.

She was so excited to tell him her news that she blurted it out. "I've seen Kicking Bird again and gave him the news I received from Jatana. And I'm to go to him in five days' time. He assured me he had everything well in hand."

Her mood was light, but Running Elk was still sullen and deep in thought. "Tell me what you know."

"You will be moved by wagon and ten armed guards."

"And the captain ... I hope," Running Elk added, looking optimistic.

Alexandria nodded her head. "Why do you want him there?"

"So that I can pay him back for the beating he gave me," he answered angrily.

It had never crossed Alexandria's mind that the captain had been involved with the warrior's beating until she heard Running Elk's icy tone.

"There are many reasons I want to see the man suffer. He beat me when I was tied up. A weak man avoids a fair fight every time he can. And yet, maybe I am angrier about him trying to keep us apart."

Alexandria was planning on moving to Running Elk's side but was stopped by a quick knock on the door before Jatana joined them.

"Running Elk, this is Jatana. I've told her a lot about you. So much that she wanted to meet you," Alexandria explained uncomfortably. She hadn't realized how difficult the situation would really be when she offered to introduce the two.

Running Elk's features turned hard when he watched Jatana approach.

Alexandria smiled an apologetic smile in hopes of calming the man she loved.

The warrior said nothing but tightened the muscles in his jaw as the woman sat beside Alexandria.

The woman smiled. "I can be trusted," Jatana offered meekly, making it clear she felt the uneasiness in the room.

Running Elk did not move or speak.

"I brought her here because she's been helpful. I know you aren't happy about this, but don't make this harder. Please," Alexandria explained in Comanche, to ensure Jatana would be in the dark about her statement.

"What you have done is foolish, Two Fires. What is it that she wants?" he asked her angrily.

"She only asked to meet an Indian." Alexandria realized her declaration was not enough.

Running Elk had told her to trust her heart, but he was making it apparent he didn't trust Jatana.

"What did he say?" Jatana asked excitedly.

"He said it was nice to meet you," Alexandria lied.

"Do not lie to the white woman," he said, growing angrier every minute.

"Then you tell her how you feel. I'm only doing what I have to do to help you," Alexandria expressed, using a tone she had never before employed with him. She was angry and hurt by the way he was speaking to her.

"What did he say that time?" Jatana asked, again interrupting the two without caring.

"He said you're a very pretty woman," Alexandria lied again.

Alexandria saw Running Elk's nostrils flare, but Jatana was paying attention to Alexandria.

"Will you tell him it was nice meeting him?" Jatana asked as she backed up towards the exit. "I must get back to the soldiers. I don't want anything ruining your time together."

The woman seemed totally ignorant that her presence had done exactly what she was trying to avoid.

Alexandria stood up, placed Little Eagle on her hip, left the basket and food where it sat, and walked out of the small, dank room without a word.

Chapter Fifty

"I will see you soon," he mumbled as she slammed the door shut.

Alexandria regretted leaving him the minute she was outside but knew she couldn't turn around and go back in. She waited impatiently for Jatana to finish her conversation with the soldiers and walked back to her friend's house in silence.

The quiet was broken as soon as they crossed the threshold. "Is everything all right? You seem upset. What happened?"

"Nothing. I'm just tired. I'm sure I'll be fine in the morning."

"Then you won't want a cup of tea before bed?" Jatana asked, not masking her disappointment.

"I'm sorry. In the morning, I'll be better company. I promise," Alexandria said apologetically as she walked down the short hallway to her bedroom.

After closing the door and seeing to Little Eagle, she sat beside him on the bed.

The reality of the last year seemed to hit her all at once. The only constant had been her love for Running Elk. She had never seen him angry at her and regretted leaving him without at least saying goodbye. What made matters worse was that she was sure her leaving the way she did had also hurt him. But it wasn't just Running Elk who plagued her thoughts. The captain had been absent most of the day. She was pleased about his absence but knew it wouldn't last. Worrying that he might very well make another appearance at her window, she found it difficult to relax enough to sleep. Instead of lying on the floor, she wrapped her arms around her son and tried to rest her mind.

Alexandria had only just dozed off when the sound of shattering glass woke her. She immediately sat up and tried to focus her eyes. It looked as if someone was clumsily crawling through her window.

"Did ya mish me?" the captain asked as he stood at the foot of her bed, doing his best not to fall.

He was clearly both drunk and angry.

Instead of answering the man, she sat in shocked silence, taking the opportunity to cover herself with a blanket.

"I mished you," he slurred as he stumbled closer.

"Go away!" she said, pushing her body against the headboard in an attempt to put more distance between the two.

"No, ma'am. Not thish time," he said, sitting on the side of the bed.

Alexandria moved across the bed, making sure Little Eagle was still sleeping between two pillows, and attempted to stand. Before she could put much distance between the two, the captain grabbed her around the waist forcefully. With every passing second, it was becoming clearer to her that he wasn't planning on going anywhere.

"You and I are gonna get together. Whether you like it or not. I'm takin charge of this sitshuation. Once ya have been wish me, you will never want that Injun again. And looky at you sleepin' on a bed. You're already makin' improvements," he stated as he held her tight with one arm and began removing his boots.

As soon as Alexandria felt his grip loosen, she made a break for it and ran towards the door. He was too quick and grabbed her again, knocking her to the floor. Her face hit the doorknob and blood immediately flowed from above her eye. She fought to free herself from his iron grip but it was proving useless. When she opened her mouth to scream, he slapped his hand over her lips. Doing the only thing she could think of to get him to move his hand, she bit him. Her actions only resulted in his grip tightening.

He pulled her closer to him as she lay on the floor before ripping her nightdress from her body.

"Please, don't do this," she mumbled into his closed hand.

Percival laid his full weight on top of her and began pulling at his trousers. Even with her thrashing and biting, he was still able to accomplish his task.

"Stop fightin' me, or I will hurt your baby. I swear I will," he threatened before quickly pulling his hand from her mouth and replacing it with his lips.

She fought to keep her mouth closed but he fought harder to open it. Alexandria could taste blood as he bit her lip.

Alexandria felt helpless. The captain had threatened to harm Little Eagle and she knew if she screamed for Jatana, they could very easily all end up dead.

"Lie still," he said trying with great effort to stop her from kicking beneath his weight. "You'll love it. I promish."

"Go to hell," she seethed as she fought him from pinning her arms behind her head. "Jatana!!" she screamed.

Percival slapped her across the mouth and smiled when she winced. "I told ya I'd kill the half-breed, and now I will," he said, moving to stand.

"Jatana!!" Alexandria screamed again.

Percival fell when he tried to walk because his pants were still around his ankles. While he was attempting to correct that situation, Alexandria moved to protect her son. She was bleeding from her eye and mouth and was naked when she picked her son up. After quickly wrapping the blanket around them, she again ran for the door.

As soon as Alexandria's hand reached the doorknob, Jatana opened the door. The woman looked horrified by the scene. "Oh my God! What happened?" she asked as she reached to embrace her friend.

"I'm leaving. I will not stay here a moment longer. Please try to get to Running Elk and tell him I love him. Make him listen to you. This will be the last time I see you," Alexandria begged as she continued to walk towards the exit.

"You can't leave. Look at you. You're bleeding and naked. You have to clean yourself up and put some clothes on."

"No. If I'm forced to look at that man again, I will kill him myself. Please let me leave. It is the last thing I will ask of you."

The panic she was experiencing had not lessened simply because she wasn't sure if the captain was passed out or not. She found herself hoping the man was dead on the floor. As frightened as she was, the main emotion coursing through her body was self-preservation. Finding somewhere where she felt safe was the only thing she could do, and Kicking Bird was where she was headed. Since stopping to retrieve her horse would only slow her escape, she wrapped the blanket around her and Little Eagle, kept her head down, and walked towards the gates of the compound.

Before she slipped through the wooden door, she heard her name being called. The pain that had been absent while she was fighting with the captain hit her hard. Her head was throbbing and her face hurt, but she forced herself to keep walking. As long as she kept moving, she wouldn't collapse, and she couldn't fall to pieces until Little Eagle was safe.

Her legs were beginning to become uncooperative when she heard a voice.

"Ha-ich-ka pomea ein?"

When she heard the question, she cautiously looked up.

As soon as Kicking Bird saw her face, his features changed. "Two Fires, what happened?" he asked before jumping from his horse. "Tell me what happened," he demanded gently.

"Please help me get away from here. He may be following me," she begged, looking around the area frantically.

"Tell me the captain didn't do this," Kicking Bird seethed as he held her close to him, cradling Little Eagle in the process.

"Please, just get me to safety," she continued to beg.

"You are safe with me," he stated angrily.

"He has soldiers at his command. I won't be safe until I'm far away from here."

Kicking Bird loosened his embrace and silently offered to take Little Eagle from her shaking arms. She gratefully handed the man her child before covering her nakedness carefully.

"We need to get you cleaned up. Can you mount a horse without causing yourself pain?" he asked, attempting to mask the worry and hatred that showed in his features.

"He knows where I will run. What if he follows me?" she asked, hoping he would have an answer that wasn't "you shouldn't have come here and endangered our people."

"Do you honestly think he will come here after doing what he did to you?" he asked, his voice full of hatred.

"I do, and that's what scares me."

"Then I will keep you safe. I will do whatever I need to do to keep the both of you safe."

"What does that mean? I can't stay here. This is the first place he'll look. I know I shouldn't have come, but I wasn't thinking straight. I've endangered your people too." Alexandria began falling into hysterics once again.

"I will take you home," Kicking Bird decided as he walked the horse Alexandria was sitting on.

"Home?" she asked, looking down at him.

"Seeing the blood and swelling on your face angers me more than I care to freely admit. It will take both time and love to put what the captain did to you behind you. It is my job to take you as far from the fort as I can. I have to take you to my people. It's the only way I can ensure that you are out of his grasp," Kicking Bird explained. "The only regret I have is not being able to kill the captain with my bare hands," the warrior added almost under his breath.

"No!" Alexandria objected when the realization of what Kicking Bird was saying sunk in. "You can't leave Running Elk. If you do, he'll die. No. You must save h—"

"I do not savor leaving my brother," Kicking Bird assured her as he interrupted. "But keeping you and Little Eagle safe is what he would want."

"I won't let you do it," she stated stubbornly.

"Two Fires, you cannot change my mind. I don't want to leave my brother, but as I said, it is what he would want. Running Elk will do his best to make it back to you," Kicking Bird said gently.

"He told me if he was unable to escape, he would die," she sobbed before falling into tears again.

All Alexandria really wanted was to be in Running Elk's strong arms. Life was not worth living without the man.

"Do not cry. He will do his best. Come down from there and get yourself cleaned up," he suggested as he helped her dismount. "White Buffalo is at a council, so you will be alone," Kicking Bird continued as they neared the entrance to the Kiowa chief's tipi. "Go inside and warm yourself. I am going to find some water and clothing for you," he said, holding the flap open for her to walk through.

Alexandria turned to take Little Eagle from Kicking Bird.

"He's better with me," he said, smiling gently.

Alexandria pulled the bloodied blanket closer to her body and sought the warmth of the fire while she waited for the warrior's return. Being inside the dwelling did little to ease her anxiety. She kept her eyes glued to the entrance. Her mind was full of fear, hatred, and regret. The brunt of her guilt was caused by the way she and Running Elk had parted. Leaving with Kicking Bird would make it impossible for Running Elk to learn what had taken place. Any hope that Jatana would relay the information to him was slight at best. Alexandria stared into the fire and said a short, silent prayer that she hadn't misjudged the woman.

"We have little time to spare," Kicking Bird informed her when he entered the dwelling. "Put these clothes on and we will clean your wounds once we are further away from the fort."

Alexandria wanted to argue with the warrior, but the sound of his voice and the quickness of his movements made her think twice. Kicking Bird had made it clear he didn't want to leave his brother any more than she did.

She dressed as quickly as her sore, beaten body would allow and watched as Kicking Bird secured Little Eagle to his strong chest. Once they were on the horse and began putting the fort behind them, she spoke quietly. "*Ura,* Kicking Bird," she said softly into his back.

"You are welcome, my sister," he said with sadness in his voice.

She was pleased the man had called her sister but was heartbroken knowing she was going to Running Elk's people without him.

Kicking Bird stopped the horse at the nearest river.

"You can clean your wounds here," he offered as he dismounted, holding his hand out to aid her.

"Are you sure he won't follow?" she asked, looking around nervously.

"If he does, he will meet with considerable resistance from White Buffalo's camp. That will give us some time, if he is fool enough to come after you at all."

Chapter Fifty-One

Running Elk was awakened by loud voices coming from the stockade. The voice was familiar to him; it was the captains. But Running Elk couldn't be sure who the man's anger was directed at. Knowing someone had caused the captain distress was pleasing. When he looked up to the lone, barred window, he realized the sun had not yet risen. Although his first thought was of Two Fires, he found himself interested to learn more about what had the captain so rattled. After slowly pulling his body as far as his restraints allowed, he listened.

"That bitch will not get away!"

Running Elk felt a chill travel through his body. His muscles tensed when he heard footsteps nearing.

"See what your woman did to me?!" the captain yelled when he threw open the door.

The soldier had scratches on his face and dried blood on his lower lip. His clothes were wrinkled and disheveled. It looked like the man had been in a fight.

Running Elk's features didn't change, but inside, his thoughts were in turmoil. He knew Two Fires was in grave danger.

"I will find her, and this time when she comes back, you'll be dead and gone. I know you understand me, so I'm gonna let ya in on another bit of information; I ain't gonna make it easy for her. She ruined any chance of that. And here's the kicker … there isn't a damn thing you can do about it!" the captain shouted with venom in his voice.

"No, Captan. I will watch you die," Running Elk promised through clenched teeth.

The captain looked shocked when Running Elk spoke but quickly recovered. "I don't think so. You have no chance of escape. Of that, I am certain."

When the officer closed the door, Running Elk fought harder than ever before to loosen the ropes. His brain knew fighting was futile, but his heart was in charge of his emotions.

As the day slowly wore on, Running Elk forced himself to calm. Two Fires would run to Kicking Bird if she were in trouble. Knowing she was with his brother gave him some comfort. If she was with him, she was in good hands, and the captain had very little chance of finding them. Kicking Bird was doing the right thing, but his brother's actions forced Running Elk to accept the fact that he would have no aid when he attempted his escape.

It was midday when the door opened again. To his surprise, he saw the white woman who was called Jatana.

The woman nervously walked inside the cell.

Running Elk said nothing but watched her closely as she neared him. He could see the woman had been crying and was still clearly shaken.

"Running Elk, I don't know how to explain this, but I feel like I must try," she said as she took a seat on the ground across from him.

Running Elk knew she was too close to him. He could have easily killed her, but she was a woman, and he had no reason to want her dead.

When the warrior didn't respond, Jatana began recounting the story in hopes that he understood English. By the time she was finished, she was sobbing into her open hands.

"Did he hurt her badly?" Running Elk asked after he was sure he could control his anger.

The woman's body relaxed when the warrior spoke. "I don't think so. She was bleeding, but I'm sure it looked worse than it was. I am so very sorry," the woman babbled.

"I need a knife," Running Elk said, looking the woman in the eye.

"I can't bring a knife here. I don't even own anything other than my kitchen knives. They'll be watching me closely now that I've helped Alexandria. There just isn't a way," Jatana protested.

"If you do not, then they will kill me, and I will never have a life with Two Fires," he said, keeping his voice emotionless.

"I'm sorry. I wish I could help, but I'm a soldier's wife. Above anything else, that is who I am," she mumbled as she walked to the doorway, avoiding his glare as she left.

Running Elk rested his head again the dirt wall and smiled in spite of all the terrible news he'd received. Two Fires and their son were safe and traveling further away every minute. His future was in the gods' hands as it always had been. He would think of a way to escape, and even if he was unsuccessful, he knew his family would be safe.

Chapter Fifty-Two

"We will stop and rest soon." Kicking Bird spoke when he felt Two Fires lean against his back.

They had been moving since they left the confines of the temporary Kiowa reservation. Conversation had been nonexistent the first part of their journey. Both were deep in their own thoughts. Alexandria was sure they were both worried about the same thing; Running Elk staying alive.

"I'm fine," she said shakily. "Maybe you can just drop us here and go back to help Running Elk," she proposed hopefully.

The thought had been with her since they left, but she had been concerned about how Kicking Bird would react to her suggestion.

Kicking Bird turned on the horse and looked at her. "I am doing what my brother asked me to. I'm keeping you and his child safe. And there is nowhere you will be safe until we are far from the fort. There is no way I can help him and also help his family. I have made my decision, and we can pray he will be able to escape without my help. My brother is a resourceful man."

Alexandria could hear the mixture of pride and sadness in Kicking Bird's voice. She fought the tears, knowing crying would only cause Kicking Bird more pain. Holding her emotions in was harder than she expected. It felt like her heart was literally breaking in two.

"How far is the camp?" she asked, searching for any topic that would lessen the pain she was feeling.

"I have no idea. It all depends on the movements of the soldiers. If we are lucky, I should be able to pick up signs in two or three moons. I do know they are tucked in for the winter. This looks like a good place to stop for the night."

"What if he's still following us?" she asked quickly.

"Then I will see him coming. Get down and I will find some kindling for a fire. You have been through a lot in a short time. You need to take care of yourself," Kicking Bird said as he untethered Little Eagle from his chest.

"My son loves you," she observed, allowing the warmth she was experiencing to enter her strained voice.

"We will take care of the fire and finding some food. You rest," he said as he pulled a buffalo robe from the back of his horse before walking away, giving her no time to object.

For the next three days, they rode as hard and fast as Kicking Bird dared. Alexandria was beginning to believe the captain was not following, and she was grateful for that. Kicking Bird's actions made it evident that his main concern was getting Two Fires and Little Eagle to his camp as quickly as possible.

Their conversation grew friendlier with each passing day. Alexandria talked much about her life before meeting Running Elk but said little about the warrior. It was good to talk to someone she could trust, but she found attempting to speak Running Elk's name was impossible without crying.

After making camp on the third night, Kicking Bird sat cross-legged across from Two Fires and sighed deeply. "I have decided you need to know my brother better. When you were with Standing Bear, what did he tell you about Running Elk?" he asked, absently pushing a stick around in the fire.

"He told me Running Elk was free to come for me," she answered as she laid her son down. After clearing her throat several times, she continued. "Why didn't he come?"

"You didn't speak of this with my brother?" he asked in an obvious attempt to give himself more time to come up with an answer that wouldn't cause Alexandria more heartache.

"There was never time. We never had any time alone … well, after the first night. I can't imagine how much stronger I would love him if I really knew the man," she said quietly.

"Two Fires," Kicking Bird said, attempting to keep her mind from wandering. "Running Elk was told you carried another man's child and that you were happy. Even after hearing that, he rode to see you."

"Why did he leave without me?" she asked, losing her battle with the tears.

"He saw Standing Bear embrace you, and you didn't appear to be in any distress," he said, choosing his words carefully.

"I wasn't happy. I was trying to protect our son," she interrupted.

"Let me finish," he said gently. "Standing Bear and Running Elk fought side by side. Running Elk was with Standing Bear when he took his last breath. And it was only after Standing Bear knew he was dying that he told Running Elk the truth."

Alexandria's head swam. It seemed to her that in the end, Standing Bear had been little better than Captain Armstrong.

"Standing Bear loved you almost as much as Running Elk does. Men do strange things when they feel so deeply. You cannot hate Standing Bear. He told Running Elk the truth, and as a result, the two of you were able to spend a little more time together. I am telling you these things so that you understand that you were never out of Running Elk's thoughts. He loves you more than he ever loved another."

"And I will love him forever," she said, wiping her cheeks dry.

Alexandria understood what Kicking Bird was trying to do, but forgiving Standing Bear was something she couldn't do. She didn't hate the Kiowa, but she would never forgive him.

"You and Little Eagle are in his heart, and I hope that gives you some comfort," Kicking Bird offered. "And I do have some news that you will be pleased to hear," he said in an attempt to bring her spirits up.

"What's that?" she asked, not sounding convinced anything he said, short of promising Running Elk would return, would brighten her mood.

"Gray Eagle seems to have found love with—"

"Abigail. I know. That was something Running Elk did tell me. While I'm looking forward to seeing Gray Eagle, I'm just not sure how I feel about Abigail now that I know the extent of her lies," she answered honestly.

"She was only doing what she was told. I'm sure she is your friend, and it will be a good thing to have someone you know to talk to. Gray Eagle holds you in high regard also."

"I was so worried that he died. I'm glad he was safe and yet another death wasn't on my head. How much further do you think it is?" Alexandria said, quickly deciding having Abigail close wouldn't be such a bad thing.

"I should have a better idea in the morning. Sleep, and I will make sure everything remains quiet," Kicking Bird said, smiling at her when she laid down.

Alexandria snuggled up close to her son underneath the warmth of the buffalo robe and slept, knowing she was safer than she had been in a long time.

***

The next morning, after a quick breakfast of pemmican, they continued their journey. They hadn't been riding more than a few hours when Kicking Bird saw a faint wisp of gray invading the blue of the sky. The sight of smoke rising caused Kicking Bird to experience mixed emotions. He was, of course, glad to be home and close to his loved ones. But he knew the questions would begin as soon as the people saw Running Elk was missing. For the first time since he'd met Two Fires, he wished the woman didn't speak his language.

"We will be home soon now," he said, turning to her.

***

She took a deep breath and smiled. "I'm ready."

"Then we will keep moving."

Alexandria's stomach was in knots as they neared the encampment. She didn't look up; instead, she steadied her gaze on her sleeping son.

"Father! Two Fires!"

The voice was one she was familiar with; it belonged to Gray Eagle. When she looked towards the voice, she saw the young warrior running towards them.

"Where is Running Elk?" he asked when he neared them.

"We will speak later," Kicking Bird answered as he jumped from the horse before handing his son the reins. "But for now, make Two Fires comfortable." He used his stern voice in hopes Gray Eagle would not speak of Running Elk again.

"Come down," Gray Eagle urged Two Fires.

Alexandria returned the young man's smile, turned, and began to lower herself. Gray Eagle held his arms out to help her reach the ground.

"I am happy to see you," Alexandria said, fighting back the ever-threatening tears.

Gray Eagle put his arms around her and embraced her. "Can I see Little Eagle?" he asked after comforting Alexandria. "I heard he was named for me."

"He was," she told him as she slowly released her hold on the young warrior.

Gray Eagle looked at the boy. He was wide awake and looking around at his surroundings but wasn't crying.

"He is a fine boy," Gray Eagle decided with pride in his voice. "May I hold him?"

"Of course," Alexandria said, unwrapping the ties holding her son to her chest.

She hadn't realized that Kicking Bird had taken the horse or that she was standing in the middle of the village.

It was a bigger encampment than she was used to, but the movements of the people were the same. Tipis lined a makeshift walkway and in the center, women were working on hides while several children ran and chased one another.

"Follow me," Gray Eagle said. "I will introduce you to my mother."

Alexandria didn't move. Her legs suddenly felt too heavy to walk forward. Gray Eagle turned when he realized she wasn't behind him.

"Are you all right?" he asked, rocking his cousin in his arms.

Alexandria didn't answer him. Her attention was focused on the two warriors walking towards her.

"Hello," the taller of the two greeted as he extended his open hand to her.

The man was tall and muscular. His features were relaxed, but his eyes looked as if they saw everything. He was dressed in leather and tassels. His long hair was parted in two and wrapped in fur and feathers. He was an impressive man with a magnificent presence.

She was taken aback but slowly moved her hand to meet his.

"I am Quanah Parker, and this is White Wolf. He is Running Elk's brother. You are Two Fires. Kicking Bird told us you were here. Welcome home. You are one of our people now." He spoke with sincerity and tenderness.

As imposing as Quanah was, Alexandria found it impossible to pull her gaze from White Wolf. The shaman resembled Running Elk even more than Kicking Bird.

Gray Eagle joined the group and stood beside Two Fires, waiting for her to say something.

"Ura," she finally uttered but didn't look away from White Wolf. "I am grateful to you all for giving us a home. I will do my best to learn your ways."

"It would appear that you already have learned much. You speak our language well. Gray Eagle, do not hold the child so tightly. Let me see him," Quanah said sternly, turning the direction of the conversation. Alexandria appreciated the man's tactics. She knew it would be for the best if Running Elk's name didn't come up. She had no answers and hearing his name only caused her pain.

Alexandria was still staring at White Wolf when he finally spoke. "Two Fires, I feel like I owe you an apology. If it had not been for me, you and Running Elk might have been together long ago. I let my feelings cloud my visions. But I am glad to finally meet you. You are indeed a special woman. We will talk more later. Now I must tell my Morning Star you have arrived," he stated politely as he backed away.

"Come with me, Two Fires. You need to meet your family," Quanah suggested gently, taking her by the hand as he held Little Eagle close to his heart with the other one.

Alexandria walked beside the man obediently, looking to Gray Eagle for support.

While they were slowly making their way through the center of the village, Gray Eagle leaned into Alexandria and whispered in her ear, "Where is he?"

"I don't know," Alexandria answered with tears filling her eyes. "I'm sure your father will tell you everything. All I can do is hope and pray he's on his way."

"I'm sure he is," Gray Eagle said cheerfully as he wiped a tear from her cheek.

Quanah cleared his throat, and Gray Eagle said his goodbyes.

Chapter Fifty-Three

The bitter cold set in two weeks later; the relentless snows came a week after that, and there was still no sign of Running Elk. Alexandria tried to stay busy with her son and new family. When she was alone, she still cried herself to sleep.

She spoke to Abigail not long after she arrived and listened to the tearful apology laced with promises of love and friendship. Abigail appeared to be truly remorseful, and Alexandria needed her as a friend.

Kicking Bird and Sparrow took her and Little Eagle into their home, and she was grateful to them. All the new members of her family wanted to spend time with Little Eagle, so she had plenty of time to explore the camp.

On one of her daily walks, she saw White Wolf approaching her.

"I was coming to ask if you would walk with me, sister," he explained with a smile.

He looked so much like Running Elk that the sight of him still caused her heartbeat to quicken until she convinced herself it wasn't the man she loved.

"I would like that," she spoke after a moment.

"Lead the way," he said, smiling.

They walked through the wet snow for several minutes in silence.

"White Wolf?"

"Yes."

"Do you think he will be back?" she asked quickly, before she lost her nerve.

"I do not know," he answered sadly. "I pray he will, but I've seen no signs. Although I have had a vision of you." He slowed his pace and waited for Alexandria to do the same.

"Me? What was it?" she asked, shocked at his statement.

"You carry another of my brother's children."

Alexandria stopped walking when she heard the shaman. "What?"

"You are with my brother's child," White Wolf repeated slower.

"It would seem the two of you cannot lie together with creating another life," Kicking Bird said, walking beside Alexandria to join the conversation.

"I have to think about this," Alexandria said, holding her hands to her stomach, allowing a plethora of emotions to run through her.

"There is nothing thinking will do. Your child will be female, and she will be proud of her people," the shaman explained while Alexandria bent over to catch her breath.

"How do you know these things?" she asked, not sure whether she believed the man or not. As soon as she asked the question, she remembered how she'd learned she was pregnant the first time. It was an old one.

"I am the shaman, and I am often gifted with visions. A gift of sight," he explained.

"Then why can't you tell me if Running Elk is alive?!" she asked before walking away from the two men without looking back.

***

"She will be overjoyed about the news once she thinks on it," White Wolf assured Kicking Bird.

"I have no doubt about that, brother, but what she needs more than anything is news of Running Elk," Kicking Bird stressed. "Have you seen anything?"

"No, but I wish I had, and I pray every night."

"I wish I could help Two Fires and calm her fears, but I feel as if my brother has passed over," Kicking Bird confessed.

"You are not the one who has sight. Your guilt is what's making you feel as you do. Now go and find Two Fires. Keep her out of the cold. She carries an important member of our nation."

"I will find her and speak to her," Kicking Bird stated as he walked away from White Wolf, leaving the shaman standing in the center of their camp, wrapped in a blanket, staring at the cloud-covered sun.

***

Alexandria pulled the thick robe close to her body to keep the bone-chilling cold out. Hearing White Wolf say she was once again carrying a child excited her, but her happiness was lessened because of Running Elk's absence. She couldn't help but wonder if she was wrong to ask for him to return to her. Wrong or not, that was what she was doing as she sat on the snow-covered riverbank. She was jolted back to reality when she heard Kicking Bird speak her name.

"It is cold out here," he observed as he sat beside her.

"I will return to the tipi in a minute," she said, knowing the warrior was actually saying she should be inside instead of commenting on the briskness. "Kicking Bird? What am I supposed to do now?"

"You will do as the gods ask. They have blessed you with another child. It was meant to be. And you won't be alone. We are your family," he declared.

"I still want him to come home," she said, standing and beginning to walk away.

"We all do, Two Fires," Kicking Bird said as she was leaving.

Alexandria returned to her adopted family's tipi and sat in silence for the remainder of the day. The only thing she did was feed Little Eagle and hold him close.

The following morning, she remained silent. She performed her daily duties of picking any vegetation that thrived in the cold and gathering the daily water supply but only spoke when spoken to.

"Two Fires?" a deep, throaty voice asked.

She knew it was Quanah.

"I wish to be allowed inside so that we may speak," he asked from the closed entrance to the home.

"Of course," she answered softly.

Before taking a seat by the fire, Quanah reached for Little Eagle. The boy was walking with help from the stakes that held the tipi. After greeting the boy with a strong hug, he settled in the center of the dwelling.

"Well ... sit down. I am not going to talk while you are moving about," the chief said as he patted the dirt next to him.

Alexandria sat down as he directed, but she didn't look at him.

"I am aware of everything that happens here. So, of course I know that you are carrying another child. You have been blessed. I am also here to tell you that there has been no reliable news about Running Elk."

Alexandria chose to ignore the word *reliable*. "Have you heard something?" she asked hopefully.

"Nothing reliable," Quanah repeated before continuing. "A trapper came to camp yesterday and informed me there had been some trouble near the fort. I do not know what trouble means. It was secondhand information. He said that both soldiers and Indians died. I do not tell you this to cause you concern. I promised myself when we met that I would hold nothing back from you. Yesterday, I sent a scout to travel to the friendlies near the fort. It will take some time before he returns," Quanah explained. "But I hope his arrival will bring answers to our questions."

"No one thinks he's coming back, do they?" she asked as she looked up at him.

Quanah watched her eyes fill with tears and tried to answer her question with as much hope as possible. "Two Fires, many warriors have made it through this war. I pray that Running Elk is one of them," he answered truthfully.

"He would have been here already if he was all right. Wouldn't he?" she asked.

"There could be many reasons for his delay," he offered.

"Quanah, I am trying to be strong, but it is so heartbreaking to think I may never see him again."

"I understand. But remember you have two reasons to attempt to be happy. The Great Spirit has blessed you. We will talk again soon," he said, standing as he finished his thought.

The war chief extended his hand and helped Alexandria stand before hugging her quickly. On his way out, he gave Little Eagle a pat on the head.

"*Ura,*" she said, thanking him for visiting.

Alexandria stayed seated and thought on what Quanah had said. He and everyone she'd met since her arrival had been kind and loving. The Comanche had adopted her and her son instantly. She knew she should be counting her blessings but couldn't allow herself to do so without knowing what had happened to Running Elk. Quanah had said the information was not reliable, but all Alexandria prayed for was that she would know of Running Elk soon.

Chapter Fifty-Four

As the days passed, Alexandria tried to take Quanah's words to heart. She spent more time with her son and spoke often to the child growing inside her. She became closer to Sparrow and gladly took all advice the woman offered. As the winter lingered, Alexandria realized just how sparse the food supply was. She wasn't going to bed hungry, but her diet consisted more of vegetables than meat. Sparrow informed her that before the soldiers came, their winters had not been so difficult to endure. The Quahadi chose to stay free, and that meant they had to make do with what they had.

Gray Eagle visited daily with Abigail steadfastly by his side. While Alexandria and Abigail visited, Gray Eagle played with his cousin. It was a comfortable routine, but she was still alone at night.

Alexandria treasured her nights. It was then that Running Elk came to her, reassuring her everything would work out.

The cold winter seemed to go on forever. Alexandria spent most of her time near the fire playing and teaching Little Eagle to talk. The boy's vocabulary was limited to Uncle, Quanah, and Ma.

She was so accustomed to her routine that she was startled one day by Kicking Bird's sudden appearance. The concern he carried on his face wasn't settling either. "Where is Sparrow?"

"She's gone for water. What's the matter?" Alexandria asked, standing and moving towards him.

"We must move very soon. The soldiers are near. I need to find her," he answered quickly.

"She should be right back. Is it my fault the soldiers are coming?" she asked, horrified by the thought.

"No. They are coming for us. They want us all on a reservation," he said as he left without a backward glance.

Alexandria sat by the fire and held Little Eagle close. Moving in the snowstorm wasn't ideal. She hoped Sparrow returned quickly because she had no idea how they were going to move the old people and children in a blizzard.

Sparrow returned alone and after laying a buffalo skin of water in a basket, she placed fresh firewood at the back of the dwelling.

"Did you speak to Kicking Bird?" Alexandria asked nervously as she followed Sparrow around.

"I did. We must start packing now. I wish we didn't have to, but we must," Sparrow answered.

"What about Little Eagle? It's too cold for him to be outside," Alexandria objected.

"We will wrap him as warm as we can. It has to be done," the woman stressed, sounding more like a mother than a friend.

"When are we leaving?"

"In the morning. We can pray the snow stops by then."

"What can I do?"

"You can go find Abigail. We need all the help we can get."

Alexandria grabbed a robe and stepped outside. The wind immediately took her breath away. After pulling the robe closer to her body she slowly made her way towards Gray Eagle's tipi.

"You shouldn't be out in this weather. Where are you going?"

The voice behind her startled her and she jumped.

"I apologize. I didn't mean to frighten you, Two Fires," the man said as he began walking beside her before putting his arm around her.

"White Wolf. I'm going to find Abigail so she can help us prepare for the move."

"Do not worry about this. You and your children will have long healthy lives. I have seen it," he informed her in a confident, calming manner.

"How will Running Elk know where we are if we move?" she asked, stopping her trek to look the shaman in the eye.

"He will know. Try not to worry about things you have no control over," White Wolf advised as he held her tighter. "Go back to the tipi. I am going to see Gray Eagle and will give Abigail the message."

"Thank you," she said, turning around, grateful for the opportunity to return to the warmth of the fire.

"Two Fires," White Wolf called to her before she had taken four steps.

She stopped and turned around.

"Look to the horizon as you walk. It holds many unspoken wonders."

"You are a strange man, White Wolf. But I will do as you suggest," she agreed, smiling as she nodded her head at the medicine man.

When she neared the lodge, she looked around the camp. The blowing snow made it difficult to see anything. Her eyes watered as she looked at the back of the tipi into the prairie that was, only a few months ago, lush and green, and now was covered in a blanket of white. She blinked her eyes to clear her vision. The wind still concealed the area so she turned and returned to the tipi.

"Sit by the fire and warm yourself. What have you been doing?" Sparrow asked with disapproval in her tone.

"I was trying to look to the horizon," Alexandria answered, frowning at the woman.

"So, you spoke to White Wolf?" Sparrow asked knowingly.

"I have. He went to inform Abigail we need her. He seemed in high spirits, even with the move coming."

"White Wolf is hard to understand. He is a wonderful shaman, but sometimes I think he looks to the horizon too much," Sparrow informed Alexandria playfully.

***

The remainder of the morning was filled with packing and preparing to take the tipi down the next day. By midday, the wind had stopped howling but the snow continued to fall. Alexandria took a minute to go back outside.

"Don't stay out there for long. We still have much to do," Sparrow reminded Alexandria.

"I won't," she answered absently.

She stood outside and quickly learned heavy snow was no easier to see through whether it was windblown or not.

She squinted her eyes one last time before giving up and returning inside. Just as she was turning to leave, she thought she saw movement in the corner of her eye. She stopped and argued with herself over the possibility that she had seen anything but snow. After convincing herself she wasn't imagining things, she squinted and looked again. For a split second, she was sure she had seen the outline of a white horse slowly moving closer to the village. Her legs felt glued to the ground, and her heart raced. She had definitely seen something. It was either the scout Quanah had sent out, or a soldier.

Her first impulse was to scream, but she knew that wasn't the right way to handle the situation. After slowly backing up, she turned and ran to Quanah's tipi.

When she reached the home, she saw the flap closed and spoke loud enough to be heard. "Quanah … someone is coming!" she blurted out as she tried to catch her breath.

The chief was beside her before she finished her statement. "Where?" he asked as he followed her back to the spot where she had seen the horse.

"I was looking out and saw a horse coming." She tried to keep up with Quanah.

"What color was the horse?" he asked, slowing his pace when he realized she was having trouble keeping pace.

"White," she answered, "I wasn't sure I'd really seen it the first time."

"If it is white, it is not Cloud Chaser. His horse is bay," he said, almost under his breath.

"Who is Cloud Chaser?" she asked, walking beside him.

"The scout I sent to learn about the incident at the fort."

Alexandria was listening, but she was also squinting in the direction she'd seen the animal. "There … can you see it?" she asked, pointing in the direction she was looking.

"You have exceptional eyesight. The man is still a good distance away. I will send someone to meet whoever it is. You have been extremely helpful," he said, looking down at her and smiling.

"Who is it?" Kicking Bird asked as he joined the pair who were still fixated on the open prairie.

"Get on your horse and find out," Quanah suggested more than demanded.

"I can barely see him," he commented as he turned to retrieve his horse.

"Go back inside and get warm. I will let you know who it is as soon as I do," Quanah promised.

Alexandria knew Quanah's request was for her own good, but she would have rather stayed with him.

As soon as she returned to the tipi, she was peppered with questions.

"I saw a rider in the distance. Quanah told me to come inside while Kicking Bird goes to meet them," she informed them as she stood by the fire, shaking from the cold.

"Take off the robe and get warm," Abigail suggested.

"No. I'm fine. I want to go back outside. I'll return if I get too chilled," Alexandria decided, before leaving the tipi she'd just entered.

Before Alexandria completely disappeared from the dwelling, Sparrow questioned her. "Are you sure you are all right?"

"I am. I just have a strong feeling whoever the rider is, he has information about Running Elk."

"Do not get your hopes up," Sparrow said gently.

"I'm not," she lied.

When Alexandria's eyes adjusted to the blinding light glaring off the snow, she saw that Quanah had not moved from where she left him. He was staring intently at the approaching man.

"Can you make out who it is yet?" she asked when she stood beside him.

"No. He is wrapped in a blanket and his head is held downward. I only know it is not a soldier. I thought I told you to get warm," he said, looking down at her.

"I can't stay inside. I'm sorry."

Quanah crossed his arms and returned his gaze to the rider. They watched as Kicking Bird neared the man. The man on the white horse kicked his mount and rode past the warrior. Kicking Bird turned his horse and gave chase.

"Get inside," Quanah told her sternly.

"Why?"

"Do as I say!"

Alexandria wanted to argue, but from the tone of Quanah's voice, she knew better. She stood at the entrance of the tipi and continued to watch with anxiety as the scene unfolded before her.

Kicking Bird's fresh horse easily caught up with the stranger, and he reached out to slow the uninvited guest. Quanah turned to Alexandria and frowned when he realized she hadn't done as he said. She didn't want to anger the chief but didn't want to miss whatever was about to happen. Alexandria couldn't help but notice the confusion on his unhappy face. Quanah was puzzled and angry but still wasn't alerting the other warriors in the camp.

The unknown rider stopped his horse near the center of the camp.

The rider was covered from head to toe in layers of fur robes, which made it impossible to see his face.

Kicking Bird stopped his mount a few steps behind the rider.

Alexandria slowly walked back towards Quanah, not caring what he was going to say.

"Who is it?" she asked quietly, not taking her eyes from the mysterious white horse and shielded rider.

Quanah remained silent. It seemed he couldn't look away from the mysterious visitor either.

Alexandria tensed when she saw the man slowly begin to remove the layers obscuring his face.

He jumped from his horse before his face was completely revealed.

Alexandria's knees went weak, but the man caught her before she fell.

"Two Fires, *nei-kamakura,* we are together again," Running Elk said, holding her tightly, speaking in the language she had grown to love. "I am home."

Fin

Thank you for taking the time to read my story. Without you, there'd be no reason to write.

Please contact me on facebook or visit my page at

ElizabethAnnePorter.com

If you enjoyed Running Elk, you might also enjoy:

The Importance of Being Prudence

The Virtue of Prudence

A Study in Scarlytt

Beauty Bedamned

Seraphina's Phyre

Roy, Vampire

A Date with Death

And coming soon to Amazon,

The Fortitude of Prudence

(Book 3 in the Prudence McDaniel series)

Printed in Great Britain
by Amazon

36184294R00213